CONTINUUM . .
I0691577

When Sophia Delaney returns to her earthly life following a near-death experience in a car accident, her awareness instantly expands far beyond the three-dimensional world. She soon discovers innate intuitive abilities, enabling her to tap into countless historic events through dreams of past lives, which over time expands her soul's journey.

As Sophia weighs her new awareness against the life she once knew, a mystical Lakota shaman introduces her to a conclave of people from around the world, called the Order of Apeiros, a culturally diverse collection of intuitive sages, seers, and shamans, whose spiritually gifted sensitivities, sacred talismans, and enlightened wisdom raise their vibrational energies in service of the earth and all her inhabitants. They invite Sophia to join them, for they are aware that she has returned to this lifetime as the most powerful oracle the world has ever known. Overnight, Sophia shifts from her everyday mundane existence to many lives of mystic wonder.

Ardyce West's Continuum Series weaves numerous interlinking stories through each book, blending a bit of self-help with metaphysical historical fiction about unsung heroes and sensitive souls from the present day and the past. The task of her dynamic and engaging characters is simple - to shift the consciousness of the world - one thought, one word, one act of love at a time. Their seemingly ordinary lives are, at times, quite astonishing through the mystery and intrigue of their mystical experiences, with interwoven stories and tales told with humor, romance, suspense, intrigue, and timeless universal wisdom.

APEIROS
COONTINUUM BOOK ONE

Writer and artist Sophia Delaney has led an average life of mixed fortune. Now divorced and coping with the impending death of her enigmatic father, Sophia is asking the inevitable mid-life questions of mortality and existence. Then everything changes in a split second on a rain-slick highway. Sophia's car hurtles into the median, and for a brief moment, she leaves her body and enters the mystical ethers of no time or space, where she realizes the wisdom within her soul's journey.

 Otherworldly entities welcome her from the next dimension, and she's given a choice to either stay or return to reconcile a life not yet fully lived. Sophia makes her choice, and from that moment on, only one thing is certain - she will never be the same.

SÍORAÍ
CONTINUUM BOOK THREE

Sophia's metaphysical awakening leads to a family she never knew existed, but she must confront a demon from the past before she may fully embrace the future. Her journeys lead her and Michael to Ireland, where they discover ancestral roots that impel Sophia to continue her recall of a past life aboard the RMS *Titanic*.

 In the meantime, members of Apeiros reunite to embrace beloved White Buffalo, who shares his noble legacy that foretells an eternal life.

FROM THE PUBLISHER

This rich and captivating story draws elements from Ardyce West's previous two Continuum novels, blending them into a compelling new slant on the metaphysical themes of spirituality, reincarnation, and eternal life. West's dynamic storytelling further fleshes out the core characters of the previous two books, Apeiros and Aeternalis, starring Continuum's heroine everywoman, Sophia Delaney, a seemingly ordinary, middle-aged American artist whose life was upended after a car accident thrust her into the ethers of eternity in a near-death experience.

Siorai – Continuum Book Three picks up in the aftermath of the tragic RMS Titanic disaster, where Sophia recalls her past-life aboard the doomed ship. Lost and cast adrift in a lifeboat, she watches the horrific demise of the great ship, which carried over 1500 souls to their icy doom, among them the man with whom she fell in love on what they believed was a voyage to a new life of hope and redemption. The story further develops Sophia's journey of reawakening as she and her beloved Michael tour Ireland and explore their ancient ancestry, while back at home Sophia's spirit guide and mentor, White Buffalo, must face his own destiny in the circle of life.

AETERNALIS

Also by Ardyce West

APEIROS
Continuum Book One

SÍORAÍ
Continuum Book Three

OUROBOROS
Continuum Book Four

I Never Heard You Cry
A Compassionate Journey Through Abortion

Children's Books:

There Once Was a Kitty Named Digit
Book One of Travels With Digit

Available at Amazon.com, BarnesAndNoble.com,
and other online book stores.

E-books also available on Kindle and other devices

AETERNALIS

COONTINUUM BOOK TWO

ARDYCE WEST

LoneWolf

Published in the United States of America
First edition published 02.01.2017 by KC LoneWolf
admin@kclonewolf.com
Littleton, CO

ISBN-13: 978-0-9969544-2-6
ISBN-10: 0-9969544-2-2

EBook edition also available on Kindle and other devices

Author contact information: admin@ardyce.org

In memory of Laurence Freedom, who consistently pursued Spirit's highest expression in every facet of his life. His perseverance, spiritual depth, and sense of humor were among his numerous qualities that enhanced the strong bond of our friendship. He lives on in me, specifically the spirit in which I write.

The Hero's Path

"We have not even to risk the adventure alone;

for the heroes of all time have gone before us –

the labyrinth is thoroughly known.

We have only to follow the thread of the hero path.

And where we had thought to find an abomination,

we shall find a god;

where we had thought to slay another,

we shall slay ourselves;

where we had thought to travel outward,

we shall come to the center of our own existence.

And where we had thought to be alone,

we shall be with all the world."

~ Joseph Campbell

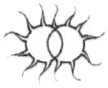

CHAPTER One

Sophia and Michael adjusted to their new life in the Rocky Mountains. For months, from early spring far into autumn, they methodically transformed Patrick and Sophia's formerly small rustic cabin into a beautiful three-story log home with a loft, complete with an outdoor wraparound deck that overlooked the distant mountains and nearby river. The centerpiece of their home was the river rock fireplace that reached into the rafters of the great room cathedral ceiling. Before construction was finished, Michael and Sophia had the foresight to install an elevator for later years when stairs would become more of a challenge. Yet, Sophia's intuition told her they would put it to good use sooner than later.

Sophia inherited the property from her father, but she always considered it hers since he bought it on her seventh birthday. Patrick purchased the property, originally built in 1932, for $7,000 cash from an elderly gentleman whose Colorado roots dated back to the late 1800s. Her father fondly recalled the transaction, made back in the days when a person's word was their bond.

"Mr. Delaney," the old-timer said, "you see them seven majestic one-hundred-foot blue spruce trees that line the property along the river? They're yours for $1,000 each. The cabin itself is free." The sale concluded with a handshake and a glass of whiskey.

Even though she knew what the old man said was in jest, Sophia felt the same reverence for the blue spruce trees, for she believed they were the greatest of earthly beings. The seven trees became her symbol of strength as they stood tall, rooted deep in the ancient Earth while reaching toward the heavens in the wind and storms of adversity. As did the many animals that took refuge among the branches of the great wooded sentinels, Sophia felt at home in their presence.

Patrick added a third story loft on the cabin, specifically for his beloved daughter. There, she spent hours painting pictures of wildlife and illustrating her short stories, beginning the life of a writer and artist at a very young age. The two of them spent most every summer weekend at the little cabin by the river, where their senses filled with the fragrance of pine and moss while listening to the continuum of the river's flow.

Colorado's high desert plain held the cabin within the intimate narrow mountain valley of lush greenery fed by a cold mountain stream. Among the plentiful vegetation were ferns, moss, aspen, fir, wild roses, blue spruce, ponderosa pine, and chokecherries, which provided shade and sustenance for everything from the tiniest of animals, to deer, elk, moose, and black bear. The stream flowed just twenty feet from the cabin's front door. During the spring, the river ran high with freshly melted snow from the Isabelle Glacier just east of the Continental Divide. In winter, the stream's shallow trickle gurgled gently under protective layers of blue shadowed snow.

On the eastern end of the property was a recess at the

river's edge, which Sophia called the Cove. It was a perfect spot for Patrick to fish, but Sophia often sat on the massive root of a blue spruce tree along the riverbank, watching the hummingbirds soar up and down the river. Mostly, she sat in quiet contemplation while the waters flowed swiftly by.

It was at that sheltered cove where Sophia began to experience her visions. Through the trees, a spotlight of sun peeked into the clear stream at her feet, the water gleaming as she peered into its depths. There, she envisioned both life-changing world events, and simpler, sweeter occurrences like sensing when and where someone would meet their soul mate, or where a friend would find a lost dog. Oftentimes, she felt an unseen presence watching over her in protection. She strongly felt that presence at the cabin, whereas at home she sensed it only on occasion, and not of the same magnitude as when she sat by the river's edge. Her dog, Buffy, seemed to sense the presence as well. When Sophia felt that particular atmosphere of love, Buffy sat up and cocked her head to one side, her long ears perked, looking like a miniature sphinx.

The synergy with Buffy gave young Sophia an added sense of better knowing herself. Her acknowledgement of how her beloved dog easily responded to love's presence helped Sophia realize that all beings lived within the protection and guidance of what she knew as God. She knew the universe supplied her with everything she truly needed. It was a sense, a knowing, and a surety that all was well.

As an adult, Sophia wondered if the presence she felt as a child was her mother's spirit watching over her. She had no memory of Elizabeth, who died when Sophia was only three years old. She concluded that the sense of security surrounding her must be the unseen assurance of a mother's love.

Sophia had all the spiritual talismans that came from sources unknown. The golden bowl was for water, the chalice with the eternal flame, the amethyst amulet that doubled as a pendulum was for air, and the hourglass, for earth. The only element not represented was ether. The use of each one enabled her to see and sense realities beyond the human realm of the five senses. She was just beginning to learn how they all worked together to assist her in the work she and Michael were doing in the world, particularly within their small enclave of the Order of Apeiros.

That summer, much like when Sophia was a child, she spent most of her time in the loft, where the dormer windows and skylights let in natural light so she could better create her best works of art to sell.

There, high in the Rockies, the air was fresh and the skies clear blue and full of mighty cumulous clouds of pristine brilliant white. From the time Sophia and her father spent their first weekend there, they followed a nightly ritual of gazing at the stars, for there were no city lights to shroud the nighttime sky. Before bedtime, they would quietly lay on chaise lounges in the middle of the yard, wrapped in heavy sweaters or a down quilt, for even in mid-summer the night temperatures were brisk. They would not return to the warmth of the cabin fireplace until Sophia completed her nightly vigil of counting five shooting stars blazing across the indigo sky.

The tradition continued, unchanged, since she and Michael made the cabin their home. Her ritual of stargazing grounded her in the reality that everything and everyone was an integral part of the never-ending expansive nature of the universe. Within this awareness, Sophia affirmed the importance of her individual contribution to the world. This was part of what she was to remind others in her writing and teaching, so people would continue to recognize their individual significance in creating a life of purpose and meaning. Knowing this created her personal accountability for making better choices, living from grander ideals, and taking a more meaningful direction, one step at a time.

One evening, while she and Michael gazed into the heavens, she looked toward the northwestern sky. A brilliant shooting star suddenly shot straight overhead and fell directly into the Big Dipper. Another instantly streaked from the northeastern skies and met at the same point in the dipper's center. From where the two seemed to meet, a third shooting star began its trek toward the southeastern sky and disappeared into the ethers, appearing as if an immense game of universal billiards just took place.

Awestruck, Sophia gasped at the celestial anomaly. "Michael! Did you see that?"

Michael snorted from a trance, bewildered and a bit less enthusiastic at the phenomenon in the night skies. "Yeah, I did," he mumbled. "See what?"

"Those shooting stars! Incredible!"

"Um hum." Michael was looking elsewhere - more likely at the inside of his eyelids.

Sophia could only smile at her slumbering bear of a man. She felt sudden delight that she might possibly be one of only a few beings on earth who witnessed the miracle in the night sky. For a moment, her thoughts turned to her mother and father. Perhaps the two shooting stars somehow represented them, she thought, with the third a symbol for – what? Sophia contemplated the question for a moment until she also dozed off.

CHAPTER TWO

Sophia scheduled several art fairs for the summer and fall that year, but the one she most looked forward to was the last fair of the season, the New Orleans Autumn Art Fair. It had been a year since she was there. For Sophia, the prior year was one of discovery on most every level, but one part of her history remained unresolved and incomplete. She could not quite fill in the gap to understand the short life of her mother who died when Sophia was quite small.

She was anxious to return to New Orleans, knowing that she was a distant relative of Darius MacPhaidin, whose American heritage went back to the antebellum days of Louisiana. Sophia had no other family that she knew of, so she hoped to dig up more roots of her southern heritage during her next visit. She had many questions and curiosities that needed answering. Michael decided to join her on the trip, not only to help her with the art fair, but he also looked forward to reuniting with his friends, Darius and Gaston. All four were a part of the Order of Apeiros, in which Sophia became an initiate the year before.

When Sophia and Michael arrived in New Orleans and joined Gaston and Darius for dinner, they felt as if they were coming home. Michael found the surrounding history of the city and the well-preserved plantation house fascinating. He also delighted in the good company of his longtime dear friends.

The dining table was set in all its finery with white linens and a floral bouquet of autumn's garden flowers surrounded by lit votive candles. Michael felt extremely underdressed, thinking perhaps his formal dinner jacket and cravat would have been more appropriate for the evening. With a grin, he reflected on the fact that his dinner jacket would smell like mothballs, which was far worse than wearing jeans and boots. Truly, he could not imagine what made him think of wearing a cravat either.

Sophia must have read his mind, because she thought about how she loved seeing Michael all dressed up in a suit and tie. Michael looked at her just as she was lost in another thought of him dressed in his well-fitting jeans, a beautifully tooled leather belt, a crisp long-sleeved white shirt, crocodile skin cowboy boots, and a fine hat. That really did it for her. She blushed at his gaze and looked away with a smile as she realized how well they read each other. Michael sat at the adjacent corner of the table and took her left hand in his right, raised it to his lips and gently kissed it. Nothing else existed in that moment but the deep love they shared, which continually grew as the days passed.

The main course included Jambalaya with crawfish, shrimp, sausage and rice, garden vegetables, fresh homemade sourdough bread and butter, and French wine. As dinner progressed, Michael said, "This meal is amazing, Darius. I'll have to extend my compliments to the chef. We rarely have the chance to eat fresh seafood. By the way, Soph, when are you going to bake *me* some sourdough bread?"

"Don't look at me," she said. "You're the chef in our household, but now that I think of it, bread *is* brown. I might be able to pull it off."

"Brown?" Darius asked.

"Sophia isn't the best cook in the world," Michael said. "Most everything she concocts in the kitchen turns out to be a collection of brown something or other. She's all about color in her artwork, but her culinary skills leave something to be desired."

"Hey - I make a mean toasted cheese sandwich with hot cocoa, and s'mores for dessert," Sophia said.

Michael shrugged. "Like I said - brown."

"Maybe we should loan you our cook," Darius said with a laugh.

They enjoyed catching up as the meal concluded with fresh berries over homemade French vanilla ice cream, paired with hot coffee. Following an after-dinner drink and small talk in the library, they retired early that night in the quiet solitude of the southern countryside.

The next morning, the sun was about to rise above the far horizon, with singing birds of many varieties beckoning the new day. Wide awake, Sophia slid quietly out of bed so she wouldn't disturb Michael. She wrapped herself in a rose-colored feather comforter that she found draped over the loveseat at the end of the bed and quietly tiptoed out onto the veranda. She stood at the second floor wrought iron railing in the cool autumn morning and watched a variety of birds flitter from tree to tree. She reveled in sights and sounds that no other time of day offered. To take it all in, she settled into one of the large wicker chairs and tucked her feet beneath her while sitting back to breathe in the beauty and grace of the day.

As the sun rose higher, she returned to the room and quietly crawled back under the covers, where Michael stirred just enough for her to snuggle up next to him. His warm body welcomed her into his embrace as she reflected on the blessings of the love they shared. It was an endless love, one in which love's freedom held the soul's everlasting power that revealed all that one needed to know as a shared sense beyond knowledge and worldly events. Sophia shared the same love with Michael that Roxana shared with Yiorgos. Such was the love held by others of her past, and she knew that more lives would reveal themselves as her awareness expanded.

Opening day of the art fair was two days away. Sophia double-checked her list to be certain she had everything ready for the set-up to run smoothly. She prepared food to enjoy throughout the day. Darius opened his wine cellar for her to gather a few bottles to offer to her potential clients. He remembered how she treated him with such fine hospitality and respect when they first met.

In addition to her abstract paintings, she chose to show some of her more realistic work. She loved painting on large canvases, for the Colorado sunrises and sunsets were like no other, and they provided her a treasure trove of outstanding subject matter. She carried her camera at all times to capture ever-changing images of the colorful Colorado skies, to later transfer onto canvas in acrylics. The change in genre attracted some of the same clientele she drew to her booth the year before. Happy to feel some familiarity, she realized that New Orleans, a city of so much diverse history, was becoming a second home to her. The next three days would be an enjoyable time for Michael and Sophia to acquaint themselves with those who visited their booth.

At the same time, the shows could be both an emotional and physical drain on the senses. Sophia had to be *on* the entire time, while remaining friendly, welcoming, and constantly able to communicate about her paintings to potential clients. Occasionally, she found herself in counsel with someone who needed a listening ear. Sophia always attracted those who would bare their souls. She treated all who entered her booth with openhearted kindness, as if they might later become a dear friend.

As the fair progressed into Sunday afternoon, Sophia and Michael grew tired and quite ready for the day to end. Michael stepped away to buy some refreshing lemonade before they began breaking down the display. Sophia was alone in the booth when a strange man quietly entered. Her heart suddenly constricted, and she felt an inner warning to beware. She sensed the man's threatening presence, feeling an urgent need to be on guard. Typically, she did not sense such negativity, but she knew all too well, if she did not listen to her powerful intuition, she would most likely regret it. The man exuded a charismatic animal magnetism with a grimy undertone of sinister and foreboding temperament. Sophia pulled out her cell phone, ready to call Michael if need be, while extending to the man a friendly but cautious greeting.

He took his time perusing her paintings, occasionally looking at her with a sideways glance. When he turned his back, Sophia slipped behind the booth and signaled a woman in the neighboring booth of her need for help. The vendors kept watch over each other with unspoken signals and codes, and the neighbor immediately understood and entered Sophia's booth, pretending she was a potential client. She stood particularly close to the man, too familiar for the stranger's comfort. Much to Sophia's relief, Michael suddenly returned and began chatting with the neighbor, unaware he had just joined a rescue party. The mysterious stranger beat a hasty retreat, and they watched him rapidly leave the fairgrounds, taking note of his distinguishing features.

"Who's the vampire?" Michael asked.

The neighbor laughed. "They do come out this time of afternoon."

"Did he say something to spook you?" Michael asked.

"You saw that face," Sophia said. "He didn't have to speak." She took her neighbor's arm. "Thank you for coming to my aid."

"Oh, honey, glad to help out," the sweet Cajun woman said. "Either of you would do the same for me. Will we see you again for the show next year? We should arrange to set up next to each other again."

"Let's plan on it!" Sophia said. She gave her a hug and bid her goodbye.

They broke down the display, packed up the booth, tables and props, and stored the paintings in the RV while keeping an eye out for the mysterious stranger. Before they rolled up the rug, Michael found an envelope, folded in half, on the ground.

"Soph, what's this?"

Sophia curiously took the envelope and read the crudely written words: *Little Girl*. "Where did you find this?" she asked.

"Over there."

"That's where that creepy guy was hanging around."

She opened the envelope and pulled out a letter, written in shaky handwriting,

> *Little girl*
>
> *I done paid the price of 40 years in prison. I want you to know I ain't sorry never have been cause she asked for it. Nobody hits me and nobody puts a hex on me neither. I been waiting a long time to find you so you better watch your back cause if I don't get you my boy will.*

"That's it," Michael said, "we're out of here." He gathered the rest of their belongings and quickly packed them into the RV. Michael's sudden departure from his usual calm demeanor unnerved Sophia. She folded her arms at a sudden chill, while she still held the letter.

"What do you think this means?"

"It means we need to go," Michael said, abruptly leading her to the RV.

"Should we call the police?"

"We'll call them from the road. I want to get you away from this place, now!"

They kept a watchful eye as they pulled out of the fairgrounds. Never had they disassembled the booth and display so quickly after a show. Once on the road and after warily deciding they weren't being followed, they began to rest a little easier. The scenery of the countryside was a soothing welcome after the three-day fair, especially following the circumstances of the unpleasant encounter.

Michael called Darius and told him about the note. Darius said he would contact the security office, because he knew the woman in charge, but he made what seemed an odd request for Michael to hold off contacting the police. When Michael asked why, Darius said he first wanted to have a conversation with them at the plantation. When they arrived, Darius called Gaston at the shop and asked that he join them for dinner. Gaston closed the shop early and immediately drove out to the plantation.

After Sophia showered and dressed for dinner, she came down the stairs and walked into the parlor as Gaston entered the house. "Gaston, I didn't know you were going to join us - how wonderful. I'm so happy you're here!" She gave him a big hug.

"Thank you, my dear," Gaston said. "Only on a rare occasion will I pass up a good home-cooked meal with the people I regard as my favorites."

"Well, look who's here," Michael said as he entered the room.

"Old friend," Gaston said with a smile and a warm handshake. "I confess I came by this evening for more than a free supper. Darius phoned and told me you had a bit of a fright today?"

"I'm not exactly sure what we had," Sophia said.

"I think we'll go with 'fright', honey," Michael said. He pulled the mysterious note from his shirt pocket and handed it to Gaston.

"Dear me," Gaston said as he read. Darius entered the parlor and exchanged a knowing glance with Gaston.

Sophia recounted her experience and described the man who entered her booth that afternoon. Darius seemed unusually uncomfortable, and without a word, he walked into his office. Shortly, he returned with a newspaper clipping that he offered to Sophia. The old yellowed clipping headline read "MOBSTER HEIR APPARENT?" over a man's photo.

"That's him!" she said. "A much younger version, but it's definitely the guy! How did you know this was the man?"

Purposely bypassing her question, Darius said, "His name is Niko. He is the son of a rather seedy local hoodlum by the name of Algernon Gillette. Forty years ago, Niko assumed his father's business when Algernon went to prison."

"Wait," Michael said, "that little ghoul creeping around our tent today is a mob boss? He looked more like a lizard in a cheap suit."

Darius could only manage a shrug. "Down this way, the criminal element rarely resembles Marlon Brando. The Gillette crime family controls the illegal drug trade, gambling, prostitution, human trafficking and the like."

"Human trafficking?" Sophia said.

"Sadly, yes," Gaston chimed in. "Slavery never really left the South. It just has a variety of different faces and additional levels of cruelty."

"Niko is not as powerful as his father," Darius said, "nor is he as well-respected among his contemporaries. But he *is* dangerous. Through Niko, Algernon Gillette still wields considerable power after all these years behind prison walls."

"And Niko is just as insidious," Gaston said. "He is truly a lowlife thug."

"But why would the father threaten me?" asked Sophia.

"Let us just say that Algernon is a superstitious man," Darius said. "He harbors old world beliefs that stem from the supernatural. It could be that he is terrified of you, or feels threatened. He may feel vulnerable, and so to pose a threat would be his way to keep ahead of the shadows."

"You didn't answer her question," Michael said.

Darius seemed unusually rattled. "Uh, yes, well you know a bully simply feels a false sense of empowerment, but only temporarily, because he is really running away from himself. He is not yet able to face his own demons. You see…"

Sophia stared at Darius and then at Michael.

"Darius," Michael said, "my dear friend. You're stalling."

Darius gave Michael a sour smile. "I was hoping you wouldn't notice."

"I do notice that you aren't much of a tap dancer,"

Michael said. "What does all this have to do with Sophia?"

"He's getting there," Gaston said.

"I do understand the concept of the bully mentality," Sophia said, a bit irritated, "which would be a good conversation for another day, but let's get back to why you think some New Orleans mobster walks into my world and leaves a threatening letter because he is terrified of me. What does he have against me?"

"Well, my dear," Darius said, "it's a lengthy story-"

"I gathered that," Sophia said. "I've never met the man, but believe me, I will not forget the face of his son, nor his oppressive energy, to say the least."

Charles, the butler, entered and announced that dinner was ready, and Darius took a deep breath, knowing the conversation was only getting started. "Why don't we first have our dinner. Then, I will explain." Darius motioned for everyone to proceed into the dining room.

Sophia was frustrated, but she let it go for the moment, determined to persist until she got her questions answered. They ate their meal with very little conversation, the atmosphere heavy with emotion.

Once they finished, they retired to the library, where Darius' ancestral grandmother Maeve's picture hung over the fireplace. Michael stood in front of her portrait, marveling at the resemblance to Sophia. Darius offered them an after-dinner drink, first pouring himself a snifter of cognac. Gaston and Michael had a glass of single malt scotch, and Sophia enjoyed a Manhattan.

"So, tell me, Darius, I am still not clear how you are related to Sophia," Michael asked.

Darius glanced at Gaston, who slowly nodded in his direction. "Michael, you are a master of the perfect segue," Gaston said.

"How's that?" Michael said.

"Come, let us sit and get comfortable," Darius said. He directed Michael and Sophia to the large divan, while Gaston took a seat in a cozy armchair. "Dear ones, I suppose this is as good a time as any to tell you both about that very topic. Gaston and I have debated this issue for some time, and we came to the conclusion that it is time that you, my dear Sophia, must learn the truth about your past."

Sophia frowned and questioningly cocked her head to one side. "What do you mean?"

Darius tentatively strolled the library, swirling his drink. "You see, Gaston and I have, shall I say 'omitted' some details about ourselves."

"We fibbed," Gaston said.

"Gaston, please."

"Well, what would *you* call it?"

"Don't help me," Darius said.

"Wait a minute," Sophia said. "What are you trying to say? That we're not related?"

Gaston chuckled, and Darius gave him another scolding glance. "Well, no," Darius said, "I mean, yes, we are related –"

Sophia put her drink on the table, fully placing her attention on what Darius was trying to say. Darius took a deep breath as he slowly and deliberately paced back and forth in front of the fireplace, inquiring within about the right words needed for that moment. He looked down at his hand as he swirled his snifter of cognac, placing his left hand behind his back, while the other three watched him in anticipation.

Chapter
Three

"Please," Gaston said, "while we're still relatively young."

"Sophia," Darius said, ignoring Gaston, "it is important for you to know how deeply you are loved. Since you were quite small, everything provided for you has been in your best interest. Since your father's death, great change has come about over these past few years. Your near-death experience revealed your innate powers that lie within your ability to know more in the broader sense of things. Your mother had similar abilities, but unlike you, she had no way to understand the immeasurable capacity of her gifts."

"Wait a minute!" Sophia interrupted. "My mother? You knew her?"

"Yes. We both did," Darius said, lifting his brandy snifter in the direction of Gaston.

Sophia looked at Gaston, who gave her a knowing smile. She shook her head. "I don't know what to say."

"My dear," Darius said, "I know this is a shock – as will be many things we tell you tonight. This is not easy for any of us, but if you will let me continue, we will sort it out together." He paused and waited for her to settle back into her chair. "Your mother had the same gift of sight that you possess."

Sophia grabbed Michael's hand. "She had - but – how did *you* know her?"

"She lived here. In fact, this is where you were born."

"In New Orleans? No, I was born in Colorado."

Darius winced and bit down on his lower lip. "I'm afraid not. You see, your mother and father lived here. Your mother was aware that she had the sight, and from her early teens into her young adult life, she served many by doing readings in the home where you were born. In very little time, she built up a large clientele who felt she understood them in ways that no one else did."

Sophia sat completely still, but her mind swirled in the new revelations about her mother.

"Now, let me make myself perfectly clear, Sophia. Elizabeth was a mysteriously beautiful, bohemian-type woman who had the ability to enable people to feel invincible. Instead of limiting her clients to their obligations and limitations, she invited them to aspire to their power and potential within their own range of gifts and talents. She simply had a way of empowering and inspiring people to take on the world."

Darius continued to pace in front of the fireplace while swirling his cognac and occasionally taking a sip. "She counseled with religious leaders, politicians, business magnates, matriarchs, and patriarchs of the South. She was most effective helping those who lived day to day, doing the best they could within the circumstances at hand. She worked with those who sought profound wisdom that might lead to a greater, more meaningful life."

"What you're describing reminds me of my dreams of

the Oracle of Ancient Greece," Sophia said.

"Precisely," Darius said. "Elizabeth worked very much in the same way, sharing her intuitive insight to guide her clients, but she was available four days of the week, instead of only one day of the month like the Oracle. She worked very hard and extended herself sometimes to the point of exhaustion. Never was she without those anxiously awaiting her counsel. Her clients paid her well beyond what she asked, making her quite wealthy."

"It makes me so sad to think that I don't have any recollection of her," Sophia said.

"You were very young," Darius said.

"And before I was old enough to know her, she became ill and died so suddenly."

Darius heaved a great sigh as he reached for his pipe and lit it. "My dear, this is an evening of astonishing revelations for you, and I regret to say there is more I must tell you that will be very painful." He paused, first turning to look into the blazing fireplace. "Your mother did not die of cancer."

Astonished, Sophia first looked at Michael and then Gaston, who looked down at his hands as if he was ashamed to have held on to such a secret. Unnerved, she moved closer to Michael and stared directly at Darius, waiting for him to tell her the whole story.

Darius took a deep breath before he continued. "One of Elizabeth's clients was Algernon Gillette."

Sophia looked at Michael, who could only say, "Gillette, a gangland mobster, was seeking spiritual guidance from someone like Elizabeth?"

"As I said, Michael, this is New Orleans, the Deep South, where many still live by centuries-old rituals and beliefs," Darius said. "Although Algernon was a ruthless businessman of great influence over the Irish criminal underworld, he was a superstitious man locked in old-world fallacies and myths."

"I don't like where this is going," Michael said.

"Darius," Sophia said, "did he hurt my mother?"

Darius took a fireside chair and placed it in front of Sophia. He sat down, facing her, so he could look directly into her eyes as he continued. "She had no idea who he was when she began their professional relationship. He spun a web of influential and nefarious business dealings – 'racketeering' as they call it. The Gillettes were intertwined with the notorious Marcello mafia family, whom many to this day believe were involved in the assassination of JFK and Bobby Kennedy. Algernon had power over the police, the river shipping industry, local government officials, and even the Catholic diocese here in New Orleans."

"So that's why you didn't want me to call the police today," Michael said.

"Paranoia, perhaps," Darius said, "for one can never be too cautious. His son may not wield as much influence these days, but back when Algernon was involved with Elizabeth, wherever he tread, he left dead bodies behind, both literally and figuratively. By the time she was aware of his notoriety, it was too late. Elizabeth was afraid to stop her readings with him in fear of what he might do to retaliate."

"Darius," Sophia demanded, "I asked you – did he hurt

my mother?"

Darius looked her squarely in her eyes. "He did."

"No," Sophia whispered, her eyes filling with tears.

"I'm so sorry, my dear," Darius said, his voice cracking as he tried in vain to swallow back a tear. "Algernon Gillette brutally murdered your mother."

Sophia could scarcely breathe. She put her hand up to her ashen face and gripped Michael's hand with the other. "What happened?" she softly asked.

"I simply cannot utter the terrible details myself, but it is important, however, that you know. If you wish, I have an old audio recording of a statement made by a woman named Ada, your parents' housekeeper, whose testimony later put Gillette in prison. She was the sole eye-witness to what happened that day - at least, the only witness who could testify."

"What does that mean?" Michael asked.

"You were there, too," Darius said to Sophia.

"I was there? I don't remember a thing," Sophia said. She was numb, and she simply shook her head. "I want to hear it."

Darius walked over to his desk in the corner of the room. From out of the lower desk drawer, he removed a small, very old cassette recorder and brought it to Sophia.

"This old thing I dare say still works, but the sound is rather scratchy. The old tape was transferred to this cassette many years ago, which is now just as ancient." He sat in the chair facing Sophia and placed the recorder on the coffee table and turned it on. The voice on the recording was that of a woman with a strong southern accent:

"*That day, Algernon Gillette wanted more from Miss Elizabeth - more than she was willin' to give. She was afraid of him and tried her best to reason with his demands, but that horrible man was used to gettin' his way. He tried to rape Miss Elizabeth. He ripped her clothes, slapped her face, and pulled her hair to force her to do his biddin', but she fought back with all her might. She raked her fingernails down his cheeks, quickly bloodyin' 'em. She pounded on his shoulders and ches' with her fists, kicked him in the shins, and stamped his foot with her high-heeled shoe, but he barely budged. You would think he was made of steel.*

"*I had already called the police from the kitchen while I held onto Miss Sophia, tryin' to protect her, but Miss Sophia could not help but hear her mother screamin' from the livin' room. I felt so helpless, but I knew it was my job to keep the chil' safe. Then Miss Sophia wriggled free from my arms so quickly, I could not catch her. She pushed through that swingin' dining room door like someone from an old western movie jus' bargin' into the saloon where all the action was about to take place. She walked into that livin' room, wavin' her arms high into the air to stop Mister Gillette from harmin' her mother.*

"*She was only three years old, but I swear God possessed her with a forceful spirit of divine power. The Almighty was in that little girl. She was completely lit up with a fire that radiated out from her very being. I am certain of it!*

"*She told Mister Gillette, in a loud and commandin' voice that did not seem to be comin' from such a small chil'. I will never forget what she said. 'You, let my mother go, now! Your wickedness has ended. Stop this minute, or you will die a horrible death, and all the pain you have done to others will be small in* comparison to the sufferin' you will feel deep into your bones!'

"She said it that way, she did. I recall it plain as day. Ain't never heard no big words like that comin' outta such a small chil'. 'Your soul will surely endure in agony' she went on,' which will extend beyond the veils of time!'

"Well, he stopped and stared at that small chil' with blonde pigtails stickin' straight out of the sides of her head like straw comin' out from under a scarecrow's hat. He looked like he seen a ghost, he did. She spoke to him, possessed by the voice of God - I am sure of it. He knew by her words that she also had the power of Knowin', just like her mother.

"Miss Sophia stood there in the center of the room, bigger than life, but smaller than a yardstick. She was dressed in her blue and green plaid cotton dress, with little white ankle socks trimmed with lace, and tiny red Mary Jane shoes. That little girl held her head high, while her arms were straight down at her sides - her tiny hands clinched into white-knuckled fists. Miss Sophia glared up at him with burning fire in her eyes. A hurricane twistin' through that room could not have budged that chil' from her stance.

"Then he took a step toward Miss Sophia. Her mother screamed out, 'Oh no you don't, you bastard!' She ran in front of him and put herself between him and her little girl. At the same time, she grabbed the heavy silver candlestick that was next to her on the table and swung it at him with all her might. Miss Elizabeth hit him with that big ol' candlestick, right in the face and split his nose at the bridge. He just stopped for a moment and stood there, stunned by the blow, reachin' up to hold his nose. He seemed surprised to see the blood gushin' out onto his hand.

"Then he was even more enraged. He grabbed the candlestick from Miss Elizabeth with his left hand and threw it to the floor.

He drew back his right hand, balled up in a fist, and with all his might he swung at her and struck Miss Elizabeth at the side of her head. She stumbled several feet across the room and fell to the floor, strikin' her head on the stone hearth in front of the fireplace. I just stood there in shock as I saw her spirit rise right up out of her body. Then, I saw a bright light that hovered over Miss Sophia. It was Miss Elizabeth's spirit protectin' her little girl.

"Mister Algernon grabbed the candlestick and raised it over her, ready to beat her with it when he realized Miss Elizabeth was already dead. She just laid there still and lifeless in a pool of her own blood.

"Then, Mister Algernon quickly grabbed a hold of the chil', slingin' her under his left arm like she was a rag doll with her arms and feet danglin' in mid-air. I screamed at him to put her down and tried to stop him by hittin' him with my broom. Miss Sophia was kickin' and screamin' so much that I was surprised he could keep ahold of her. He began to run out the front, just as the police busted through to meet him head on. Mister Algernon then ran toward the kitchen. The police shot him twice in the leg to stop him from runnin' out the back door with the chil'. He stumbled to the floor and dropped Miss Sophia at the same time. She came to me and hid behind my legs. Then the police grabbed Mister Algernon.

"I went with Miss Sophia in the ambulance to the hospital where they treated her for shock. Her poor father met us there after he heard the news. Before we left for the hospital, I saw Mister Algernon carried away, strapped to a stretcher. He was moanin' in pain from the gunshot wounds, but he threatened to take revenge out on Miss Sophia, never to leave her among the livin'. I don't believe she heard what he said, but I did."

Darius turned off the recording.

Sophia could not hold back the tears. She shook her head in denial. "I have no memory of this. You'd think I would recall such a horror. My poor mother - I don't remember her at all. She tried to save me, and it got her killed." She leaned into Michael, who held her while she sobbed deep tears of despair. Gaston brought her a box of tissues and poured her a glass of water.

"And you think he believes a three-year-old put a curse on him?" Michael asked.

"You'd be surprised at the number of people here in the South who still believe in the occult," Darius said. "Algernon has always been a superstitious man with beliefs that stem from the supernatural. His familial history is steeped in black magic. Remember, the Irish are a people historically attracted to the mystical realm."

"A three-year-old leprechaun casting a spell on a mob boss," Michael sarcastically said. "That's a new one."

Gaston chuckled. "A *paranoid* mob boss, my friend – as if there is any other kind. Mix the constant fear of gangland reprisals with a little black magic spell-casting, and you have Algernon Gillette."

Darius agreed. "A person like Gillette's heartfelt beliefs eventually can become his reality no matter how unreasonable or illogical. We believe life is good - that is what we see, and therefore that is what becomes of our lives. But when someone believes the opposite, they live in the depths and downward spiral of small thinking, which leads to a life of negativity. I believe Algernon remains terrified of what you said to him that day. After all these years, he still fears what he believes was a spell or some kind of hex you put on him."

Sophia blew her nose until it was raw, and she wiped the tears from her eyes. With tissues balled up in a pile on her lap, she took a sip of water. "My head is spinning with so many questions. Darius, why did you keep this from me?"

"Until Patrick died, it was not my place to tell you," Darius said.

"My own father deceived me all those years," Sophia said.

"Before you judge him too harshly, Sophia, there is much more I must share, if you feel up to it tonight."

She sighed and braced herself. "I might as well hear it all now."

"It gets worse, I must warn you," Darius said. "But I promise we are here to bring you to a much brighter conclusion, once you've heard everything."

She inched closer to Michael, her protector, her rock. He purposely did not hold or put his arm around her, but instead just sat beside her, still and strong, empowering Sophia to move through the pain on her own. She would have many moments later to discuss and process these new truths, as the old ideas fell away and the new information made a home in her heart.

"Very well," Darius said. "You recall earlier when Michael asked about the precise nature of our kinship?"

Sophia tried to smile. "Distant cousins, many times removed, to the third power or some such thing – yes, I've confused both of us many times trying to figure it out."

"Well," Darius said, "it will indeed confuse you, but in actuality it's not complicated. Sophia, your sweet mother Elizabeth – was my daughter." Darius could not hold back his tears.

Sophia gasped, utterly speechless.

"My dear Sophia, I am your grandfather."

"What?" Sophia said.

"My god," Michael whispered.

Darius pulled his handkerchief from his inner coat pocket and wiped the tears away, quickly composing himself.

Sophia looked down at the floor, shaking her head, entirely dumfounded. "Why am I just finding this out now? I don't understand."

"We wouldn't expect you to," Gaston chimed in, himself dabbing tears with a kerchief.

"Oh, good," Sophia said. "Now *you* have something to say. Why would I expect you to sit quietly over there? I suppose you're going to tell me you're my long-lost brother or something?"

"Close!" Gaston laughed but quickly looked away when Sophia's glare nearly sliced him in two.

"Gaston, you're not helping," Darius said.

"Where were you when I was growing up?" Sophia demanded.

"I'm about to explain-"

"Why did you lead me on like this?"

"I can see you're upset-"

"Upset?" Sophia said. "I haven't even *started* to get upset! I have to get through startled, dazed, and confused first! My whole life I don't learn *one thing* about my mother, or any of my family for that matter, and then Dad dies, and you waltz into my life like some dapper benefactor and tell me you're giving me this entire plantation, the hotels-"

"I know," Darius said, "I know-"

"It's best if you let her go for a second," Michael said, giving the bewildered Darius a reassuring wink and a nod.

"You introduce me to the Order of Apeiros, which incidentally included my father – which I didn't know about – and then I find out some lunatic Irish mobster, who killed my mother, by the way, wants *me* dead because he thinks I'm a damned *witch!*"

"Ok," Michael said, "I think we're getting there."

"Is that enough to upset me?" Sophia said. "No! Because now you tell me you are my grandfather! You want to see upset? Oh, it's coming – and then stand by for angry!" Sophia suddenly stopped. She gave everyone a good stare and then exhaled a deep breath.

Darius reached for Sophia's hand. "I do say, dear girl, you *are* your mother's daughter."

Sophia took another deep breath and instantly calmed down. A tear welled in her eye. "You're really my grandfather?"

Without missing a beat, Darius continued. "I really am."

Sophia gently put her hand on Darius' face, fighting

back tears of love. "Grandfather," she whispered, as she looked tenderly into his eyes. "I'm so sorry – so sorry. How terrible for you to lose her that way. How terrible for my poor dad. He never told me any of this."

The library grew deathly silent. In a moment, Sophia felt a dark pall fall over the room. She pulled her hand away. She looked at Darius and then at Gaston, who simply could not hide from Sophia's intuitive awareness. She spoke softly. "There is more," she flatly said.

"Yes," Darius said, still sitting across from her. "I believe I should first explain a little more about our family, and I shall begin with Gaston. He is your granduncle."

"How do you do," Gaston said.

"You're brothers?" Sophia said.

"Stepbrothers, actually," Gaston said.

"But when we first met, you told me you were brothers-in-law."

"Yes," Darius said. "And that is true. I just did not mention we also are stepbrothers."

"I feel like I am in a live soap opera here," Sophia said. "You want to run that by again? Gaston, wouldn't you be my step granduncle?"

"Oh, no," Gaston said, "that would be too simple. We intermingled even more."

"Gaston, perhaps you might help now?" Darius said as he walked over to the bar to refresh his cocktail.

"Of course," Gaston said. "My mother died when I was a child. Darius lost his father also when he was quite young. Soon thereafter, my father courted and married his mother, making Darius and me stepbrothers. I had an older sister, Lianne, who was Darius' age, and as we grew up together – well, let us say nature took its course and Darius fell in love with Lianne. He was wisely smitten by the pure fruit of my family tree."

"Gaston," Darius said, "just please tell the story."

"Of course," Gaston said. "Darius and Lianne married and soon had a lovely baby girl, your mother, Elizabeth. So, after all our co-mingling, you are directly related to both of us."

"I need another scotch," Michael said, and the room erupted in laughter.

"Shall I just leave the bottle?" Darius said.

Without a word, Michael snatched the bottle and poured himself a double.

"So," Gaston said, "I am your granduncle, and Darius – your grandfather."

Sophia took all the wadded up facial tissues in both hands before she stood up. "Tell me where I can find a wastebasket."

"Behind the desk," Darius calmly said. He whispered to Michael, "Is she taking this well? I can't tell."

Michael drank. "I'll let you know."

Sophia threw the tissues away and came back to sit down next to Michael, but not before she poured herself a glass of scotch and took a good drink.

"What I don't understand is why my dad always told me I was born in Colorado. He told me that all of my grandparents were dead, and we had no other family. Why didn't he ever tell me about you? Why didn't he tell me the truth about my mother?"

"My dear," Darius said. "This is going to be even more difficult to explain." Taking his brandy snifter in hand, Darius again sat facing Sophia. With a heavy sigh, he continued. "Patrick was not your biological father."

"No," Sophia said. "Don't tell me that." She looked at Michael and grabbed his hand. "This can't be happening."

"Darius?" Michael said.

Darius heaved a hard sigh. "Your real father was also murdered."

Sophia closed her eyes and dropped her head.

"I am so sorry, Sophia," Darius said.

"Was it-"

"Gillette? Yes," Darius said. "At least, we believe it was someone associated with him."

"But – my dad," Sophia said, her head spinning. "Who was-"

"Patrick was Gaston and Lianne's uncle – your great-granduncle."

Sophia rubbed her eyes as if it might make this surreal nightmare go away. "And my real father?"

"He was a lovely man," Darius said.

"Amen," Gaston said. "God rest his soul."

"Thomas Gallagher – Tommy, we called him," Darius said, his voice quivering. "A big, strapping Irishman very much like your Michael. Oh, how Elizabeth loved him – love at first sight, they both said."

"And they killed him?" Sophia shakily said, the tears coming again.

Darius sadly nodded. "Tommy was a longshoreman. He was working when Elizabeth – well, he was so enraged when he heard, he flew off the handle and went to the police station, looking for Gillette. Of course, Gillette was locked up, but Tommy made quite a scene. Word got back to the wrong people that Tommy wanted revenge, and the next day, he was found dead up in the Avondale shipyards. No one was ever arrested."

"I can't believe this," Sophia said.

"We were devastated," Darius said, "and terrified for your safety. You were a witness, and rumors were flying about this absurd curse that Gillette imagined you put on him."

"She was three years old!" Michael said, the scotch igniting *his* Irish.

"That didn't matter," Gaston said. "If given half a chance, that cretin and his murderous minions would have done away with Sophia without any conscience whatsoever."

"We didn't know what to do," Darius said, "but whatever it was, we had to do it quickly. And then, like a brilliant white knight – or more like an angel – our dear Uncle Patrick appeared."

Gaston laughed. "Cowboy Patrick – my offbeat, eccentric uncle."

"Tell me more," Sophia said.

"He was the epitome of the free spirit," Gaston said.

"He was the youngest of his family, a maverick who left the rigors of working in the Louisiana oil patch in his late teens and ventured west to seek his fortune."

"He came running when he heard that your mother and father died," Darius said. "And when he learned of the danger you were in, without hesitation he took you away from this place like a bandit in the night, telling us only that you would be safe and cared for as if you were his own. We agreed it was best that we did not know precisely where you went, to protect you from Gillette's long reach.

"Ada, your parents' housekeeper, was put in protective custody during Gillette's trial, and she packed up and left town after his conviction. For many years, Patrick occasionally sent me some form of message – a discreet postcard, letter, or a brief phone call to let me know that you were safe and well, but for your protection, he made certain your tracks were covered. We later learned you went to Colorado, where he changed his name to Delaney, after my distant grandfather that I told you about, Luciano Delaney from Ireland."

The mention of Luciano was enough to shift Sophia's thoughts for a brief moment: *Luciana and Nostradame. We truly are all one in this family.*

"All the years growing up," Sophia said, reflecting upon her enigmatic father, "I never had any suspicion that he wasn't my real dad."

"Ah, but he was," Gaston said. "Indeed, we all adored Tommy – no one more than Patrick. He loved him and Elizabeth, and I assure you, when he adopted you, he loved you like the daughter that he never had."

"Some of this makes more sense now," Sophia said. "Daddy was such a happy, gregarious man, but whenever I brought up the subject of my mother, he got very quiet and elusive. He just said that she died of cancer, and he couldn't talk about it without it breaking his heart."

"Well," Gaston said, "there *was* a grain of truth to that."

"How so?"

"Patrick married a beautiful woman around the time when Elizabeth was born. In his letters home, he rarely if ever mentioned any women prior to meeting her, but from the moment they met, he wrote volumes. They planned to have a family, but sadly, she passed away just two years after they married."

"Oh, my God," Sophia said. "Cancer?"

"Indeed," Gaston said. "After that, he was never quite the same. He never expressed any interest in another woman."

Sophia nodded. "I remember one time I asked him if he ever thought about getting married again, and he said that falling in love was a solitary experience for him. I just didn't realize he wasn't talking about my mom."

"Indeed," Gaston said. "Patrick was a deeply devoted and spiritual man."

"Yes, he was," Sophia said. "And how did his induction into the Order of Apeiros come about?"

"Ah," Gaston said, "so much that is new for you to learn."

"Ah," Sophia said, "so many riddles my Uncle Gaston loves to exasperate me with."

Gaston laughed. "Another piece of the puzzle, my dear. You will find the answers in your dreams."

Sophia simply rolled her eyes to Michael. "Do you believe these two?"

Michael simply shrugged. "Hey, they're *your* relatives."

Darius continued, "Suffice to say, we knew the time would come when we would meet again. I had hoped, after all these years, you could reconnect to your heritage without the added baggage of New Orleans gossip. This unexpected appearance of Niko Gillette has thrown us a considerable curve, however. I wonder how in the world he found out about you."

"I don't care about him," Sophia said. "I still don't understand why you could not come to Colorado to visit."

"Algernon Gillette had too many people working for him on the outside; too many poisonous tentacles wrapped into the New Orleans community, and for that matter, the entire South. To err on the side of caution, we all agreed it better to have no association with you. Back then, Algernon made sure his wretched men harassed us, trying to find you. What you said to him that day apparently haunted him, so much so, that he believed if you were dead, the spell you placed on him would die with you."

"Spell!" Sophia said. "To think a three-year-old child would frighten a grown man so."

Darius placed the snifter on the end table next to Michael, but not before he downed a good sip of cognac. "There is more on this tape that you should hear."

He turned on the recorder:

"Like I said Miss Sophia was only three years old, at least her little body was. That tiny girl stood there, like Moses on the mountaintop, stronger than any adult I have ever seen in my days. There was this golden swirl of energy surroundin' that chil'. I could not believe my eyes. I even reached out to touch it and felt it movin' through my fingertips, like water flowin' from a cascade. There she stood with a pillar of brilliant white light comin' right out from the top her head, straight into the ceilin' above her. It was as if the angels were shinin' their light on her, protectin' that little girl. Mister Gillette's eyes were as big as saucers. His face lost all color. That little tiny chil' put fear into him as if God was about to strike him down. When Miss Elizabeth came between Sophia and him and struck him with the candlestick, it seemed to break the spell. That is when Mister Gillette raged to full force and struck poor Miss Elizabeth down to her death."

Darius turned off the recorder. "Although still in prison, Gillette is apparently as dangerous as ever. He has a prosthetic leg, because there was too much damage from the gunshots to save it. Algernon remains determined to make you suffer for his downfall."

"So, my legal name is Delaney, but Daddy's real name was Menard?" Sophia said.

"Actually, it is Delacroix," Gaston said. "I took the name Menard, which was my mother's maiden name, when you and Patrick left for Colorado. It seems silly now, but I was frightened of Gillette."

"Okay, Sophia Delacroix Gallagher."

"MacPhaidin," Darius said. "As your grandfather, I must insist on top billing."

"Sophia MacPhaidin Delacroix Delaney Gallagher," Sophia said, finishing with an audible gasp for air.

"I think you have the western European continent covered," Michael said.

Sophia shook her head. "This will take some time to process. I was an orphan. Adopted."

"Don't forget - loved then, and loved now beyond your imagining," Darius said.

She looked around the mansion. "Now that I think about it, I knew the first time I came here, this house seemed familiar. I just thought maybe I recalled it from a dream."

"You were just three when you were here," Michael said, "but you probably have some small recollection."

"Now it makes sense why my father never spoke of my mother." Sophia paused, putting all the pieces together. "He couldn't speak of her without taking the chance of revealing to me what happened."

"He was protecting you," Gaston said, "and, if you didn't know, there was no chance you might inadvertently tell the wrong person."

"I suppose," Sophia said, "as I got older, it was easier for him to live the lie rather than the truth. I would probably have done the same thing if I were in the same position."

"It was a terrible burden," Darius said.

"It also explains the protective loving energy surrounding me, which I've felt since I was quite small," Sophia said. "I always wondered if it was the spirit of my mother. I guess I was correct."

She suddenly felt it again, filling her with loving warmth. She smiled and nodded in acknowledgement of her mother's spirit. In another moment, she began to sense a second presence, which she recognized as Tommy Gallagher, her birth father.

"There's one more thing, Gaston," Sophia said. "When we all first met, Darius told me a story about a couple that came into what was then your father's shop many years ago. You said they were visiting New Orleans on their honeymoon. Your father gave the golden bowl to the woman as a wedding gift."

Gaston smiled. "I knew who you were that day. I recognized you by the way you affected the amethyst amulet, which now hangs around your neck. Not to mention that you looked just like Maeve. I felt compelled to introduce your mother in a way that when you finally discovered the bowl on your own, you would know it was she. Then, when you finally knew the truth, perhaps it would not come to you as much of a shock."

"So, it was another fib about them visiting New Orleans."

"Yes, a white lie, but one that was necessary at the time. Your mother and father were actually living here, but what happened that day was true. Your parents came into the shop, and your mother *did* hold the bowl and affect the energy in the room. My father gave her the letters, originally written by Maeve and her daughter Alannah. Then they disappeared before our very eyes." Gaston looked up at the portrait hanging over the fireplace. "It appeared that Elizabeth was acting out some kind of mime as she folded the letters, which were apparently visible to her, and carefully put them into her handbag. Quite extraordinary! My father and I wondered if we had simultaneously lost our minds, because the letters were visible when my father handed them to her. Then, suddenly, they vanished."

Sophia looked at Michael and smiled. He remembered witnessing the same thing with Luciana's letter that Sophia had found hidden in the bottom of the wooden box that held the golden bowl, which she found at the cabin. He never doubted that Sophia could see the letter, but it helped him to know that others witnessed the same phenomenon.

"To answer your question about Patrick being a member of Apeiros - White Buffalo, Darius, and I were already members. Patrick came into the fold when we reconnected with him several years after he took you to Colorado. The gathering seemed to hold greater meaning for the four of us than to the other nine in the group. When we were alone, Patrick showed us pictures of you and shared with us the news of your accomplishments. So, you see, we kept up with you throughout the years."

"So, all this time, White Buffalo has known about me?" Sophia asked.

"Yes, he has," Gaston said.

"The trauma of that terrible day apparently caused you to block out the memory of your mother's death," Darius said, "and Patrick was content to spare you the agony of knowing what really happened. This, in my opinion, was to your advantage. Had you remembered, you might never have developed the abilities that you now have because of guilt and fear. White Buffalo became the safe link between us, because he lived with his wife in Colorado. He kept track of you, knowing the right moment would make itself available to reunite us."

Darius stood and walked over to the fireplace. He turned his back and looked down into the flames, feeling the enormous weight of emotion release itself. It had been over forty years of holding the grief and pain at the loss of his only daughter and son-in-law, and wondering if he would ever see his granddaughter again. Tears flowed from his eyes as he released his burden.

Sophia slowly stood and walked up to Darius. He turned to face her. She lifted the folded handkerchief from his breast pocket, shook it free, and gently wiped his tears. She put her arms around his shoulders, kissed him on the cheek, and tenderly said, "My dear, dear Grandfather. How I love you so."

Chapter
Four

Over the next few days, Sophia and Michael rested up from the physical exhaustion and emotional upheaval of the previous weekend's events. They spent quiet time on her grandfather's plantation, walking through the woods, sitting by the lake, and acquainting themselves with the occasional rabbit, fox, or deer. Nothing brought Sophia more peace.

The newfound information about the murders of Elizabeth and Sophia's biological father, Thomas Gallagher, as well as the revelations of Sophia's family connections took some time to settle into her mind, although oddly enough, none of it seemed entirely out of place. Since she could remember, there was always a mystery about the unknown life of her mother, and for some reason Sophia felt a sense of serenity in accepting that Patrick, the man she had always loved and known as her father, was actually her great-granduncle.

For the first time, Sophia went by herself to the family plot, surrounded by a wrought iron fence on the other side of the woods, far from the plantation house. With a bouquet of flowers in hand, she passed through the squeaky gate and quickly spotted a large headstone that read: GALLAGHER, and under that, the names Elizabeth and Thomas – *Forever in Eternity*. For several moments, she simply stood and wept both tears of sadness for the tragedy of her parents' short lives, and joy for this spiritual reunion that forever erased the mystery of who she was in this lifetime.

She then sat down under an old oak tree for several hours and talked to her mother's spirit as if to catch up after forty years of being apart from one another. That one-sided conversation helped Sophia feel connected to some of her untapped roots. First on that list was to acquaint herself with the man who rested beside Elizabeth – Thomas Gallagher, the man whom Darius tearfully and quite lovingly called 'Tommy'. He was a stranger to Sophia, but she sensed an incredible loving energy come over her at the thought of him. More importantly, she felt Patrick's warm blessing to thoroughly explore the lives of Elizabeth and Thomas without fear, despite the dark specter of Algernon Gillette.

Deep within her soul, she heard Patrick's voice: *You are still safe. No harm can come to you, for you are protected . . .*

Sophia felt a deep sense of liberation, now finally free to inquire about her ancestry without question of who she was. She would think about all the new family revelations when she had more time, for she and Michael were re-framing how the news would affect their lives, knowing it would certainly bring change. Some would say the past is gone and has nothing to do with the present, but Sophia knew differently because of her many past-life experiences. She knew her task was to unearth the buried secrets, which would clearly change the story.

The shrouded mystery of her mother was no longer a secret. With this new awareness, Sophia finally had some sort of reference about the life of her mother *and* father, which opened the portals into her own personal insight. She also had a greater understanding of the solitary nature of Patrick. The death of Elizabeth and Thomas obviously weighed heavily on Patrick's heart and mind as he assumed the role of father and protector of his great-grandniece. As she became better acquainted with Darius and Gaston, she knew they would reveal the story of her mother and father. The past automatically altered, as truth shed its light upon the darkened mystery.

Laughing to herself, she thought this was how life worked - a series of questions, which lead to more questions, never actually arriving at an answer. Yet, what White Buffalo called the Circle of Life was ever unfolding into greater understanding and evolvement. Sophia was evolving as her life became more transparent from out of the mystery of what she once knew, into the realization of what was the truth - at least as much of the truth that she could comprehend.

However, Sophia found herself asking the inevitable questions of *what if, if only, and why,* to which even if there were answers, none would ease her weary mind and broken heart. *That type of inquiry,* she told herself, *would only keep me spinning. As the questions fade, so will the extreme pain.*

I am here to do what those who were here before me could not accomplish. I am here to celebrate my rich heritage. I honor my mother, father, and Patrick's memory, and the memories of the many who preceded me. I do my best, using my gifts and talents for the greater good...

"Could you use some company?"

Sophia perked and saw Michael standing at the gate.

"Always," she said with a loving smile.

Michael stepped onto the sacred ground and looked at the many headstones signifying the legacy of Darius MacPhaidin's family. He walked up and gently touched the Gallagher monument. "At last, we meet."

He joined Sophia under the tree, and she curled her arm inside his. "Dad said he scattered her ashes at the summit of Long's Peak. We climbed up there several times to pay homage to her. I guess maybe those ashes were actually his wife."

"The ceremony was all that mattered," Michael said.

"All my life, she didn't really exist except for in my mind, and my heart. And now – Tommy – what do I do with him, Michael? He's my father, but I don't even know him."

"You will, honey, but he understands it will take time. I mean, look at him – he's beside the love of his life. He's not going anywhere."

Sophia tried to laugh. "No, I guess not."

"They've both been here all this time, but more importantly, they've always been in your heart. This will be your legacy someday, and you'll all be together."

"*We* will be together," she said, squeezing his arm.

"I was hoping you'd say that."

"I've been sitting here, talking to them – telling them about my life with Dad. It seems strange calling him that in front of Tommy, but I can't think of him as 'Uncle Patrick'. He's Dad, and that will never change."

"And that's ok," Michael said. "They were taken from you, and Patrick took their place. He was your angel. He *was* your dad."

Sophia smiled and shook her head. "He was something, you know? Forty years, give or take, and as much as I thought I knew him, he still had his little mysteries."

"Oh, as if he had *you* all figured out," Michael said, nudging her.

Sophia laughed. "I drove him crazy! Are you kidding? That man was solid black and white - no gray tones - and I was pure 365 gigapixels of color. Dad was a mining engineer, a brilliant numbers guy, but his thoughts were very linear. Oh, the many times he would say 'I just don't understand the way you think.'"

"I'm a little slow on the uptake myself sometimes, babe," Michael said. "You're a 200 miles-per-hour Ferrari in a 30 miles-per-hour world."

She giggled as she looked off into the distance. "But he kept up with me. He was my great-granduncle, so he was older than the parents of kids I grew up with, but I never gave that any thought. He was in his sixties when I was a teenager, but he was one of those people who didn't look or act anywhere near his age. Gosh, he took me on my first climb up Pike's Peak when I was sixteen, and I had to stop about a dozen times to rest before I got to the top. I swear he would have jogged up if not for me huffing and puffing all the way. Really, he only began to slow down about two years before he died at ninety-six."

"And remember what he told you when he died?"

Sophia's eyes widened as she shook her head. "Oh, my gosh. 'Know thyself.'"

Michael had to laugh. "Any doubt he's Gaston's uncle? In and out of the shadows, talking in playful riddles?"

Sophia nodded with a smile. "There was always a subtle sense of mystery about him, and although I loved him deeply, I sometimes wondered if I really knew him. There was nothing sinister about it by any means, but I just knew he had secrets – things he refused to share."

"It makes perfect sense now, doesn't it?" Michael said.

"I know. I feel bad now, because I pressed sometimes about my mother, wanting something – *anything* - from him. But that old stubborn mule wouldn't budge. He'd say, there are some things we just don't talk about. Little did I know the double meaning. He was protecting me from my past down here, while at the same time hiding from his own grief over the death of his wife. Why didn't he tell me the truth once I was old enough to understand? I could have helped him."

"He was a protector, sweetheart," Michael said. "We take the world on our shoulders no matter how badly it crushes us."

"He was sometimes gregarious, and other times quiet and introspective, and since he never cared to discuss my mother, or any of his family for that matter, I simply accepted his reticence as normal."

"He was deeply devoted to you," Michael said. "That's all that was important."

"No father could love a daughter more. He *was* my father." She smiled and leaned back against the tree. "I guess now I know why we really didn't have much in common, except the cabin. That was the one place where we were perfectly in-sync. No matter how much stress he was under on some mining job, he was in hog heaven when we went up there – and so was I. We went up almost every summer weekend. It's funny, he went to relax, but he'd be up at dawn to go fishing, and then he worked all day, clearing brush, cutting wood, fixing the pump – there was always something to do."

"I'll bet he put you to work, too," Michael said.

"Oh, yeah. As far back as I can remember, I was responsible for tending the fire in the fireplace all weekend, adding a log here and there and banking the fire at bedtime with coal so a bit of kindling would easily re-start the fire the next morning. At the end of the weekend, I had to clean out the fireplace before we left for Denver. I'd scoop the ashes into a metal bucket and carry them to the ash pit at the end of the property, where I dumped them into a pit. Then I'd pour in several ladles of river water and stir everything into a gray soup with a stick. There wasn't gonna be any forest fire on my watch, I'll tell ya. Smokey Bear had nothing on this girl."

"Keeper of the fire and water? You still have that job now, just on a tad larger scale."

"Yeah, how about that? Back at the cabin, I'd crumple up newspapers in the fireplace and finely layer it with kindling and pinecones, topped with larger split logs so it would be ready to light the next weekend. When I got a little bigger, Dad taught me how to split logs with an axe and a wedge and sledgehammer. He taught me basic survival skills so he would worry less when I was outside in the woods on my own. With every little bit of new knowledge, I felt more confident out there.

"Whenever I went hiking alone, I always told him where I was going, and we'd agree on a specific time for me to come back. I felt so important hiking out there with my backpack loaded with food, first aid kit, compass, rope, Swiss army knife - anything I might need in an emergency."

"Sounds like he taught you well."

"He taught me that knowledge was power. He'd say, 'practice creates confidence and courage to go the distance, which propels you to keep your feet firmly planted on the ground while you reach for the stars.'"

Michael gave her that loving smile.

"What?"

"Nothing. Go on, tell me more about him."

"Well, we rarely went up to the cabin during the winter months, you know-"

"No running water," Michael said. "I know because it cost us a fortune to plumb the place last summer."

"Exactly, but we did go up once in awhile to check on the place, and sometimes we'd even spend the weekend if it wasn't too cold. From the paved road, we'd trudge across the bridge through four feet of snow. We'd haul river water, one bucket at a time, from a hole chipped through the ice. Before drinking it, we boiled it in a metal bucket on the old iron cook stove. And, you know before we remodeled and added onto the kitchen, there was that bare concrete floor? Well, if you spilled water on it, you had an instant sheet of ice. It took my dad quite a bit of reasoning to convince his inquisitive daughter not to intentionally create a skating rink there on the kitchen floor."

"Something tells me you spilled a drop or two anyway."

"Daddy would get so mad," Sophia laughed. "It wasn't until now that I realized taking a header on a concrete floor when you're over fifty isn't anywhere near as funny as when you're ten."

"Those were undoubtedly the rare moments when he wondered if he shouldn't have left you in down here in Louisiana."

Sophia's smile faded, and a tear began to well in her eye. "Can you imagine? He wasn't whole after his wife died. He was a lonely man in his fifties, resigned to spending the rest of his life alone. And suddenly, when this traumatized little three-year-old needed a dad, there he was – he raised me without any help, without his family to support him – all because he was protecting me. My God, Michael, he was such a wonderful man."

Michael put his arm around her and let her squeeze out a few more healthy tears. "I think he needed you just as much as you needed him."

"He was always there for me, the single parent at the piano recitals, the softball games, graduation, my wedding – my divorce. And all of those holidays – just the two of us, or maybe a dinner with the family of friends. He sacrificed so much for me."

"Granted, he saved your life," Michael said, "but you saved his, too. It sounds like he had very little to live for until you needed him. And remember, you were the bond between him and Apeiros." He held her for another few tears. "So what else did you do up at the cabin?"

Sophia unceremoniously sucked back the tears. "Oh, winter up there – you know how beautiful it is."

"Yeah," Michael said. "Beautiful, and a bit treacherous if you don't have a Humvee with a plow blade."

"I'd scramble up the hillside ledge, where I could jump and bury myself in eight-foot snowdrifts. I'd have to come in and change several times. I'd hang my wet clothes with wooden clothespins on a rope that extended behind the hot iron cook stove. Oh! And I built an igloo once."

"A real igloo?"

"I learned about the Inuit tribes of the American Northwest in my sixth grade Social Studies class. We watched a movie about them, and I learned how they constructed an igloo from 18" blocks of snow, one icy brick at a time. To finish the exterior, they smoothed handfuls of snow over the outside seams, which created a flawless rounded surface. One really snowy winter, the snow was perfect for building a tiny three-foot-high igloo just big enough for me and my dog, Buffy."

"Buffy?"

"She was this cute Beagle-Basset, with short front legs and the long ears of a Basset Hound, and the head and long back legs of a Beagle. From a side view, she stood at a downward slant."

"Buffy the Beagle Basset," Michael said.

"That's right. So, when Dad and I finished the igloo, I

urged Buffy through the icy entrance. She wanted nothing to do with it and scrambled out, so Daddy climbed in and got stuck about halfway in. Oh, I cried laughing, because he made a big deal out of it, screaming from inside that igloo – 'Get me out! I'm gonna die in here!' He was usually pretty stoic, so whenever he cut loose like that, he was hilarious."

"What about the summertime? Did you hike around there a lot?"

"Oh, yeah. During the warmer months, I scampered along the mountainside, hauling a knapsack packed with water, a drawing pad and colored pencils, a camera with an extra film cartridge, a peanut butter and jelly sandwich, potato chips, and plenty of dog biscuits. Man, Buffy and I were set for the day. We spent much of the time on the mountainside at an outcropping of large boulders that I called the Fort. I created a hideout by building a wall to enclose the space. I built a foundation wall from rock and mud to support a few timbers that held an old screen window frame I found in the shed. I layered pine boughs overhead to make a five-foot-high slanted ceiling. The interior was just large enough for Buffy and me to spend hours pretending we were bandits hiding out and conjuring up our next train robbery."

"Barbie dolls really weren't your speed, I take it?"

"No. I had a dad and no mom, remember? When I wasn't drawing or painting, I was climbing mountains, or fixing some gadget, or painting an old chair on Dad's workbench. You know, there was an artistry to the skills he taught me. I remember once I built a stone stairway up the steep mountainside from the cabin to the Fort, first digging horizontal flat indentations into the earthen hillside. I put these smooth rocks I found along the river's edge into the foothold and mudded them into place. The stairway project took a few weekends to finish as I hauled each rock up the hill to its new destination. I probably spent even more time chasing tumbling rocks down the mountainside. I was certain the runaway rock intentionally wiggled its way free from the foothold, just because it wanted to be by the stream. Then, you know me - even as a small child, I was all about making everything pretty. I covered each stone step with a carpet of green moss, believing the transplant would easily grow."

"So you inherited Patrick's engineering skills, but botany wasn't quite up your alley."

Sophia laughed. "For several weekends, I watered every mossy step, making numerous trips up the hill with a two-liter bottle of river water, but before too long I finally figured out maybe I needed to watch another movie in class about the finer points of moss-growing."

"So, it sounds like the two of you didn't do much relaxing on your relaxing weekends at the cabin."

"Actually, we did at night. After a supper of trout that we caught ourselves, we usually played several games of Canasta or Gin Rummy while listening to records on an old hi-fi stereo. Daddy loved the music of the forties and fifties – Sinatra, Dean Martin, Sammy, the Mills Brothers, Ella Fitzgerald, Nat King Cole – oh, gosh, we listened to all of them. I made popcorn, tossed with melted butter and salt into a big bowl, and we'd have a bottle of pop. Daddy would sneak a shot of whiskey into his drink when he thought I wasn't looking, but he didn't fool me. Then he would call the last game 'The Championship of the Evening', and he always let me win.

"And then, we went outside and wrapped up in blankets, just like you and I do now, and we sat and watched the stars and just talked. Michael, I cherish those talks. Even when I was little, I'd prattle on about little girl things and he would listen as if he were conversing with a queen. He was always interested in everything I had to say. And when I got older, he would talk about so many fascinating things – many things related to the Order of Apeiros, but I just didn't realize it then."

"I think he was preparing you for the time when you joined us. At least, by the time I knew him, it seemed apparent."

Sophia gave Michael a suspicious eye. "So, did you know about all this family stuff Darius and Gaston hit me with?"

"Not a clue," Michael said. "I always thought Patrick was your real father, and I knew nothing about your mother's death. Those two characters and White Buffalo don't let me in their inner circle."

"What do you mean?"

"Well, you see how Darius and Gaston are locked at the hip, despite their bickering?"

"Yes," Sophia agreed. "They're brothers and they've been together for about seventy or eighty years."

"Yeah, well, you'll see when they come to stay with us for the Order of Apeiros. When they get together with White Buffalo, it's kind of like hanging around a geriatric fraternity house."

Sophia laughed.

"And I'm their pledge – you know, not quite in the club."

"Oh, that's funny. Careful now, you're talking about my relatives, such as they are. You know, I fell in love with them the minute we met. In a way, it's almost like I have three fathers here on earth, and two more here in my heart."

"So, a typical night at the cabin with your dad ended with stargazing. No roasted marshmallows?"

"Well, of course, sometimes – or s'mores. Then we'd go back inside and Dad would catch up on his reading, while Buffy and I fell asleep on the rug in front of the blazing fireplace. He'd carry me to bed and tuck me in, and we said a prayer every night, counting our blessings." The tears began to well up again. She stood and looked at her parents' grave, touching the headstone as Michael wrapped his big arm around her . . .

Sophia and Michael had three days before they planned to return to Colorado. They decided to spend the day with Gaston in his antique shop, *Nothing but Tyme*. Since she now knew he was her granduncle, Gaston's charming shop held even greater significance for her.

"We need some furnishings for the cabin," Sophia said.

"Quite a few pieces, actually. In particular, we need a dining table and chairs for when we host Apeiros next month," Michael said.

"I must run some errands," Gaston said, "so why don't

you make yourselves right at home. If you would like to move pieces to the center of the room to get a better look at them under the skylight, feel free to do so. On my way back, I will stop by Café du Monde to get us some beignets and coffee. I'll be gone for about an hour."

When they first walked into the shop, Sophia noticed an exquisitely hand-carved walnut library table with a lustrous dark patina. The piece seemed to call out to her as she imagined where in the cabin she would place it. They rebuilt the cabin with good-sized rooms and vaulted ceilings to accommodate such a fine piece. Sophia decided the library table would go nicely in the great room behind the sectional sofa that sat in front of the fireplace, where it would be a primary piece at the center of the home.

A pair of French carved walnut throne chairs caught Michael's interest. He thought they would be beautiful on each end of the large rectangular dining table made of Goncalo Alves, a tropical two-toned hardwood from South America. With all the leaves in place, the rich red grain would make a stunning statement in the dining room. They moved the table to the open space and placed the throne chairs on both ends. They tried out different styles of chairs until they arrived at seven pairs that worked together well. In the next couple of weeks, Sophia would reupholster the seats in coordinating fabrics to complement their mountain decor.

Sophia chose several pairs of sterling silver candlesticks and candelabra to group on opposite ends of the dining table, which would beautifully enhance the ambiance of any dining experience with various sizes and shapes of ivory candles. The character of an unusual old-world wrought iron chandelier caught her eye. Beautiful crystal pendants added a touch of elegance as they hung from the chandelier's arms, catching the light in contrast to the black ironwork. Sophia was all about ritual, ceremony, and making things pretty. The atmosphere of their home would be conducive to all three.

For the master bedroom, Michael found a beautifully hand-carved mahogany poster bed, with posts tall enough to spiral to the ceiling. It was a must-have item on his list, for it was large enough for a king and all his courtiers. Perhaps his choice was more about the courtiers, but nevertheless the bed was big enough for his towering height. He would no longer need to hang his feet off the end of the bed. To balance the size of the piece, he selected an eight-foot-high mahogany armoire for the opposite side of the room.

For the windowed alcove, Sophia discovered a small oval table that doubled as a desk and chair. The table opened up to reveal an upholstered red velvet seat, hinged on the inside to a half round desk with a drawer beneath the tabletop. Sophia just loved unusual pieces that told a story, and she thought that this little desk must have been legendary.

Every piece they selected complemented the mountain decor along with their contemporary furnishings, making their home an eclectic mix of styles and history. They could have spent days at Gaston's shop searching for just the right pieces, but for the moment, a few more accessories would complete their search until they returned to New Orleans the following year.

Sophia never went out into the world without wearing

her amethyst amulet and her aquamarine ring. The amulet connected her to other like items of similar resonance, and the ring provided a field of protection around her. She never knew when she would need the safeguard, but that day proved to be one of them.

There was a small room in the back corner of the store that Sophia had not noticed before. Draped over the doorway was a Persian throw, held back to one side by a large tasseled rope, appearing as one of the accessories in the shop. The small room possessed a numinous quality that drew her into its atmosphere, and yet she thought twice before entering. Sophia felt a sense of reverence for the small space, as if she was trespassing. She carefully pushed the drape aside as she ducked into the darkened recesses of the windowless space. There was just enough light leaving a gleaming reflection on the round crystal ball at the center of a draped table with chairs all around. She reached out and lightly touched the crystal ball, which caused images to flash through her mind of the people once served by its use. The protective quality of her aquamarine ring kept her safe, knowing that, at her convenience, she could tap into their stories. When she stepped away from the room, Sophia wondered about the mystic life of her Uncle Gaston.

Whenever Sophia came near the glass display cases, her amethyst amulet began to vibrate. Of course, her curiosity was piqued. She would have to wait until Gaston returned to discover the mystery, for he had taken the keys that unlocked the cases. Before he returned with coffee, she went to the case where the vibration was strongest. No jewelry was inside, but rather, it held a wide variety of small collector's items, such as pocketknives, snuffboxes, candle snifters, and figurines. Nothing called her immediate attention, but she had to admit she was more preoccupied with furniture and accessories for the cabin. Yet, the vibration of her amulet kept her searching for the piece with which it best resonated. Just then, Gaston returned with coffee and beignets from New Orleans' famous Café du Monde.

"Gaston, when you get a chance, would you please unlock this glass case? Evidently, there is something of interest in here. My amulet just won't stop quivering."

Of course, he already knew which piece it was. He was just waiting for her to find the small golden cast of an ammonite. "At the center is a labradorite, which is a stone of protection," he said. "The ammonite represents the ethereal plane of infinite expansion. My grandfather gave this to my grandmother as an engagement piece."

"So, that would be my great-grandfather, right?" Sophia said.

"It would," Gaston said with a wink. He took the golden ammonite out of the case and handed it to Sophia. "The labradorite protected our grandmother in a very crucial historical moment. Its history will come to you over time."

"Getting to the point isn't your strong suit, is it, Uncle?"

"Exasperating, isn't it?" Gaston said.

"Very much so."

"Just be patient, my darling, for there are reasons for everything. Now, take a look - the expansive nature of the ammonite represents the never-ceasing continuum of life and how we continue to grow and evolve through our many lifetimes, to infinity. The cast of the ammonite itself, I believe, is the same golden metal in all of your talismans. As you know, I cannot identify the metal, but the chain holding the ammonite cast is 18-karat gold."

"I have a feeling everything I am attracted to in this shop came from your lineage, or from Darius' family," she said.

"Yes, there is some truth to that. In this case, the piece's history is connected to the Delacroix family – your flesh and blood."

The piece resonated with her amulet and her ring, as the spirit of all three joined as one. The familiar sound rang out, and the room lit up, filling the space with light more brilliant than sunlight. The ammonite found its home with her. Sophia, however, could not help but wonder about the ammonite's validity, recalling the letter from Luciana that mentioned only five items, the ring among them, but she wondered - why would the ammonite attune with her ring and pendulum if it weren't authentic?

On the other hand, she remembered Yeshua telling Rachel there were many pieces that would enhance her life's work. She knew that Rachel's work was not for her alone, but for all of the descendants of her lineage, beyond time and space. She quickly concluded this ammonite must be another true talisman. According to Gaston, it connected to the ethereal realm, completing the five elemental pieces of earth, air, fire, water, and ether.

She peered into the stone's labradorescence, with its multi-dimensions of color, similar to the vibrant iridescent tones of violet, blue, turquoise, green, and gold tones of a peacock feather. The physical world disappeared around her, and she found herself in an unfamiliar atmosphere. Nothing she dreamed of yet took her to such a place of awareness. She transcended the physical realm, and yet she was in an environment of her soul's knowledge. It was a realm similar to that of her near-death experience. The feelings were the same, but the atmosphere was different.

Gaston and Michael watched her body fade from view for several seconds as she looked into the labradorite set into the ammonite's center. Michael grabbed for her arm, but his hand passed right through her.

Knowing she would soon understand more about this new awareness beyond time, Sophia made a conscious choice to come back. Time would reveal where she journeyed, with the help of the ammonite. Michael felt helpless, and was quite relieved to see her return. Soon afterward, however, his fear turned to anger. His pupils turned black as he stared at Sophia.

Taken back by his response, she quickly said, "Michael, I'm in control of these ventures. I am always at choice to return. That is part of my power. So, please don't worry."

"Well then, I feel so much better now," Michael sarcastically said. He switched to a defensive posture, speaking in clipped tones. "That is so easy for you to say. So, you're telling me that I'm supposed to stand back and watch you fade away? I'm the one person who hears all your dreams and visions, and believe me, it's challenging for me, knowing that I am supposed to be your protector."

"Michael, it's your presence that protects me - it is your heart. The love you have for me protects me and brings me back home to you, which is far more powerful than anything you can do. It's not always in the action you take, but the soul's connection between us that does the protecting. That is what pulls me back to you each time. I have been guided many times to know this."

"I'm aware of that," he said. "You are protected, guided, and supplied with all you need. So, if that is the case, why am I your appointed protector? Tell me that!"

"It's our soul's connection that helps to protect me, but truly it is who you are - it is *you*, my love."

Sophia smiled, knowing she needed to remain strong. She loved Michael so greatly and wanted to make sure he was all right with the changes she was going through, for they affected them both.

He knew he was not going to win this argument, but after hearing about her mother's murder, he was even more on edge. For a few moments, Gaston stayed silent, observing their exchange of energy. He knew that all would be well.

Then Gaston said, "Michael, if I may I remind you, there are eleven others to help you protect Sophia in the same way that we are here to support each other. And, of course, as you know, in the greater sense of things we are never alone." Gaston placed his arm around Michael's shoulder. "That is one of the reasons for Apeiros. We each have our individual calling, and yet we are here as a collective whole."

"I know that," Michael said with a sigh. "And thanks for reminding me. I've just been worrying so much about this thug, Gillette."

"Tell me about it," Gaston said. "He scared me so

much, I changed my name!"

"I've been pondering this," Michael said, "and I wonder what you two would think about presenting our concern about Algernon to the group when we meet in Colorado? If we participated in a collective healing, maybe we could counteract his negative energy."

"It's a splendid idea!" Gaston said. "Sophia?"

She shrugged. "I'm a believer."

"Then that is precisely what we shall do," Gaston said. "Oh, I so look forward to coming to your new home. I have never been to Colorado, and I don't believe anyone else in the group has either, except of course White Buffalo."

"That's why we selected this table and fourteen chairs," Michael said as he settled down. "Let's talk it over with Darius and solidify our plans to join together at the cabin in a month. I think we can pull it off, don't you, Soph?"

"Yes, by then we will have everything ready," she said.

Gaston walked over to the library table. "I would like to point out that you have selected a significant piece of family history here."

"This table does look familiar," Sophia said. "Haven't I seen this at the plantation, in the library?"

"You don't miss much do you?" Gaston smiled. "Darius wants you to have it. We moved it here last night, hoping you would choose it for your home. It just so happens that Uncle Patrick carved this table in his senior high school shop class. He carved it from a single block of walnut. It is quite the masterpiece with the acanthus leaf motif on the legs. Very few people create such pieces anymore. It is truly a work of art. So, Sophia, the table is yours."

Sophia felt her emotions rise. "Gaston, this is overwhelming."

"Uncle Patrick wanted to be a woodcarver as a young man," Gaston said. "This exquisite table was the most prized of all his pieces."

"I used to love watching him work with his hands," Sophia said. "He was very talented. I wonder why he didn't take this with him to Colorado."

"Actually, it was a wedding gift for your mother and Tommy. That is why Darius wants you and Michael to have it. He put me up to it, because he said if he gave it to you at the plantation, he would blubber like a baby."

"Oh, my gosh, now I'm crying," Sophia said. "I'm so happy to have it. It truly is a beautiful piece." She ran her hand along the tabletop, admiring Patrick's artisanship. "I wish he could have seen it placed in the cabin. It will be stunning in our great room."

While Michael paid Gaston, Sophia took the silver candelabra and the smaller pieces to the RV. Gaston gave them the family discount - a much better deal than either of them could possibly imagine – and he would make the necessary arrangements with a moving company to ship the furniture to Colorado. Sophia returned to the shop with a couple of her paintings.

"Uncle, I want you to have these to sell - just to make up for all the discounts you gave us."

"My dear, I don't know what to say."

"Say yes, Gaston," Michael said, "otherwise, you'll have a fight on your hands, and we'll be late for dinner."

"They're beautiful," Gaston said. "Thank you. You know, I sold the two you gave me last year within a month. Why don't I display some of your other pieces, too? I could clear some space and create a little gallery."

"Would you?" Sophia said. "How wonderful! And what a lovely excuse to come visit you more than once a year, but I insist you take 40% from the sales, just as any other gallery would. Deal?"

"Very well," Gaston said.

"Michael, would you mind getting the paintings out of the RV? I'll wrap it up here with Gaston."

Sophia walked past another display case, when something caught her eye. She took particular interest in a blue and white porcelain teacup and saucer trimmed in gold. She noticed on the inside of the cup a printed white star on a red flag, and underneath was a printed scrolled ribbon that read, *White Star Line.*

"Wait! Gaston, what is this?"

Gaston coyly smiled as he walked up. "Something catch your eye?"

She looked inside like a child peering into a candy case. "The cup and saucer in here – White Star Line? Is that *the* White Star Line?"

Gaston smiled as he unlocked the case. "Well, let us see, shall we?" He pulled out the delicate cup and saucer and placed it on the counter.

Sophia picked it up as if it were a delicate flower. She

suspiciously looked at Gaston. "This isn't from the *Titanic*, is it?"

Gaston simply smiled.

"C'mon, Uncle. It's a replica, right? Or it came from another White Star Line ship – the *Olympic* maybe? Was this set an extra piece left behind? Or was it brought up from the bottom of the ocean? Gaston! You're making me crazy here!"

"Actually, one of the survivors brought it from the ship the night *Titanic* sank," Gaston said.

"Oh, my goodness," Sophia said. She turned the teacup in her hand as some of its history flashed through her mind. She saw a woman dressed in a winter coat and hat. Over the coat, she wore what appeared to be a white canvas lifejacket. As the woman walked out of her elaborately decorated stateroom, she carefully wrapped the cup and saucer in a red scarf and placed them in a small black leather bag.

"What 'cha got there?" Michael asked, as he returned with an armful of paintings.

Sophia intentionally brought herself back into the room.

"Just one last item for the road," Gaston said. He took the cup and saucer and carefully wrapped them for her to carry.

"More stuff?" Michael said. "The bank's gonna make Gaston cut my credit card in half if we don't slow down here."

"No, no," Gaston said, handing the package to Sophia.

"It's another gift. This is quite valuable, as you might imagine, so don't sit on it on the way home. Its story, and to whom it is connected, will soon reveal itself. Enjoy!"

"Soph?" Michael said, waving his hand in front of Sophia's blank face.

"I'll tell you about it when we're on the road," Sophia said.

Life was never boring for Sophia. The excitement of the ammonite talisman opened her to another dimensional portal, allowing for the broader perspective that she needed to process all the new information about who she was in the world. She was primed and ready for new adventures into territories she had not yet imagined, and the cup and saucer were about to catapult her into a past life that most people only dreamed of, yet would never truly want to experience.

When she and Michael returned to the plantation, Sophia placed the cup and saucer on the nightstand. She went to bed early the next couple of evenings, with the revelations about her family history taking quite a toll on her emotions. The history of the cup and saucer began to reveal itself, beginning in her dreams that first evening. She briefly recalled a past dream she had months earlier of a woman who sailed on the *Titanic*.

Sophia no longer needed to wait for her dreams to lead her to other dimensional fields, but she did not want to take time away from Michael or her family during the day. She chose to wait until her dreams easily allowed her right of entry into a deeper sense of who she once was. Not only did she have access to her past, but she could also connect to the history of pieces that she touched. This way, Sophia tapped into the lives of her ancestors, and even some strangers, who at times were simultaneously inner-woven into the many layers of her past.

Sophia was beginning to understand that life contained the entire universe as an intricate web of journeying souls. When peering into its vast wholeness from a distant perspective, fractal patterns of sacred inner-connectivity emerged like the symbols and varied colors of a mandala - as the grand design of life ever unfolding.

CHAPTER Five

*S*ophia welcomed into her dreams the vision of her life as Jocelyn Brewster Davis. It took her from the immediate worries about Algernon and his son, into another memory of who she once was in another time and place. She had no difficulty recalling the history connected with the cup and saucer, beginning with Wednesday, April 10, 1912. *Titanic* began her maiden voyage from Southampton, England, heading across the English Channel with 922 passengers aboard.

Belfast's White Star Line did not christen its ships. By that time in history, christening a ship by breaking a bottle of champagne over her bow at her launch was more of a Catholic tradition. Belfast was a Protestant city, and perhaps that is why the White Star Line, comprised of Protestants loyal to the British crown, did not christen its ships. However, some who were superstitious believed that if such a blessing had taken place, *Titanic's* fatal history might never have come about.

At the beginning of the voyage, a near disaster occurred in Southampton when the massive ship passed by the moored ocean liners, SS *City of New York* and *Oceanic. Titanic's* enormous size displaced so much water that a swell arose high enough to drop both ships into a trough. The strained mooring cables of the *SS City of New*

York snapped, forcing the ship to swing around toward *Titanic*. Captain Edward J. Smith ordered *Titanic's* engines full astern, and the two ships barely avoided a collision by a mere four feet. The tugboat, *Vulcan*, came to the rescue and towed the *SS City of New York* back to the dock, delaying *Titanic's* departure by an hour.

Titanic crossed the English Channel, traveling 77 nautical miles toward Cherbourg, France. The weather was windy, cold, and overcast. Cherbourg's docking facilities were not sufficient for a ship the size of *Titanic*. She was 882' 9" long and ten decks high, measuring 104 feet from the keel to the top of the bridge, while holding 900 tons of baggage and freight. Ship's tenders were required to transfer passengers from shore to ship.

On the dock in Cherbourg, motor cars lined up bumper to bumper, each filled to the limit with luggage and steamer trunks piled so high on car tops and rumble seats that only a webbing of heavy rope could hold each mass together. Dozens of horse-drawn carts overflowed with provisions waiting to be loaded onto the ship.

Jocelyn Brewster Davis could hardly think straight. The noise was deafening, and there was very little order - only chaos. Hundreds of people moved in every direction in the blustery cold. Gathered on the dock were crewmembers, hired drivers, dockworkers, and passengers' servants, in addition to the 247 passengers who waited impatiently for transfer by the tenders.

Men barked orders at those unloading carts with the ship's cargo and provisions. Taxi drivers left their customers' baggage stacked in piles for the dockworkers to transfer onto the dinghies. There was very little room to stand without getting in someone's way. It was half-past six, and the spring sky was growing dark.

After Jocelyn's taxi driver unloaded her luggage onto the pier, she paid him the fare plus a generous tip. She gathered her smaller bags and quickly turned to join the crowd, accidently colliding with a dockworker who seemed to come out of nowhere. She dropped her black leather valise, her makeup case, and handbag.

The dockworker swiftly straightened his jacket and gathered himself, then bowed at the waist and tipped his hat in her direction. "May I beg your pardon, Mademoiselle? I am such a fool." They both knew she caused the fracas by not paying attention where she was going. "I am dreadfully sorry for causing you any distress."

Although it was dusk, Jocelyn could not help but notice how he towered over her. She guessed him to be about 6' 3" tall, nearly a foot and a half taller than her diminutive height. The dim lighting from a faraway lamppost reflected on his face, and she quickly took note of his distinguished good looks. Appearing in his early thirties, he was dressed in a dockworker's uniform of dark woolen pants and heavy peacoat. His dark blonde hair held sun-streaked waves, which complemented his healthy tan. By the sound of his dialect, she assumed he was French.

"That's quite alright, Monsieur," Jocelyn said, straightening her tri-corner hat and taking out a four-inch hatpin to weave it back through her hair. "With so many people gathering about, it's difficult not to bump into one another."

Jocelyn bent down at the knees to pick up her handbag

just when the dockworker leaned over to assist her. They collided again, hitting heads and knocking her to the ground.

"Oh, Mademoiselle, again, I *do* beg your pardon!" He bent down to help her to her feet, lifting her by the arm.

This time, her response was not as amiable. Jocelyn rose to her full height of 4' 10" tall, and immediately became a formidable adversary. She wrenched away from his grip and proceeded to brush the soiled spots from the dark brown satin cuff on her woolen tweed jacket. She then brushed the satin inset on her skirt and hem. She also noticed the scuff on her button boots, which brought her additional distress.

The man leaned over to pick up her hat, and she quickly snatched it away from his grip. "Mon Dieu! I am so terribly, terribly-"

"Sorry! Yes, I know! I heard you the first time!" She firmly placed her hat on her head, making her hair even more disheveled. She had to remove her gloves to tuck the stray wisps of auburn hair back under her hat.

"Mademoiselle, please forgive me."

Jocelyn looked at him with fire in her green eyes. "It is *Madame*. And if you will be so kind to hand me my bag and my valise without dropping them on my foot, I will be on my way."

"Oui, of course." He gathered her things and nearly fumbled them again. "I am such an idiot."

She almost smiled at this ridiculously charming oaf as she quickly put her gloves back on, challenged by fitting the snug calfskin along each finger, which provoked and agitated her more. When he handed over her bags, she impatiently grabbed the valise away from his grip and tucked the makeup case under her arm. She turned on her heels to join the crowd of passengers waiting for the ship's tender to transport them aboard. The dockworker cut his losses and sheepishly disappeared into the melee.

Jocelyn took a deep breath and calmed down as she waited in the long line to board the tender. She could not help but again notice a feeling of dread that hovered over her for weeks. Jocelyn had a strong intuition and mystical abilities of knowing. She received many intuitive nudges warning her *not* to sail upon *Titanic*.

Jocelyn wondered if her intuitive warning was due to the delay of *Titanic's* initial departure date due to her sister ship, *Olympic*, colliding with the *HMS Hawke* the previous September. Captain Smith was in command of the *Olympic* at the time of the collision. The propeller shaft from the *Titanic* replaced the broken piece to make the necessary repairs for *Olympic* to set sail again. The repairs took two months to mend the enormous triangular hole in her starboard side near the stern. Then, in February 1912, *Olympic* threw a propeller blade on her return from New York. Again, it was necessary to utilize *Titanic's* resources to make the repairs, delaying her maiden voyage originally set for March 20, 1912.

This was not enough to keep Jocelyn from sailing aboard the *Titanic*, but in addition to the ship's near collision with the *SS City of New York* in Southampton, a national coal strike in the United Kingdom lasted thirty-seven days, finally ending April 6th, just four days before *Titanic's* departure date. The strike disrupted railroad and shipping schedules, causing many cancellations. The British government finally intervened by passing the minimum wage law. Many travelers postponed their plans until the strike was over.

The full capacity of *Titanic* was 3,547 passengers and crew, leaving her maiden voyage under capacity, with 2,229 people aboard - 1,316 passengers and 913 crewmembers, of whom most were not seamen, but rather, engineers, firemen, stokers, stewards, and galley staff. Ninety-seven percent of the crewmembers were male, and three percent were female.

The operation of *Titanic* required 825 tons of coal per day. Because of the coal strike, four days was not enough time to transfer coal from the mines. *Titanic* was only able to sail due to the transfer of coal from other International Mercantile Marine Company vessels in Southampton, putting the other IMM ships out of service, one of which was the *SS City of New York*. Some passengers that were booked to sail on those ships turned to *Titanic* instead.

Jocelyn dismissed her intuitive warnings, thinking her emotions were residual effects of her long period of grief over the loss of her beloved husband. New life was calling her forward, and she had many ideas brimming in her mind. She could not take action on them until she returned to New York City.

While standing in line, Jocelyn reflected on rumors she overheard that started in Belfast. The greatest rumor regarded the switching of *Olympic* with *Titanic*. It was one of the most common forms of marine fraud, to switch names and fittings with another identical ship when the damage of one ship was beyond repair and no longer insurable. The damaged ship would sink at sea, thus making an eventual insurance claim for the ship thought to be the one insured. *Surely there could not be such a devious plan for this ship,* she thought.

Jocelyn conceded that warning signs could be small. She had to wonder if her collision with the Frenchman was just such a warning. She continued her justification for moving forward on the journey because she paid a substantial fare to travel in a First Class suite on the maiden voyage of the world's newest and most luxurious ocean liner, and she was not going to pass it up. *Titanic* held a total of 840 staterooms, of which 416 were for First Class passengers, 162 for the Second Class, and 262 for Third Class. The most expensive fares for a First Class Parlor Suite cost $4,350. Jocelyn splurged, knowing she would never again partake in such extravagance.

In Sophia's time, the cost of the fare would translate to $100,000. A $150 berth in First Class - $3,500. First Class children and dogs traveled for half-fare. A Second Class Berth cost $60, translating to $1,375 in Sophia's time, and a $15 to $40 Third Class ticket would cost $350 - $900.

It took years for parents to muster the finances for their entire family to voyage across the Atlantic Ocean to a new life in America. Among the Third Class passengers were two families of eleven people each, and one of eight. There were no cheap seats on *Titanic.*

Despite the chaos, it only took ninety minutes to load the cargo, baggage, and passengers onto the leviathan of a ship. *Titanic* left Cherbourg's port at 8:00 p.m., heading for Queenstown, Ireland to pick up the remaining passengers the next day before setting sail across the Atlantic Ocean for New York City.

Captain Smith greeted all First Class passengers as they boarded the ship. Five of the eight-piece orchestra played festive melodies, immediately impressing the passengers of the ship's opulent celebratory atmosphere. A steward escorted Jocelyn to her First Class Parlor Suite, located mid-ship on the Bridge Deck or B Deck, where the rocking motion of the ship was less bothersome. She tipped the steward half of his gratuity, with a shilling, requesting he promptly deliver her steamer trunk and other luggage. She assured him that she would match the tip if he did so. He looked down at the generous amount in his hand and happily complied.

Her suite contained a bedroom with a wardrobe, and a small parlor. The rooms, stylishly decorated in an Old Dutch style, were quite elegant and sumptuous. The furnishings, woodwork, and paneling were of light walnut, inset with rose-colored flocked wallpaper. The upholstery and bed linens were color coordinated with the plush carpet. Jocelyn's bedroom appeared fit for royalty, appointed with a four-poster bed luxuriously draped at the corners, a dressing table and bench, and a chest of drawers. A beautifully upholstered chaise lounge sat opposite the bed. At the center of the bedroom was a small round table with two chairs. Jocelyn was pleased, knowing she would be more than comfortable during the weeklong voyage.

She also enjoyed the luxury of her own private bath, complete with a vanity and bathtub with hot and cold running water. The private bath was the main reason she chose to stay in a suite. On past voyages across the Atlantic, she shared bath facilities with other passengers, so she was truly stepping up in the world of travel on the most luxurious ocean liner in the world.

Despite the cozy opulence of her suite, she could barely quell her excitement to go out and explore the beautiful ship. Since her steamer trunk and luggage might not arrive for a while, she decided to freshen up and go out with the clothes she was wearing. *No one will know the difference,* she thought. She sat at the dressing table flanked by electric lights on either side of the mirror. She checked her cosmetic case, relieved to know nothing broke when that silly Frenchman knocked her down at the dock.

She almost laughed. *Buffoon,* she thought. *If he had not been so frightfully handsome, I might have given him a piece of my mind.*

She took off her hat and removed the hairpins holding up her tangled mass of waist-length hair. She brushed it out and twisted it into a chignon at the base of her neck, winding the sides around the bun to make her auburn locks presentable again. When she finished, she looked into the mirror and put a faint tint of rose rouge on her cheeks. She then lightly powdered her face, followed by a bit of matching rose-colored lip tint. She felt presentable again and ready to make an appearance to any eligible millionaire bachelor who happened to look her direction.

Jocelyn was starting over. Two years of grieving from the devastating loss of her dear husband, Henry, to influenza left her a young, childless widow in search of a new beginning. Henry had a good mind for business and established himself in the steel industry as an up-and-coming steel baron. Jocelyn also had a flourishing career, rare for a woman of her time. They owned a beautiful home in Pittsburgh, and traveled among the elites of the Industrial Revolution. For a time, they had it all until they made the fateful decision to travel to Europe on holiday.

Jocelyn spent the last two years picking up the pieces, finally facing the inevitable conclusion to move on with her life. She sensed her beloved Henry gave his blessing, for she felt a certain surprise at the prospect of entertaining new suitors. She longed for male companionship, even if in the beginning it was only to attend public affairs together. At twenty-seven, Jocelyn had many years left to live a full life and once again find love. Nothing, she insisted, would hold her back from a bright future.

The First Class Dining Saloon closed at 7:30 p.m., but the Café Parisien was open from 8:00 a.m. to 11:00 p.m., where she could choose from the à la carte menu. It happened to be located on the same level as her suite on the Bridge Deck, making it easy for her to keep her bearings that evening. She planned to arise early the next morning and take a tour through the ship before it arrived in Queenstown at 12:30 p.m. This would give her plenty of time to become acquainted with the various First Class Amenities.

Jocelyn left a note and another shilling for the steward, and took one last look into the mirror before she left the suite. Her excitement at making the voyage meant more than crossing the Atlantic. She was beginning her life again with fresh new dreams to expand her custom dressmaking business into one that would potentially bring tremendous commerce for New York, Chicago, London, Rome, and Paris.

As a designer of Art Nouveau couture, she developed

quite a reputation for her beautiful designs on both sides of the Atlantic, but times were changing and she wanted to expand her business into producing stylish ready-to-wear clothing for men, women, and children. The concept of the modern department store was building momentum, and she intended to capitalize on the trend by offering attractive, affordable clothing items for all classes of people, while continuing to design her custom pieces. *A modest dream*, she thought, *by which I intend to conquer the New York garment district!*

As she left her suite, she turned to lock the door, but the skeleton key slipped from her hand as she pulled it from her handbag. Seemingly from nowhere, a steward suddenly appeared. Jocelyn was more than surprised to see the same man who ran into her at the departure gates an hour before. He was smartly dressed in a steward's uniform, quite different from the dark wool she saw him wear earlier.

"Allow me," he said as he quickly leaned over to reach for the key.

"You again? Don't you even think about it, Monsieur!" Jocelyn said. "With thousands of people on board, what are the chances that we would be in each other's presence again? Leave the key to me, please. I don't care to be upended again." She bent down and snatched the key.

"As you wish," he said. He straightened up and stood back, leaving her to her business. "By the way, *Madame*," he was sure to place emphasis on her title, "it appears I shall be one of your stewards during the voyage, so please know that I am at your service in the event that you need someone to pick you up off the floor."

She tried not to smile. "I will do my best to keep my distance from you. Otherwise, I might need medical assistance. Good evening to you, Monsieur." She locked the door, dropped the key back into her handbag, and swiftly proceeded down the hall toward the public areas.

The Frenchman watched her hasten down the long corridor and rapidly disappear around the corner. A smile curled his lips. "You Americans leave little to be said."

He could not help but like her sassy nature. This might be a more exciting voyage than he originally planned. Who knows what might happen?

Chapter Six

Café Parisien, situated directly outside the First Class À la Carte Restaurant, was the only restaurant on the ship with large picture windows for diners to enjoy a view of the sea. Never before had a British ship offered such an amenity for its passengers. During the day, the sunlit veranda captured the atmosphere of a sidewalk café in Paris, charmingly decorated with wicker tables and chairs and French trelliswork, all painted white. Climbing ivy vines and other green plants added to the garden ambiance.

The À la Carte Restaurant was the most intimate dining experience on board, with its own reception room located next to the aft Grand Staircase. The room, decorated in elegant Louis XVI style, displayed walnut paneling and lit picture windows. Crystal lamps held intimate candlelight at each table, which seated from two to eight people in Georgian style armchairs and settees upholstered in Carmine red silk. The tables were set with white linen tablecloths, porcelain dishware, gleaming silver flatware, and crystal goblets. A stringed orchestra played classics from composers such as Puccini and Tchaikovsky.

The restaurants, served by subcontracted chefs and their staffs, offered luxury dining for First Class Passengers at an additional cost beyond the passenger's fare. The menus were the same for both restaurants, featuring caviar, lobster, quail, plover's eggs, oysters, salmon, roast duckling, sirloin of beef, pâté de foie gras, hothouse grapes, fresh peaches, and chocolate and vanilla éclairs. Jocelyn chose a small meal of pâté, with fruit, bread, and cheese, paired with a nice Chardonnay.

The restaurants were nearly full that evening, offering Jocelyn many opportunities to hobnob with fellow passengers sailing across 'The Pond'. Her trepidation over the voyage yielded to her renewed lust for life, as she felt a rush of excitement at her discovery of the many influential people on board. Some were quite famous, like mining heir, Benjamin Guggenheim, who was traveling with his mistress, an unknown woman whom, according to the *Titanic* grapevine, was a French cabaret singer.

Seated at the table next to Jocelyn was John Jacob Astor IV, builder of the famous Waldorf-Astoria Hotel and reportedly the wealthiest man in the world. Although Jocelyn resisted most of the gossip bantering about, she did raise an eyebrow at Astor's new nineteen-year-old wife, Madeleine Force Astor, whom every woman on the ship could tell was quite pregnant. The middle-aged multi-millionaire had divorced his wife for Madeleine, and the two were returning to New York after an extended honeymoon in Europe, away from the scrutiny of New York society.

Jocelyn was thrilled to learn that the owner of R. H. Macy & Co., Isidor Straus and his wife, Ida, were also aboard. They retired for the evening before she could introduce herself, but Jocelyn put it in the back of her mind to engage Mr. Straus in conversation about her concept of affordable ready-to-wear apparel. She believed her idea was perfectly suited for Macy's, the largest department store in the world. With more than one million square feet of floor space, Macy's certainly had room for her clothing designs, and Jocelyn determinedly resolved to sell Mr. Straus on her idea before they docked in New York.

In the reception room, outside the À la Carte Restaurant, Jocelyn introduced herself to the well-known London fashion designer, 'Madame Lucile' and her husband, Sir Cosmo Duff-Gordon, a dashing Scottish landowner and fencing champion who served on the organizing committee for the 1908 Summer Olympic Games in London. His family founded Duff-Gordon sherry in Spain during the latter part of the 18th century. He and Lucy, also known as Lady Duff-Gordon, were traveling incognito under the assumed name of Mr. and Mrs. Morgan.

Lucy founded the British-based haute couture fashion house, famously known as *Lucile Ltd*. She was the first to achieve international acclaim among a trend-setting clientele, most of whom were of noble birth, royalty, and celebrated personalities of stage and film. She owned design houses in Paris and New York, and planned another in Chicago. Her best-known designs catered to women's desires of sensuality and romance. They were simplified, yet elegant silk and lace lingerie, tea gowns, and eveningwear with risqué slit skirts and low necklines.

Lucile was the first to introduce the IT Girl - the first professional models of outstanding beauty - displayed on what Lucy called the 'mannequin parade,' the forerunner of the fashion show, which included a curtained stage with a catwalk, mood lighting, and a small orchestra to set the atmosphere of supreme elegance. Clientele sat along the edge of the catwalk enjoying tea and cookies, while the IT Girls appeared on the stage wearing *Lucile's* latest couture fashions.

Although a bit intimidated by *Lucile's* success and fame, Jocelyn did not pass the opportunity to tell Lady Duff-Gordon about her design ideas. To Jocelyn's delight, Lady Duff-Gordon was fascinated and invited Jocelyn to meet her for tea the next afternoon at 4:00 p.m.

Among the other passengers Jocelyn met that evening, was one First Class woman who certainly stood out among the rest. Margaret Brown, the wife of a wealthy Colorado gold miner, also embarked from Cherbourg, having spent a portion of her holiday traveling in Egypt and France with John and Madeleine Astor. Jocelyn noticed Margaret earlier that day while waiting at the dock for the ship's tenders.

Mrs. Brown was a large woman in every sense of the word, large in girth, large in countenance, and large in voice, unafraid to speak her mind. Quite confident, she left little guesswork of her opinions, and yet, Jocelyn found her very affable and friendly. Many of the wealthy elite on the ship snubbed her, for she was 'new money'- a person of a lower social pedigree with newly acquired wealth. That haughty attitude made Jocelyn, a bit of a bohemian herself, want to get to know Margaret all the more.

As Jocelyn finished her meal, a waiter serving the guests at a nearby table caught her eye. He was quite handsome, Jocelyn thought, but she suddenly realized he was that clumsy Frenchman again - the same man who knocked her down at the dock and who also attempted to assist her with her key at the door of her suite.

Their eyes met, and noticing the puzzled look on her face, he bowed slightly with a polite nod and quickly walked toward the galley with several menus in hand.

She had the fleeting thought that, since the ship set sail so soon after the ending of the coal strike, they were unable to hire all the needed crew on such short notice. Perhaps crewmembers were cross-trained to work many different duties.

It was getting late. Jocelyn wanted to unpack and ready herself for the next morning's activities. She shook the unimportant queries from her mind and quickly gathered her belongings and left for her suite.

She was pleased to find her luggage waiting in the suite, neatly placed for her convenience. She turned on the electrical heater to ward off a chill in the air, and she removed her hat and jacket and went to work unpacking her bags and large steamer trunk. Placing everything into the brand new drawers and wardrobe made her feel more at home, for after all, the suite would be her residence for the next week.

When she opened her black leather valise, she was suddenly dismayed to find inside a compass, pencils and eraser, a ruler, protractor, and French curves. "Oh, what is this?" she angrily said. She found a small notebook filled with drawings of room details and various styles of buildings.

This black case was nearly identical to her bag, which actually once belonged to her husband - one of his last possessions that she kept. Keeping it with her on her travels helped her feel as if Henry was still with her. Although her rational mind told her this was a simple mistake and her case would be located, she felt in her heart a sense of panic at such a personal loss.

A sudden knock on the door struck Jocelyn with relief. *My bag!* she thought.

She quickly opened the door and felt both relief and surprise at who stood in the doorway, again wearing a steward's uniform. Embarrassed, the Frenchman smiled, holding up Jocelyn's black leather valise.

"Well, if it isn't the accidental gentleman. You certainly are a busy bee, aren't you?"

"Have you grown weary of me yet, Madame?"

"Not this time," she said with a laugh. "Please tell me that's mine!"

"Oui," he said with that charming accent. "And I believe you have my valise?"

"*Your* valise?" she said.

His eyes darted to and fro. "Oui – yes, it is mine. What a coincidence, no? They are so similar."

Jocelyn didn't care. She was just happy to get her bag back. "I apologize that I opened it, but I thought it was mine. The contents look like you might be an architect?"

He simply smiled. "Merci. Is there anything else I might assist you with, Madame?"

Jocelyn thought it more than peculiar that she had seen him in three different uniforms, working three different jobs in less than four hours. "Dockworker, steward, waiter - architect. My, what a Jack of all trades you are," she said.

"Jacques? No. I am Gaston, at your service." He awaited a smile that didn't come. "Ah, yes, architect. I am re-locating to New York to work for a prominent architectural firm."

Jocelyn leaned against the doorway and folded her arms. "Just a poor French vagabond architect working his way across the Atlantic, aboard England's most prestigious ocean liner bound for a lucrative job in America?"

"Very continental, no?" There was that playful smile again.

"How nice for you." She handed him his bag. She admitted to herself this man *was* charming and very handsome, but she had been single long enough to be leery of bright shiny packages. "Well, I *am* in the middle of unpacking. If you do not mind, might you give me my valise, please? I will be saying goodnight."

"Oh, oui, of course," he said. He handed her the valise and turned to leave.

"You seem to work all over the ship, Monsieur."

"It certainly appears that way, does it not? Bonne nuit, Madame. Fais de beaux rêves."

She stopped and looked at him. "Yes. Goodnight."

He smiled and closed the door. Jocelyn pondered for a moment. She had learned just enough French to be dangerous in Paris. Goodnight, he said. Sweet dreams.

The Frenchman walked down the hallway, wondering what it would take to warm her up. Maybe it was not his to do. He would certainly lose no sleep over it. It had already been a very long day.

CHAPTER Seven

Jocelyn slept soundly for several hours until an unfamiliar woman came to her in a dream. The woman appeared in her early twenties, quite beautiful, with blue eyes and dark hair tied back away from her face. She stood in a misty gray veil, lovingly holding a baby. She said, "Please tell François to no longer grieve. We are both happier than we could ever imagine. Let him know, when it is his time, we will be waiting to welcome him. Tell him he is deeply loved."

Jocelyn suddenly awoke, still feeling the strong presence of the woman in her room. Having had experiences as a medium since she was a young child, Jocelyn knew she would soon understand this vision, and to whom the woman was referring. She was often receptive to spirits who had a message to pass along to their loved ones.

The visitations did not frighten her, but they did arouse her enough to make it difficult to fall asleep again. She got up and put on her woolen bathrobe, and turned up the heater. For such occasions, she pulled out a small flask of cognac, which she hid in the dressing table drawer. She pulled the table up next to the bed and poured her own form of spirits into a teacup and then plumped up the pillows and crawled back under the covers. With a big day planned for Thursday, she hoped the cognac would calm her enough to sleep well until morning.

She awoke around 6:00 a.m. and decided to take a walk in the brisk morning air on the Promenade before bathing. Along the way, she met a young Irish priest from Cork, Reverend Francis Mary Hegarty Browne, who was taking photographs of a young boy playing with a top on the First Class Promenade. People tended to open up to Jocelyn for reasons she knew not why, but most of the time she truly enjoyed the conversations.

Father Browne told her how his uncle, the Bishop of Cloyne, raised him after the deaths of both his mother and father. As a gift, his uncle gave him the camera and a ticket for a holiday cruise on *Titanic's* maiden voyage from Southampton to Queenstown. He stayed in a First Class cabin on A Deck and spent most of his time taking photographs throughout the ship. As they walked together, they chatted as if they were old acquaintances. He took photographs here and there, including Jocelyn in a few.

"I met the most lovely couple at dinner last night, Americans they were," Father Browne said. "I suppose I bantered on so much about how I wanted to go to America some day. Well, we got on so well that they generously offered to pay my way to New York and back, just because they had enjoyed our time together. Can you imagine such a thing?"

"How sweet," Jocelyn said. "Are you going to take them up on it?"

"Sadly, no," he said. "I used that Marconi telegraph contraption to send a message to my superior, asking for permission, but he said no. I must stay with my original holiday plan and get off at Queenstown."

"More's the pity," Jocelyn said. "Maybe you will get there someday."

"Perhaps," Father Browne said. "I suppose I just didn't have the luck of the Irish this time."

Before they parted ways, they exchanged addresses, and since she would soon be moving from Pittsburgh to New York City, he asked her to write when she settled in. He promised to send her some of his photographs of the ship.

After her walk, Jocelyn took a bath in her private bathtub, using the French bubble bath she bought while in Paris. Rarely had she enjoyed endless hot running water, but on the ship, there was plenty for her pleasure and delight. If only she had a bottle of champagne to enjoy while soaking in the suds, she could complete the feeling of absolute decadence.

Feeling revitalized, she styled her long hair in a loose chignon at the base of her neck, lightly rouged her cheeks, and powdered her nose. She added just a touch of lip rouge to brighten her face. She chose an outfit comfortable enough to walk around the ship - a light gray woolen skirt, and a jacket with a smart white silk blouse underneath. To keep the chill out, she wore over her shoulders a red pashmina shawl made of soft cashmere wool. She brought a book for when she had some time to herself, wondering if the particular book she bought at a Paris used bookstore would be entertaining reading, considering *Titanic* would soon set sail across the Atlantic . . .

Sophia awoke in the middle of the night, reflecting upon the peculiar notion of dreaming of another who also had a dream that she herself could see. It felt like wandering through a maze of mirrors. She laid still, wrapped in the down comforter, with the cool autumn night's air blowing through the room and displacing the images of Jocelyn on the *Titanic*. Michael slept soundly next to her, snoring like a freight train.

With a sigh, she carefully arose from the bed, so as not to disturb him, and slipped on the plum colored silk robe that she laid out on the armchair the night before. Draped over an arm of the loveseat was a slightly faded red pashmina shawl. As she picked up the shawl, she thought, *No, it can't be.* She wrapped it around her neck and shoulders and stepped out onto the second story veranda outside their room. While standing at the black wrought iron railing, she closed her eyes and breathed in the cool scents of autumn's beginnings. She then curled up on a padded wicker loveseat and wrapped herself in a quilted afghan she found there, reveling in the added comforts of Southern hospitality. The soothing song of crickets put her into a deep meditative state, and Sophia quickly returned to the *Titanic*.

Chapter
Eight

Sophia drifted halfway between her own world and Jocelyn's, again viewing life on the *Titanic* through Jocelyn's eyes. Sophia thought it an amusing parallel, sitting on the veranda of the antebellum house while seeing herself as Jocelyn eating breakfast in the famous ship's Verandah Café.

The Palm Court, a mirror image of the Verandah Café, was on the other side of the Second Class stairway, which divided the two rooms. Jocelyn enjoyed a light meal of fruit and a breakfast roll with copious amounts of coffee and cream. She always strived for that perfect caramel color that cream brought to a good cup of coffee, so very appealing to her taste. Lunch and dinners aboard *Titanic* offered more than a generous amount of food, but a simple breakfast of fruit and a roll was all she needed that morning.

After breakfast, she briefly perused her book, but her eyes could not help but wander over the pages and into the splendor of her lavish surroundings. *Faux reading*, as she called it, gave her plenty of opportunities to observe with discretion those traveling in First Class. When not surveying her fellow travelers, Jocelyn actually enjoyed the book she found at the *Petite Paris Librarie*, a small used bookstore, a few days before she left for Cherbourg.

Written in 1898 by American author, Morgan Robertson, *Futility or Wreck of the Titan* was the story of a ship that hit an iceberg and foundered in the North Atlantic, 400 miles south of Newfoundland. She laughed to herself, thinking it might be wise to conjure up a different synopsis if anyone aboard should ask. *How fortunate that Titanic is an unsinkable ship,* she thought.

At noon, *Titanic* stopped for 90 minutes to board the remaining passengers at Queenstown, Cork, Ireland. As in Cherbourg, the water at Queenstown Harbor was not deep enough for the *Titanic* to dock, so passengers were ferried on the tender ship *Ireland*. The *Ireland* delivered bags of mail and 123 Irish passengers bound for new lives in America. Jocelyn's new friend, Father Francis Browne, was among the disembarking passengers. He carried the telegraphed dispatch he received from his superior when he asked for permission to accept the offer to sail on to New York - a note with five words that read, "Get Off That Ship - Provincial." He disembarked at Queenstown, having captured quite a number of photos of *Titanic's* grand interiors and the exterior. Father Browne placed the note in his wallet, where it remained for the rest of his life.

Three passengers - a man, his wife and child - were the only First Class passengers to embark at Queenstown. Those remaining were Second and Third Class passengers. Every Third Class passenger that boarded underwent an inspection for ailments and physical impairments that could possibly deny their entry into the United States.

Aboard *Titanic*, lunch in the First Class Dining Saloon would soon begin. Jocelyn returned to her suite to freshen up. Later, she planned to wear her best day dress for high tea with Lady Duff-Gordon. She took one last look in the mirror before leaving her suite, seeing a healthy spark in her eyes reflected back. The sea air must have done her some good.

The Saloon Deck, or D Deck, held three large public rooms. As Jocelyn descended the fore Grand Staircase, she came into the First Class Reception Hall. At the base of the staircase hung an Aubusson tapestry, *La Chasse du duc de Guise*. Decorated in Jacobean style, the walls were white with embellished moldings. Thick wall-to-wall carpeting covered the floor. Wicker chairs and tables filled the area with seating for 600 people. The ship's bugler alerted passengers with the call to lunch at the Dining Saloon, which served from 1:00 p.m. to 2:30 p.m.

The First Class Dining Saloon extended the entire width of the ship and could accommodate over five hundred passengers in one sitting. It was located between the second and third funnels for the smoothest ride on the ship. There were only a few two-top tables available, with more intimate dining for two available at the À la Carte Restaurant on the Bridge Deck. Most tables seated up to twelve people, all with white linen tablecloths and comfortable upholstered armchairs. The intricate tile pattern on the floor resembled a Persian carpet.

Although Jocelyn arrived promptly at 1:00 p.m., the Dining Saloon was quite full. Nearby, she noticed a table with one vacant seat and asked the others if she could join them. They were all pleased to welcome her with introductions all around, including, to Jocelyn's delight, Mrs. Margaret Brown. Among the other six guests seated at the table was a wealthy American couple, millionaires evidently, who continued their conversation.

"Mrs. Davis," the gentleman said, "I was just telling everyone about a charming young Jesuit we met last night."

"Father Browne?" Jocelyn said.

"Why yes! You know him?"

"We met this morning on the Promenade. What a coincidence! He mentioned you!"

"Oh, a lovely man. He was so thrilled to be here. He carried his camera wherever he went. I am so interested in learning about photography myself."

"My husband even offered to pay his fare to continue to New York and back," the gentleman's wife said with a laugh.

"What a generous gesture," Jocelyn said.

"Well, he knew so much about that camera," the man said, "so I thought he would be absolutely enchanted with New York. They take a vow of poverty, you know, and he may never have an opportunity to see America. He said his superior in Dublin would never allow it, but I did try to pull some strings."

"Appealing to a higher power?" Jocelyn said, pointing upwards with a wink.

The others at the table joined in laughter. "One never knows until one tries!" the man said. "I began a little lower, however. I took Father Browne to the Marconi Room and helped him send a telegraph to his Provincial. Unfortunately, his response was very clear – a resounding no. 'Get off that ship,' he said. I had my knuckles bloodied by enough nuns in school to know not to argue with that!"

"I can tell you he was very grateful for your offer," Jocelyn said.

"We insisted to see his finished prints when we arrive back home. He said he took many photographs of the ship and passengers. He even took a picture of the Marconi Room. We will love to have those prints to remember this wonderful crossing."

Jocelyn was so pleased to meet Margaret Brown, who also went by 'Maggie'. She found Maggie's down-to-earth self-confidence and chutzpah quite intriguing. Jocelyn had already heard a few 'new money' whispers around the ship, regarding Maggie. For that reason, and her unabashed gall, Maggie was not widely accepted among some of the ship's elite, which Jocelyn found distasteful and decidedly rude. Fortunately, at this table, the other diners seemed genuinely interested in her.

Maggie told the story of her humble beginnings. Most wealthy people with whom she rubbed elbows had no concept of the challenges of being poor. She felt it was up to her to enlighten them with an entertaining tale or two.

"I was born on the banks of the Mississippi River in Hannibal, Missouri. When I was 18, I traveled with some of my family to Colorado and ended up in Leadville. I did cookin' for several of the miners, one of which was 'Leadville Johnny' Brown, who was a big, charismatic Irishman. Oh, I must say he did have such a way about him." She gazed off into the corner of the room with a look in her eye as if she saw him standing there. "Mmm, mmm. What a man! He just swept me off my feet, and we married three weeks later. J. J. was 37 at the time, and I was 19."

"My word, Maggie," Jocelyn said, "that must have caused a stir!"

"Nobody much cared up there in the mountains. When it's twenty below zero and the wind is howlin' down your neck, it doesn't much matter how old the feet are next to yours, as long as they're warm!"

The diners at the table erupted with laughter, garnering a few stares from around the dining room.

"You know, I wanted a rich man, and when I met him he was just as poor as we were, and had no better chance in life. But I loved Jim, and I decided I'd be better off with a poor man who I loved than with a wealthy one whose money lured me on. He was smart as a whip, though. He'd worked hard for twenty years in the minin' business, learnin' everything there was to know about engineerin', geology, and gold and silver. And he had a good enough job in Leadville to keep food on our table."

"Mrs. Brown," the American gentleman said, "I would judge, by your presence on this grand ship – and your lovely countenance, I might add – that Mr. Brown's fortunes turned?"

"Dang right," Maggie said. "Jim was partner and supervisor for the Ibex Mining Company. They owned a property called the Little Jonny Mine that they believed had gold in it, but when they started diggin', they hit a layer of sand that was too loose to support a mineshaft. Well, Jim invented a way to use baled hay and wooden timbers to keep the mine walls from cavin' in."

"Quite ingenious," the gentleman said.

"When they opened the Little Jonny, they found

enormous quantities of copper and gold. An investor from London said it was practically a lake of ore. They discovered a gold vein so pure, it was the world's richest gold strike at the time. They mined 135 tons of ore per day. For J. J.'s ingenuity and hard work, he earned 12,500 shares equalin' 12.5% of the company's stock, plus a seat on the board. It only took twenty-some years for Jim to be an overnight success!"

"Hear, hear!" the gentleman said.

"My J. J. is one of the most successful minin' men in the country, with twenty million in gold and silver. Growing up, I'd never seen twenty *dollars* all piled up in the same room, let alone with all those extra zeros behind 'em. It's beyond me - all that money, but I sure have no problem spendin' it while I am travelin' the world." She gave a hearty laugh, and those at the table could not help but join in her mirth.

"I dare say you'll not find many of us on this ship who built their fortunes with their own two hands," the gentleman said.

"Well, most of you all act like makin' a fortune, rather than inheritin' it, is some sort of a poor man's curse."

"Sadly, that seems so true," Jocelyn said.

"Certainly not at this table," the gentleman said. He raised his glass in toast. "Mrs. Brown, to you and the Little Jonny."

"Don't forget Big Jim!"

"To Big Jim!"

Everyone followed suit and toasted the Browns.

"You know," Maggie continued, "the newspapers love to make fun of me – the rich bumpkin from Hannibal."

"That's cruel," Jocelyn said.

"No, honey, I love it! Growin' up, nobody ever said *nothin'* 'bout me. These days, I see my picture in the society pages from Denver to New York. They once made up a story that I accidentally burned up hundreds of thousands of dollars in a cast iron stove. Never happened, but I don't care. It makes a damn good story!"

"Maggie!" Jocelyn laughed, covering her mouth.

"Oh, well excuse my French! But I really don't care what they write about me, as long as they write *somethin'*."

"You are such a delight," Jocelyn said. "So, why isn't Mr. Brown on holiday with you?"

"J. J. spends most of his time in Leadville workin', while I travel around the world spendin' his money. We have a beautiful home in Denver, too, but the social world and city life is not for him - kissin' up to all them society folks. Oh, how I love that man, though. I miss him so, but I must admit he would be terrible miserable travelin' to all these fine places with me."

Everyone at the table was enraptured with Maggie Brown. Jocelyn could have listened to her for hours, but lunch was over. It would soon be time to dress for High Tea. Jocelyn wanted look her best for her meeting with Lady Duff-Gordon. She excused herself, agreeing with Maggie to sit together at dinner, where they could become better acquainted. She then returned to her suite.

While dressing, Jocelyn needed the assistance of a ship's stewardess to help lace her corset. Jocelyn stood, holding the bedpost in her silk stockings and ivory leather button high-top shoes, while the stewardess yanked the laces up tight in the back. Jocelyn sucked in as much air as her little lungs could hold, to the point of nearly fainting.

To finish off her ensemble, Jocelyn wore one of her own creations - a lavender gown with several layers of chiffon descending to the floor, accented with fine French ecru lace at the neckline, sleeve edges, and hemlines. Her auburn hair, gathered in a cluster of wavy curls at the base of her neck, set the tone to finish off the outfit with a wide-brimmed ivory hat. The underside of the hat brim was finished in lavender, complete with a band in lavender chiffon to match the gown. She wore pearl earrings given to her by her late husband, Henry. Long cream gloves over her elbows added a final, elegant touch.

Jocelyn felt optimistic about this meeting, for she had many ideas that had not yet come to fruition. She was a creative visionary with a strong, reliable intuition that gave her a distinct advantage in the competitive fashion industry.

Jocelyn and Lady Duff-Gordon enjoyed tea in the reception room on the Saloon Deck. They sat on the starboard side near the five-piece orchestra, which included a beautiful Steinway grand piano. Lady Duff-Gordon purposely chose a table away from the main traffic of passengers, as she and her husband were traveling under an alias, as Mr. and Mrs. Morgan.

"We really do not mean to be snobbish," she told Jocelyn. "But our name seems to garner more attention than our faces!" They laughed together. "It is much easier to travel in anonymity so we may enjoy this wonderful liner."

"Well, I certainly recognized you the moment I saw you," Jocelyn said. "I hope I didn't intrude last night, but I have so wanted to meet you."

"Not at all, Mrs. Davis. In fact, I am surprised we haven't crossed paths before. I greatly admire your Art Nouveau couture."

"Oh my, thank you. Such high praise coming from you."

"Your designs are highly celebrated in Paris, London, and New York. But please tell me more of what we spoke about last night."

They shared many ideas, particularly Jocelyn's thoughts about designing attractive and affordable ready-to-wear clothing for women, men, and children. Men's ready-to-wear military uniforms were first mass-produced, owing to advances in technology during the War of 1812, but the 19th century women's fashions were far too complex and remained largely dependent on individual styling and alterations. Jocelyn saw the Industrial Revolution taking place across the world and knew that mass-production of fashions, specifically for women and children, could open up new markets for all economic classes, rather than just for the wealthy.

Jocelyn captivated Lady Duff-Gordon as they brainstormed together many new possibilities. "American women are leaning away from European styles, not to disparage your designs, of course. But they want American styles manufactured within our own apparel industry."

"Yes, of course," Lady Duff-Gordon said, "and who better to introduce this to America than a wonderful

American designer – with just a slight European taste of spice provided by her British partner."

"Oh, I love the sound of that!"

"There is so much to discuss. And I know right where we can begin – right here on this ship."

Jocelyn's eyes alighted. "Mr. Straus?"

"Isidor will love your ideas, I assure you."

"I so hoped that you knew him!"

"For many years. You will adore him."

"Perhaps we will find the opportunity to briefly chat with him?"

Lady Duff-Gordon took Jocelyn's hand. "We will more than briefly chat, I promise. He is accustomed to listening to me, for I corner him sometimes for hours at a time!"

At the end of teatime, they stood. "Lady Duff-Gordon, this has been such a pleasure," Jocelyn said.

"Please, call me Lucy."

"And I am Jocelyn."

"I will see you at dinner tonight, after I speak to Isidor."

Jocelyn was thrilled. She reached out to shake Lucy's hand, and instead, Lucy leaned over and gave her a hug. She smiled at the younger woman and patted her on the cheek, an unusually demonstrative gesture of kindness. "Jocelyn, you remind me so much – of me!" They laughed together and then bid each other good afternoon.

Jocelyn could not have been more pleased as she retired to her suite before dinner, ready to celebrate her good luck. She believed that all those previous feelings of despair and worry over sailing on *Titanic* must have been residual feelings of her two years of grief at the loss of her husband. She now believed that nothing could possibly get in the way of her dreams. *The Ship of Dreams,* she thought. Sometimes, they do come true . . .

CHAPTER
Nine

*D*inner in the First Class Dining Saloon was extraordinary, not only because of the opulent menu choices, but because every woman came to dine in her finest gown and jewels, and each man was dressed his absolute best. If it were a royal event, the women would not have been more opulently bedecked than they were that evening. Unlike at lunchtime, assigned seats were the tradition for the evening meal.

Jocelyn found her table before her other dining mates arrived. She sat down and simply took in the beauty of the room. The portholes, obscured with inner leaded-glass windows lit from behind for greater ambience, gave passengers the impression they were eating on shore instead of at sea. Jocelyn was so preoccupied looking around at all the various fashion styles that she did not at first notice a man who approached, impeccably dressed in a smartly-fitted tuxedo. She turned and looked up, startled to see her "accidental gentleman" grinning at her.

"You?" she said.

"Well, Madame, since you are clearly following me, I suppose we should make our acquaintance."

"*I'm* following *you?* I hardly- wait – now you're the maître d'?"

"No, no," he said, pointing at the placard next to her seat. "We are seated together. It must be *kismet*, no?"

She looked at the placard. "What is this?"

"Kismet – you know . . . fate."

"I *know* what kismet is," Jocelyn said. "You are dining here?"

"Permettez-moi. François Delacroix, at your service." He bowed and extended his hand. "As I bow, you may rest assured of your safety, for you are already in your chair and out of danger."

She tried not to smile as she placed her gloved hand in his. "Monsieur, I am Jocelyn Elaine Brewster Davis."

He gently kissed the back of her hand. "What a distinct pleasure to finally make your acquaintance." He motioned to the chair next to her. "If I may?" She suspiciously watched him take his seat and delicately situate himself. "Isn't this a grand setting? And how fortunate I am to be in your lovely company, Madame."

She hoped he did not notice her blush. She could not help but feel the goose bumps on her arms, relieved to be wearing gloves that reached above her elbows. When she felt the tingle and thought - *Follow the goose bumps!* - she knew they were a sign of her intuition nudging her in a direction that would be to her advantage. Twice, in his presence, she found herself caught off-guard by such a nudge.

"So," she said, also regarding her inner voice that continued to urge caution. "Mr. Delacroix is it?"

"Oui, and please, call me François."

"Um hmm," she said suspiciously, "but last night you called yourself 'Gaston,' if I'm not mistaken?"

"I did? Oh! Yes, I suppose I did. You see, Gaston is my middle name. I sometimes call myself that because Gaston was my father's name, and we look so much alike that I sometimes confuse me for him!"

That was it. Jocelyn couldn't help herself. She had to laugh.

He rubbed his hands together. "So, what is on the menu tonight? I am famished."

"Well, you were a waiter last night. Don't you know?"

François gave that marvelous smile and then looked up. "Oh, look who is here!"

The ship's Chief Purser, Hugh Walter McElroy, approached. "Mr. Delacroix! Good evening!"

Jocelyn rolled her eyes as François stood and shook his hand. "Chief Purser, Mr. McElroy. Have you met Mrs. Davis?"

McElroy bowed. "Mrs. Jocelyn Brewster Davis, I presume? I have so looked forward to meeting you."

"Thank you," Jocelyn said, quite flattered that McElroy knew who she was.

"You will be joining us tonight, yes?" François asked.

"Indeed, it shall be my pleasure. If you will excuse me for a moment." McElroy walked over to greet other arriving guests. Other than Captain Smith and White Star Line Chairman Bruce Ismay, he was the only other officer that dined with the passengers. A gregarious and charismatic man, McElroy entertained his guests with his good sense of humor and vast knowledge of the grand *Titanic*. Many First Class passengers often requested to sit at his table for each meal.

"Charming man," François said. He sat back down and smiled again. Jocelyn stared back, but she was beginning to smile more. "Mrs. Davis, so many questions, but for now may we just sit and enjoy?"

Dinner was beyond compare, with thirteen courses, offering choices beginning with Punch Romaine, made of wine, rum, and champagne. Oysters, consommé, and cream of barley soup began the meal, followed by a choice of poached salmon with mousseline sauce and cucumbers, filet mignon, chicken Lyonnaise and vegetable marron forci, lamb with mint sauce, roast duckling with applesauce, or roast sirloin of beef. Side dishes included chateau potatoes, green peas, creamed carrots, boiled new potatoes, roast squash and cress, cold asparagus vinaigrette, and pâté de foie gras with celery. Dessert offerings were Waldorf pudding, peaches in chartreuse jelly, chocolate and vanilla éclairs, French ice cream, finishing with fresh fruit and cheeses. Coffee, Port, and cordials ended the meal, while the men had their choice of cigars.

The conversation at the table was lively and interesting throughout the evening. Indeed, Jocelyn wanted to interrogate Mr. Delacroix, wondering just who – or what he was. From the moment they met on the Cherbourg dock, this peculiar man had worked his way from crewman to sophisticated First Class passenger in 24 hours. Clearly, something was amiss, but Jocelyn did not sense any clear and present danger that she might otherwise feel in the presence of such a stranger. Instead, all she felt were *goose bumps* – unsettling and quite exciting all the same.

At one point, Lady Duff-Gordon stopped at the table and excused herself for the interruption before she whispered into Jocelyn's ear to meet her after dinner for cordials in the À la Carte Restaurant at 10:00 p.m. Jocelyn smiled and nodded.

Jocelyn turned her attention back to the table as Mr. McElroy spoke. "Tell me, Mr. Delacroix, what brings you to sail with us to New York?"

"Well, you might guess I am from Paris. Until a year ago, I lived there with my wife, who was expecting our first child, but she became ill quite early in her pregnancy, and I lost them both before our child was born." The women at the table moaned in sympathy. Jocelyn's nagging doubt about François instantly disappeared when she saw the sorrow in his eyes.

"That must have been very difficult," McElroy said.

"Oui, c'était. I am beginning my life over in New York – I have secured a position with a prestigious architectural firm. Comment dit-on en Englais? An opportunity of a lifetime for me. There, I will begin again in a new city and country. I must say, I am looking forward to the opportunity."

Jocelyn suddenly recalled the visitation in her dream the night before and immediately understood why she felt the goose bumps. *François!* She wondered why she didn't make the connection until now. Entirely disarmed of all suspicion, she concluded it was time to reconsider her skepticism and be genial to this man.

The orchestra played until 9:00 p.m., but dinner concluded long after that. As waiters began clearing tables, Mr. McElroy invited the men to join him in the Smoke Room for conversation, cigars, and a fine glass of gin or scotch. François gladly accepted the invitation and turned to Jocelyn. "It was my pleasure being seated next to you, Madame. Will your husband be meeting you when we arrive in New York?"

"No," Jocelyn said. "I am afraid I am a widow. My husband passed on two years ago from influenza while we were visiting his family in Wales."

"I am so sorry for your loss, Madame. I know too well the bonds of grief."

"Thank you. I appreciate your empathy. We keep meeting, so will you please call me Jocelyn?"

"It will be my pleasure, Jocelyn." When he said her name with his French accent, it reverberated through her as if she had never heard her name spoken before.

"Well, good evening, François."

He leaned in close to her, so others would not hear. "I am neither one for cigars, nor one to pound on my chest in competition with other men. So, I will join them for appearances and perhaps to acquaint myself with one or two, to at least say I know someone in New York. I must confess that I know not a soul on that side of the Atlantic."

"You now know me."

"Yes," he said. "For that I am grateful. May I assume we have moved on from our rather awkward first encounter?"

"Yes. I must apologize for my temper."

"You *are* a high spirited one, well able to hold your own." They both laughed.

"One more thing, François. I recall that you mentioned unanswered questions?"

She detected a slight blush. "Oh, oui . . . yes."

"It is a long voyage," she said, "and since we are in the habit of running into each other, perhaps you'll have time to answer a few before the end of our journey? That is, if you don't anticipate a promotion to Captain of the ship anytime soon . . ."

François did not miss a beat. "I assure you, Jocelyn, if that happens, I would still be delighted to find time to see you again. For now, I bid you a pleasant evening." He bowed and again kissed her hand.

At the À la Carte Restaurant, Jocelyn found Lucy seated with Mr. and Mrs. Straus.

"Jocelyn," Lucy said, "may I introduce Mrs. Ida Straus and Mr. Isidor Straus - Mrs. Jocelyn Brewster Davis."

Jocelyn first shook the hand of Mrs. Straus. "It is such a pleasure to meet you."

Mr. Straus stood and pulled a chair out for Jocelyn and motioned for her to take a seat as he reached out to shake Jocelyn's hand. "We are honored to meet you as well, Mrs. Davis. Lucy has told us so much about you."

Isidor and Ida were everything Jocelyn expected – a lovely, stately couple in their late sixties who exuded elegance and grace. It was clear to Jocelyn how much they adored each other, and she could not help but feel pangs of desire to have the same type of relationship.

Straus and his brother acquired the R. H. Macy Company in the late 1800s and turned the lower Manhattan dry goods emporium into the world's largest department store after relocating in 1902 to Herald Square on 34th Street, the first store to have an escalator for its eleven floors. Jocelyn had long envisioned mass-producing her ready-to-wear designs for Macy's, and here it was - the opportunity was unfolding before her, which left her with a calm sense of confidence and assurance.

They talked for over an hour, and Straus concluded that Macy's should exclusively contract with *Lucile Ltd.*, with Jocelyn as the company's head designer for women's, men's and children's ready-to-wear. Jocelyn looked at Lucy, who seemed quite satisfied and not nearly as stunned as Jocelyn felt in that moment.

Straus leaned forward and studied Jocelyn. "Mrs. Davis? Does that sound satisfactory?"

"Yes! Of course!" Jocelyn was embarrassed. "Forgive me, I am just a little taken aback. This is quite sudden."

"Your proposal is sound," Straus said. "Lucy loves your designs, and I have full faith in her judgment. I see no reason to dawdle with a decision."

"Yes, I agree," Jocelyn said.

"We shall see that Jocelyn's custom designs, under the umbrella of *Lucile Ltd.*, will be protected under our agreement."

"I'm not sure I understand," Jocelyn said.

"It is a common legal stipulation, my dear, " Lucy said.

"Although we will sell your clothing with our label, you will retain the rights to all of your designs in the event that we might someday part ways."

"Part ways?" Jocelyn said, laughing. "I just started working for you!"

"And I hope you will for many years to come," Lucy said, "but your life changed the instant you boarded this grand ship. There will be many opportunities for you to grow while working for *Lucile*, but your clothing designs, sold solely at Macy's, will bring you worldwide exposure."

"The day may come when we all will be working for you!" Straus said.

"You just offered me the opportunity to work for one of the most prestigious design houses in the world," Jocelyn said. "I dare say I shall be grateful and quite satisfied to remain with you for as long as you'll have me."

Jocelyn simply could not believe her good fortune. It was as simple as that. She recalled what Maggie Brown said: *It only took twenty-some years for Jim to be an overnight success!*

"Lucy and I shall telegraph our attorneys in the morning," Straus said. "We will draw up the papers and have everything in order upon our arrival at port next Wednesday."

"So soon," Jocelyn said, a bit breathless.

"There's little time to waste," Lucy said. "We are already producing our fall line."

Jocelyn could barely contain herself, but she remained enthusiastically reserved, harking back to her strong

Brewster lineage. Her ancestors were the famed William and Mary Brewster, who, along with two of their children, were among the 102 pilgrims that traveled to the new world on the Mayflower. Fifty-one people from the Mayflower died from the plague within six months of their arrival. Miraculously so, the entire Brewster family survived, unaffected by the plague. Europeans brought the smallpox plague when they settled Jamestown in the early part of the 17th Century, having killed most of the Indian population on the east coast who had no immunity to the disease. Brewster, deemed 'The Patriarch of the Pilgrims,' was the ruling elder and religious leader who helped the Mayflower survivors build the Plymouth community into one of stalwart means.

Jocelyn was made of the same strength and fortitude as her ancestors. She was a survivor, having already overcome much sorrow. Nothing, in her mind, could take her down. Before her was the opportunity of a lifetime to live the life of her dreams.

"I cannot tell you what a pleasure it will be to work with both of you," she said. "I shall find a flat near the store and get settled directly."

"If you will allow me," said Mrs. Straus, "I shall put you in contact with a friend of ours who is a concierge. He has connections to everything in New York. You may send him a telegram tomorrow, and he will have a furnished flat waiting for you." She wrote down his name and address on the back of one of Isidor's calling cards, and handed it to Jocelyn.

"Wonderful! I am truly so grateful to you all," Jocelyn said.

"This calls for a celebration!" Straus said. He summoned a waiter and ordered a bottle of Perrier-Jouet. The waiter soon brought over an ice bucket with the champagne and four chilled champagne goblets. He popped the cork and ceremoniously poured the champagne as it bubbled to the top of the goblets.

Straus lifted his glass and the others followed suit. "To new enterprises. May we all continue to live and love well, and may we be remembered for our great contributions to the world."

"To new enterprises!"

When they finished, Lucy stood and said, "Well, tomorrow morning Mr. Straus and I will get everything in order, but for now I bid you all a good night." Jocelyn stood with Lucy and they left the room together. Mr. and Mrs. Straus ordered a pot of tea before they retired for the evening.

Delirious with joy, Jocelyn returned to her room and fetched her coat and hat. She needed a brisk stroll in the cool night air on the Promenade before going to bed. Her head spun with the excitement of the evening. Walking would help to release some of the pent-up energy. Otherwise, she would not sleep for hours.

Chapter
Ten

Jocelyn happily walked the long Promenade, listening to the steady push of the ocean along *Titanic's* hull. She thought she was alone until she noticed someone standing ahead at the railing. She slowly drew near and recognized François. She marveled at how their paths kept crossing.

"Good evening, François."

He perked, genuinely surprised as if he had not noticed her approach. "Madame – Jocelyn."

"I hope I am not interrupting," she said.

He turned her direction, obviously deep in thought. "Why, no. As a matter of fact, I welcome your presence. I did not remain in the Smoke Room with the other gentlemen for long. Many of them like to brag about their financial wealth, comparing their big houses and their automobiles. I find it to be boastful and small-minded."

Jocelyn smiled and marveled at his wistful eyes. "So what *do* you like to talk about?"

"I prefer talking about forward-thinking ideas. I enjoy talking with others about their ventures, where they have travelled, who they have met, and what they have learned along their journeys."

"You sound like a philosopher. The field of architecture

is one of logic, not one of the heart."

"In actuality, the combination of the two makes my job much more interesting. I first become well acquainted with my clients. Then I design them a building of their dreams, which not only meets their physical needs, but also meets their hearts' desires, where they can reside in comfort and do business effectively. You are a designer. You must understand, no?"

"Oh, yes," Jocelyn said. "I suppose I do the same with my custom clothing designs. I try to create something that will make a woman feel as if she is better represented from the inside out."

"So, you see, we are not so different, are we, Jocelyn?" He curiously contemplated her countenance. "You know, as I look at you in this light, you are so radiant. Your cheeks, they are blushing perhaps?"

Jocelyn laughed. "Oh, it is just I am simply overcome with what has happened this evening."

"Oui? Tell me."

"I was offered – as you put it earlier – an opportunity of a lifetime. It is a business venture with Lady Duff-Gordon and Isidor Straus."

"Merveilleux!" François said. "I am so happy for you!"

"Thank you. But I am much more curious about you. Tell me who *you* are, François."

He smiled and looked out toward the dark ocean.

"You know," she said, "you have a very charming way of avoiding my questions, but I'm on to you, sir."

"On to?" he said, innocently. "What is this 'on to?'"

"No you don't. You are very fluent in English, and you may stop pretending, because you keep running into me wearing many different uniforms, as if you are working all over the ship. And tonight, I catch you posing as one of the wealthy passengers at the dinner table."

François threw a heavy sigh. "You know, it was – how do you say – just my luck to keep running into the same person on a ship this size." He disarmed her yet again with that marvelous smile. "And yet, I consider it very good luck at the same time. I know you may be thinking I am some sort of uh-"

"Criminal?"

"Well, I was going to say 'charlatan', but before you decide to call the Master at Arms-"

"François, just tell me without the lengthy preamble."

"Oui, well, my wife and I planned to immigrate to America, but when she fell ill, everything we saved went to her medical care. I devoted all of my time to her, and I had difficulty finding work. This offer of a position in New York came to me through a colleague, who recommended me on the condition that I arrive as quickly as possible. They did not offer to pay for my passage, and I regret to say I have very little money."

"You're a stowaway?" Jocelyn said.

"Well, I was going to say 'seafaring vagabond', but essentially, you are correct."

"I knew it! The moment you bumped into me on the dock, I knew there was something peculiar about you!"

"When we first met in Cherbourg, I was posing as a

dockworker so I could smuggle my luggage aboard."

Jocelyn laughed. "Such a relief to know you didn't steal that lovely tuxedo from Mr. Astor."

"No no, this is mine. Dashing, no?"

"Yes, quite debonair. But how did you get aboard? Where are you staying?"

"I simply took my trunk to the cargo hold and wandered around there until we sailed. You would be surprised how many crewmen on this ship do not know each other. If you look busy, no one even notices you."

"Are you sleeping down there, in the hold?"

"On such a luxurious ship as this? Mon Dieu, no! I have a cabin in First Class."

"What?"

"While posing as a steward, I found a master key hanging on a hook in the steward's room. This deck is not fully occupied, so I found an empty cabin and unlocked the door. Then I delivered my trunks to that room. In fact, that was when we met for the second time, at your door."

Jocelyn could not help her laughter. "But wait? You successfully got on board and secured a cabin – why did I see you later that evening masquerading as a waiter in the Café Parisien?"

"I was hungry? Madame, I had been working hard all day, and I didn't feel like dressing for dinner."

"But of course!" Jocelyn said. "And how have you managed to endear yourself to the Chief Purser, who regards you an equal to the Astors and Guggenheims?"

"Oui," François said, polishing his fingernails on his

lapel. "I met him earlier and said I was so delighted to see him again. He will spend the rest of the crossing embarrassed for not remembering a First Class passenger. I would imagine we will be dear friends by the time we reach New York."

"So why did you call yourself Gaston?"

"Well, Gaston actually *is* my middle name, but yesterday, whenever I encountered another crewman, I gave them a different name just to enhance the masquerade."

"My word, you are very resourceful, Monsieur Delacroix, and quite devious, I might add."

"Jocelyn, s'il vous plaît, I am ashamed that I told you a, how do you say-"

"Lie?"

"I was going to say fib, but essentially, yes. Will you forgive me?"

Jocelyn touched his arm. "I believe you are being just a little hard on yourself, François."

He looked down. "As they say, desperate times call for desperate measures. Since Madelyn died, it seems I walk every day in despair. If I can just get to New York and give my heart to making a new life, I vow I will someday repay the White Star Line."

"The ship of dreams," Jocelyn said. "That is what they call it. And, of course I forgive you."

François smiled. "Now that I have established myself as a First Class passenger, I hope I may complete this journey as myself. Unless you give away my secret, no one will know."

"I see no reason to give you away, François. You are not bringing harm to anyone."

"Merci, Jocelyn - thank you for trusting me, especially considering how we originally became acquainted."

"I always believe that everything happens for a reason – even if it hurts a bit." They paused, looking out at the clear, starry night over the dark Atlantic. "I have something else to ask you, François. When I found you here tonight, you seemed deeply enraptured in thought. Is everything alright?"

"I was thinking about my wife. She was so worried about the birth of our child. Sometimes I believe that our thoughts create our very reality. Could it be that her worries eventually caused her death and that of our child? She was prone to melancholy, and I could not find any way to help her."

"I must say I understand," Jocelyn said. "I cannot tell you how many times I have changed my very circumstances with a shift of perception. For example, when you bumped into me at the dock, I was rude and unwilling to accept your polite apology. But now, because I was fortunate to become acquainted with you, I realize that you were being kind and simply trying to help me. I was the one who made my circumstance so challenging, not you. If my change in perspective had not occurred, we would not be standing here, looking at the stars on this glorious night."

"It is a pleasure to find common ground, is it not?"

"François, I have something important to share with

you. It may seem odd at first, but I think it will bring you some peace."

"Qué est-ce que c'est?"

"I have the ability to connect with people who have moved on to their next life. They sometimes come to me in my dreams." She awaited a response, expecting the usual skepticism that generally followed when she shared this revelation.

Instead, François inquisitively raised his brow. "You are a medium, yes?"

"That's right."

"My wife had the same abilities. Tell me more, if you please."

"Well..." She hesitated and took a deep breath. "Last night in my dreams, a woman whom I have never met came to me. She was petite, with dark hair and blue eyes - quite pretty. She wore her hair tied loosely at the base of her neck."

His eyes widened in disbelief. "That sounds very much like my wife!"

"I feel I may be intruding into your personal life by mentioning this-"

"No, s'il vous plaît. If she came to you as a visitation, it must be important. I would like for you to continue."

"At dinner tonight, when you mentioned your loss, I suddenly recalled the dream and was certain it was she. I believe you said her name was-"

"Her name was Madelyn."

Jocelyn closed her eyes and silently asked Madelyn if

she was the one who visited her the night before. The answer immediately came through, *Yes!*

"Very well, then." Jocelyn opened her eyes and turned to François. "She said, 'Tell François to no longer grieve. We are happier than we could ever imagine. When it is his time, we will be waiting for him. Tell him he is deeply loved.'"

Tears welled in his eyes, and perhaps for the first time since Jocelyn met him, François was speechless.

Jocelyn looked up at him with a warm, empathetic smile. She knew the grief that overtakes a person to the point of not knowing any longer who they are. She found herself gently placing her gloved hand on his arm just as he broke down in tears. He wrapped his arms around her, with the need to be close - just to know someone understood his sorrow. She held the giant of a man with all her emotional strength and reserve. He was silent, but she could feel him tremble as he released long-held grief and sadness.

He gathered himself and pulled away from her, reaching into his inner coat pocket to find a handkerchief. "I do not know what overcame me. I normally do not weep like that."

"Perhaps you should start doing it more often," Jocelyn said. "You suffered unimaginable loss, and it does great damage if you don't allow your grief to release."

François nodded with a shrug as he unceremoniously blew his nose. "We men do not cry. We choose to simply die over and over again without a whimper. I still grieve for Madelyn so, but it helps me to hear that she is well.

Maybe she is finally happy. It does my heart good to hear that she came to you."

"François, she came to you, through me. I am only the deliverer of the message." They paused for a moment as François regained his smile. "You know, I have some fine cognac in my suite," Jocelyn said. "Would you care to join me for a nightcap?"

"Oh yes, I would welcome that. Thank you, Jocelyn."

They slowly walked back to her suite in silence. When they arrived, they entered the sitting room, which could accommodate a second bedroom for additional passengers. For this voyage, the room contained no bed, which under the circumstances made Jocelyn and François feel at bit more at ease. The room contained a lovely settee and an armchair placed by a low table.

"Please, have a seat," Jocelyn said. "I hope I do not sound terribly forward, but if you will permit me, I must change into something more comfortable to wear. I simply cannot breathe in this corset."

"But of course," François said, amused by her delightful openness. "Please make yourself comfortable." He wandered around the suite, taking in the sheer opulence.

Jocelyn went into the wardrobe to change into a lovely dressing gown. When she returned, François could not help but notice Jocelyn's radiance. He politely looked away so his interest might not be overt.

"Thank you for allowing me to change. Corsets are certainly a bane of existence for women." Jocelyn smiled, knowing that François was clearly uncomfortable as she sat next to him.

"Well," François said, clasping his hands together, "you mentioned a nightcap?"

"I did," Jocelyn said. She retrieved two brandy snifters, which she obtained earlier in the day, and a bottle of Courvoisier XO, a very old blend of fine cognac. She poured and lifted her glass to him. "To life!"

"Oui, à la vôtre!" he responded, touching his glass to hers.

Each took a small sip and let it slowly take off the chill of the night air. Jocelyn held the snifter in her palm, the cognac warming with the heat of her hand.

"I am curious," François said. "Would you mind telling me more about your visitations? Does this happen often?"

Jocelyn watched the rich amber cognac swirl in her glass, allowing its sweet aroma to fill her senses as she pondered how to answer his question. "The visitations are but a small part of what I experience. I am what some would call a seer, a medium, an intuitive. From what you tell me, your wife possessed the gift?"

"I should say it possessed her," François sadly said. "I sometimes believe I understood and accepted it better than she."

"It can be overwhelming if you don't understand – even frightening," Jocelyn said. "Two centuries ago, many deemed us witches, as was the fate of my ancestral grandmother in 1692. She healed many people in her community near Salem, Massachusetts, but because she was beautiful and had great knowing, a jealous wife branded her a witch." Jocelyn swirled her snifter, watching the cognac churn inside her glass. She breathed in the sweet aroma before continuing. "She healed both her accuser's husband and child. The boy's fever refused to break until she simply laid her hands on his head and commanded the illness to leave, claiming for him his innate health to return. By the next day, both father and son were nearly well, soon going about their business as if nothing had occurred. And for that, death at the hand of her community was her recompense."

François closed his eyes. "We have not progressed very far, but thankfully we have emerged from those dark days."

"My grandmother's belief was so strong that no illness could prevail in her presence. Her belief was not in her own powers, but in the eternal presence of God that knew all, was all-powerful, and was ever in the present moment at all times. She was so clear, as in the wisdom spoken by Jesus: 'These things ye shall do and even greater things still.' Those words were a promise of what life could be if one believed. My grandmother knew and believed that very power was also in her, and so that is how she healed - simply by knowing."

"Are there others in your family who possessed such gifts?" François asked.

"The women of my family pass down to their daughters what I call the 'knowing' - the ability to heal and see beyond the physical world. In my lineage, there are gypsies, mystics, seers, prophets, Delphic Oracles - all healers. It is my hope there will come a day in the near future when being a healer will be widely accepted, beyond the esoteric domain, particularly for women."

Jocelyn offered to pour François another cognac. "When that happens, we will be easily able to use these God-given powers that lay in our hands of the all-knowing, all-powerful Universal Intelligence."

"That might not sit well with some," François said with a grin. "If we all should apply the ability to 'heal thyself' as the Bible teaches, it might eliminate the need for doctors."

Jocelyn smiled. "Healing occurs when people believe more in their health, rather than their illness. We must learn to utilize the love that emanates from our hearts, which is where the true power of all that is good resides. All we have to do is believe and understand there is always a solution that is greater than the problem. To believe is to receive, both as a healer, and as the one in need of healing."

She arose from her seat and turned on the electric heater to take the chill from the room. François felt a longing in his heart as he observed her graceful movements while her back was turned. As she sat again at the table, she caught him shyly looking away. She gently smiled.

"S'il vous plaît, may I ask about the visitation from Madelyn?"

"Oh, yes, of course," Jocelyn said. "Sometimes I perform a séance to call in the spirits, but on most occasions, someone comes to me in a dream and communicates a message to pass along to their loved one, just as Madelyn did. If we open to the energy, we find that there is a very thin veil between this world and the next. Heaven is right here, right where we are, and in this present moment it is everywhere."

"Oui, I believe that she and our child are still with me

here, in my heart."

"Millions of beings surround us at all times," Jocelyn said, "those who have known us from our past, and I believe into our future as well. They help to support and guide us in all we do - that is, if we let them. It is up to us."

"Yes, the concept of time is only a part of the material realm," Francois said.

Jocelyn's eyes lighted. "A dock worker, a waiter, architect, and a philosopher - Monsieur Delacroix, you are a man of many mysteries."

François smiled. "It is a human limitation, but we can rise above and reside in the infinite realm where time, in and of itself, does not exist."

"So true, is it not?" Jocelyn said. "It is there where we realize the mysteries and miracles. If we allow this awareness to be our way of life, then we no longer fear death, for it is not the end, but instead is a portal to a new existence. Beyond that, to a greater degree, we are not afraid of fear itself, for we have already transcended into the realm of absolute awareness - which is love."

François laughed as he swirled his drink. "My dear Jocelyn, having met you on the dock yesterday, I certainly would not have considered the possibility that we would be sharing at such depths this evening."

"Kismet?" Jocelyn said with a lovely smile.

"Oui! Kismet!" They offered their glasses in toast. "Would it surprise you if I told you I have some intuitive abilities?"

Caught by surprise, she said, "I'm intrigued!"

"I, too, come from a lineage of healers. My family lived for generations in the south of France in Saint-Rémy-de-Provence, not far from Marseilles. A very famous seer lived there. He is my ancestral grandfather, Nostradamus."

"Yes, of course! I have read his quatrains. Do tell me more."

"He used the light of a candle reflecting into a water-filled bowl to do his readings – and to see into the future. He healed many who suffered from the plague, and yet he never contracted the disease himself."

"Such a fascinating lineage," Jocelyn said.

"I do not pretend to possess his remarkable vast insight," François said, "but my judgment is most always correct when I heed my intuition."

"I believe that we all have such powers," Jocelyn said. "Religion and science have reduced and homogenized healing to something offered by old men who only do what they are told, with theories only proven by limited repetition. It is our faith in the unseen that creates true healing – the recognition of something greater, beyond the manifest realm of the world as we know it."

"Some of us have naturally come by these powers, piquing our interest to learn more," François said. "This is what I have done for many years. I often anticipate future events, as Nostradamus did, based solely on understanding the present. It helps me in my design work, foreseeing what people need long before they are aware of their needs themselves. It is not of my own doing, but through my intuition that I am able to pass along what I see to my clients."

Jocelyn agreed. "A seer must ever remain open to the possibilities, for therein lies the solution. I once knew a seer who divined a very bleak future for the world. She interpreted this to mean that a world event or disastrous illness would leave everyone in peril, or perhaps lead to the end of life itself. She soon grew ill with diabetes, followed by total blindness. What she saw were her own limitations. It is not a problem to see into the future, because the problem lies in the interpretation, from the level of limited perspective. As seers and people of the spiritual gifts, we have a great responsibility to hold the highest truth for those we serve, including ourselves."

"With that, I must share something," François said. "For some time, I have experienced visions of an extreme disaster, where hundreds of people lose their lives. There is a feeling of urgency, as if it is going to happen soon. I keep seeing nothing but dark skies filled with stars and no moon. It is frigidly cold - so cold that people live only minutes. This event will change history."

Jocelyn could not help but recall her own recent feelings of dread. "I must admit, for some time, I too have felt similar warnings. In fact, I almost reconsidered taking this voyage. There have been several major occurrences on the ship prior to sailing that I suspected were warnings."

"Such as?"

"For one, in Cherbourg I overheard two crewmen talking about a rumor regarding the switching of the *Titanic* with her sister ship, *Olympic*, another White Star liner."

"I don't understand," François said. "They were saying that this ship is actually the *Olympic*, and not *Titanic?*"

"It was a rumor. But I did read that the *Olympic* collided with the *HMS Hawke,* which put it out of service for two months, and it later threw a propeller blade on the way back to England from New York. The repairs should have taken hours, but instead it was out of service for two more weeks. The crewmen discussed rumors that the two ships were switched because the *Olympic* has been involved in three major incidents and is no longer insurable. These incidents were all related to why the *Titanic's* maiden voyage was delayed until April."

"This is troubling," François said. "I do not understand why White Star would do such a thing."

"I don't know," Jocelyn said, "but it gave me even more to think about concerning the warnings I received not to sail. I heard that the ship almost collided with the *SS City of New York* when it was leaving Southampton, not to mention the British coal strike, which caused many challenges in the days before it sailed. François, this might sound silly, but I even think about our little tiff when we met."

"You cannot mean that our disagreement was a warning not to take this voyage," he said.

"It is possible. I am certain you know when something is right, or in alignment, situations happen seamlessly and easily fall into place. When out of alignment, the opposite occurs with warnings both big and small. Oftentimes, if we are paying attention, all we need to do is make a slight shift toward what comes more easily for us. Then we come into alignment with our soul's calling. This is the way of the universe, and I strongly believe in paying attention to such happenings, but I must admit I have not been heeding the many warnings about this voyage. I have been so preoccupied with my good fortune meeting Lady Duff-Gordon and Isidor Straus – and you."

"Do you believe we will have problems as we cross the Atlantic?" François asked.

"I am more concerned now that you speak of troubling visions of a disaster with great loss of life. That may be an even stronger indication that something may happen. I have to say, I am able to see people's life force, which in this case, I am not so certain I can consider it a 'gift.'"

"How so?"

"When people are of a low energy, they have no aura, or very little light surrounding them. Some of those people are approaching the end of their life. Likewise, when people have a strong life force, the light surrounding them is powerful, and the colors are vibrant. I have to say that many of the people I have seen on this ship have no aura about them, particularly those among the crew. There is something prodding me to connect with them in some way. I do not know how or even why, but my intuition has been guiding me to do so. As with all things, if I set a clear intention and believe it to be so, miracles will make themselves known."

"And what do you see for me?" he asked.

"You are a mystery - a conundrum. When you were on the deck this evening, lost in your grief, I saw very little light surrounding you, but here in the room, I see you fully surrounded in a brilliant glow. That tells me it is up to you. It is *your* belief in life that will carry you, not mine - it is all about your perspective and the choices you make. If you knew the ship was in peril, what do you think would be your chance of survival, François?"

"At this moment, quite good, actually. I find that I have a renewed zest for life. I have you to thank for your presence here this evening. I am weary of grieving, which seems to come from nowhere at times, but each time it arrives, I choose if I am going to participate in the memory or not. I must say, I do so appreciate our conversation this evening."

She blushed, with more goose bumps as he took her hand and kissed it.

"I have a grand idea," François said. "Let us shift our fears to a positive energy for the future. No matter what happens, let us agree to meet for dinner at the St. Regis Hotel in New York City on April 30th. We shall celebrate our new beginnings with a lovely evening together. Shall we say dinner at 7:00 p.m.?"

"Now, how do you know of the St. Regis?"

"My new employers arranged for me to stay there. As long as I can get to New York on my own, they said I can stay as their guest for as long as I desire. Of course, your meeting me there makes it much easier. Just do not ask me about anything else in New York City."

"May I assume you will be dining with me rather than serving?" she said with a wink.

François laughed. "I promise." They pensively acknowledged their agreement with a final toast and then finished their cocktails. "I must say, I hoped a nightcap might help me sleep well, but I am not certain that is what I accomplished. This makes every moment seem so important, does it not?"

"Perhaps we've found each other to remind us of that very notion, François."

"I must ask, do you think Madelyn came to you because I am about to die, and she wants me to know she and my child were waiting for me?"

"I believe our loved ones are ever waiting to welcome us into the home of heart," Jocelyn said, taking his hand. "They are not in the realm of time and space, but rather within the realization that love is ever-present. Your wife and child are right here, just not in the same denseness of our worldly existence. Those who love us are around us at all times, ever within our field to support and guide us. We do not have to die to realize their presence, nor do we have to die to reside in heaven with them."

"Oui, I do believe they will always exist in my heart."

"Every moment of our lives carries within it the opportunity to recognize either heaven or hell," Jocelyn said, "which is within our earthly existence and not out there somewhere in the clouds. It is through our choice - through our perception - that we create the reality in which we live. We choose, in every moment, either heaven - the existence of love's presence, or the fear-based hell, which is the lack of love.

"I believe Madelyn came to give you the gift of life. If, in fact, this ship is in peril, perhaps she came to let you know there is nothing for you to fear. If we do not succumb to fear, then we let go of the darkness and bask in the light that is already ever-present in everything we do. That light - the life force - supports us. Instead of doom, where there is only a downward spiral, we must seek the revitalizing opportunities coming our way."

"We do have so much to look forward to, yes?" François said.

"I think we are here for a very important reason," Jocelyn said. "You are to see into the possibilities of what the future will bring, and I am to connect with the souls who are about to leave. In a way, perhaps I am a bridge to help them ease over to the other side. What better way could we be of service than to love these many people right where they are, even though they have no awareness of what is to come."

"Yes, but on that soul-level they may know," François said, "even though their minds may not be aware of it. Jocelyn, the next few days must be used well." Their eyes reached into each other as they reluctantly released their touch.

Jocelyn smiled. "We must get our rest and prepare to be in service to ourselves, and to the many souls on this ship."

They stood, and François gently kissed her hand. "Thank you, Jocelyn – merci. Until morning, I pray you rest well . . ."

CHAPTER
Eleven

*I*t was Friday morning. *Titanic* departed Queenstown the prior afternoon and was now well out to sea. Jocelyn walked to the Purser's Office on C Deck and wrote a telegram and paid to have it delivered by pneumatic tube to the Marconi Room. From there, Radio Officer Harold McBride transmitted it by wire to Mrs. Straus' concierge. Jocelyn marveled at the advancement of present day technology, knowing that within minutes her telegram would arrive in New York and soon be on its way, most likely by bicycle messenger, to the concierge. By the next day, she hoped she might receive confirmation of a new flat waiting for her in Manhattan. Despite her conversation with François about their common concern for the fate of the voyage, she felt excitement and hope for a promising future.

As she left the Purser's Office, she came across Lucy and Mr. Straus, who leisurely strolled the promenade, undoubtedly discussing their new business plan. Straus tipped his hat and said, "Jocelyn, you look lovely this morning. I trust you slept well?"

"I dare say hardly a wink," Jocelyn said. "I have so many ideas running through my head!"

"We are creating a new and exciting venture together,

are we not, ladies?"

Both women smiled, and Jocelyn said, "I cannot wait to begin! If I may be of assistance before we arrive in New York, please let me know."

"Did you wire the concierge?" Lucy asked.

"I did, and please thank Mrs. Straus again for the referral. Now, if you will excuse me, I must run. I have a breakfast engagement. May you both have a most pleasant day!"

"Thank you, Jocelyn, and may I extend the same to you," said Mr. Straus. Lucy smiled and nodded in acknowledgement as they parted ways.

François was waiting for Jocelyn at the Café Parisien. Their conversation the night before brought them together with a powerful common calling. Even though their time together was limited before their scheduled arrival in New York the following Wednesday, that did not stop François from being a gallant romantic. At the table was a lovely bouquet of flowers with a card that read:

To my dream girl,
The universe awaits you
with every possibility for
a bright future.
Yours, François

Jocelyn was more than surprised. It had been years since a man demonstrated such interest in her. She had to admit she liked the attention, knowing she too felt her heart stirring in his direction. She leaned over and lightly kissed him on the cheek, something not considered proper etiquette in the Edwardian era, but, she thought, who really cared anyway? Certainly, no one in the café appeared to be bothered.

After breakfast, they took the flowers back to her suite and placed them on the table. Jocelyn arranged the stems to be certain they were perfectly symmetrical. François watched admiringly until Jocelyn caught him. "What?" she said.

"Oh, nothing. I'm simply mesmerized."

"You are?"

"S'il vous plaît, Jocelyn, I wonder if you might indulge me for one moment? You see, last night I was overcome by a passionate desire to kiss you goodnight before I left."

"You were? And why did you not?"

"Well, I felt perhaps it was too soon, considering just a day earlier we were virtual strangers wrestling around on the docks of Cherbourg."

"Yes, such a sudden transition would hardly be proper," Jocelyn said.

"But now, more than eight hours have passed, and I wonder if you might consider that we have been acquainted long enough to indulge in that first kiss?"

"I might," she said with that marvelous smile.

François gathered her into his arms and leaned over as she rose on her tiptoes to join him in a kiss. It was a sweet moment - one that seemed timeless in its inception, and one without any calamitous collision between them.

He then took her by the hand, and they left the suite to tour the ship. "Why don't we start on the uppermost level on the Boat Deck and work our way down through the levels of the ship," he suggested.

"I'm glad you know where you are going," Jocelyn said. "The ship is so enormous, I'm afraid I'd get lost."

"Oui, but don't worry, I worked here for two days. I learned my way around."

She laughed and took his arm as they arrived on the Boat Deck. "Oh, look," Jocelyn said, pointing ahead. "Isn't that the captain?"

"It is," François said. Up ahead, Captain Smith stood, conversing with Second Officer Charles Lightoller. The discussion appeared rather animated. François stopped and put his finger to his lips as he looked at Jocelyn, and they maneuvered to the side of a lifeboat so as not to intrude on the discussion. They overheard Captain Smith admonishing Lightoller, believing they were alone and out of earshot.

"What is the status of the fire in the coalbunker?" Captain Smith impatiently asked.

"No change, sir," Lightoller replied.

"It has been smoldering since we departed Belfast, and you haven't made any progress?"

"Sir, the firemen *have* made some progress clearing the bunker, but they have not yet reached the source of the fire, for it is buried very deep in that hold."

"I'm concerned about the hull being exposed to such heat now for almost two weeks."

"Yes, sir. I am told that the corner of the watertight bulkhead next to the coal chute under bunker number six is red hot."

"Those bulkheads could be warped by the heat," Captain Smith said. "Not to mention the danger of fires igniting in the adjacent bunkers."

"We are wetting down the outside walls of the coal chute to cool the steel, but we cannot simply pour water in the bunker itself."

"I am well aware of the physics of a coal fire, Mr. Lightoller!" Captain Smith nervously paced. He turned and looked Lightoller in the eye. "The coal strike forced us to scavenge barely enough coal for passage to New York. I must order the final boilers lit to bring the ship to full speed, for we are under great expectations of the company to arrive on, or ahead of schedule. That fire is consuming precious fuel."

"The firemen are confident they will have it under control within the next twenty-four hours."

"Do you share their confidence?"

"I do. The fuel loss should not impact our supply."

"Very well, Mr. Lightoller. See to it."

"Yes sir."

Jocelyn and François heard Captain Smith take his leave around the corner, while coming up the stairs behind them were Chief Purser McElroy and another man dressed in civilian clothing. Lightoller approached and impatiently but politely stopped at the convergence. François and Jocelyn at first acted as if they had not heard any of the captain's conversation with Mr. Lightoller, yet Jocelyn knew this was another confirmation forewarning the ship's peril. She knew when something was not right, many things happened as warnings prior to disaster.

"Well, good day, Mrs. Davis, Mr. Delacroix," Mr. McElroy said in his typical jovial manner. He patted François on the shoulder. "François, you are looking fit as a fiddle this morning."

"Good day to you, Mr. McElroy," François said. He smirked at Jocelyn, who rolled her eyes.

"It is a pleasure to see you both again. May I take the opportunity to introduce you to Mr. Thomas Andrews, the naval architect in charge of the design of the *Titanic*, and Mr. Charles Lightoller, the ship's second officer. Mrs. Jocelyn Brewster Davis is a couturier of fine women's clothing, and Mr. François Delacroix is an architect, about to resume his career in New York City."

"Yes. It is a pleasure to be sure," François said.

"Walking about, are you?" Mr. McElroy asked.

"Yes, we thought we would start on the Boat Deck and explore the ship," François said.

"Well, enjoy your day. If you will excuse me, Mr. Lightoller and I have some business to attend," Mr. McElroy said, tipping his cap toward Jocelyn.

Lightoller acknowledged them, and he and Mr. McElroy politely took their leave.

Turning his attention to Mr. Andrews, François said, "Mr. Andrews, my congratulations on this wondrous achievement."

Andrews shook both their hands in greeting. "Thank you for the compliment, Mr. Delacroix. I am certain some of your designs are just as fine. Since I am about to take a gander through the Boat Deck and then down to the Promenade Deck, I would be happy to be your tour guide. Would you care to join me?"

"That would certainly be a fortuitous opportunity." François looked at Jocelyn for her approval, at which she smiled in agreement.

As Lightoller and McElroy left the bridge, Andrews turned in their direction and noticed the look of concern on their faces.

Jocelyn decided to tell him what they overheard. "Mr. Andrews, we must confess we just overheard a conversation between Captain Smith and Mr. Lightoller about a fire in the ship's coalbunker."

"Oh? Well, please don't concern yourselves, for you may be assured that the crew is handling the situation."

"Mr. Andrews," François said, "what could cause such a fire?"

"I can't say for certain, but it was most likely spontaneous combustion."

"I'm not sure I understand," Jocelyn said.

"Well, coal provides an abundant source of energy to run the ship," Andrews said, "but it is highly combustible, and under certain conditions, a chemical reaction with oxygen can cause it to ignite spontaneously if not properly ventilated and cooled. Ideally, coal must be stored cool and dry, which is a challenge in the extremely hot environment of the boiler rooms, and that is why smoldering coal fires are fairly common aboard large vessels. *Titanic's* coalbunkers are three stories high, and each hold hundreds of tons of coal, so it is taking some time for our firemen and stokers to burrow in and extract the burning coal, which can exceed temperatures of 500 degrees."

"Extract the coal?" François asked. "Why not just spray water on the fire?"

"No," Andrews said, "although that seems logical, water contains oxygen, so wetting burning coal in that confined space will generate heat, toxic gas, and steam, which can create more problems. The best course of action is for the crews to dig out the burning coal, load it into wheelbarrows, and throw it into the furnaces."

"Mon Dieu," François said. "Such terribly difficult and dangerous work."

"Indeed," Andrews said. "As you can imagine, the crews must move slowly and cautiously."

"Mr. Andrews," Jocelyn said, "we overheard Captain Smith say the fire has been smoldering for some ten days."

"Yes?" Andrews said. "Well, it is not my place to disagree with him, but it is hard to know precisely when it began. The coal was loaded into the bunkers in Belfast, so it started sometime between then and the point when crews noted signs of a fire."

"Forgive me," Jocelyn said, "but why did they not immediately notice when it started?"

"Coal can smolder for a great length of time without detection, particularly when it is buried deep inside bunkers as large as *Titanic's*."

"But clearly," François said, "the captain knew about it before the passengers boarded and we set sail, no?"

"Yes, Mr. Delacroix, that is true."

Jocelyn pensively looked at François, who shared her concern.

"I deeply regret this has alarmed you," Andrews said. "I must reiterate, coal fires aboard ship are quite common, and while this particular fire has been a bit more stubborn than Captain Smith or the crew expected, he would never have set sail if there was any reason to believe we were in danger."

"I suppose," François said, "your presence here is reassuring, no?"

Andrews laughed. "Yes, and don't forget the chairman of the White Star Line is also aboard. Now, I must ask, however, if you would be so kind as to not speak of this to your fellow passengers."

"Of course not," Jocelyn said.

"Thank you for your discretion," Andrews said. "Please call me Thomas. May I call you François and Jocelyn?"

"By all means," Jocelyn said.

"If you would like, after we finish here on the Boat Deck and then on A Deck below us, let us go down to the Café Parisien for a cup of coffee and a biscuit. Afterward, I will be happy to give you the grand tour. I walk through the entire ship twice a day to assure that all is in working order. If you would care to join me, I can take you into areas not for the average passenger's eyes. They are quite interesting, especially for a fellow architect."

"We will be delighted. Thank you, Thomas," François said. "So, you are the chief designer of this glorious vessel."

"Well, certainly not by myself," Andrews modestly said. "I am the Managing Director for Design at Harland and Wolff, the ship's builder. I am here as part of the Guarantee Group, which consists of nine men, all experts in their field at the company. We are inspecting *Titanic* and vetting the ship for inevitable issues that arise on a ship's maiden voyage. Each man holds a key position, such as plumber, electrician, draughtsman, fitter, and designer. Needed changes are repaired onboard or noted for when we arrive back in Southampton."

They walked along the Boat Deck. At the fore end, the Bridge stood eight feet above the deck, and the wheelhouse, separated by windows, was above and behind it. The captain's and officers' quarters were located behind the wheelhouse. François found it interesting that the sides of the Bridge were open, somewhat like on a sailing ship. There were neither walls nor windows to keep out the elements, especially in the rough, cold waters of the North Atlantic.

Andrews pointed out the raised forecastle, located forward of the Bridge Deck, which accommodated the number one hatch - the main opening leading down to the cargo hold - the anchor housing, and many pieces of machinery. From the Bridge Deck, he showed them the raised Poop Deck toward the aft, at 106 feet long, used as a promenade for the Third Class passengers. Both the forecastle and Poop Deck were separated from the bridge by the recessed well decks.

"*Titanic's* center anchor, the largest ever built, is over eighteen feet long and weighs fifteen tons. Most of the links in the anchor chain are up to three feet in length. The ship carries twelve hundred feet of chain for her anchors. *Titanic* weighs forty-six thousand tons - the largest moving object ever built."

"That is almost unfathomable," François said.

Andrews explained the ship's advanced technology, which included the Marconi Room, situated at the aft end of the Bridge. Jocelyn was interested to learn that radio officers were not crewmembers of *Titanic*, but rather were in the employ of the Marconi Wireless Telegraph Company. Their sleeping quarters were in a separate room to the starboard side of the Marconi Room.

Just past the entrance to the Grand Staircase, they came to the First Class Gymnasium, a sunlit room with many windows. They took notice of several women using the rowing machine, electric camel, electric horse, and cycling machines. The only exercise equipment not in use at the time was the punching bag.

"If you want to use these facilities, you may purchase a ticket for a shilling from the ship's purser for one session. Permit me to introduce you to the physical educator." Andrews motioned for the man to join them. "Mr. McCauley, may I introduce Mrs. Davis and Mr. Delacroix."

"At your service," McCauley said. He nodded and bowed in acknowledgement. "I am available for physical education instruction during all gymnasium hours. Ladies may use the facilities in the morning from 9:00 a.m. to noon. The gentlemen's hours are from 2:00 p.m. to 6:00 p.m. Children may come with a parent from 1:00 p.m. to 3:00 p.m. Please let me know if I may be of assistance."

"A pleasure to make your acquaintance," François said.

As they walked along the First Class Promenade, Andrews continued, "There are four separate promenades on the Boat Deck. One is strictly for officers and another solely for First Class passengers. The third is for engineers, and the last promenade is for Second Class passengers. No lifeboats are stored on the First Class Promenade so as not to obstruct the ocean view."

"According to what I can see, there are not many lifeboats on the ship," François said.

"That is an astute observation, François. *Titanic* has the capacity to carry up to 64 wooden lifeboats - enough for 4,000 people, more than the ship's capacity. I designed her to hold 40, but the White Star Line made the decision to carry only one-third of the capacity, in compliance with Board of Trade regulations. That leaves 20 lifeboats total; 14 standard for 65 people each, 4 collapsible for 47 people each, and two emergency cutters for 40 people each, totaling space aboard the lifeboats for 1,178 people."

"So, there is less capacity on the lifeboats than there are numbers of passengers and crew?" François said. "I happen to know that *Titanic's* crew surpasses 900, *and* there are far more passengers than crewmembers aboard, are there not?"

"I understand your concern, François," Andrews said. "Let me just say, the number of lifeboats aboard *Titanic* complies with Board of Trade regulations, based on the gross tonnage of the ship. That is, in shipping vernacular, the total enclosed revenue-earning space of *Titanic*. Beside the point, the route across the northern Atlantic is well traveled, and it is believed that many ships would quickly aid any ship in distress. Therefore, the Board of Trade calculates that the required number of lifeboats is adequate to ferry passengers from a ship in peril to a rescue ship with plenty of time to spare."

What Andrews did not mention was that, due to the recent British national coal strike, very few British ships were crossing the North Atlantic at the time. The 37-day strike ended on April 6, four days before *Titanic* set out on her maiden voyage. Three days was not enough time to transport coal from the mines. Instead, the International Mercantile Marine transferred coal to *Titanic* from several of the company's ships docked in Southampton, leaving them out of service. Last minute crewmember hires for *Titanic*'s maiden voyage came from the IMM ships in Southampton that were temporarily not serviceable.

They all walked down the Grand Staircase while Andrews told them where to find the other staircases. "As you now know, the fore Grand Staircase entrance is located between the first and second funnels, just before the gymnasium. The highest level of the aft Grand Staircase goes up to the Promenade Deck, where we are going next, between the third and fourth funnels. The moderate Second Class staircase is toward the stern and extends to the Boat Deck."

As they came to the next level, Andrews continued, "Here we are on the Promenade, or A Deck, which is the longest extension along the length of the ship at 546 feet. It is for the exclusive use of First Class passengers, which houses the six palatial staterooms, or Parlor Suites, featuring their own enclosed First Class Promenades. Each suite has two bedrooms and two wardrobe rooms, private baths, a telephone for room-to-room calls on the ship, electric heaters disguised as small fireplaces, gimbal lamps designed not to tip over in choppy seas, table fans, and the most important feature - call bells for the stewards.

"Tonight, Mr. Bruce Ismay, the Chairman of the White Star Line, is hosting a party in his suite, which is actually three suites joined together. He always makes a point to accompany his ships on their maiden voyages. In appreciation for their patronage to the White Star Line, he hosts a festive gala for the most influential passengers aboard. I would like to invite you both as my guests. It will commence at 9:00 p.m. following dinner."

Jocelyn looked at François, glowing with excitement at the chance to rub elbows with the ship's most influential people. "Oh, Thomas, we would be honored to attend. Thank you for the invitation."

"Very well, then. You may meet me in the Parlor Suite B-52 around 9:00 p.m. It will be a formal black tie affair."

Jocelyn began imagining what she should wear. She desired to make a good impression, for she could potentially create some business interests with those attending the party, most importantly, society's upper class women.

"Let us continue," Andrews said. "Many First Class cabins are located on the Promenade Deck. There is a special clothes-pressing room for First Class passengers' maids and valets. Stewards and stewardesses quarters are on the First Class deck so they are readily available when summoned."

They walked to the center of the Promenade level, where there was less turbulence than at either end. "Here we have the First Class Lounge. It is the primary public gathering space with access to a bar. You will notice the large bookcase at one end and fireplace on the other to offer passengers a warm, inviting place to gather. The room's decor is in the Louis XV style with details derived from the Palace at Versailles. Very comfortable upholstered seating is set around small four-top tables, making it an inviting place to gather for cards, conversation, and reading. Ah, I see over there in the corner is Mr. and Mrs. Straus - a particularly lovely couple, I might add."

Isidor and Eva Straus gave the party a wave.

"Yes, I had the pleasure of meeting them last evening," Jocelyn said as she waved at the couple in return.

"As we walk through the room, we come to a door at the end, which leads from the lounge to the Reading and Writing Room. You will notice the large bow window on the port side, just off the Promenade. It is the most femininely decorated room on the ship with beautiful furnishings. As you can see, we have yellow sofas, and pink and red chairs. The panel walls are painted white, with white floor-to-ceiling Corinthian columns, and elegantly beautiful white floral plasterwork around the chandeliers on the ceiling. Graceful velvet curtains flank every window throughout the room. The White Star Line did not scrimp on the ship's decor. It is of the highest quality. Good day, ladies," Mr. Andrews said as they walked by two tables of women who chatted over tea. They politely nodded first at Andrews and then at Jocelyn and François.

As they walked by, Jocelyn giggled when she overhead one of the women say to another, "That man looks just like the handsome waiter at dinner the other evening."

"We are coming toward the aft Grand Staircase," Andrews said, "where we find the First Class Smoke Room. Jocelyn, you might just be the first woman allowed entrance into the men's inner sanctum." He winked at her as he held the door for her to enter.

"Are you certain it is all right?" Jocelyn said.

"Of course," Andrews said. "This room is intended for gentlemen only, similar to that of a private men's club on shore, but I don't believe we shall shatter the sanctity of man's eminent domain if you pass through."

Andrews led them into the lounge, where a dozen or so elegant gentlemen smoked, drank, and conversed. Jocelyn's presence indeed caused little stir. In fact, several men looked up and politely nodded.

Andrews spoke softly, "You will find the elegant carved mahogany panel walls inlaid with mother of pearl. The paneled four bay windows have inset leaded glass with etched mirrors that hold the images of world ports and White Star Line ships. The room also has two lavatories."

"This is where I joined the men last night after dinner," François said.

"Here you will find the only working fireplace on the ship," Andrews said. "The room is U-shaped, designed to vent smoke out through the fireplace. Above it hangs the Norman Wilkinson painting, *Approach to the New World*."

"Magnificent," Jocelyn whispered. "And I do so love the beautiful tile flooring."

"All handcrafted," Andrews said. "The table tops are

marble, and the armchairs are made of leather. Stewards provide drinks and cigars for the men's enjoyment, and this room stays open until midnight, one-half hour later than the First Class lounge."

They approached a table where John Jacob Astor sat playing cards with three others. Jocelyn recognized one of the men as Benjamin Guggenheim. She excitedly nudged François.

"Good day, Mr. Astor," Andrews said. "I hope we are not intruding."

At the sight of Jocelyn, all four gentlemen half-stood and nodded to her before sitting back down. "Not at all, Mr. Andrews," Astor said. "The room brightened considerably when your lovely guest came in. Well, hello, François."

"Good morning, Jack," François said.

Jocelyn's eyes popped at François.

"Are you winning?" François continued.

Astor shrugged. "I am gaining their confidence before I swoop down upon them."

"Which is to say, no, he is losing," Guggenheim said.

Everyone laughed, and Andrews led François and Jocelyn away.

Jocelyn looked at François. "Jack?"

François shrugged. "That is what his friends call him. He insisted."

As they stepped away from earshot of the table, Andrews said, "As you might guess, this room is the preferred spot for gamblers. We have to be wary of professional cardsharps using aliases, who travel upper-class ocean liners. We warn passengers in advance, but they gamble at their own risk."

Jocelyn had yet to let this go. "And I suppose you played cards with him last night?"

"No," François said, "but from the sound of it, I wish I had."

Andrews laughed as he continued the tour. "As we walk toward the aft, we have the Verandah Café and the Palm Court, located on each side of the Second Class Staircase. We designed them to simulate an outdoor sidewalk café, brightly lit by large windows and double sliding doors that open onto the First Class Promenade Deck. As you can see, wicker chairs and tables sit over the black and white checkered tile floor. We have many varieties of outdoor plants throughout the room, including palm trees and ivy covered trellises. Here in the café, we offer refreshments to the passengers, but no full meals. However, you may order a light snack, as you would in a continental sidewalk café."

A familiar voice rang out. "Jocelyn! Hey, honey, over here!"

"Hello, Maggie," Jocelyn said, greeting Margaret Brown, who sat at one of the tables nearby. "I can see that you are enjoying this beautiful room. Mr. Andrews, may I introduce Margaret Brown, of Denver, Colorado. Margaret, this is Mr. Thomas Andrews, the ship's architect."

"Well, I'll be! This is a fine accomplishment you have here, Mr. Andrews - a fine accomplishment indeed!"

"I thank you, Mrs. Brown," Andrews said. "Charmed

to make your acquaintance."

"And may I also introduce Mr. François Delacroix - Mrs. Margaret Brown."

"It is my pleasure, Madame," François said, taking Margaret's hand and kissing it.

Hearing his charming French accent, she responded, "Je suis heureux de faire votre connaissance."

"Parlez-vous français?" François asked.

"Oui. Je pasee mes étés en Paris," Margaret said.

"We must find some time for you two to get to know each other," Jocelyn said.

"Yes, let's do. J'aime apprendre á mieux vous connaître. Mr. Andrews, Mr. Delacroix, it was a pleasure," Margaret said, smiling at Jocelyn with her inimitable confidence. As they departed, Margaret elbowed Jocelyn and gave her a wide smile, pointing at François. Jocelyn winked and brushed her off.

"Let us walk down to the Bridge Deck or B Deck, which is located at the uppermost level of the hull," Andrews said as he motioned to the stairway.

"*Titanic* has thirty-nine parlor suites, of which thirty are here on the Bridge Deck, and nine more are on the Shelter Deck. Each has up to two bedrooms, two wardrobe rooms, and a private bath."

Jocelyn's suite and François' cabin were on the same level as the À la Carte Restaurant and the Café Parisien, where they sat down to take a break from their tour. While enjoying coffee, François said to Andrews, "How did the *Titanic* come about? Could you give us some history?"

"Of course," Andrews said. "As you may know, J. Bruce Ismay is the President of the IMM - the International Mercantile Marine Company. He is also Chairman and Managing Director of the White Star Line, succeeding his father, Thomas Ismay, who was the founder and Chairman before him. Mr. Ismay Senior believed that more passengers would more likely make longer journeys across the Atlantic if the vessel were spacious and well appointed, with at least the comforts of home. J. Bruce Ismay intended that *Titanic* offer the sophistication of an elegant European hotel for the wealthy.

"Harland and Wolff, out of Belfast, have been shipbuilders for the White Star Line since 1867, having built the largest and fastest luxury liners in the world - that is until Cunard's *Mauritania* and *Lusitania* came about." Andrews poured cream in his coffee and stirred it before he took a sip.

"In 1907, Mr. Ismay met with Lord Pirrie, partner and Chairman of Harland and Wolff, to instigate the concept of the largest and most luxurious ocean liners in the world, giving rise to three Olympic Class liners, of which *Titanic* is the second completed ship. At the time, speed was of lesser concern to Mr. Ismay than size and luxury. Later, he made it the long-term goal of the White Star Line to attain the highly acclaimed, yet mythical Blue Riband, which is an unofficial award for the record of a passenger liner's highest average speed. Only passenger liners in regular service crossing the Atlantic Ocean on a westbound route can obtain the Blue Riband. The *Mauretania* currently holds the coveted prize, and while White Star's Olympic Class liners are too large to match it in speed, Mr. Ismay intends to someday achieve the Blue Riband with a comparable liner that will exceed Cunard's liners in size, luxury, and speed as well."

"I am most interested in your background, and how you came to design *Titanic*," Jocelyn said.

"Well, I began working for Harland and Wolff as an apprentice when I was sixteen years of age, and in 1901, I became a member of the Institution of Naval Architects. Lord Pirrie, who is my uncle, hired me because of my background as a naval architect. My first job was to prepare the scale drawings so Harland and Wolff could begin building *RMS Olympic* and *RMS Titanic* side by side. Both ships are fifty percent larger than those of Cunard's line, with *Titanic* slightly larger in its tonnage than her sister ship. I am in charge of design as the principle architect of the project, and I am now the Managing Director at Harland and Wolff.

"*RMS Olympic* made its maiden voyage on June 14, 1911. *RMS Titanic,* as you know, is the second ship, and the third is *Gigantic,* which is currently under construction. For the most part, all three ships are identical."

"Excuse me for interrupting," Jocelyn said, "but being an American, I am not certain what RMS stands for. Is it Royal Merchant Ship?"

"Actually, at one time, that was what RMS stood for, but now it is Royal Mail Steamer, because both the *Olympic* and *Titanic* carry mail under the support of His Majesty's postal authorities. Our postal clerks process sixty thousand pieces of mail per day."

"Well, I guess that certainly qualifies as a mail ship,

does it not?" Jocelyn said.

Andrews smiled as he continued, "All three ships were constructed in Belfast in specially-designed shipyards to accommodate their massive size. Of the fifteen thousand workers at Harland and Wolff, three thousand labored for over three years to build *Titanic* alone. They used two thousand one-inch-thick steel plates to form the hull, held together with three million iron rivets, with 2,000 portholes so passengers have many opportunities to view the sea. She is 833 feet long and 104 feet high, with ten decks, of which eight are for passenger use."

"What kind of wage does a worker earn in a week?" François asked.

"A skilled worker earns two pounds, which is the American equivalent of $10.00 per week, while an unskilled worker earns one pound weekly," Thomas said. "The cost of *Titanic's* construction came to 1.5 million British pounds - or 7.5 million dollars to build."

In Sophia's time, the cost was the equivalent of 179 million U.S. dollars.

"Although the White Star Line, itself, has not claimed *Titanic* to be 'unsinkable,' she was labeled as such by *The Shipbuilder*, a prestigious British shipping trade journal. There are sixteen watertight bulkheads, accessible through steel doorways that close with a flip of the switch. If two of these bulkheads are flooded, she can still stay afloat. Actually, the first four bulkheads could flood, and she would remain above water, but I cannot imagine anything that would cause such a catastrophe. No such disaster has yet befallen a ship anywhere near the size of *Titanic*," Andrews said, shaking his head at the thought.

"Her construction began March 31, 1909, and was completed on May 31, 1911. During the last year, she has undergone all the fittings - with the engines, funnels, and of course, all the details of her extravagant interiors."

"One might think they were traveling aboard a luxurious floating hotel," Jocelyn said.

"Yes, it was quite an accomplishment of thousands of people who helped it come about. The White Star Line has great plans for the three ships. This voyage is the first of many cross-Atlantic journeys between Southampton, England; Cherbourg, France - which services continental Europe; Queenstown, Ireland; and New York. *Titanic, Olympic, and Gigantic* will set sail once every three weeks. From Southampton, one ship will sail every Wednesday, leaving at noon. Another will leave from New York each Saturday for its return to Southampton, by way of Plymouth, and on to Cherbourg. This offers the traveler weekly sailings in each direction across the Atlantic."

"I look forward to traveling frequently now, considering my new enterprise," Jocelyn said. She looked longingly at François. "New York, France, and England."

"Oui," François said. "With all those travel plans, you might require a private valet."

"Perhaps you know of someone who could accompany me?" They smiled like two teenagers on a first date.

Andrews cleared his throat, and the two lovebirds perked. "Jocelyn, in the event you have employees who will be traveling with you, you might be interested in the Second Class accommodations."

"Yes, of course," Jocelyn said. She winked at François

as they followed Andrews.

As they walked down the stairs to the next level, Andrews said, "Take note of the natural light flowing in through the glass dome overhead, which crowns the aft Grand Staircase. There, you will find the pianist playing each evening. As in the fore Grand Staircase, the two ceilings are works of art, as premier examples of the ship's luxuriance. Wrought iron framework holds the glass together in an artful crown over the stairway's six descending decks, from the Boat Deck, down to E Deck. The distance from the lower landing to the glass dome is sixty feet.

"The walls along the stairway are paneled in oak, with detailed carvings and paintings in the William and Mary style. The Grand Staircase descends all five decks from the Boat Deck, which is the uppermost deck, down to E Deck."

"My word," Jocelyn said. "Earlier, we were discussing how easy it would be to get lost around here."

"Indeed," Andrews said. "We instruct our stewards to keep an eye out for lost passengers, especially children. Now, below us, the staircase ends one floor down at F Deck, merely as an ordinary stairway. At the base of the E Deck stairway, on the middle railing, stands a bronze cherub that serves as a lamp base. The fore Grand Staircase at mid-landing between the Boat Deck and Promenade Deck exhibits a fine grandfather clock surrounded by intricately carved woodwork of two facing figures depicting *Honor and Glory Crowing Time*. Here at the aft Grand Staircase, on the same level, we have a clock, which is not quite as elaborate."

"Ah, but still quite beautiful," François said.

"The ornate bronze grillwork on both stairways is intricately decorated with ormolu garlands, with an application of finely ground, high-karat gold-mercury amalgam applied to the ironwork of the banisters. The balustrade is inspired by the French court of Louis XIV."

"Their features are most exquisite," François said as he gazed at the many beautiful details. "They are the crowning jewels of *Titanic*."

"Behind the fore Grand Staircase are the three First Class elevators that travel from A Deck to E Deck. For your convenience, each holds a chair and mirror."

Sophia awoke to Michael's restlessness. He swung his legs out of bed, drenched in sweat, with a spike of pain in one of his hips that extended up his back and down to his knee. Sophia got up and sat behind him to rub his back.

"Those spikes are getting worse. Can I get you something for the pain?" Sophia asked.

"How about a glass of scotch and a new hip?" Michael said. "The right one hurts tonight, as usual, but my left one is not much better."

"Well, the hip part of that request needs to be on our agenda when we return to Colorado," Sophia said.

"Yep. One of these days, I'll have to get to the doc."

"Yep," she sighed, "and as long as you put it off, the pain will only get worse. The cortisone injections don't help for very long anymore."

"Yep," Michael said as he leaned over on his elbows rubbing his hands through his hair.

"In the meantime, how about I get you a hot pack for the pain and that glass of scotch for the rest of what ails you."

"I'd appreciate that. Me and my hips will be not-so-patiently waiting."

Sophia returned after five minutes, finding Michael tucked back in bed, sound asleep and snoring like a bull elephant.

Sophia shook her head. *How does he do that so easily? One minute he's in excruciating pain, and the next he's out like a light. I wish it was that easy for me to fall asleep.*

She put the hot pack next to his ailing hip, plugged her earplugs in, and downed the scotch herself before drifting back to her dreams.

Chapter
Twelve

Thomas Andrews continued the tour, next through the Second Class Smoke Room located on the Bridge, or B Deck. Men filled most of the tables, enjoying a game of checkers or poker. In the same way that Second and Third Class passengers could not access First Class, neither could First Class passengers access the lower deck facilities.

"As you can see," Andrews said, "this room is quite spacious and handsome, decorated in the Louis XVI style and paneled in carved oak with upholstered dark green Moroccan leather. You may have noticed throughout the ship are various patterns of linoleum on the floor? It is the latest in floor coverings - perfect for the shipping industry - lightweight, colorful, and durable. This room is also for men only, as in the First Class Smoke Room."

"And here I am intruding again," Jocelyn said. "I feel like I am trespassing secretive territory of an exclusive men's club in London."

"That is precisely the intention," Andrews agreed. "It is a private place for men to lose their shirts while playing cards." He lowered his voice to a whisper and leaned close. "Here they can gather to boast and tell tales without their wives to remind them of how ridiculous they are."

They tried to laugh quietly. "You men," Jocelyn said.

"How do you stand yourselves?"

"I don't know," Andrews said. "My wife often asks that question, and I am hard pressed to provide an answer. All right, now from here, the Shelter Deck, or C Deck, runs uninterrupted from bow to stern. At the Grand Staircase on C Deck, and at the aft Grand Staircase on E Deck, are the Purser's Offices, which are actually a suite of rooms. There, passengers can purchase tickets for the Turkish baths, deck chair rental, swimming bath, electric baths, or book time in the gym, squash court, and photographic darkroom. One can also fill out a telegram to be sent to the Marconi Room via pneumatic tube."

"I did that very thing this morning," Jocelyn said. "I am looking for a flat in New York. Mrs. Straus referred me to her concierge, who will have something waiting for me when we arrive next Wednesday. Fascinating – quite exciting."

"Yes, isn't it a modern miracle?" Andrews said. "We can thank the British for laying the submarine cable system so the wireless radiotelegraph will work across the Atlantic. The Marconi Room's radiotelegraph has a range of 400 miles during the day and 1,000 miles at night. The Purser's Office also houses a miniature printing office, operated by office clerks. You may have read the *Atlantic Daily Bulletin*, printed with news gathered by the Marconi Room, which contains ship's news, weather updates, and society gossip. There you will find stock prices, horse racing results, and on-board tournament results, along with all the ship's facilities hours, and of course, advertisements. So, Jocelyn if you want to reach a wealthy clientele, you could place an advertisement in the *Bulletin* to promote your ladies couture designs."

"If I knew before I came on board, I might have done just that," Jocelyn said, "but I will take that into consideration each time I cross the Atlantic in the future."

"You may want to speak to the *Bulletin* editor. He will give you the information you need. As we leave this level, the last room of interest is the photographic darkroom near the Purser's Office for amateur photographers who would like to develop their photographs of the voyage right here on the ship."

As they descended the Grand Staircase to D Deck, Andrews continued. "In the middle of the ship are the majority of the First Class cabins and the Second Class Library. The First Class Barber Shop is located at the foot of the Grand Staircase, where it doubles as a lounge for passengers' maids and valets. As you can see, there is a bench on one side of the room, and chairs for cutting hair on the opposite side. Souvenirs hang from the ceiling and on the walls, such as penknives, banners, dolls, hats, tobacco, and ribbons embroidered with *RMS Titanic*. It doubles as a small gift shop."

He further explained that, on the same deck, was open space for Third Class passengers. First, Second and Third Class passengers had cabins on D Deck. Berths for firemen were located on the bow. D Deck was the highest level reached by eight of the fifteen watertight bulkheads.

C Deck housed some of the crewmembers below the Forecastle. Their berths were very much like that of the Third Class berths, painted in white enamel with mahogany furnishings and linoleum tiled floors. Each housed two, four, or six people per room. All had bunk beds, a small amount of wardrobe space, and a sink with fresh water.

"Let us tour through the Second Class Library," Andrews said. "It has a similar style as the Smoke Room, except with sycamore paneling, upholstered chairs, and carpeting. The Library is primarily for Second Class women and children, since the Smoke Room is solely for men. It is the equivalent of the First Class Reading and Writing Room. Here they serve afternoon tea and coffee, or one can also have tea on the Second Class Promenade, located on the Boat Deck.

"A good many First Class amenities aboard other shipping liners are not as well-appointed as those of Second Class aboard *Titanic*. She sets a new standard for transatlantic travel. You will find Second Class accommodations over seven decks, with an elevator that services all. The White Star Line is proud to provide both comfort and style for all passengers who travel with them."

Jocelyn thought they must have seen most of the 285 Second Class passengers in those two rooms. It was rather chilly that morning on the Promenade Deck, and not many people were outside strolling in the cool spring air. She made it a special point to tap into the presence of every person she saw, as either a passenger or crewmember, taking note of whether or not she could see their energy. It was of vital importance to follow through with her ability to sense their life force.

On the Saloon Deck, or D Deck, they walked through the Main Galley, which serviced both First and Second Class dining facilities, located between the two dining saloons. There was a large number of kitchen crew preparing the lunchtime meal for about 600 people.

"You might find it interesting to know that *Titanic* uses fourteen thousand gallons of drinking water every 24 hours. The ship's galley holds several rooms," Andrews said. "There are serving pantries, a butcher shop, and a bakery, where fresh bread is baked daily, among other delectable baked goods. Vegetable kitchens are where all the vegetables and fruits are stored and prepared for the meals. Several cold storage rooms hold wines, beer, and oysters. We also have specialized rooms for silver, crystal, glass, and china. As you can see, there are massive storage bins that hold tons of coal needed to fuel the nineteen ovens, cook tops, ranges, and roasters."

Jocelyn watched the galley activity in awe, wondering how they could possibly produce the mass of food for all the passenger meals on the ship.

"Also here on the starboard side of D Deck, you will find the ship's hospital facilities, comparable to the best small hospitals in Britain and America. *Titanic* has a twelve-bed hospital for First and Second Class passengers, and a six-bed infectious ward in two separate rooms. On C Deck, there is a four-bed hospital for the crew. Both have surgery and treatment rooms. We have a surgeon, assistant surgeon, a medical steward, and nurse/stewardess, along with a matron in charge of immigrants. She teaches them how to use the toilet, which many have never seen, nor used. If they have medical needs, she contacts one of the surgeons to care for them.

"The doctor charges extra for treatments if the health issue occurred before embarking on *Titanic*. Consequently, there is no charge if the passenger becomes ill on the ship.

For example, one of our First Class passengers slipped on a piece of food and fell down the stairs, breaking her arm. The ship's physician placed her arm in a plaster cast, and because she incurred the accident onboard, there was no charge for her medical services. All medications are free, regardless of the circumstance.

"Anyone with an infectious disease will not be allowed entry into the United States, and will be forced to sail back to their homeland. So, all Third Class passengers, prior to coming aboard any White Star Line passenger ship, will undergo a health inspection. The doctors search them for lice and infectious diseases, particularly tuberculosis."

Andrews proceeded with the tour, "The Second Class Dining Saloon can accommodate 564 Second Class passengers, but for this voyage we have half the capacity of 285 Second Class passengers aboard."

Again, Jocelyn took special notice of the facilities, because she would most likely bring along her assistants who would travel in Second Class. She was already convinced that they would be more than comfortable.

"As we enter the Second Class Dining Saloon, you will notice the Sunday Evening Menu is already posted outside the entrance." It listed a menu fit for a high-class restaurant, with several choices for that evening's dinner. "As you can see, the decor is quite nice with the walls lined in oak paneling. The long tables are set with white linen tablecloths, and passengers sit in crimson leather and mahogany chairs."

"I see the chairs and tables are bolted to the floor. Is that in case of bad weather and rough seas?" François asked.

"Yes, and the same is true for the Third Class Dining Saloon. In this room, you will notice the piano, used for the diner's entertainment, is actually better than in the First Class Dining Saloon, where the band plays before and after dinner only. We also have a special dining room off to the side for the First Class passengers' maids and valets, where your people eat their meals. They are served the same meals as the Second Class passengers."

Jocelyn laughed, "Well, neither one of us have 'people,' Thomas. We *are* our people." They all laughed.

The Third Class public rooms were located below the Poop Deck on the Shelter, or C Deck. The General Room and Smoke Room had white enameled walls and long wooden benches with individual tables and chairs, all in teak wood. Both rooms had plenty of electric lighting and portholes, which let in the natural light. Also on the same level was the Third Class Promenade, located on the Poop Deck.

A man approached. "Mr. Andrews, sir. May I interrupt you to say that my family and I are most impressed with your ship. Thank you for making this such a pleasant voyage for us to start our lives in America."

"Tell me your name, good sir," Andrews said, "and where will you be settling?"

"Fredrick Goodwin. My wife and six children are traveling with me to Niagara Falls, where I will join my brother to work at the power plant."

"I am so pleased that your voyage is a pleasant one. My best to you and your family, and thank you for sailing with us."

"Thank you, sir," Goodwin said as he bowed slightly and backed away to join his family.

Third Class accommodations were luxurious compared to most liners. They were not the large dormitory-type rooms found on older ships, but individual two- to six-berth closed cabins. In all, there were eighty-four, two-berth cabins. Jocelyn took note that the majority of the 706 passengers were currently gathered in both of the public rooms. Only a few were out on the Poop Deck that morning at the back of the ship.

Upper Deck, or E Deck held berths for the cooks, seamen, stewards, and trimmers. Crew and passengers were not to meet at anytime during the voyage.

A lengthy internal passageway used by Third Class passengers and crewmembers was nicknamed Scotland Road, referring to the famous street in Liverpool. The E Deck also held mostly Second Class, two- or four-berth rooms and also sleeping quarters for stewards, waiters, and cooks. None of the rooms had private baths, but large facilities were available, designated individually for women and men. Off the aft Grand Staircase was the Second Class Barber Shop.

The Middle Deck, or F Deck, was the last complete deck with Second Class, and Third Class accommodations, along with those for several departments of the crew. Mr. Andrews walked Jocelyn and François through two vacant cabins in Second and then Third Class. The Second Class cabin was similar to the least expensive First Class cabin. Two bunk beds were in each cabin, with a settee, a small wardrobe space, writing desk, and fresh water with a makeup or shaving mirror over the sink.

Third Class cabins had two, four, or six bunk beds per room, all with mahogany furnishings and painted white enamel walls. Provided daily for the First and Second Class cabins were clean sheets and pillowcases. However, in Third Class, only mattresses and pillows were provided. Third Class passengers brought their own linens. Large, clean bath facilities were available, but for the 1,000-person capacity, there were only two bathtubs on hand, one in the women's bath, and the other in the men's bath.

The cost of a Third Class ticket equaled three to four weeks wages of a skilled laborer, which was quite steep for the current economy, especially considering many travelled with several family members. In Sophia's time, that price would equal $900.00 per ticket.

"Most shipping lines do not think it necessary to provide much more than transport for Steerage passengers," Andrews said, "who are required to bring their own bed linens for their bunks and also enough food for the duration of the passage across the Atlantic. Their large quarters hold several bunks for sleeping, leaving little or no privacy. They think because most people traveling in Third Class are immigrating to the United States, and would most likely not be on a return voyage, what would be the point to make special allowances for them.

"However, the White Star Line has a different policy. They know many people are leaving Europe permanently, and their families will soon follow. The White Star Line wants to create a pleasant experience for Third Class passengers, with individual, private rooms for no more than six people, along with spacious, clean restrooms. White Star provides several public spaces, including nice dining facilities and outdoor areas that invite the Third Class passengers to begin their new lives with a fresh start - one that would be a pleasant beginning for them. I must say, such consideration is also excellent for business, since the majority of the ship's passengers travel Third Class, which is a ship's greatest source of profit."

Andrews toured them through the Third Class Dining Saloon, split in two by a watertight bulkhead. It had the joint capacity of 473, with two seatings available. For the initial voyage, 706 Third Class Passengers were aboard, nearly three-quarters of capacity.

"Breakfast, dinner, tea, and supper are served in these two rooms, prepared in the Third Class Kitchen and Pantry behind the wall of the Dining Saloon. The well-lit dining saloon's walls are painted in white enamel, with rows of end-to-end tables. Again, you'll notice the tables and wooden chairs bolted to the floor for rough seas." He lowered his voice, "You might notice only wooden seating is available throughout the Third Class facilities, because lice are unable to live in the wood like they can in upholstery."

Jocelyn instinctively stepped away from a nearby chair.

"The food served here is simple but plentiful. Each day the ship offers a similar dinner menu, serving rice soup, fresh bread, biscuits, roast beef with gravy, sweet corn, boiled potatoes, ending with plum pudding, sweet sauce, and fruit. Many of the passengers are from all over Europe, Russia, China, Belgium, and Great Britain. Those from Finland, Norway, and Sweden, where fresh fruit and vegetables are scarce, are not used to such plentiful offerings. I have heard that a good number of Third Class passengers think the food here is decadent, for it is far beyond what they are accustomed to eating."

"It seems to me that these facilities are most likely better than where these people have been living," François said.

"Yes, most of these people do not have electricity, running water, or indoor plumbing in their homes. The ship, for them, is quite elegant and offers them a good start for their new life in America.

"Now we are coming to the most enjoyable part of the ship. If you are able, you must take advantage of the Swimming Bath. It is a six-foot-deep, heated, saltwater swimming pool - the largest of its kind on any ocean liner. For your convenience, there are several changing rooms located off to the side. Did you bring bathing suits?"

"I did," Jocelyn said. "François?"

"Oui, I must come down for a swim," he responded, hoping she might be game to join him.

"We also have the Turkish Bath, or sauna. Lucky for us, there are no passengers in here right now, so we may tour through. As you can see, the elaborate decorations are of an eastern Moorish theme with walls lined in ornate blue and green tiled panels. Personally, this is my favorite place on the ship. Cairo curtains disguise the portholes with elaborate latticework."

"How much time should we allow to use these facilities?" Jocelyn asked.

"With the use of the Swimming Bath, and the facilities here in the Turkish Bath, I would suggest a minimum of three hours," Andrews said. "There are lounge chairs available for your comfort. You can purchase a ticket from the purser for four shillings, or one dollar, for the use of the room and all the amenities. It offers a steam room, hot room, temperate room, cooling room, shampooing rooms, and toilets. The morning hours are for women, while men use it in the afternoon and evening. Inside the Turkish Bath are the Electric Baths, an ultra-modern innovation of individual enclosed beds with ultraviolet lights overhead.

"Also available is the Squash Court on the Lower Deck, and above it is the spectator gallery on the Middle Deck. Frederick Wright is the supervisor. He will provide you with racquets and balls, and will serve as your opponent if you need one. Are you game, François?"

"I have never played squash."

"Oh, come now, François," Jocelyn said sarcastically. "You *never* try new things."

"Ah," François said, "you did not let me finish. I *would* be willing to try." Jocelyn laughed and grabbed his arm. "Perhaps, with Frederick's patience and expertise, I might become a champion – how you say – squasher?"

"The Squash Court is also for First Class passengers only," Andrews said, "at the cost of 50 cents. If others are waiting to play, one hour is the limit. Your ticket, again, can be purchased from the purser."

As they walked away from the Squash Court, Andrews spoke softly so as not to be overheard by Fredrick Wright, "He earns only one shilling per day, the equivalent of 25 cents, American. Tips are greatly appreciated for all those in service at the Squash Court, pool, Turkish Bath, and exercise room."

The highest salaries on the *Titanic*, at that time, were for

Captain Smith, who was well-paid at 105 British pounds per month, converting to $12,348.00 in Sophia's time. The lowest earnings were for the stewardesses, at three pounds 10 shillings per month, converting to just $427.75 in Sophia's time.

Andrews took Jocelyn and François through the remainder of the lower deck, or G Deck, divided into rooms for food storage, with the exception of the Squash Court, Baggage Rooms, and the Post Office.

"In our Post Office, you will find our five mail clerks sorting letters and parcels for delivery when the ship docks on Wednesday. We have three Americans and two Brits who work thirteen-hour days to process over 3,000 sacks of mail.

"The next two decks are the Orlop Deck and the Tank Top, neither of which you are allowed to see, but I can tell you the Orlop Deck houses all the meat and fish in cold storage, weighing in at 125,000 pounds, not to mention most of the other food stuffs and beverages. The bottom level of the ship is the Tank Top, which holds all the engine rooms, boiler rooms, electrical panels, fresh water tank, and coalbunkers - where the smoldering fire is going on that we discussed earlier. *Titanic* uses 825 tons of coal per day to keep the ship powered, the water hot, including the Swimming Bath, and electric heat throughout."

The Orlop Decks and Tank Top, the lowest levels of the ship, were below the waterline. The Orlop Decks also housed the cargo spaces. The Tank Top was the inner bottom of the ship's hull. Platforms held the ship's boilers, turbines, electrical generators, and the engines that stood four decks high, housed in six compartments. There were twenty-nine boilers, supplied by 159 furnaces, generating pressures up to 215 pounds per square inch. The twenty-nine boilers enabled engines to gain up to 15,000 horsepower. To make it easier to work in the boiler rooms, the double-bottomed hull did not continue up the sides of the hull.

"The Orlop Decks and Tank Top are not accessible to passengers," Andrews said. "Stairs connect it to the higher levels of the ship via twin spiral stairways near the bow. If you would please wait here at the base of the stairs for me, I will return in about ten minutes. Here are two wicker chairs for your comfort. Then if you like, I would enjoy your company for lunch in the Café Parisien - my treat. We can watch the sea roll by as we enjoy each other's company."

"Yes, of course, we will wait," said Jocelyn. Andrews then took his leave.

"How fortuitous that we happened to meet him today," François said.

Jocelyn, a visionary and always thinking of new opportunities, said, "You never know, François, your meeting him here today may create business opportunities for you. He is now widely known in Britain for his architectural achievements, and I would think the United States would be clamoring for his talents, as well. Both you and I know that those whose personalities work well together make the greatest collaborations. Talent is secondary. It seems to me, this is a good start to a promising alliance between you and Mr. Andrews."

"Oui, one can always hope," François said.

CHAPTER
Thirteen

François and Thomas Andrews filled their time at lunch with tales of architectural feats. Jocelyn found their stories fascinating, because their creative process was similar to hers when she designed a custom piece of clothing for a client. For her, it all began with first getting to know the client well and discovering their likes and dislikes, but more-so Jocelyn had to get a feel for her client's personality. Without that edge, her designs would be without that unique essence needed to create a distinctive art form that would fit the character of her client. Once Jocelyn found those precise qualities, the design virtually created itself. The fabrics seemed to avail themselves, and the finishing touches jumped out at her with an intuitive knowing of just how to accomplish every detail. When she did her preliminary homework well, Jocelyn never failed to astound her patron with the finished piece.

François and Andrews were so enraptured in conversation that Jocelyn wondered if they noticed she was still sitting at the table. She wasn't insulted, however, for she rather enjoyed reflecting on her own dreams of the life she intended for herself, knowing what she was about to embark upon would unfold when she arrived in New York. She was also truly happy for François, for he and Andrews were finding such common ground. Perhaps they would be of assistance to each other's careers when they reached their individual destinations.

As she sat, listening to the two of them, the one thing she did not want to admit to herself was the aura she perceived around Andrews was practically nonexistent. When he spoke of the *Titanic*, an accomplishment of which he was rightfully proud, he lit up. Otherwise, his life force energy dimmed down to near nothingness.

Her observation of him caused her to reflect inward on the thought that, if the ship was indeed in peril, she possessed a sense of certainty that she would survive. She wondered how she knew such a thing, but she also knew she must not doubt the assurance within, which was akin to questioning her intuitive nudges. If she questioned her intuition and failed to follow her inner guidance, she would most certainly later regret allowing her thinking mind to get in the way of her heart's direction. She had already gone against her intuition warning her not to take *Titanic* across the Atlantic, but it was too late for regrets now.

To hold the critically important task to which she felt charged was enough to give her a greater sense of purpose for the time being. With each passing hour, it became clear that she must tap into each and every soul on the ship and carry them in her heart, knowing that whatever was their destiny, their souls would be forever remembered. That was enough of a task to carry her onward, beyond the fear of her premonition.

She quietly prayed that nothing bad would happen, and that her misgivings were just a product of the intensely emotional upheaval of the last year mixed with her elation of the last few days. *After all,* she thought, *I am starting my life anew, and I just met a most wonderful man who has captured my heart, and I have a career ahead of me, of which until now, I could only imagine.*

She looked longingly at François, and as if on cue, his eyes alighted on her with pure, tender love. She smiled hesitantly. For the moment, a sheer bright aura surrounded him but then quickly faded.

They concluded lunch, having thoroughly enjoyed every minute of the tour. "Thank you so much, Thomas," François said. "I cannot tell you how you have helped me better understand this incredible ship. You should be very proud."

"It was my pleasure," Andrews said. They shook hands, and Andrews turned to Jocelyn and took her hand. "Until this evening's soiree?"

"Oh, yes, Thomas," Jocelyn said. "We shall see you then."

She tucked her hand in the crook of François' arm as they watched Andrews leave. François looked at her, at first smiling, and then her smile faded. "Jocelyn?"

François, of course, had no idea the entire time during the tour that Jocelyn was connecting with as many souls as possible, particularly those whose life force was dwindling to near nothingness. Jocelyn always marveled how God worked. She set her intention to connect with these souls and had no idea how she would accomplish it, but she simply knew it would happen, because all things noble come about in miraculous ways. Her divine counterpart in her task was none other than Thomas Andrews, the ship's architect - of all people - who took them on the tour to accomplish exactly what Jocelyn needed to do. She was humbly grateful, knowing that answers to her prayers came about with grace and ease.

"Jocelyn?" François again said.

She suddenly perked. "Yes – yes, François."

"You looked as if you were somewhere far away."

She lovingly smiled. "Oh, I do that occasionally. Come – we have some time before dinner. Take me for a walk."

"Avec plaisir."

They decided to take a stroll on the Promenade. The day had warmed up, and it was good to be outside in the fresh, crisp afternoon air and sunshine. Jocelyn was feeling introspective and said very little along the way.

"Cheri?" François said. "I know you are troubled. Do you wish to talk?"

"Two-thirds of the people I saw today have no light around them, particularly the people in Third Class, and also the crew," Jocelyn said. "There are so many children - so many." They stopped by the railing and looked out at the ocean. Jocelyn kept recalling some of those tiny faces. "Do you remember Mr. Goodwin from Third Class?"

"Oui, the nice man who greeted Thomas."

"With a wife and six children," Jocelyn said. "They are moving to New York. François, he had no light around him, and I sense that none of his family do either." She rubbed her arms in the chill and looked around. "There is a ubiquitous emptiness upon this ship. As busy as people are, it is as if most everyone is just going about their lives and duties, finalizing what they came here to do."

"But at times, you seem happy and more relaxed."

"Yes, I know. It moves in an out of my consciousness. I am so elated one moment, and suddenly anxious the next."

"Are you certain these feelings aren't just the anxiety of this new life you are pursuing, or perhaps some innate fear of our isolation out here on the vast ocean?"

"Well, I have sailed before, and I sometimes do feel a slight apprehension about the water, but never have I ever felt such an ominous warning like this. François, something big is approaching, and there is nothing you or I can do, except be as present as possible - to take in every soul's essence - to carry it onward. Somehow, I know this is the most important task I have ever done."

François sighed. "I suppose I am just trying to wish this away, for I must admit that, even though I cannot see their energy like you can, I too sense something ominous."

"Should we tell someone? Captain Smith? Should we warn him?"

"I do not know what we would say. Look around, everything appears so normal. Everything is running smoothly."

"What about the fire? Could that be what I am feeling? The captain said he was concerned that the intense heat might damage the hull."

"And if, indeed, that is what is going to happen, they are already aware. The crews are working to prevent it. For now, it seems best that we wait and be very aware of what goes on."

"It so frustrates me at times," Jocelyn said, "this feeling I get. Sometimes it turns out to be nothing, but this time it is so strong."

"You well know that, even if you tell Thomas of your visions, he will most likely greet it with skepticism."

Jocelyn reluctantly agreed. "And yet, *you* believe me without hesitation."

François gently kissed her. "In addition to dock worker, steward, waiter, philosopher, and architect, I am also a very good judge of character."

She smiled at him as they continued their walk along the Promenade. "I listened to your conversation with Thomas and thought about how I create my best work. It is only when I almost absorb the soul's essence of my client, can I then represent a portion of who they are in the dresses I design for them. I heard both of you speak of the same thing, he in his ship designs and you in your buildings. We almost become the people we serve and certainly join souls with them when we create something magnificent on their behalf.

"I suppose that is what I did this morning as we toured through the ship," Jocelyn said. "I was able to capture the embodiment of not so much each individual, because there were so many, but more-so a cooperative body of souls."

François gently wrapped his arm around her shoulder as they walked.

Jocelyn felt a profound sadness overcome her. "It is my belief that these people have gathered together at this time, as a collective whole, to give of themselves, knowing on a deeper level that they are changing the world. Their sacrifice is about to alter history. It will shift the current reality like no other event in time. Future generations will remember them. Least of all, the shipping industry will benefit by the changes that will immediately go into effect."

François stopped and looked into her eyes. "You have seen more?"

"I am seeing it now, even more clearly. And so do you."

He looked out toward the ocean, pensively regarding his visions of a cold sea.

"You and I are here to honor them," Jocelyn said. "I think we are a bridge by which they will go from this earthly domain to the next. We are here to remember who they came here to be, and to utilize their essence in the work we do, so they will not be forgotten."

They began to feel the chill in the late afternoon air. "Let us go to the lounge and get something warm to drink," François said. "Perhaps some hot buttered rum? What do you say?"

Jocelyn smiled up at him as she slipped her gloved hand into the crook of his arm. They walked quietly and reverently inside . . .

Dinner was a magnificent thirteen-course affair. Everyone in First Class dressed in their finest of gowns and tuxedos, as if they had absolutely no cares in the world. At that very moment, none of them did. All the hard work and preparation of the crew behind the scenes made dinner a model of perfection. Nothing seemed out of place.

Jocelyn and François remained in the Dining Saloon until 9:00 p.m., but a good majority of First Class passengers remained until 11. They joined Thomas Andrews for the party in the suites of Bruce Ismay. The decor was exquisite, with details like that of the highest quality suite of the Waldorf Astoria in New York, built, of course, by one of Ismay's honored guests. Beautifully prepared hors d'oeuvres were wondrous works of art, although very few of the guests were eating because of their sumptuous dinner beforehand. However, the champagne and spirits flowed freely.

Thomas Andrews introduced Jocelyn and François to many of the society elite. Jocelyn's creation of a stunning mahogany, teal, and sea foam green gown, with a matching floor-length duster of burnt velvet and beaded trim, brought more attention to her talents than any form of introduction. Several of the guests gave their calling card to Jocelyn and asked her to call on them. One woman wanted her to design a gown or two for the upcoming holidays. Of course, Jocelyn was thrilled to have future business opportunities for when she settled in New York City.

Andrews introduced François to many notable business magnates from both sides of the Pond, making sure that he mentioned François' architectural achievements in Paris. Most inspiring was John Jacob Astor's invitation for François to call on him once he settled in New York. François was more than impressed with Thomas Andrews, who had plenty of accolades of his own. Not once did he draw attention to his own achievements, one of which was the ship they were on - the greatest industrial marvel in the world. Rather, he called attention to both Jocelyn and François, making sure to introduce them to the people who could help catapult their success in New York.

During the evening, Jocelyn could not help but take notice of their host, J. Bruce Ismay, whose towering height of 6' 4" and handsome, dark good looks caused him to stand out amongst most of the partygoers. However, he appeared to have an introverted demeanor, which was contrary to not only his bigger-than-life appearance, but to the success of his professional position.

After two hours of rubbing elbows with the ship's elite, Jocelyn and François took their leave of the grand soirée, but first thanked Mr. Ismay for his hospitality. He was cordial, yet proper with his British reserve, but she caught him off-guard and made him blush when she put out her hand for him to take.

"Mr. Ismay, we so appreciate being invited this evening. May I say, your achievements go beyond compare in this marvel of a ship. You sir, are to be commended, for *Titanic* is certainly a glorious reflection of who you are."

He was taken by the petite American woman, thinking to himself, *My goodness, what self-assurance this woman possesses in saying such things.*

Ismay smiled at her, all the while still holding her hand. The red cast across his face was hidden somewhat by his generous mustache. "Mrs. Davis, I am confident your couture designs will take New York by storm - that is, if your charm and American air of confidence has anything to do with it."

"I hope you are right."

"It was my pleasure to meet you, Madame. May your journey on *Titanic* bring you lasting memories. If I may be of further service to you and Mr. Delacroix, please do not hesitate to call on me. My offices are at 1 Broadway, in New York City." He bent over to kiss her hand.

"Thank you, sir." She smiled and then turned her attentions to François as they bid goodnight to Thomas Andrews. "Thomas, what an astounding day this has been." Despite her haunting visions of peril aboard this ship, she was certain their brief association with both Andrews and Ismay would forevermore affect their lives.

"I am so glad you enjoyed yourselves," Andrews said. "I wish you both pleasant dreams and trust we'll have more time together before we dock next week."

From the Parlor Suite, Jocelyn and François found their way out onto the fifty-foot private promenade, romantically lit for the overflow of the party. It was quite chilly in the late evening on the waters of the North Atlantic . . .

Jocelyn did not invite François to her room at the conclusion of the evening, because she did not want to reveal her feelings for him before he stated his own intentions for her. Love was such a conundrum, containing many complicated facets, yet it came so easily. The greatest task was to keep that love pure and unencumbered from residual impediments. François was relieved that Jocelyn did not suggest they go to her suite, because he was certain he would too easily show the passion he felt for her. He did not want to act improperly by pursuing her before they were both ready. As they bid each other goodnight, they shared the same thoughts, wondering what was holding them back from declaring their love.

It was clear that they both wanted the intimate company of the other - both hungry for acknowledgement. At the same time, they resonated with the other's pain, grief, and loss of their loved ones. Both were ready for newness and a fresh start. They both thought to themselves, *Tomorrow...!*

"Your feelings tonight," François said, "are you still in dread?"

"It comes and goes," Jocelyn said, "as if this ship is drifting in and out of danger - like every decision being made upon the bridge, in the engine room, on the decks, is conspiring to decide our fate."

"Perhaps I *should* go and impersonate the captain, no?"

Jocelyn laughed. "You would be the most handsome, dashing officer in the White Star fleet."

Reluctantly, François bid her goodnight at the door. "I wish this night could last forever, Cheri, but we shall have many more."

"That is my wish."

He leaned down to kiss her too quickly. She stood on her tiptoes, and they hit heads.

"Oh, my goodness!" Jocelyn laughed.

François stood back, holding his head. "Madame, that was *your* fault this time!" They both laughed until they cried. "Oh, mon Dieu," he sighed.

"We are going to have to learn how to do this more easily. You are too tall, and I am certainly too short.

Somewhere in the middle, we need to learn to gently meet."

"I will summon the ship's carpenter and have him bring a box for you to stand on."

"Alright," she said, "let us try this again." She carefully stood, looking up at him and not moving. He cautiously bent over and kissed her. Then, he took her room key from her hand, unlocked her door, and opened it.

"Bon nuit, mon cheri."

She demurely smiled as she stepped inside her suite and turned to face him. She then slowly closed the door.

François lingered and listened to Jocelyn burst into laughter on the other side of the door. He smiled and put his hand on his heart with a loving sigh. Before he walked to his cabin, however, he paused and suspiciously looked around, yielding to a sudden, cold chill. The gentle hum of *Titanic's* engines whispered that all was well, but for some reason, François felt little comfort in that reassurance . . .

CHAPTER
Fourteen

Jocelyn unpinned the curls from her hair and brushed out her long auburn locks. She removed her makeup with coconut oil, which easily melted away all the powder, rouge, kohl, and color, leaving her skin clean and gleaming. Then, she brushed her teeth with a mixture of salt and soda. Even though she traveled the world, she still liked to use simple, natural remedies and concoctions for beauty and health.

She finally felt liberated of all her uncomfortable formal wear. It took some time to unlace her corset and unveil her body from the layers of lace, satin, cotton, and linen. She could have employed the services of her stewardess, but she preferred to undress alone. Finally liberated of the societal encumbrances of all her undergarments, she stepped into her nightgown, robe, and slippers, enveloped in a sense of freedom, warmth, and comfort.

It was late. Jocelyn wanted to use the swimming pool and Turkish bath the following morning, but she also had something very important yet to do that evening before she went to sleep, and she needed time to prepare.

Her bed, already turned down by the steward before she returned to her cabin that evening, was prepared for her to lay her head down, but she was not yet ready to retire. Earlier in the day, she borrowed from one of the chefs an eight-inch-diameter bowl, which he would have used to serve vegetables. Jocelyn filled the bowl with water and placed it on the table in front of the chaise lounge, where she had already lit a single taper candle. She sat on the chaise lounge with her feet tucked beneath her, wrapped in the eiderdown quilt that she found folded at the end of the bed. With the table in front of her, she picked up the bowl and placed it in her lap. She cradled the bowl with both hands as the candlelight cast a reflection on the surface of the water. With closed eyes, she prayed:

"Dear God, please allow me to see beyond my limitations and my fear. Give me the sight, so I may envision what it is that concerns the majority of the people aboard this ship, whose light is no longer present. May I be open to see clearly, so I may best be of service to all. My God, to you I surrender."

Jocelyn opened her eyes, seeing the reflection of the candlelight upon the surface of the water. She relaxed her gaze to witness a vision beyond that which she could see with her eyes alone. All the veils parted.

Her eyes widened in shock, as tears instantly welled up. From a distance far away, she envisioned a great ship, filled with hundreds of people soon to be swallowed up by the sea. There was no moon, but millions of stars twinkled in the blackened sky. She saw the horrific scene of hundreds of people in their muslin cork lifebelts, flailing about and bobbing on the ocean's icy surface. Those in the lifeboats were, for the most part, eerily still as they watched in shock, most of them already grieving the loss of at the least one loved one or friend. Tipped downward with the bow below water, it was not long before *Titanic*'s lights flickered out, followed by the sound of an underwater implosion. Amidst crackling of wood and bending of metal, she heard a cacophony of deafening screams filling the once still night. The upright stern turned to the starboard side like a corkscrew, with its end tipped high into the air for a brief instant before the last vestige of *Titanic* sank forevermore, swallowed up in the glassy sea's abyss.

Stunned, Jocelyn broke away from the vision. Her heart hurt, knowing the fate of those aboard *Titanic*. There was no doubt in her mind why two-thirds of the people had no light about them. They were about to perish, along with the greatest ocean liner on earth.

She sobbed into her pillow to stifle the shock at what she envisioned so as not to call the attention of those in the rooms flanking hers. After she thought she could cry no more, she dried her tears with a handkerchief and then readied herself to be about her work.

She took several deep breaths, closed her eyes, and held her hands out, palms up. Breathing deeply several times, she felt the energy in her hands increase, signaling she was ready to pray. She turned her hands over, and from her mind's eye, she held the crown of each individual's head in her hands in a blessing as she remarkably recalled each person's face pass through her memory. She whispered her prayer aloud while tears continued to roll down her cheeks.

"God is all there is - expanding, evolving, and becoming something even greater still - always in and as Love. This Love for the world manifests in and as every being, and as peace, joy, compassion, kindness, caring, abundance, oneness, harmony, and synchronization. That which is of discord is merely an illusion in the process of change. Change transforms to that which is peace-filled, elegant, and graceful. All this is inclusive within Love's embrace and Its Absolute Awareness.

"Every one of us voyaging across the Atlantic tonight is blessed beyond our comprehension with a journeying of the soul that knows no end. In our Godliness, we live as an expression of that which created us. From our choices, we have decided how to live out that privilege of life to vistas beyond our imagining. We express the divine attributes to celebrate heaven on earth. Without really knowing we do so, we rejoice, praising that which is greater than ourselves.

"Tonight, I state a blessing upon every soul who is sailing on this ship. Each one is of tremendous importance. None of us are lost, forgotten, or without purpose. To the contrary, we will prevail to live out our dreams yet realized, if not here, then in some other place and time. All are important. We, who will continue to remain upon the earth will live to tell the tale as the storytellers, remembering deep into our bones the sacrifice of so many who made it possible for us to live on. We will carry on and honor those left behind, for their lives are so freely given out of sacrifice and love. Each contribution to Life is, and will ever be, recorded in the book of Life.

"This event will change the world, remembered by every future generation. Souls will prevail and rise to heights where all realization takes form, where everything is known, and nothing is out of place. In this reality, all who have ever loved us will be awaiting our arrival, to join with them as the watchers of all existence. I bless us all for what is about to occur. I hold this radiant knowing as an embrace for all of us, for we will live on in some way or other.

"As did Jesus, I give thanks for this blessing, in advance, knowing it is already done. In gratitude, I leave it to the God of the Universe, who knows all, is all-powerful, and all knowing; who takes it into the field of all possibility, setting this blessing into motion.

"And now I release this prayer, knowing it is already activated by the Mind of God, in which we all reside.

"And so it is, Amen."

CHAPTER
Fifteen

Sophia awoke with a smile on her face. She was pleased to recall in her dream the prayer Jocelyn said on behalf of those on *Titanic*. Sophia, of course, was aware of the fatal outcome of the ship, but it was good to know that someone held a blessing for everyone aboard, whether Jocelyn and François remained among the living, or transitioned into their next level of existence.

It was the last morning of Sophia and Michael's visit to New Orleans. The events of the last few days were emotionally exhausting for Sophia, and both she and Michael were more than ready to return to their mountain home in Colorado. The night before, they said their goodbyes to Gaston, who arranged to have the antiques delivered a few days after their return. They enjoyed a lavish breakfast with Darius, and then bid him a deeply emotional farewell before they took to the road in their RV. It was indeed a sad goodbye, but they took heart knowing they would reunite in Colorado in a month for a gathering of the Order of Apeiros – a visit that Sophia and Michael promised would have a few wonderful surprises.

Sophia would miss having the luxury of someone else to do the cooking for her. They both put a few pounds on while staying at the plantation, but Michael would just have to deal with her less than ordinary cuisine when they returned home. She was no cook, Michael conceded, but she *could* build a hell of a fire in the fireplace, perfect for late night s'mores.

A week later, when the furniture arrived, they were excited to place the beautiful pieces they selected throughout the cabin. Michael, who was handy around the house, had the electrical wiring ready to hang the wrought iron crystal chandelier in the dining room, but not before Sophia removed each and every crystal and washed and polished them to gleaming brilliance.

They placed their brand-new king-size mattress and box springs on the oversized frame of the four-poster bed, finding that it fit perfectly. At the foot of the bed was a plush bench. Sophia placed the small oval table that doubled as a small desk and chair, leaving it half-open in front of the window. She placed a decorative lamp on the table, one that at least looked like an antique. She had a beautifully reupholstered chaise lounge from her single days, which sat in the corner. With the mahogany armoire in place, all they needed were a few small chairs to complete the ensemble.

The dark walnut library table added a beautiful ambiance to the great room. If Patrick were still alive, he would be pleased to know his greatest piece of artful handiwork was finally at the cabin, where he enjoyed life at its best. The dining table, with its contrasting grain, was exquisite. Combining various styles of chairs was Sophia's idea, which added tremendous charm to the room. When they placed the sterling silver candleholders on the table with various sizes and shapes of ivory candles, their fiery radiance lit up the room, making it a welcoming ambiance for the best of any impressive gathering. The wrought iron crystal chandelier overhead reflected the candlelight in hundreds of crystal facets.

Over the next two weeks, Sophia reupholstered the fourteen chairs in four different coordinating fabrics. Some of the fabrics she repeated in accent pillows and throws for the foot of the beds throughout the cabin, which delighted Digit, who tried out each one.

They finished working out the many details, for there were so many particulars to consider as they finalized their plans for the Order of Apeiros to gather. There were travel details, transportation, accommodations, and meals - including special dietary needs, and the daily itinerary, leaving both Sophia and Michael quite busy up until the scheduled date of the gathering.

Michael had a surprise for Sophia before the group arrived. She had her mother's set of china, crystal stemware, and sterling silver flatware, but nowhere to display it properly. It remained in boxes, some of it never taken out of its original wrapping. Back in New Orleans, Gaston helped Michael select an exquisite china cabinet made of Malle Burl, over ten feet tall, with curved glass doors that flanked its corners. Michael made some fancy clandestine arrangements with the movers, who delivered the cabinet to the next-door neighbor's garage. His task was to figure out a creative way to get it inside without Sophia finding out.

One morning, Sophia walked to the Riverside Inn down in the village to finalize the arrangements for eight of the people to stay when they came for the gathering. Although the cabin was quite large, it could only accommodate eight people comfortably. They decided it was best for White Buffalo, Darius, and Gaston to stay with them at the cabin, while the rest would stay in the best rooms in the five-star Riverside Inn.

Sophia and Michael knew the Kelly family, who were the third-generation proprietors. Sophia grew up with Jameson Kelly, whose grandparents originally owned the property. Jameson and his wife, Karen, upgraded the inn, making it a destination place for weddings, special occasions, or a simple getaway for anyone wanting to enjoy a night or two in the Rockies. Jameson was more than happy to accommodate Sophia's requests. She would leave a specially prepared welcome basket for each guest's room that she would create herself, just to make their stay even more enjoyable.

After talking over the details with Jameson, Sophia said, "Well, I think that's about it, unless you can think of anything I missed."

"Wait!" Jameson said. "You have to see our new activity center. You can't go until you do."

"I didn't know you had one," she said.

"Hence the word 'new'. Get over here! Come see!" Sophia had to laugh. Usually Jameson was so calm, but he seemed overly excited to show her the building, so she could not refuse. They took the long way behind the inn to a large new outbuilding.

"Oh my gosh," Sophia said. "When did you do this?"

"Been working on it this year. We've talked about expanding for so long that I decided to get it done before I die."

"Jamie, you're not that old," Sophia said. "At least you better not be – we grew up together."

"Yeah, I figured thinking about it would motivate me. Come, check it out. We have an exercise room, an indoor-outdoor swimming pool with the wave feature, and a hot tub on the left side – really cool during a blizzard."

They stepped inside. "Oh, this is really nice," Sophia said.

"Ya got your great room here in the center of the building with a sectional sofa and end tables in front of the fireplace for small parties. Got a wet bar and fridge over there. Back there is a game room with a billiard table, poker table, ping-pong, darts, and plenty of seating for guests. Over here on the right side is a separate theatre room with an eight-foot screen, DVD player, and several comfortable reclining theatre chairs. We got a library of movies, or the guests can play their own. There are also two washers and dryers in the back utility room."

"This is great," Sophia said. "When our guests stay here, would you allow the rest of us to join them for a movie?"

"Oh, whaddya kidding? Of course, anytime, Sophia. We got the movie schedule printed in the lobby. In fact, you and what's-his-name come by any time ya want."

Sophia laughed. "Michael."

"Yeah, Michael. We also got popcorn and soda machines - a movie's not complete without popcorn, huh? Movies start around eight, give or take."

"You're such a good friend, Jamie. It's almost like when we were growing up - always finding something fun to keep ourselves occupied."

"Yeah, where'd the time go, huh? We're all grown up now. Your dad's gone, my folks are both gone now. Yeah, what the hell, huh? Hey, c'mon out back. I forgot to show ya something else."

As they left the building, he showed her the large outdoor gas grill, with picnic tables, and two horseshoe pits. They walked back to the lobby, again taking the long way around. Sophia wondered why Jamie was adding all the extra mileage, but she really didn't care. She wanted to walk off a couple of pounds anyway.

"Oh, I almost forgot," Sophia said. "I need to give you a credit card number to cover the expenses for their stay. They will join us for their meals at the cabin, but for the first night, since we will be getting here in the late afternoon from the airport, let's plan to all come down here for dinner at your fabulous restaurant. We will be thirteen. Please put the dinner and a 20% gratuity on this card."

"Oh, hey yeah, you got it. We'll certainly create a Rocky Mountain feast they won't forget. You call me if ya think of anything else."

"Great! See you soon. Give our love to Karen." She gave him a hug and left to walk back up the road. When she entered the cabin, she noticed Michael standing in the great room with a cheesy grin on his face. "What are you up to? Did you break something? What's wrong?"

"Follow me." He led her into the dining room and turned on the dimmer switch to the crystal chandelier.

She jumped when she saw the china cabinet. "Oh, my – Michael, you did this for me? I remember this piece! It's so beautif-" She quickly put her hands over her mouth to keep him from seeing her cry the "ugly face." Too late. She burst into tears.

"I'm sorry, honey. If you don't like it, I'll send it back." She shook her head and laugh-cried, and then full-out cried. He smiled and placed his big arms around her. So much had transpired in the last few weeks, and he thought her reaction was a combination of pent-up emotions, especially about the revelation of her parents' deaths. Sophia normally held back the tears, but the dam broke that afternoon, and she just stood there in his arms and sobbed.

"I'm getting snot all over the front of your shirt," she finally managed to say. She walked over and grabbed several tissues to mop up. "Oh, gosh, Michael, this was such a surprise. How can I thank you?"

"Let me cook tonight."

She laughed and blew her nose. "How in the world did you get this in here so fast?"

"I called Jamie and told him to stall you. The cabinet was up the road at the Langs. He and I hauled it down here."

"Wait a minute," Sophia said. "*You* carried it?"

"Jim Lang and I did, yeah."

"With those hips?"

"Oh, man, here we go . . ."

"And I suppose your hips hurt now, right?"

"Oh, yeah – like hell. They're ok, I took some-"

"Michael, when are you going to figure out you can't be

lifting heavy things like that? I swear, you're just like my dad was. You think you're invincible. And another thing . . ."

The cabin was at last ready for everyone to arrive. The china cabinet displayed Elizabeth's china and crystal beautifully. With all the final touches that they gathered from Gaston's shop, Sophia honored Patrick's, and her mother and father's spirits. The cabin was Sophia and Patrick's special place for forty years. She and Michael customized the cabin to make it theirs, and of course, it was home for Digit, too.

They were so pleased to host the enclave of distinguished members of the Order of Apeiros. The next day they would go to Denver International Airport and pick up everyone in two SUV's, and bring them 85 miles, through Denver, Golden, and Boulder, to their home by the stream in the Rockies.

Even though the mystic vision of Jocelyn Brewster Davis and the doomed ship *Titanic* again drifted into her dreams that night, Sophia slept surprisingly well.

CHAPTER
Sixteen

Jocelyn awoke early Saturday morning. She wanted to arrive at the pool by 8:00 a.m., and happened to be the only one there to enjoy a private swim at that hour. She felt herself slide through the warm salt water with rejuvenating ease until four other women eventually showed up, making the pool a bit too crowded for a peaceful swim.

In the Turkish Bath, Jocelyn took the benefit of every offering, beginning with the ultra violet lights of the Electric Bath. She then went from the Steam Room, to the Hot Room, on to the Temperate Room, and finally laid back on the chaise lounge in the Cooling Room, surrounded by the exquisitely Moorish designed atmosphere, with walls covered in blue and green ceramic tiles. She took advantage of the luxury of a private massage. Following a final dip in the pool, she had her hair washed by Annie Caton, one of the ship's stewardesses. Never had she felt so pampered. It seemed an extravagance, but she knew it would be quite a long time before she would ever get the chance to take pleasure in such indulgence again.

Despite the luxurious morning, Jocelyn could not fully purge from her mind the terrifying vision from the night before. Just as that moment was dark and foreboding, this morning seemed contrarily serene, as if two forces played against each other. It so disturbed Jocelyn to feel death surround her one moment, and the next feel joy and tranquility. The women who joined her in the Swimming Bath, and Annie Caton as well, all seemed to exude a bright aura of light. Jocelyn could not determine if the danger to the ship may have passed, or if these women simply were among the fortunate few who would live on.

Jocelyn was to meet François at noon for lunch, but she would have to postpone for thirty minutes. She asked Maude, the other stewardess, to pass a note to Mr. Delacroix, telling him of her delay. Maude, as well, appeared in a bright aura of light. Jocelyn simply shook her head and took a deep breath, deciding it best to move on with her day and try not to worry too much. She reveled in what a delightful morning it had truly been. She was so relaxed and yet she was famished. Besides, she was looking forward to spending time again with François.

They met at the Café Parisien. "You must go to the pool and the Turkish Baths," Jocelyn said. "They are truly decadent. It's an experience you should not miss."

"I already bought my ticket from the purser. I will go this afternoon. Did you sleep well last night?"

"I spent quite a bit of time in contemplation before I retired." She told him about the sacred ritual she performed using the water-filled bowl, but she stopped short of telling him about the disturbing vision.

"Nostradamus also used a bowl in his visioning," François said. "It is said he learned this practice from a woman healer he met when he traveled to Italy. She was a descendant of the Delphi Oracle. She taught him to open a window into his future, along with his visions for healing. Much in the same tradition, I too use the bowl to strengthen my connection to the Divine. What, may I ask, did you see?"

Jocelyn paused, unsure if she should tell him, but because he already envisioned the moonless night, and saw people perishing in frigid temperatures, she decided he should know. She looked around the crowded café. "There are so many here. I should not want anyone to overhear. When we are finished with lunch, let us walk along the Promenade, for I have much to tell you."

As they walked in the cool sea air, she told him about her vision of *Titanic's* doom. François fell silent and turned an ashen gray. He was shocked, even though he had known the truth on some deeper level. "Do you think it is the fire? Was there an explosion?"

"I saw no fire," Jocelyn said, "just the ship sinking quickly in cold darkness, and hundreds of people in the water."

He stopped at the railing, and she took his arm as he peered out across the vast Atlantic. "The lifeboats," he said. "There are far too few. Not more than half can survive if this ship founders before help arrives."

"We talked about this before, François. I truly believe we are both here to hold the peace and harmony for those about to perish. On some higher level, I believe it an honor to know in advance what is about to happen."

"But is it possible we can alter our fate?" he asked. "Can you recall any greater detail as to what causes this disaster?"

"No," Jocelyn said in frustration, "only the aftermath. All I could see was black everywhere with brilliant pinpoints of starlight. There were people in the water, while I heard terrible cries for help. François, our intuition warned us both long before we embarked upon this voyage. If we could affect fate, would we not have been able to do so already?"

François rubbed his forehead and took a deep breath. "If only we stayed in Cherbourg, we would not be here at risk, but the opportunity to change our lives for the better would not have availed itself if not for this voyage. And we would not have found each other. Such a circuitous dilemma."

"I think we are both here for bigger reasons. We know these may be the last moments for some – maybe even for us. Perhaps we are here to act as a bridge for those who will not survive. I propose we make the best of our time, here on the ship. Let us make it memorable for us . . ."

Dinner that night was elegant, but before the dessert course, Jocelyn and François decided to leave the Dining Saloon. François asked one of the stewards to deliver a bottle of champagne and two champagne glasses to Jocelyn's suite.

Their love affair was one that could have inspired poets to write of their passion. The timing of their union, which normally would have taken months, developed partly because of their common-felt grief at the loss of their respective spouses. In addition, the insight that each knew about the impending events generated swiftness of action. Both Jocelyn and François felt the immediacy of living in the moment.

When they arrived at her suite, François uncorked the champagne. He lifted his glass to her. "Jocelyn, je'taime ma chère."

Knowing only a bit of French, Jocelyn was pleased to respond, "Je t'aime aussi."

They took a sip of champagne and passionately embraced, then fervently kissed, finally coming together after much contemplation. Neither had been intimate with another since the death of their spouses. The ardor they felt was an explosive fire generated by their liberation from enduring grief.

Their insight of the ship's impending doom made them mindfully aware to cherish each moment well, for this might be their last. Being together was all that mattered.

Jocelyn walked to the dressing table and sat in front of the mirror. She unpinned her mass of curls and began to brush out her waist-length hair. François quietly moved behind her and took the brush from her hand. He proceeded to finish what she had started, running his fingers through her hair.

As she turned around on the bench to face him, he leaned over and kissed her on the lips. He then knelt down on one knee at her feet and unlaced her boots, lifting them gently off her feet. He slowly ran his hands under her skirt, up her legs to find the garters that held up her silk stockings. He gently pulled each garter down her legs and off her feet, and then removed her silk stockings one by one. She stood, looking up at him in the dim lighting of the room. He realized she was even tinier without her additional two-inch heels as he towered above her.

Jocelyn followed his lead. "Sit down on the bed, my love." She knelt on the carpet and removed his patent leather slippers, and his sock garters and socks. She lit a candle next to the bed and turned off the electric wall sconces. In the faint candlelight, they undressed each other, peeling away the layers of pomp and pageantry important to French society's tradition. Passionate kisses interrupted the unveiling of each layer of clothing, which brought them closer to revealing their nakedness, not only of body, but also of mind and soul.

François loomed above the petite Jocelyn, both liberated of their clothing. He scooped her up in his arms and gently laid her down on the bed. He then lay down next to her. While leaning on one arm, he ardently drank in her beauty.

He leaned over to tenderly kiss her throat and nuzzle her neck as his hand gently caressed her breasts. He moved his hand to the small of her back, pulling her body towards his. Jocelyn tipped her head back and opened her mouth to meet his tongue with hers.

François then dipped his finger into his champagne glass and proceeded to outline the features of her body, beginning with her lips. He lightly licked away the sweetness and kissed her lips with tenderness. He proceeded down her neck with his tongue, circling her nipples, on down to her belly. Jocelyn arched her back in pleasure and shivered with arousal, which she had not felt for two years. François placed his hand on her waist to still her as he poured a bit of champagne into her belly button. He positioned his body so he could lean down to lick it from her tiny well.

She giggled as she pushed him back onto the bed, taking possession of their passionate encounter. François smiled at her taking charge, already knowing they would be as good in bed as they were in conversation.

François was skillful in his passion, realizing he had not forgotten how to be a good lover. He was equally pleased to find Jocelyn to be as practiced. Her fingers played with the hair on his chest, and she slid her hand down to his waist while she slowly kissed him, moving incrementally down his body, only to stop and linger at the soft space where his leg met his torso. There she licked and kissed the tender area, bringing him fully to arousal. She artfully moved her hand, gently stroking him as she straddled his body and placed herself in a position to easily receive him. She paused on purpose, feeling his pulse in her hand while looking deeply into his eyes with a smile he would never forget.

She arched her back, catching her breath, as they joined in ecstatic union, moving into a natural rhythm as if they had been practiced lovers for a lifetime. He held her waist as she braced herself against his powerful chest. Then François raised himself while holding her securely on top of him. He bent his right leg and rotated her onto her back. He shifted her to lie on the bed below him while facing the opposite end of the bed. He proceeded to make love to her, holding her hands above her head, her legs wrapped around his torso. François' skill in lovemaking allowed him to wait until they were both ready to reach climax together, making their union one of simultaneous ecstatic joy.

The instant they culminated their union, she knew she conceived their child. There was no doubt in her mind.

Jocelyn was certain she was pregnant. Tears welled in her eyes - tears of great happiness and joy. If these were her last days, they were perfect. The love she felt in that moment was beyond anything of her imagining.

They lay in each other's arms, wrapped in a cocoon of blankets with the feeling that nothing could steal their joy. They made love once more before dawn, and then they arose to take a bath together in her private bathtub. Then they readied themselves for breakfast, later to attend the Sunday morning service in the Dining Saloon. Both Jocelyn and François felt tremendous gratitude that morning.

CHAPTER
Seventeen

Captain Smith presided over Sunday's Anglican Church Service, conducted in the First Class Dining Saloon. If the captain's duties prevented him from attending, a minister from First Class stepped in. The ship's quintet provided music for the service.

Following his message, the congregation sang the Naval Hymn, *For Those in Peril on the Sea*, led by Chief Purser McElroy. As the singing proceeded, François and Jocelyn looked at each other knowingly, for the hymn was true to the vision they had seen of *Titanic's* demise.

Eternal Father, strong to save,
Whose arm hath bind the restless wave,
Who bidd'st the mighty ocean deep
Its own appointed limits keep;
Oh, hear us when we cry to Thee,
For those in peril on the sea!

Oh Christ! Whose voice the waters heard
And hushed their raging at Thy word,
Who walked'st on the foaming deep,
And calm amidst its rage didst sleep,
Oh hear us when we cry to Thee,
For those in peril on the sea!

Most Holy Spirit! Who didst brood
Upon the chaos dark and rude,
And bid its angry tumult cease,
And give, for wild confusion, peace;
O hear us when we cry to Thee
For those in peril on the sea!

O Trinity of love and power,
Our brethren shield in danger's hour;
From rock and tempest, fire and foe,
Protect them wheresoe'er they go;
Thus evermore shall rise to Thee
Glad hymns of praise from land and sea.

Earlier at breakfast, Jocelyn and François agreed that the time had come to stop trying to reason their fears away. Jocelyn's warnings of intuition were simply too strong and precise to ignore, and François was more certain than ever that his dark thoughts of disaster were very real. At the conclusion of the service, they spoke with Captain Smith, who stood at the door of the Dining Saloon as everyone left the room.

"Captain Smith, my name is Jocelyn Brewster Davis."

"It is my pleasure to meet you, Madame." He looked at François, who introduced himself. "Mr. Delacroix, how do you do. Are you enjoying the voyage?"

"Captain Smith," Jocelyn said, "I wonder if I might trouble you for a private moment? We simply *must* speak to you on a matter of utmost urgency."

Smith appeared genuinely concerned. "Oh? Yes, of

course, Mrs. Davis. Come, let's meet over here." He directed them back into the dining room, which was finally empty. "Now, Madame, Monsieur, how may I be of service?"

Jocelyn began. "Captain, this may seem a bit strange, but I have had a very strong premonition that *Titanic* and all aboard are in grave danger."

"How so?"

"It is very hard to explain without you thinking I might be overreacting, or perhaps mad."

Smith allowed a tempered laugh. "Mrs. Davis, I assure you I would never suggest such a thing. You know, you are not the first passenger who has ever expressed such a concern while out at sea. It actually happens quite often."

"It is more than a concern, captain," François said.

"Well now, Mr. Delacroix, perhaps you would-"

"We know about the fire in the coalbunker," François said. "We overheard your conversation with Mr. Lightoller the other day."

Smith became less jovial. "Well, I am so very sorry that we alarmed you, but our firemen successfully extinguished the fire yesterday and will continue to monitor it the rest of our voyage. So, you see, there is certainly nothing to worry about."

"Then it is something else," Jocelyn said. "Captain, I know you find this hard to believe, but I *know* something terrible is going to befall this ship. It is just that I cannot tell you precisely what it is, or when it will happen, but we both agreed that we should warn you to beware."

Captain Smith measured Jocelyn and François before he spoke. "I would never dismiss your concerns, and I am very sorry this has distressed you so, but may I reassure you that I cannot conceive of any disaster so large to cause this vessel great harm. The design advancements in modern shipbuilding have come so far as to entirely prevent a disaster."

"Captain," François said, "we do not intend to cause any stir of panic aboard, as I assure you we have not spoken of this to anyone. All we ask is that you consider what Mrs. Davis told you as you continue to navigate this journey."

Captain Smith nodded. "Thank you, I will. Please, not to worry now – everything will be just fine. Go on about your day and enjoy the voyage. *Titanic* has many offerings for your pleasure and enjoyment." He bowed slightly and exited the dining room.

Jocelyn watched, never looking at François. "He doesn't believe me."

François took her arm. "Jocelyn? What is it?"

"There was so little light around him that I could barely see his face . . ."

Following lunch, Jocelyn and François silently walked along the Promenade, noticing a deeper chill in the air than what they felt the day before. In concert with the frigid sea breeze, they felt a pending heaviness in the atmosphere surrounding them. A simple walk along the Promenade would not cure the mood that grew darker as the day progressed. They encountered a few passengers who braved the chill in the air, and each face told a different story to Jocelyn as they passed. It was not long before they returned inside to the Palm Court for tea. The hot beverage was welcome to help assuage their foreboding feelings.

Prior to dinner, they went to Jocelyn's suite and made love as if it was the last time they would ever experience the passion of each other, for they had no idea of what would soon occur. They engulfed each other in both body and soul, knowing that it would not be long before all aboard the *Titanic* would be in peril.

At dinner, they made the best of it, enjoying yet another spectacular thirteen-course meal. They sat with Mr. and Mrs. Isidor Straus, Sir Cosmo and Lady Duff-Gordon, and Margaret Brown. Sir Cosmo and Lucy exuded a bright aura, as did Maggie Brown, but one look at Isidor and Ida caused Jocelyn to shudder, and she barely glanced at them again the rest of dinner.

Already the works were set into motion for Jocelyn to join in a new business venture with Lady Duff-Gordon and Mr. Straus at his Macy's Department Store once they landed in New York. Both Mr. Straus and Lady Duff-Gordon, known professionally as *Lucile Ltd.*, had notified their legal advisors, via the Marconi telegraph, of the alliance to utilize Jocelyn's designs at Macy's Herald Square store, under the wide umbrella of the *Lucile* name. Straus took no issue with doing business with women, for his predecessor, R. H. Macy, was the first retailer in history to promote a woman to an executive position at Macy's.

The greatest of Jocelyn's expectations were rapidly coming to fruition. However, her thoughts were just as swiftly tumbling down into the vortex of knowing that

Titanic was cruising full-steam ahead into a dark, perilous abyss.

During their dinner conversation, another business venture nonetheless lit aflame. *Lucile* was the most notable name in the fashion industry as the leading fashion designer of the late nineteenth and early twentieth century. Times were changing, with war looming on the horizon. Lucy was looking to expand and unify her design houses across the globe. The discussion fell onto François. Lucy said, "It is my understanding, Monsieur Delacroix, you are a celebrated architect from Paris, about to begin your life in New York, working for an architectural firm in the city?"

"Please, Madame, call me François. Yes, I am to start work a week from tomorrow with Willborough and Johnson."

"François, I am in need of facilities to house my new ventures in New York, Chicago, London, Paris, Rome, and perhaps San Francisco. May I ask your professional opinion of how I might go about such an undertaking?"

François almost didn't hear the question as his mind drifted to thoughts of *Titanic*. He at last perked. "Oh, oui, if new construction is what you desire, might I suggest that you build each location from the same blueprint. You could standardize precisely what you want to achieve - how many employees, designers, and managers per location, and how your business would be best run to increase production and efficiency."

"That *would* simplify things," Lucy said.

"Oui, your initial outlay would be high, for you would be building each from the ground up. You certainly could refurbish each building you now have, but if you started from scratch, in a few years the overall efficiency of a new facility would make up the difference and most likely surpass your current level of production."

Maggie Brown interjected, "Now *there's* a man with a good head on his shoulders!" She winked at Jocelyn, who barely responded. "Honey? Are you ok?"

Jocelyn looked up from a haze. "Oh, yes . . . yes, I am fine."

"Have you any experience in retail or fashion, François?" Lucy asked.

"Not directly, but principally it is no different than any other business venture. By providing a service well, ideally what you create is a profit-making business with exponential growth. With an efficient and pleasant working environment, your employees will look forward to coming to work. They will be more productive and generate a better product. In the long run, your clients will return to purchase the tremendous creative endeavors generated by employees who love what they do, and do what they love."

"François," Mr. Straus said, "should you ever decide to change professions, I would certainly hire you to manage my employees." Everyone politely laughed, but François and Jocelyn were uncharacteristically somber.

François continued, "Here is a thought - each one of your fashion houses could specialize in a specific market, say ladies' fashions, from Paris. Chicago could house children's, toddler's, and infant's clothing. Rome could specialize in men's fashions, and so on."

"François, with your visionary ideas, you could be my general manager," Lucy laughed. She pondered a thought, looking at Mr. Straus, who gave an approving nod. "François, would you consider designing my projects?"

"Well, Lady Duff-Gordon, I must say you have caught me by surprise. You know nothing of my work."

"Oh, on the contrary, François, I am quite familiar with your architectural achievements in Paris. I believe we could do magnificent things together. What do you think?"

Never ambivalent, Lucy was certainly not one to dally. This type of offer for François most likely would never occur again. The door opened quickly, and one had to step in with confidence in the vision of their desire before it shut. This was how great opportunities came about - immediate - and with rapid force. They were rarely ever something one would recognize coming their way. It was as if all the stars were in alignment for this very purpose to come about.

François felt this alliance could change the direction of his career beyond his imagining. If he were to remain with Willborough and Johnson in New York, he would likely be a junior architect for some time before opportunities for advancement arose. With *Lucile*, he would be his own boss, and would rise to new opportunities for growth and change throughout the world, in conjunction with her fame.

If only we make it to New York, François thought.

He knew he had to make a quick decision, because this opportunity would not be available again. The door would slam shut if he didn't say yes that very moment.

"I gratefully accept your most generous offer, Lady Duff-Gordon."

"Oh, how marvelous!" Jocelyn said, her eyes gleaming with surprise and wonder.

"Splendid! Oh, please call me Lucy. You can begin working for me Monday next." She handed him a calling card. "I assume Willborough and Johnson paid your fare on the *Titanic*?"

"No, actually," François said, certainly not wanting to tell his new employer he was enjoying First Class accommodations on *Titanic* as a stowaway, "they *have* arranged hotel accommodations upon my arrival, however."

"Well, I will make a compensatory offer to help assuage the inconvenience I have caused." She turned to her husband. "Cosmo, darling, might I borrow your fountain pen and notebook, please?" She tore out a blank page and wrote down a few words, signed it, then folded it in half and handed it to François.

"Would that suit you, to begin with? If this alliance works well for the both of us, we will renegotiate after a year." The paper read:

François Delacroix is under the employ of *Lucile Ltd.*,
from today, 14 April 1912, until 30 April 1913,
at which time his contract will be renegotiated.
Earnings will begin at $850.00 per month
or $10,200.00 annually, plus travel and expenses.
~Lady Duff-Gordon, a.k.a. *Lucile*

When he looked at the note, François quickly sat back in his seat, attempting to maintain his composure, for the offer was more than four times that of the job awaiting him. He nodded, and smiled. "Oui, that will be more than satisfactory."

"I will notify my office of your employ tomorrow morning, via telegraph. There, it is done," Lucy said. She waved for the waiter. "Would you be so kind as to bring us three bottles of nicely chilled Heidsieck Blue Top, please? Tonight we shall celebrate new beginnings."

François was overwhelmed by the dichotomous nature of his feelings of joy and ominous foreboding, but not so much that he could not enjoy the celebration. However, Jocelyn's attention was momentarily diverted as she sat back in wonder at the self-assured nature of Lucy. She did business with a confidence in which there was no pomp and circumstance. Lucy knew just what she wanted and fervently, yet efficiently, went about to get it. Jocelyn would more than enjoy working with her. She would soak in every bit of her wisdom, with the intention to be as successful.

Jocelyn and François felt a strange sense of cautious elation. Their lives were changing beyond their wildest expectations, of that they were certain, but the nature of that change was shrouded in a dark cloud of trepidation drifting over the night. Contrarily, their dinner mates laughed and conversed as they had every night since they first set sail. Captain Smith and Mr. McElroy met and greeted the diners, clearly happy and confident without the slightest hint that might suggest trouble lurking behind their calm demeanor. In short, nothing suggested that the maiden voyage of *Titanic* was anything but the grand experience that everyone expected.

By late evening, the dining room began to empty, and Jocelyn and François were quite exhausted from the emotional upheaval of the day. They excused themselves and bid everyone goodnight, and then François discreetly offered to escort Mrs. Davis to her suite. Perhaps they had fooled Mr. and Mrs. Straus, but Lucy and Maggie Brown shared knowing, yet approving glances that said Mrs. Davis and Mr. Delacroix were fast becoming a juicy item to hang on the *Titanic* grapevine.

The time was approaching 10:30 p.m.

Throughout that Sunday, the Marconi Room received five different messages warning *Titanic* of icebergs drifting uncharacteristically farther south than normal for that time of year. The Marconi system had been out of order for a good part of Saturday into Sunday morning, and operators Jack Phillips and Harold McBride were woefully behind in their transmissions, unable to keep up with the backlog of outgoing messages. Captain Smith did receive the iceberg warnings, however, and ordered the ship southward another ten degrees, but he maintained the order to remain at full speed ahead.

Jocelyn and François enjoyed making love again, and simply laid in the solitude of the ever-present hum of *Titanic's* great engines.

"I've never felt so curiously contented," François said, "and yet, there still exists such a pang of dread. How is it that we have such good fortune mixed with something ominous that we cannot actually see?"

"I have given it so much thought, my love," Jocelyn said, "and there is but one conclusion. There are simply forces in the universe we cannot alter. We can only be in the moment and hold the light for ourselves and all the souls aboard."

"Jocelyn, I asked you if you see my fate, and you said it is my belief in life that will carry me. Has that changed?"

"No, François. Although I know somehow I will carry on, I see an aura about you that burns intensely bright, but sometimes wavers. That is quite unlike many people about whom I see little or no aura at all. I believe that you will face a challenge to survive very soon, but it is a challenge over which you can triumph depending on the choices you make." Tears welled in her eyes as she took his hand. "If we are separated, you must come back to me, François, for I do not know how I can survive without you now."

They shared a long, passionate kiss and held each other for what seemed an eternity. François then slipped into the darkness of the suite and retrieved something from his jacket pocket. He quickly returned with the small item in his hand.

"I want you to have something that was handed down through the generations to my ancestral grandfather, Nostradamus, who gave this token of affection to my ancestral grandmother, who then passed it along to their daughter and on through my ancestral line until it came to me."

Jocelyn caught her breath when he opened his hand to reveal something she had never seen before, but found so incredibly beautiful. "It is stunning, François. Tell me about this piece, and the stone set in the middle."

"It is a golden metal cast of an ammonite, with a gleaming labradorite in the center. The ammonite is an extinct ancestor of the nautilus."

"That is a sea creature, is it not?"

"Précisemént. It exhibits a ribbed spiral shell - the Golden Spiral – which is the mathematic perfection of nature's enfoldment. We can see this very spiral in most everything in nature - the unfolding fern, and the perfect spiral growth of a sunflower. We see this spiral in tornadoes and hurricanes. It is everywhere in the natural world. The gold metal cast of the ammonite is of unknown origin, but the chain from which it hangs is 18-karat gold."

"And the labradorite?"

"The stone was first discovered in Labrador, Canada, on the island of Paul in 1770. Inuit tribes believed that the northern lights were trapped inside, making it a magical stone. This stone was set into the middle of the ammonite by one of my later ancestors in the early 1800s. In metaphysics, labradorite is the most powerful protector of the mineral kingdom. It is the stone, particularly that of shamans, diviners, and healers who seek more profound knowledge and guidance. It stimulates awareness of the inner spirit, awakening the mental and intuitive nature of clairvoyance, telepathy, and prophecy. It assists one to communicate with the Divine and helps one in psychic readings and past-life recall. You might say it helps one to tap into all that is known.

"For those who use the power of touch to heal," Francois said, "labradorite helps develop sensitivity in the hands. It also unites all the chakras, enabling one to align with the Divine. Some believe that its labradorescence is of extra-terrestrial origin, enclosed in the mineral to bring the evolved energies from other worlds to the earth. It enables one to travel into otherworldly dimensions, bypassing time and space.

"Jocelyn, with your intuitive powers of communication with those who have gone before us, and your ability to see auras around others, you should have this to enhance your abilities."

"I cannot take this from you," Jocelyn said. "It is far too important a piece, especially since it was passed down from Nostradamus."

"But, Jocelyn, you have said you are certain that you will survive whatever is coming. Although I want you to have this, as my gift to you, it is also important that this piece survives with you."

She embraced him, and they shared another long kiss. "You must come to me," she whispered.

"I assure you that I never plan to leave your side once we arrive in New York. We already have quite a future carved out for us, yes?"

CHAPTER
Eighteen

Sophia awoke before sunrise, reveling in the recall of her dream. While she felt deep empathy for Jocelyn, François, and all the souls aboard *Titanic*, she could not help her excitement in the revelation of the golden ammonite with the labradorite mounted in its center, undoubtedly the very ammonite she found in Gaston's shop. A stone of protection, Sophia recalled Gaston saying, *a gift from his grandfather to his grandmother!*

She could not wait to tell Gaston with almost a first-hand account of Jocelyn and François, as she prayed the veils of time would continue to pull back and reveal their fate.

Sophia and Michael bathed and dressed before they ate a quick breakfast and departed for the airport. They first stopped at the Riverside Inn to borrow Jameson's SUV. Michael would drive it, following Sophia in their vehicle to DIA. The drive would take about three hours, and the return ride back up into the hills through heavy traffic even longer. The members of the Order of Apeiros were all due to arrive from Chicago at 10 a.m., where they came together from faraway places across the globe.

Their reunion in the center of the airport baggage claim garnered happy stares from other passengers, who could not help but be enraptured in the feelings the group exhibited for each other. They came from around the world. Markos and Christofer came from Santorini, Greece, and traveling with them was Shoshana, originally from Israel, who led the archeological excavation at Akrotiri. Lestari came from Bali. Ananta was from India. Yesinia traveled from Peru, while Anja flew in from Senegal, West Africa. Of course, Darius and Gaston came from New Orleans, and Irina flew in from Romania. The only missing member was White Buffalo, who lived in Golden, just west of Denver on the eastern edge of Colorado's Front Range. They would pick him up on their way back from the airport.

They ate lunch at a hillside restaurant in Boulder, which overlooked the plains. It was a clear day, allowing them to see fifty or sixty miles from their vantage point. Following lunch, it took only another forty-five minutes to reach their destination. Eight of them settled into their rooms at the Riverside Inn for the afternoon, while the elders, Darius, Gaston, and White Buffalo stayed with Sophia and Michael at the cabin.

White Buffalo often visited Sophia and Michael, but this was the first time Darius and Gaston visited their river rock log home. Gaston was so pleased to see the many antiques they brought from his antique shop, *Nothing But Tyme*. Every piece fit well into the rustic, yet elegant mountain setting.

"The dining table with all the different dining chairs is perfect," Gaston said. "I was not sure how they would work together, but you chose well in the varied fabrics for the upholstery."

"A little rule I always follow," Michael said, "is that you may impugn her culinary skills to your stomach's content, but never – *ever* question Sophia's artistic eye for design!"

Gaston laughed. "Well said, my friend! I say, who would think this wrought iron crystal chandelier would look so fine in the rafters of a mountain home? This all turned out so beautifully."

"Why, thank you, dear Uncle," Sophia said as she wrapped her arms around Gaston and planted a big kiss on his cheek. She turned to Darius. "Grandfather, what do you think of this?" She led him into the great room. Tears came to his eyes when he saw the trestle-footed library table placed as the centerpiece of the room. It was an exquisite display of a woodworker's skill, with legs specifically detailed in hand-carved acanthus leaves. He fondly recalled when Patrick gave it to Elizabeth and Tommy at their wedding.

Darius simply smiled. "It couldn't be in a better setting, here in the home of heart that Patrick - your father, I should say - created for both of you."

"I know," Sophia said. "I'm still getting accustomed to thinking of him as someone more than just good old Dad."

"How about Uncle Dad?" Gaston said with a wry smile.

"That's cute," Sophia said, "but he will always be Daddy."

"And he deserves that, my dear," Darius said. "Raising such a precocious child as you must have been quite a challenge for a single man. He would be so proud to know what you and Michael did with this lovely home."

"Well, why don't we show you the rest of the cabin, and we'll take you upstairs to your rooms?" Sophia said. "You may have either a view of the river or the mountains, and there is one corner room with both. The three of you may fight over which one you want."

"I will Indian wrestle you for the corner room," White Buffalo said.

Darius rolled his eyes. "I shall be delighted with *any* room."

Gaston looked at Michael. "Sonny, get our bags, will you?"

Sophia escorted them to the elevator, while Michael shook his head and struggled with the luggage.

"An elevator - how marvelous!" Gaston said, looking at all the bells and whistles.

"We thought we had better make the place senior-friendly for our latter years," Sophia said. "If you would like to rest in your rooms from your travels, feel free, or you can join us down here in the great room before we meet the others for dinner."

They all got on the elevator together.

"I believe a cocktail is in order," Darius said.

"Hear, hear," Gaston said. "White Buffalo?"

"I feel like a sarsaparilla."

"We have your favorite brand!" Sophia said. "Michael, sweetheart, why don't you fix the drinks, and we'll be back down in a minute."

"Yes, dear boy," Darius said. "That will be two scotches for Sophia and myself, hers on the rocks, mine neat.

Gaston, a Courvoisier for you?"

"Yes, and be generous with it," Gaston said.

"A generous cognac for my lush brother," Darius continued, "and the sarsaparilla, my friend?"

"Frothy," White Buffalo said. "A dab of vanilla ice cream, if you got it."

The elevator doors closed, leaving Michael outside with four suitcases at his feet, and three carry-on bags draped over his shoulders. He dropped everything and walked to the bar, mumbling, "I guess we aren't too worried about poor old Mikey's hips *now*, are we?"

In the elevator, Gaston searched the control panel to activate the car. "What a splendid idea. An elevator right in your home." He accidentally hit the emergency button, and a loud bell went off. "Dear me," he said.

Sophia reached over and calmly turned the bell off, and hit the '2' button. "It's a great benefit for me, not having to carry my big canvases up and down three flights of stairs."

"Well, brother," Gaston said, "now you won't have to complain about your aching knees. You'll have to find another pastime."

"Yes," Darius said, "and most likely, it will be slapping your hands away from all those buttons, specifically the emergency bell. I am certain you will find many reasons to go up and down in the elevator, as you have yet to grow up."

"You know," White Buffalo said, "I love these gatherings mostly for when I return home, for after being with you two, I marvel at the blissful silence that surrounds me."

Sophia just rolled her eyes and said nothing . . .

The cocktail hour was full of great conversation and laughter. The other ladies rested and freshened up in their rooms at the inn, but as if guided by radar, Markos and Christofer showed up just as Michael began pouring drinks.

Earlier in the day, Sophia cut the last rose in full bloom from her garden and placed it in a clear crystal bud vase as an offering to the Divine for the altar she created on the library table. Around the rose, she placed all the elemental pieces - the golden bowl, as the vessel for water; the golden chalice bore the eternal flame of fire; the ammonite cast in the same golden metal, in lieu of eternality, bearing the protective stone of labradorite. She removed her amethyst amulet from around her neck and draped the golden chain over the tripod, which held the hourglass containing the sands of time from Ancient Greece, on behalf of earth.

That night, at 5:30 p.m., all thirteen came together for an early dinner at the Riverside Inn, where Jameson's chef prepared a special Colorado cuisine with a variety of dishes made just for the occasion, paired with Colorado wines from the Western Slope's Palisade and Grand Valley wine region. Jameson prepared a special 'mocktail' for White Buffalo, a Hocus Pocus Fizz.

"There is not a place where we go when you aren't served the most delectable soft drinks," Markos said to White Buffalo. "It almost entices me to quit drinking alcohol. Almost."

Following the delicious meal, the group returned to the cabin for the initial opening ceremony of the Order of Apeiros.

They walked the half mile up Riverside Road to the cabin just as dusk settled in. Amber lights lit the windows of the mountain homes strewn along the road, in salutation to the night's dimming blue light. The aroma of the wood-burning fire beckoned them inside from the cool autumn air. As each member entered their home, Michael and Sophia welcomed them wholeheartedly, for they had become dear friends and family of choice.

Following tradition, the thirteen wore white on the first night, in humble reverence of the clarity and grace of the Divine Intelligence, the Infinite Field, Allah, and Great Spirit, to honor whatever name each one referred to as their God and Source. They opened the gathering with the ceremony of the rings. They stood facing each other in a circle before the fireplace, each wearing an aquamarine ring set in gold. They each placed their ring hand straight toward the center, like the spokes of a wheel. Their individual radiance joined at the center and became one column of brilliant golden white light, extending from the floor at their feet into the vaulted ceiling overhead. This was their connection to the eternal realm, representing to each that they were a conduit of the Divine. They joined with the angels and the Divine Intelligence, all for the same purpose - to hold the consciousness of heaven on Earth as the Order of Apeiros - the cause of all unity and the measure of all things.

In ritual, each member walked around the circle to anoint the others with oil, bestowing a blessing upon them, using their individual calling for that year. White Buffalo began with Balance, as he blessed Michael for his calling of Health. Michael, in turn blessed Darius for Truth and so on around the circle. Irina was Harmony, Shoshana - Order, Gaston - Abundance, Anja - Peace, Christofer - Oneness, Lestari - Compassion, Ananta - Joy, Markos - Beauty, and Sophia - Love and Absolute Awareness. Yesinia, with her calling of Grace, concluded the ceremony with a prayer of benediction, spoken in Spanish.

Around the wooden table, they all toasted the gathering with Colorado wine. Both Gaston and Darius were French wine connoisseurs, and Christofer owned a very successful vineyard in Santorini. All were impressed with the quality of the local wine.

Michael made White Buffalo an Emerald Palmer.

"Hey Michael, this green stuff is pretty tasty. What's in it?" White Buffalo asked.

"Cucumbers, lemon juice, basil, mint, agave nectar, and maca powder."

"O—-kay! Remind me not to ask about the ingredients. If it tastes good, that's all that matters."

For the duration of the gathering, Sophia hired a private chef who that night served a lovely dessert of shortcake with whipped cream and fresh peaches, another of Colorado's gifts to the world.

"If I did the cooking," she said, "you might never return, no matter how beautiful this mountain setting."

"Sophia," Gaston said, "having never partaken of your cooking, I have trouble believing it is so terrible."

"Trust me," Sophia said. "Michael does most of the work in the kitchen, just to save himself the trouble of constant indigestion. I may have held the attribute of

Absolute Awareness for the last year, but it does not extend to any form of logic in the kitchen."

"Michael," Gaston said, "you are rather quiet here. Have you anything to add?"

"Yes," he said. "When I was about thirteen, my mother taught me a valuable lesson that I remember to this day. She said, 'Mike, you will do well in life if you always recognize the proper time to speak, and when to keep your big mouth shut.' More wine?" Everyone laughed as Gaston bowed to Michael.

They all spent the evening catching up with individual events and experiences over the past year. To spare her the heartfelt difficulty of telling the story herself, Michael agreed to tell about the terrible deaths of Sophia's mother and birth father at the hands of the New Orleans hoodlum, Algernon Gillette. Darius revealed his and Gaston's relation to Sophia, as well as the startling revelation of Patrick Delaney's true identity. The room was abuzz with shock and surprise at all of the revelations. Each of them knew Patrick as one of their longstanding elders of Apeiros.

Sophia then suggested the group participate in a blessing for Algernon. "I once heard the story of an African tribe that would celebrate a new birth with the song of that child," she said. "Even before their birth and throughout their lifetime, they sang that individual's song, which was unique to them. It helped them remember who they were. If at any time in their life they strayed from their truth by committing a crime or a social injustice, the tribe surrounded them and sang their song to heal their soul, bringing them back to their true self again through love.

They gathered in love and compassion, using peace, grace, joy, and harmony. They used the attributes of the Divine much in the same way that we do."

Sophia took Michael's hand as tears welled in her eyes. "This man, Algernon Gillette, lives a life of decadence. I seriously doubt that anyone has ever surrounded him in grace and compassion, but I believe that if we do this, not only will his consciousness shift, healing will occur as well. Everything he is about will shift, affecting thousands of lives. Would you please join me in blessing Algernon?"

"As you might know," Anja said, "I come from Senegal, in West Africa. I grew up in my community doing this very thing. Thank you for the reminder, Sophia. It is no wonder that this group calls to me, for what we do is in the same spirit as in the traditions of my people. Yes, I would be so pleased to bless this man."

"Well then, Anja, tomorrow would you lead the blessing?" Sophia asked.

"It would be my honor," Anja replied.

Everyone agreed in turn. The group believed they could generate Love and Awareness on Algernon's behalf without him being physically in the room. They could shift the consciousness in which he existed, affecting his mental state and the physicality in which he resided as well.

Sophia said, "I know the blessing will bring me to forgiveness – so I can better release my anger and resentment toward him."

Darius walked up and embraced Sophia with tears in his eyes. "I seek that liberation as well, my sweet granddaughter."

"Together, we shall set Mother's and Father's spirits free, no longer held back by the negativity of their violent deaths," Sophia said.

With that decided as a beginning for their work together the next day, the eight returned to the inn to get a good night's rest, while the three elders stayed at the cabin.

Late that night, White Buffalo awoke to find Digit snuggled next to him, curled up in the crook of his arm. He smiled and gave her a pat on her tiny black head, only to fall easily asleep with a contented smile on his face. Sophia and Michael slept well, wrapped in each other's arms, as Sophia returned to her dreams of the life of Jocelyn.

CHAPTER
Nineteen

Jocelyn sat on the bed, wrapped in the blankets and enjoying the ammonite's unusual beauty as the light caught the labradorescence of the stone with each turn of her hand.

François placed his hands over hers. "I do not suppose that I expressed my intentions clearly."

She looked up at him. "What do you mean?"

"Jocelyn, I gave this ammonite to you as my solemn promise. I feel such a sense of immediacy, it is important that we live each moment as if it will be our last. Jocelyn Brewster-Davis, will you do me the honor of spending the rest of your life with me?"

Jocelyn sprang from out of the covers and flung her arms around his shoulders, nearly knocking him over. She straddled his lap, cradling his face in her hands, and kissed him passionately. "Yes! Yes, François, without a doubt!"

He enveloped her in his arms as they passionately, in near desperation, made love to the steady vibration of the ship at full speed of 22.5 knots. Time stood still, if for only a brief moment, as their bodies intertwined and all their fears melted into the darkness.

They suddenly felt a deep, subtle shudder that continued for several seconds, interrupting the ship's momentum. The walls almost imperceptibly rattled, and a low unearthly metallic groan echoed through the suite. If they had not been living in the expectancy of some type of catastrophe, they might have dismissed the experience as some harmless seafaring anomaly common to a large ocean liner.

"François," Jocelyn whispered.

François put his hand to her lips, their eyes penetrating. "Jocelyn, my love."

They untangled as the shudder faded. François sat up and reached for his pocket watch on the nightstand. The time was 11:40 p.m.

For a moment, they laid together, wrapped in the eerily silent darkness. Silence – it was something to which they were unaccustomed aboard *Titanic*. The engines had stopped, and the ship was perceptibly slowing to a crawl. Under ordinary circumstances, the odd but gentle change might have barely warranted concern, but for Jocelyn and François, this was beyond an extraordinary circumstance. The greatest ship in the world, with more than two thousand souls aboard, was standing silent in the middle of the dark and frigid North Atlantic.

"It begins," Jocelyn whispered.

François held Jocelyn in his arms, knowing that these might be the last private moments they would share. They gently smiled at each other, holding the other's gaze. Silently, they embraced in the timeless eternality, which would carry them far into their soul's journey beyond time and space.

In the silence, they both calmly dressed, readying

themselves for the inevitability of *Titanic*'s demise.

At 12:15 a.m., a frantic young wide-eyed steward knocked on the door. "Mrs. Davis!" he called, knocking harder. Jocelyn opened the door, and the steward pushed in. "I am so very sorry for the intrusion, but the captain has ordered all passengers to proceed immediately to the Boat Deck. Dress warmly." He walked to the wardrobe and pulled out the single lifebelt stored there. "Put this on, Mrs. Davis, and you, sir, will find a lifebelt in your cabin."

"What happened?" François asked.

"It is likely precautionary," the steward said, "but the captain's orders are clear. Leave all personal belongings in the suite, and do not dally. Time is of the essence."

François grabbed the young man by the arm and glared. "Unsatisfactory answer. Tell me what has happened."

The boy's eyes revealed fear. "The ship struck an iceberg, sir. I hear we are going down by the head. I can't believe it myself, but the lifeboats are being deployed. Go to the Boat Deck as fast as you can." He quickly exited.

François looked at Jocelyn. "An iceberg," he said, shaking his head.

He quickly secured the ties on Jocelyn's bulky muslin, cork-filled lifebelt, which felt to her like wearing a lightweight protective box. She had put on every piece of valuable jewelry that she could stuff underneath her fur coat and hat. She placed what remained in her black leather valise, for she thought it would be small enough to hold on her lap. Oddly, one of the last things she placed in her bag was a teacup and saucer, inscribed with *White Star Line*, carefully wrapped in her red pashmina shawl.

"Jocelyn," François said, "a teacup?"

She looked at him with what he was beginning to recognize as *that* look. "It is something we will show our grandchildren when we tell them about tonight."

He smiled. "Come, we must go."

Just as they were about to shut the cabin door, she grabbed the small flask of cognac from the dresser drawer, and the eiderdown quilt from the bed. On their way down the corridor, François quickly went to his cabin to get his lifebelt, coat, hat, and comforter as well. He reached in his coat pocket and grabbed his informal contract drawn by Lady Duff-Gordon and placed it into his wallet, handing it to Jocelyn to place in her bag. He gave her his passport and small items of value, every bit of cash he had with him, and lastly his gold pocket watch. Everything else would remain behind.

They quickly walked up the Grand Staircase and took one last look at the beautiful workmanship surrounding them before they ascended two levels to the Boat Deck. Thousands of people's vision, artistry, and hard labor went into creating the largest, most impressive piece of working machinery of humankind. Jocelyn and François wanted to remember every possible detail, knowing at some point in their future they would recall and utilize from their memories the essence of RMS *Titanic* in some creative form of their own . . .

Because the British coal strike ended just days before *Titanic's* scheduled departure, not enough newly mined coal was available to satisfy the giant ship's requirements in time. Most of *Titanic's* coal was harvested from other IMM ships in Southampton, putting them out of service. Many of the out-of-work crewmembers from those ships hired on to *Titanic,* but they had little or no time to familiarize themselves with the brand-new vessel. Passengers who were also displaced from their original plans to sail across the Atlantic aboard the canceled IMM ships booked last minute passage on *Titanic.* With so many changes taking place simultaneously, many details such as lifeboat drills did not take place.

Captain Edward John Smith, formerly commanding the RMS *Olympic,* took command of the *Titanic* on 1 April 1912, succeeding Captain Herbert Haddock, who left *Titanic* only a few days after signing on. White Star appointed Henry Tingle Wilde as Chief Officer, who held the same role under Captain Smith on the *Olympic.* Wilde did not join *Titanic* until April 9th, one day before she sailed.

With Wilde coming aboard, the other officers shuffled about. Chief Officer William Murdoch dropped to first officer, which demoted Charles Lightoller to second officer. David Blair, the original second officer, lost his position from the command roster, and he inadvertently left *Titanic* with the key to the crow's nest locker, which contained a pair of binoculars. Little thought was given to the missing binoculars until some later speculated that they might have been used in the crow's nest to perhaps spot the iceberg.

It was a moonless night. Other than starlight, blackness prevailed. The sea was like glass, reflective, still, and smooth. For a split second, in spite of the surrounding terror, Jocelyn could not help but notice the clear celestial beauty, shining like crystalline reflections more brilliant than she had ever recalled. Never before had she seen such magnificence from the heavens, causing her to stop and take notice. *How is it that there can be such spectacular evidence of nature, when at the same time, what occurs in tandem is an act of human tragedy beyond compare?*

In the cold, clear air, the celestial heavens shined with brilliant points of starlight down to the horizon line, where the sea's blackened stillness quenched their radiance. Jocelyn leaned over the starboard railing and looked back toward the stern, noticing the field of stars that shined down toward the sea, interrupted by a large black mass on the sea's edge. The temperature was 31 degrees, but the sight of the iceberg made Jocelyn break out in a cold sweat. From the little she knew about icebergs, this one was small by comparison. She overheard a crewman say he estimated the iceberg was 400 feet long, and 100 feet above sea level, not as tall as the ship's bridge. Even at that, Jocelyn knew what was seen above the waterline was only one-tenth of its full size, which made it far more intimidating to think of its mass beneath the sea's surface.

The solid, icy behemoth had floated so far south that the sun rendered it more clear than white, thus reflecting the darkness of night like a mirror. This type of clear iceberg was termed a 'blackberg,' because it was far more difficult for mariners to spot in the dark. The danger on that night increased twofold, for there was no moon to cast light on the berg, and the dead calm sea produced no visible whitecaps against its base. Instead, the silent mountain of ice stealthily blended into the black waters until it drifted directly into the path of *Titanic*.

At 12:45 a.m., one hour after the collision, Captain

Smith spotted a ship's light on the northern horizon and ordered Fourth Officer Joseph Boxall to signal it with a Morse lamp. In reality, there were two ships to the north, one much smaller than the other. Neither ship responded, with one of the ships turning away and disappearing from sight. Quartermaster George Rowe, directed by Captain Smith, launched a distress rocket toward the larger ship. The rocket soared 100 feet into the air, high above *Titanic*'s decks, and more were fired in five-minute intervals thereafter.

The first lifeboat deployed one hour and five minutes after the collision. Chaos brewed on the Boat Deck in large part because the crew was not properly trained in lifeboat deployment. Many crewmen had no idea how to operate the newly designed davits - the small cranes used to launch the lifeboats – for there had been no dry runs or drills to help the crew develop the necessary problem-solving strategies for just such an emergency. The ropes, also brand-new, were stiff, and the newly painted pulleys made them stick, leaving the officers and crew unable to launch the lifeboats with ease.

On the port side, Lightoller followed Captain Smith's orders to the letter, allowing only women and children into the lifeboats, with the exception of one male passenger with sailing experience to command the boat. If no more women or children were present, Lightoller refused to board available men, and launched many lifeboats that were only partially full. At one point, Lightoller approached one of the lifeboats already filled with men, some who were crewmembers. He threatened them with gun in hand, ordering them out of the boat at once. When the boat was again empty, he filled it only half-full with women and children before launching.

Captain Smith ordered the crewmen of the first lifeboats to row toward the light that was seen on the horizon, estimated to be only a few miles away. They were told to leave the passengers on that ship and row back to rescue more passengers. One boat began rowing in that direction, but could not make enough headway, realizing the ship in the distance was too far for them to reach. They soon decided to row back toward *Titanic,* where they could see more lifeboats lowered down to the sea in five to ten minute intervals.

At that time, it was not yet clear to all of the officers, and certainly not to the passengers, that *Titanic* was in imminent danger of foundering. The initial belief was that, although clearly disabled by the collision, the ship's watertight compartment design would enable the crew to isolate the breach in the hull and prevent catastrophic flooding. The deployment of the first lifeboats occurred as a precautionary measure, with the belief that approaching rescue vessels would pick them up, or the lifeboats would then return to *Titanic* once crewmen secured the ship. Unfortunately, the suspension of other IMM vessels due to lack of coal drastically reduced the number of ships sailing in the Atlantic shipping lanes that night.

After fully sounding the ship, the officers in charge of launching lifeboats were late to learn that Thomas Andrews discovered the extensive damage from the collision had compromised the first five forward compartments. Andrews informed Captain Smith that *Titanic* was doomed and would sink, deeming it "a mathematical certainty."

As *Titanic* slowly dipped lower into the sea, the ill-prepared crewmembers began to feel the same sense of panic as did the passengers. Their lack of authority and disorganization, for the most part, added to the pandemonium of the passengers' frenzy. Sadly, no single officer or crewman knew precisely what to do. They had believed *Titanic* was unsinkable, leaving no room for a contingency plan.

Jocelyn and François learned from Thomas Andrews, during their ship's tour, that only 20 lifeboats were on the ship - four more than required by British regulations, when in truth, *Titanic* was originally designed to carry 42. The maximum capacity aboard the 20 lifeboats was for 1,178 people, but there were nearly twice that number of souls aboard at 2,229.

With each departing lifeboat, panic on the Boat Deck grew. There was now a noticeable portside list to the ship, making it clear she was quickly sinking. The ocean was inexorably crawling up the bow and would soon spill over into the well deck and swallow the great ship whole. Officers in charge frantically pulled women and children into the lifeboats and threatened the men to stay away. Women and children first was not a steadfast rule of the sea, but rather a point of honor.

François looked at Jocelyn in the grim realization they would soon have to split up . . .

Chapter
Twenty

The next night at Sophia and Michael's cabin, the members of the Order of Apeiros enjoyed another sumptuous meal together. After they cleared the table, everyone walked into the great room to commence with a ritual to surround Algernon Gillette in love. They would call forth and remember who he truly was at the soul level, beyond the appearances of the life he lived.

Theirs was the mystic life, which accessed spiritual wisdom beyond the logical reasoning mind, melding the spiritual realm into their earthly experience through Love and Absolute Awareness. Meditation, contemplation, and study were a daily practice, while each member worked with their individual spiritual teacher, who helped them evolve into a higher realm of awareness by releasing known or unknown illusions about the truth of their being.

Not one of them believed they had arrived at an enlightened awareness. In fact, each knew that the divine attribute each individual held in their daily walk was needed to understand themselves more fully, for they recognized the value of being both student and teacher, or novice and master. Without a deeper understanding of their own lives, they could not be a witness to another's greater good.

As a member of Apeiros, each went about their days within their communities, some with families and careers, and most doing what would seem normal everyday work or service. Each of the thirteen lived their lives as a shaman, a sage, a light-worker, or a metaphysical spiritual practitioner. They were tremendously humble, calling no attention to their extraordinary abilities, for they believed the same awareness they possessed existed within all beings. It was their task to help others realize the greater truths about themselves, and to hold in their very being, Love for the entire world. Each member's elevated energy affected those in their presence in exponential ways, in the same way a tiny pebble thrown into a pond creates ripples that flow to the far banks.

Their energy expanded far beyond their physical presence. What they knew through their consciousness and heart's expression allowed each to individually *Know Thyself*, so they could perceive a deeper meaning beyond external appearances. They learned to focus on a greater expansion of the invisible divine eternality - the essence of everything and source of all things - the all-inclusive nature of both material and ethereal domains. Thus was the definition of Apeiros - eternal, boundless, infinite, endless expansion - the cause of all unity and measure of all things.

The purpose of the Order of Apeiros was to play a great sacred role, not only for the world as it was, but also for the vision of life beyond human perception of time and space. As teachers, healers, and light-workers, some were speakers, writers, and spiritual guides. Others held a specific role as sacred teachers and counselors throughout their soul's journey of many lifetimes. They were interested in conversation and participation in the quality of life beyond the mundane surface facts of what seemed to be of worldly importance - ever probing for the underlying principal of truth in all things.

For the Earth herself, they held the highest vibrational consciousness for her peaceful evolution, believing that humanity and the animal kingdom must reside with her in communion. The members of Apeiros had his or her task for the year, each a quality of love, which aided them to think, speak, and take action from that quality. By doing so, they respectfully and peacefully shined the light throughout the world where darkness prevailed.

That evening, White Buffalo, a Lakota chief, spiritual leader, and shaman, gathered the group in a circle before the fireplace. He asked everyone to leave their ego outside the door, and then smudged each person with the smoke of sage to bless and cleanse them of worldly energies. He spoke a prayer in his native tongue to call in the four directions. Everyone followed along, turning their bodies in unison to each of the four directions, then to the sky - the ethereal world of Great Spirit - and lastly to Grandmother Earth.

The resonance of his blessing permeated everyone. Although they did not understand his language, each deeply comprehended the essence of his prayer. The prayer's high vibration was so elevated, all felt transported into an altered state as the events of the evening commenced.

"I will tell you the Seven Lakota Virtues," White Buffalo said, "which are the qualities of the Creator, Wakan Tanka, Great Spirit. Walking and praying with these in your heart - listening with both ears, seeing with both eyes, and speaking with one mouth - will help you to live in a good way. I invite you to take these virtues into your meditation and prayer work, adding one each week, until all seven fill your mind and heart. It is not an easy task, but one that will bring you great reward.

"*Wocekiya* - Prayer

Waohola - Respect

Waunsila - Compassion

Wowicake - Honesty

Wawokiye - Generosity

Wahwala - Humility

Woksape – Wisdom"

He concluded by singing a Lakota prayer to fully invoke the presence of Great Spirit throughout the evening.

Gaston then invited the group to join him at the dining table. He asked that all the lights be turned off, including the chandelier overhead. On the dining table were the two clusters of silver candleholders, lit with varied sizes and textures of ivory candles. The fire in the fireplace continued to burn brightly in the great room. Everyone sat down, held hands, and closed their eyes as Gaston spoke in Creole to call in the spirit of Algernon.

Soon, the atmosphere grew heavy and thick. Everyone remained seated, but some squirmed in their chairs, clearly uncomfortable. Gaston continued to speak in Creole, as a visible dark blur formed at the center of the table, churning about like a heavy storm cloud. It hovered between the clusters of candles, making them flicker. Everyone opened their eyes to the intense atmosphere, which was a physical gray presence hovering before them. Those seated opposite each other could not see the person across from them. Gaston then spoke in English, so everyone would understand his directions.

"Each of you will speak to the entity of Algernon. Coming from your calling, speak directly to the energy to raise its vibration. First, stand and let those on either side hold hands behind you, so you are included in the circle. Anja, if you would be the first to start."

Anja stood and placed her hands out, palms nearly touching the dark cloud. She closed her eyes and, in her deep African dialect, she spoke a prayer of Compassion for the soul of Algernon.

"Praise Allah, the magnificent and wonderful. In this moment I call upon the heart of Compassion to fill this space - to fill every heart that is here this evening for the soul of Algernon Gillette. I know that I am a divine child of Allah, the magnificent and wonderful, and my word holds true as I speak on behalf of our brother. No one is unworthy. We are all deserving, and this is true for the soul of Algernon Gillette. I speak, knowing that the understanding Compassion of the heart not only surrounds him, but also is now set into motion, raising Algernon above the conditions of which he has believed as his truth, until now. I now speak for Algernon to rise above, to become transparent as the light shines through him and as him. I call forth the remembrance of his soul, and I know that he is now identifying with who he truly is. I hold gentle, merciful, Compassion for Algernon now, knowing it is his to live in Love, to love himself, and to remember who he came here to be. And so I pass."

They went around the table, each speaking from the Divine Attribute of their personal representation. Ananta confidently stood before the group. "The Hindu gods are here tonight. I stand with them in Joy. It is clear that, up until now, Algernon has not known true joy - no elation of the heart - for humanity, for the earth, and mostly for himself, but now that darkness is gone. I now declare Joy to fill the mind, body, and soul of Algernon, bringing him to a state of mind which is happy and fulfilled."

She held her hands out, her palms holding the living truth while feeling with every ounce of her body the delight of blissful Joy. "I feel in my entire being the enchantment of the gods. In my mind's eye, Algernon is filled with that same elation. There is laughing, singing, and dancing in the music of Creation. In the center of this is Algernon, overflowing with his pleasure-filled essence that is no longer held back. I declare, on behalf of Algernon, that all is well, for it is now done!" Ananta finished her prayer, certain that it was already taking effect.

The dark gray cloud at the center of the table roiled up as if something inside was spinning like a top.

As each of the thirteen spoke, the darkness grew lighter. The agitation of the entity became more peaceful. Gaston was the eleventh to speak, followed by Darius, who included a prayer for the souls of his daughter, Elizabeth, and his son-in-law, Tommy. Sophia spoke the final prayer as the one most personally affected by Algernon. All agreed it appropriate for her to bring the final blessing upon his soul.

She brought to the table a large tray holding the sacred elemental talismans and placed it in the center between the candelabras. The eternal flame caused the dark cloud to rise above it, as if to distance itself from the fiery chalice.

Sophia then held her hands in front of her, palms up. "I call all the elements for their strength and power - the golden bowl - for water; the chalice holding the eternal flame; the hourglass with the sands of time for Earth; the amethyst amulet - representing air; and the ammonite - for the ethereal realm, set with the labradorite - a stone of protection. Every aspect of our earthly and ethereal world is represented by these symbols."

There was yet another shift of energy in the room.

"Everyone here tonight brought to the soul of Algernon healing and wholeness," Sophia said, "honoring his soul's journey for this lifetime and for its future. What occurred this evening not only affects him, but also affects everyone touched by the energy of Algernon. Change has commenced tonight. History has been altered and the future transformed, as light shines through what was once dark."

The cloud was nearly gone.

"From my heart, I now forgive Algernon for my mother's death. I let go of the heaviness I held onto since the day her life was taken. The pain of her death has remained in my mind and heart, unbeknownst to me all these years. Now that I know of its origin, I declare the evil of that day's events no longer has power over me. It is done. It is gone. I forgive him.

"From my heart, I now forgive Algernon for my father's death. I let go of the heaviness I have felt since the moment I learned his identity. For depriving me of the father whose love I never knew, whose kiss I never felt, and whose warm heart shall only beat inside of me, I declare the evil of that day's events no longer has power over me. It is done. It is gone. I forgive Algernon.

"I now feel only love and compassion for Algernon. What he once believed as his destination in life is not the truth of him. Principle stands strong, never to be altered or diminished, and Love operates all principles as the foundation of everything. In all things, Love generates the action of God, the Divine.

"And so tonight, as a divine conduit of the God Most High, I hold Love for the soul of Algernon Gillette, which will continue on for lifetimes, evolving to its highest order of Grace and Absolute Awareness. This Love permeates all boundaries, penetrates the hardest of hearts, and enlightens all to the clarity of their soul's journey to horizons beyond their greatest dreams. For this, and so much more, I declare this Love to not only change and alter the soul of Algernon, but for him to be Love incarnate. This Love is all there is.

"And so we collectively hold this Love in the exuberance of blissful Joy. The elegance of grace prevails. Compassion of the heart permeates all as kindness and mercy. Peace of mind is a knowing that all is well now, as demonstrated in stillness and tranquility. Harmony's accord plays as the symphony of all people working together for good. Order and Balance - with all in its place - fills life with ease and grace. Every moment contains Beauty, with its wonder of the exquisite nature of God's creation. Oneness and inclusion is being in union with the Divine. Abundance in all things and the material realm expands with the circulation of prosperity in receiving and giving within the opulence of wealth. Truth in its clarity always leads to and from the heart. Full Health is of the mind, body, and soul. For these truths, I am so very grateful to live in the appreciating qualities that never fade and ever prevail. All this is the Absolute Awareness of the soul and life of all, which includes the life of Algernon Gillette. And so It Is!"

Just then, Digit jumped up on the table and walked up to the golden bowl and began lapping up the water. Everyone around the table smiled as Michael stood and reached over to pick her up, but Sophia put her hand out and stopped him. He quietly sat down as Digit walked over to Sophia and sat straight up directly in front of her. The tiny black cat looked up at her human with her almond-shaped golden green eyes.

Those familiar with ancient Egypt reflected on how Digit appeared like *Bastet*, the Egyptian Cat Goddess, who was the giver of blessings to the good, and a deliverer of wrath to the evil. The room was completely silent with the exception of the resonant purr of Digit, who held everyone's attention. Sophia picked her cat up and held her close just as the wisp of fog at the center of the table shifted into a glowing golden light, emitting such brilliance that it joined with the radiance of the thirteen who sat around the table.

There was no delineation of individual souls. The group focused their energy so Algernon's soul became concentrated in a swirling mass of rotating golden luminosity, like a brilliant ball of fire. The cadence of Digit's purr set the fire's energy into a deep pulsating rhythm like the beat of a thousand drums. Each one there felt it through their heart, deep into their cellular levels, for this blessing was not only for Algernon and everyone he had ever affected, but also for everyone present. This is how they were to work with any concern that came their way - holding their individual spiritual calling within the group, united as one, as a whole with the Divine.

The fire of Algernon's soul then rose above the table and slowly dispersed into the air. What remained was a sense of tranquility and peace - a harmony so blessed that each one simply sat quietly in the glow, with the exception of Digit's continual purr.

With the evening's events concluded, Michael and Sophia walked with the eight people who returned to the inn, leaving Darius, White Buffalo, and Gaston to sit with Digit in front of the fire. When Michael and Sophia returned to the cabin, they sat in the yard for their nightly ritual of searching for shooting stars, wrapped together in a down comforter. One so bright and brilliant shot across the sky, as if to say all was well. And it was.

Two days later, Gaston showed the group a news item from New Orleans. Niko Gillette was just indicted on racketeering charges of human trafficking, gambling, prostitution, and murder. The district attorney's office was confident it had enough evidence to put him and his associates in prison for life, essentially ending the reign of one of Louisiana's most notorious crime syndicates. The thirteen knew they had something to do with his arrest.

Even though her mind was at rest, Sophia did not sleep well that night, for again she recalled Jocelyn at a pivotal moment in her life aboard *Titanic*.

Chapter
Twenty-one

On the Boat Deck, people frantically pushed and shoved toward the dwindling lifeboats. Jocelyn and François went to the port side of the ship, where women and children were boarding under Mr. Lightoller's direction. With the panic now clearly palpable, the crewmembers could not ready the boats fast enough. They launched each one in five to ten minute intervals, but time was growing short as the ocean filled up to the forecastle.

François and Jocelyn watched families part, as cold inevitability began to assault their senses. Women silently looked into the eyes of their men, knowing it would most likely be their final memory of their husbands. The men, some deciding not to wear their lifebelts, courageously held their children close, imploring them to be brave so they could take care of their mother and siblings. The younger children were unaware that they would not likely see their fathers again.

Jocelyn overheard one man tell his young daughter that she and her mother would go out on the lifeboat for the time being, and by morning, they would be back on *Titanic* in time for breakfast. His wife, who then stood by her daughter's side holding her hand, briefly let go to place her arms around her husband's neck. He held her close. They whispered words into each other's ears that only they could hear - their last words - which would remain with them forever. The woman pulled away, a single tear rolling down her cheek as she looked into the eyes of her husband. She then took her daughter's hand and boarded the lifeboat.

Men stood stoically on the deck, watching their families slowly lowered in the lifeboats to the sea, knowing that their chances for survival were slim to none, lest they jump overboard and take the chance of swimming to an available lifeboat.

Third Class passengers had no single stairway leading from the lowest levels of Steerage, eight levels below, up to the Boat Deck. There were no maps to guide passengers to the top levels in an emergency. Instead, several stewards spread out through the lower levels of the ship, directing Third Class passengers to the next steward, who would lead them up toward the Boat Deck. Steerage passengers and crewmembers from the lower levels had to walk through several public rooms leading to hallways, and then up staircases, only to go through more rooms leading yet to another stairway, before they reached the Boat Deck. Those who spoke little or no English had even greater difficulty finding someone to help them traverse *Titanic's* internal maze.

Many Third Class passengers were traveling across the Atlantic with everything they owned. Some attempted to carry luggage and trunks up the stairs in an effort to save what little they had. Others remained behind, unwilling to leave their belongings. A number of Third Class passengers made it to the Boat Deck, only to decide that the thought of drifting in a lifeboat on a dark, cold ocean was even less safe than remaining on *Titanic*, and so they returned to Steerage to pray for rescue.

Out of the 322 stewards, only 44 served the 706 Third Class passengers, more than the number of passengers in First and Second Class combined. John Hart, a Steerage steward, led two different groups of passengers from the aft Third Class cabins located near the stern, up eight levels to the Boat Deck. Some of those in his charge were among the many who chose to return to their cabins. For those remaining on deck, Hart made sure that each one safely boarded a lifeboat, thus saving at least 50 people that night. Without his assistance, most would have likely perished. Of the 706 Third Class passengers, only 178 would survive. John Hart saved nearly one-third of them.

First Officer William McMaster Murdoch, in charge of the lifeboats on the starboard side, ordered Hart to get into the lifeboat to help row, whereas the 39-year-old Murdoch remained behind to carry out his duty until the end. Murdoch, a Scottish sailor, was known as a consummate professional, who was gallant and relentless in his dedication to his career. He was described by many who knew him as compassionate, kind, gentle, and sincere - a true gentleman. Every lifeboat in his charge on the starboard side entered the water filled to capacity with women, children, *and* men. He would place more people on lifeboats than any other officer that night.

It was difficult for Jocelyn and François to fathom all that ensued that evening, when only two hours earlier many were enjoying the end of another glorious day at sea, having libations in the ship's lounge, placing bets on the exact time *Titanic* would arrive in New York, or retired to their rooms and sleeping in a warm bed. The ship was slipping away into the North Atlantic, which was clearly inevitable, and although distress rockets still fired, there was no sign of a rescue ship in sight. Soon all the lifeboats would be gone, leaving more than two-thirds of the passengers and crew still aboard to fend for themselves.

In his nightmares, François knew this time was coming. It did not require the skills of an architect to complete the calculations. He was staying behind. Even if he had known that Murdoch was allowing men on the starboard lifeboats, he would not have boarded until every woman and child was off the ship. He did not deem it any act of nobility. He simply thought that if his wife and child were aboard, he would remain behind, so there would be room for them on the lifeboats.

He turned to Jocelyn and looked into her marvelous, loving eyes. "It is time, mon cheri."

François enveloped Jocelyn inside his coat and held her close. In spite of the deafening panic surrounding them, she held her head to his chest and listened to his steady heartbeat. Somehow, its resonance would stay with her. As long as she felt his heartbeat, although apart, she knew he would remain safely among the living. Of this, she had no doubt.

He took from his pocket the ammonite that dangled from the chain and placed it around her neck. "Remember, labradorite is a stone of protection. The ammonite represents the eternality of the universe, which is ever-expanding and becoming greater. What needs releasing eventually disappears, because it is no longer of importance. Both the ammonite and labradorite exemplifies *aeternalis* - without end. I promise that you and I will soon begin our life together. We have too much to live for. We will find a way."

Jocelyn closed her eyes while she held the ammonite in her hand, feeling a warm golden presence surrounding them. All noise dissipated, and she heard a voice say, *You are protected, guided, and sourced.*

"We will come out of this and do great things together, my love," she said. "Until we see each other again, we must remember all on this ship tonight. Most will no longer walk the earth, but their souls will remain with us. We will carry on, ever connected to each one. You are my beloved, François."

"Je t'aime plus que la vie elle-même." He touched her face. "More than life itself."

They had tears in their eyes, not wanting to release each other. They kissed, and with their last embrace, Lightoller firmly gripped Jocelyn's arm and guided her into the lifeboat.

"We must hurry, Madame," Lightoller said. As she settled into her seat, Lightoller gave the order, "Right! Lower away!"

Jocelyn gripped the ammonite as the lifeboat gave a hard jerk and began descending to the sea. The women and children around her desperately cried out to their husbands and fathers. As the boat lowered to the water's surface, Jocelyn could see the life force surrounding those few who would survive, but more so, she could see that most of those on the ship had no such aura. She felt such sorrow, knowing these were the last moments for the majority of people left behind. But François stood apart. As before, Jocelyn saw a light fade in and out around him.

Jocelyn then experienced a moment of utter panic, as she briefly recalled another lifetime when her life was at stake in a small boat heading out to sea.

François quickly disappeared from Jocelyn's view as the lifeboat rowed a safe distance away from the ship. A pall of bleak darkness befell her heart, for even though she was in a boat of many, she felt entirely alone. She looked up and saw *Titanic* listing dramatically to the port side, now at a steep angle with the bow well underwater. Many people aboard screamed in terror, as some slipped or jumped overboard into the water hundreds of feet below. Most died instantly on impact, but Jocelyn could see some thrashing about for a few minutes before succumbing to the water's icy temperatures. The ship took on 400 tons of water per minute, tipping to an eleven percent grade and making it quite difficult for crewmembers to drag the remaining collapsible boats up the slanted deck to the davits.

On board, in the chaos of the passengers and crew, Mr. Murdoch attempted to finagle one of the collapsible lifeboats onto a starboard davit. *Titanic* suddenly shifted, causing a huge wave to wash him overboard. Not wearing a lifebelt, he disappeared into the watery darkness and was never seen again.

François remained on the port side, assisting Lightoller and other crewmembers as they helped the women board the last of the lifeboats. Over the chaos, he suddenly overheard a crewmember and Isidor Straus attempt to convince Mrs. Straus to board. Ida would have nothing to do with it, desiring to remain behind with her husband. Before her newly appointed English maid, Ellen Bird, stepped onto the lifeboat, Ida removed her fur coat and placed it around Ellen's shoulders, telling her that she no longer had any need for the coat. Isidor and Ida held onto each other, telling the shipman to give their seats to younger passengers, two of whom were young brothers.

Only Collapsible D remained, which was the last lifeboat to launch, with a capacity of 47, while well over 1,000 people still remained aboard *Titanic*. As François approached the edge of the Boat Deck, he witnessed three more acts of courageous sacrifice among what he believed were hundreds, perhaps thousands that must have already occurred that night. François briefly thought to himself how appropriate it was that the word courage came from the French *coeur,* which meant heart.

Before Frederick Hoyt put his wife on Collapsible D, François overheard him tell her that he estimated the direction and distance the boat would row. He thought if he jumped ship, he could swim to her lifeboat and they would pick him up.

First Class passenger Edith Evans already sat in the last available seat and noticed there was no room for her friend, Caroline. Edith promptly took her leave from the lifeboat and told the crewman to give the available seat to her friend, who had children. As it happened, Caroline was the last woman to board a lifeboat. The men left standing on the deck stood in respectful awe beside Edith, knowing there were no more lifeboats, and she, like them, would go down with the ship.

Then François found himself next to a man who

seemed to stand out amongst the rest. The man stood silently on the deck as he watched his two small boys, ages two and four, placed into the boat next to the daughter of an American banker, who was able to save her small dog. François quickly handed his quilt to one of the boat's crewman, instructing him to tuck the blanket around the boys to keep them warm. Time seemed to cease, as he witnessed the father's stoic silence that spoke in strident volumes beyond what ears could hear.

Their father then turned to look at François, slightly smiling in gratitude. "Merci, Monsieur."

François nodded in acknowledgement. "Ce sont vos enfants?"

"Oui. Se sont mes garcons," he said.

They silently stood next to each other, watching the boys in the eighteenth and last lifeboat successfully launched down to the sea's surface. On A Deck, one deck below the Boat Deck, there were women who chose to stay behind with their husbands. Only men, with the exception of Edith Evans, remained on the port side of the Boat Deck.

François caught his breath in reverence as he stood still for just a brief moment, aware of only absolute silence.

Chapter
Twenty-two

The Colorado gathering of the Order of Apeiros could not have begun more meaningfully than with the grand blessing and forgiveness of Algernon Gillette. The other members helped Sophia and Darius purge the darkness and shed welcome light on their beloved Elizabeth and Tommy, something for which they were eternally grateful. Knowing well the love and support her friends would bestow upon her, Sophia had enlisted Michael's help to plan a special surprise to express their gratitude. Sophia told the group at breakfast the next morning.

"I know, with the exception of Michael and White Buffalo of course, that this is the first time any of you have visited Colorado," Sophia said. "So, we thought it would be fun to charter a bus and conduct our meetings while on a grand tour of our beautiful state." The group greeted her surprise with great enthusiasm. "We're going to show off our mountains and some wonderful towns and historical landmarks, and take you on a road that's over twelve thousand feet in elevation!"

"Dear girl," Darius said, "I remind you that your uncle and I hail from New Orleans – which is several feet *below* sea level? My brother gets a nosebleed even when he ascends a staircase!"

"I take offense at that," Gaston said. "I don't deny it, but I *do* take offense."

"Well, we will bring some extra tissues," Sophia said with a laugh. "But I know you will love this, for you all came here during the height of the fall color season. The golden aspen trees are beautiful right now."

With the tour set to commence the next morning, Michael broached a subject at the evening meeting, which he had been contemplating for some time.

"I have been thinking about how each of us holds our particular attribute upon which we place our full attention during the year. While what we do is noble and good, I think we can simplify it to create a greater collective power as the Order of Apeiros. Simply put, if we all embrace Love and Absolute Awareness as our work, we will automatically come from the other divine attributes, which up until now we have each embraced throughout the year."

"Are you suggesting that we no longer hold our individual calling?" Irina asked.

"Just hear me out. For instance, when we come from Love, joy generates feelings of bliss. Love, as peace, envelopes us in its tranquility. Love, as compassion, directs our thoughts and actions in support of another, and so on. In this way, Love is at the center of all we do in each moment. Wherever we are across the globe, we will energetically join in oneness from the only power, which is Love itself.

"An easy way to remember this is with the symbol of the cross. Each of us stands in our individual vertical field, in the present moment, where we anchor to the center of the earth, while our energy aligns with the zenith above, to infinity. At the same time, our communal connection upon Earth is the horizontal plane, in recognition of our oneness with all beings. Where the vertical and horizontal planes meet is at the heart - our individual center, right here in the present moment. I believe this was the work of Yeshua, and all the enlightened teachers throughout time, centered in the here and now, and united from the heart through Love. We know it as the Sacred Way of the Heart.

"Our challenge is, we must retrain our minds and remember to love ourselves by dropping our energy from our mind to our heart, and to extend that love for anyone and anything that comes. We continue to collectively hold the divine attributes in our hearts, each enveloped in love. This is our only task - to be Love."

"Brilliant! Absolutely brilliant!" Darius said.

Everyone began to talk at once, all in agreement with Michael's suggestion.

"We can discuss this further on our tour," Michael said.

"I think your idea will both simplify and empower us even more," Markos said.

"We should all get some sleep now," Michael said. "The van will be here in the morning. If we have anything more to discuss about this, we can do it on the road. So, let's meet down at the inn at nine for breakfast, and then we'll be off!"

Everyone bid each other goodnight, and the others walked down the riverside road to the inn, excitedly discussing the new direction they were taking. Gaston and Darius enjoyed a nightcap with White Buffalo, who sipped on a milk - straight up - in front of the fireplace before retiring, while Sophia and Michael sat outside under the stars, which seemed to radiate more brilliantly than ever. At one point, Sophia looked away from the heavens to take in the wonder of Michael's heart and mind, feeling an even greater love and respect for him.

The van arrived the next morning to take the group on a nine-day personalized tour of Colorado. Sophia and Michael spared no expense, chartering a luxurious Mercedes small touring van, driven by a charming driver named Sam Baker, who also served as concierge in arranging touring, lodging, and dining accommodations along the way.

From the cabin, they drove to Copeland Lake, near Allenspark, providing a great opportunity to take photos of the shimmering golden aspen trees. The van wound its way up into Rocky Mountain National Park, where they spent the remainder of the day hiking around Bear Lake and Sprague Lake, taking photos and enjoying a picnic lunch prepared by the chef. As the sun dropped into late afternoon, they drove back down toward Estes Park, passing a large field far down below the road.

"Look! How unusual!" Lestari said, pointing out the window. Everyone looked down at the meadow, where there appeared a large outcrop of dark boulders. From the road several hundred feet above, it was difficult to make out precisely what they were looking at. "Those rocks look almost identical in size and placed evenly apart."

Michael asked Sam to pull over, and everyone climbed out. They stood outside the van, looking down at the field below. Markos shaded his eyes from the setting sun and squinted. "What in the world? Those don't really look like rocks," he said.

Michael smiled. "Sophia? If you will . . ."

"Your attention please," Sophia said. She walked to the edge of the road, and in a not-so lady-like fashion, she put her fingers to her lips and gave a shrill whistle. Suddenly, all the 'rocks' below simultaneously lifted their heads and looked up the hill in their direction. They were dozens of elk beginning their evening meal on the plentiful field of cool grasses. Everyone looked at Sophia in astonishment and laughed. She simply smiled and got back on the bus.

They stayed at the historic Lodge at Estes Park for the night. It was Saturday, and the 140-room hotel hosted two weddings that day. The front desk clerk, who looked no more than seventeen, had difficulty finding available rooms for everyone, even though Sam had pre-arranged guaranteed reservations well in advance. There were no bellmen to help with the luggage, and everyone had to tote their bags up the stairway to the third and fourth floors because the only elevator in the hotel was overworked with wedding parties, service carts, and hotel guests. The group took the inconvenience in good humor, although Sophia did rein Michael in once or twice before he told someone what was really on his mind.

When Sophia and Michael settled in their room, Michael called down to room service to order a bottle of champagne for the evening, but no one answered the phone.

Michael stared at the receiver incredulously. "An answering machine," he said. "Room service has an answering machine."

"Well, leave a message," Sophia said.

"Leave a message? Who leaves a message for room service?"

"Well, maybe you should just yell out the window," Sophia said.

Michael shrugged and spoke into the phone. "Hi, how are ya, this is room 311 calling. When you get a chance, give us a call to see if there is anything you can do for us, ok? Some champagne maybe?"

He tried several times over the next hour to no avail, only able to leave three more irritated messages that embarrassed Sophia even more. No one ever called back or delivered champagne. By Michael's fourth message, Sophia figured the room service people were afraid to return his calls.

Rather weary from a big day of touring, the group all decided to meet downstairs at the restaurant for an early dinner so they could get to bed at a decent time. When they arrived, the young, wide-eyed hostess had the grueling job of informing them that the hotel had run out of food.

"Excuse me?" Michael said.

"I'm sorry," she said, "but we stopped serving fifteen minutes ago."

"It's five o'clock, and the restaurant is out of food?"

"We really weren't expecting such a large crowd this late in the season," the girl said, apologetically.

"Well, of course," Michael said. "Who would have thought two large wedding parties and a hotel full of guests would get hungry?"

"Michael," Sophia said, "easy, tiger."

"There's a coffee shop downstairs," the hostess said. "They have bagels."

"Bagels and spaghetti, I hope," Michael said.

"Michael, heel!" Sophia said. Everyone laughed. "It's not her fault."

"You're right," Michael said. Just the look on his face made the teenage girl appear as if she wanted to crawl under a rock. He bowed to her. "Thank you. Perhaps we'll stop by in the morning to see if the chickens replenished the egg supply overnight."

White Buffalo, the most stoic and thoughtful of the group, turned and unexpectedly did a wonderful Groucho Marx. "Well, that's the most ridiculous thing I ever heard."

If Michael had put any tension in the air, it quickly broke as everyone laughed at White Buffalo, who never cracked a smile.

"I'd complain to the manager," Michael said, "but it's probably past his bedtime."

Both Michael and Sophia knew the hotel's failure was an anomaly, because typically, the Lodge was an exceptional place to stay. Wherever they traveled, they seemed to dance between the raindrops, and rarely did they have any issues, but this time they were caught in a deluge and stuck in the mud.

"Alright," Sophia said. "Plan B. Let's find Sam and ride into town for dinner."

"I'd be content with a scotch or two in the lounge before retiring," Darius said.

"Now we're getting somewhere!" Markos said.

"No, no," Gaston said. "With you, a scotch or two before dinner turns into five or six, and you know what a bad influence you are on me."

"Me, too," Michael said. "After all, we're family. Let's go."

"I'll drink to that," White Buffalo said. "I want to try one of those Peach Paradise Spritzers."

The boys stopped in their tracks to look at White Buffalo.

"What?" White Buffalo said. "I read about it my room. They use fresh Colorado peaches. If you haven't had one, you really have no reason to live."

Markos and Christofer laughed and followed, but the revolt was suddenly shut down by Sophia's shrill whistle. In fact, the entire hotel stopped its orbit, including eighty members of a wedding party.

"Gentlemen," Sophia said, "the ladies and I are hungry."

So, everyone hopped in the van in search of a good restaurant for dinner.

CHAPTER
Twenty-three

In the heart of Estes Park was a charming little Italian restaurant that, to everyone's relief, actually *had* food, served by a woman of adult status. She more than compensated for the hotel's inadequacies and helped everyone enjoy a great dining experience.

"What kind of mocktail do you have that will go well with Italian food for our fine friend here?" Christofer asked, pointing to White Buffalo.

"I have just the thing. It's called an Italian Smooch," the waitress said.

"Oooh, does that come with red or pink lipstick?" Gaston asked.

"It comes in a glass, with ice, muddled lemon, cola, and ginger ale."

"Well, if I can't get an Italian Smooch with lips attached, a glass will be second best," White Buffalo said.

With the wine poured and orders taken, Sophia suggested, "I know very little about some of you. How about, each night at dinner, we go around the table and tell something unusual about ourselves that might be of interest to everyone." They all agreed, and Sophia suggested Shoshana be the first.

"Again, I have the good fortune of receiving another generous grant to continue my work at Akrotiri," she said.

Christofer was obviously happy that she would remain on the island for at least another couple of years. He put his arm around her and gave her a kiss. "You would not believe how much more of the village Shoshana and her team of archaeologists have unearthed beneath all those layers of 5,600-year-old volcanic rubble. Sophia, you wouldn't recognize the place."

"Actually," Markos said, laughing, "may I remind you that Sophia is one of the three of us who *would* recognize what they uncovered."

"Sophia, we have found what may have been Roxana's home," Shoshana said. "I would suppose only you might know its precise location, but according to what you indicated on the map, I believe we found it."

"Oh, my goodness," Sophia said. "I can't wait to go back and see it."

"Once we dug through layers of volcanic rubble, we discovered the buildings in that particular area were well preserved. Their interiors were only affected by the volcanic ash that fell before the lava sealed the buildings. It was easy to reveal beneath the ash many personal items still intact and in excellent condition."

"How exciting!" Sophia said. "You must feel a sense of satisfaction finding such treasures."

"Yes, it has been a rewarding several months. Actually, I brought something for you." She took from her purse a small royal blue silk pouch and handed it to Sophia. "This goes against the rules, for everything we find must be catalogued and stored. I made an exception in this case, however, because these probably belonged to you. I thought you should have them."

Sophia loved receiving gifts. She felt the anticipation as she pulled apart the drawstrings that held the pouch closed. She poured out a pair of golden hoop earrings, handcrafted from the purest gold she had ever seen. They were simple in design, and made for pierced ears. "Oh, I remember these! They are exquisite, aren't they? I remember not intending to leave them behind, but there was so much chaos, with the fear that the volcano would soon explode. All I took with me were layers of clothes and my sacred talismans – and, of course, Theo." She looked across the table at Markos, who raised his glass in her honor. "All I cared about was getting my people safely off the island. I left many items of value behind that day." She excused herself and walked to the restroom, where she could put the earrings on and see herself briefly in the mirror as a young Roxana with long, flowing ebony hair and bronze eyes.

She returned, showing off her new ancient earrings. "Oh, thank you, Shoshana. The memories are coming back to me from when I wore these. What more did you find?"

"I wanted to be certain the earrings were yours, and since they are, here is a bracelet we found next to it." It was Roxana's beaded bracelet with elegant gold and lapis beads.

"This is truly lovely!" Sophia said. "It fits as if someone made it for me now. Look at the beautiful artisanship - and to think that someone made this over 5,600 years ago. This bracelet belonged to my grandmother, who passed it on to my mother. She gave it to me when I became high priestess. Thank you for bringing it to me. What a wonderful gift. Please thank your people for me, Shoshana."

"Well, this is something we will keep to ourselves," Shoshana said. "I am stretching my ethical boundaries by giving these to you, so let us keep this our little secret, alright?"

"Yes, of course," Sophia said.

"We have found many items like these throughout the excavation, so they are not anomalies. Otherwise, I would not have given them to you, but I am so happy you are pleased."

"Other than my aquamarine ring and amethyst pendant, they are now the loveliest pieces of jewelry I own. Thanks again!" She leaned over and gave Shoshana a big hug.

Shoshana smiled, knowing she did the right thing by returning the jewelry to Sophia.

"So, tell us more about you," Sophia said.

"What I have to share is more about my father," Shoshana said, "but what I learned from him remains with me. It exemplifies what we do here in Apeiros. As you all know, I was born in Israel. I am Jewish, and was raised Hebrew, but I spent much of my childhood in Syria. My father, who was a professor at Georgetown in Washington D.C., became a U.S. citizen when I was a small girl. He tells the story of how he attended a holiday party, when the President's chief of staff approached him to become the ambassador to Syria. My father was taken aback and respectfully suggested the man was out of his mind."

"How does one respectively tell a man of such power that he is crazy?" Yesinia said, laughing.

"Evidently, it did not come as an insult, because my father did take the post. There is one story he tells, which I will always remember. It teaches me everyday how I am to be in the world.

"As ambassador, my father was the key mediator between the military and political leaders of Syria and Israel among other surrounding Middle East countries. Many times, he would pass a communication from one side to the other only as a verbal message, at great risk to his own safety. One time, it took many days for him to deliver a special message from a Syrian general for the Aluf, a lieutenant-general in the Israeli army. When my father finally reached him, he whispered in his ear, 'He wants you to know that he sends you his love.' My father then returned to Syria to reciprocate a similar message to the general.

"You see, the two men grew up together as neighbors, having been dear friends on opposite sides of the border. These two men were able to continue their love for the other, in spite of their political differences. My father taught me that the most important relationships are those of family and then our neighbors, because they consist of our communities of heart, which continue throughout our lifetime. He taught me how to live and how to love - seeing everyone as family - as a member of my community of souls."

Christofer put his arm around Shoshana and kissed her on the forehead. "I love you so," he said.

Shoshana smiled and then turned to Markos. "Markos,

why don't you tell everyone what you've been doing since we were last together."

"Well, I am no longer in the rental car business," Markos said with a laugh. "Christofer and I are working to increase tourism in Santorini, which will help boost our challenged economy. Part of our plan includes lodging in Christopher's boutique hotel in northern Santorini.

"Here's the news: not far from the Akrotiri excavation site, we are developing a re-creation of what Akrotiri would have looked like before the eruption. From the top of the hill, where the village will be, a road will lead down to a small harbor. There, we will have two replicas of the Cycladic ships, similar to those seen in the *Flotilla Fresco*, which was on the wall in the West House. They were beautifully decorated pleasure ships at the time, rowed by slaves. These boats are a good re-creation, however they *are* motorized without the oars or the slaves, of course. We will have morning, afternoon, and sunset cruises."

Everyone at the table was intrigued with the plan.

"Most of the restaurant and business owners on the island are thrilled to be part of our venture. Many are offering special incentives for the tourists, resulting in more year-round opportunities that will sustain the island's economy throughout the year, and not just for the summer season. Akrotiri is also benefitting from the increase in tourism, and with the expansion of the site, there is much more for people to see.

"Sophia, we could use your help. You can describe details that Christofer and I cannot remember. As Theo, I was only five years old when you whisked me off the island, and Christofer, as Dimitios, was either venturing to other ports with his father, or painting a fresco inside many of the homes. So, you are our best advisor."

"Whatever I can do, I would be happy to help," Sophia said.

"We'll just tell you the basics now. Later we can show you a copy of the plans. The village will be about one-quarter the size of what they have uncovered in Akrotiri. We are using the same grid of the buildings along the main street that were originally uncovered at the site. We will build the village with modern technology, of course, but in the same design as the original construction." Markos took his pen from his pocket, and on his napkin he drew a rough grid similar to the village that was unearthed. "Replicas of the frescoes on the walls will be painted by Christofer."

Christofer stood from his chair just enough to take a slight bow. They all laughed and mockingly applauded.

"Humbly, of course," Markos said. "We will sell olive oil and wines, available in small ceramic amphorae. Initially, the wines will be produced in Christofer's winery, and as demand increases, we will use other vineyards on the island."

"We cannot make wine in the old tradition," Christofer said. "Plus, it is not good wine by today's standards, but Santorini has some of the world's oldest vineyards, so in a sense we are still being true to the island's history. Wine is one of Santorini's greatest commodities, and putting a historic bent on it by selling it in an amphora-type container, which will create more of a draw. When the amphora is empty, it will make a great art piece for the home."

Christofer continued, "We also have artisans who will make jewelry items from gold, silver, copper, bronze, gemstone beads, and with cabochon jewels. We will have nothing made of iron or steel, as the Iron Age did not occur for another 2,400 years. The jewelry, somewhat like the pieces that Shoshana brought to you, Sophia, will be one of our greatest successes. Tourists love to buy jewelry."

"We also have artisans making clothing items," Markos said, "such as peplos, chitons and colorful woven sashes, constructed in similar brilliantly dyed fabrics, such as hemp and linen. Long woven skirts in beautiful multi-colored stripes will be available, along with the fitted open vests, which women wore at the time. If women customers wish to wear the vests with their breasts exposed, as they were illustrated in the frescos – well, why break tradition?" He shrugged as everyone laughed. "However, we *will* have cotton blouses available to wear under the vests, if customers are feeling a bit shy."

"5,600 years ago," Christofer said, "there was much trade with Crete, Egypt, and Anatolia, which is now Turkey. However, the primary navigators and traders of the time were the Canaanites, later called Phoenicians, who lived in the ancient city-states along the Mediterranean Sea - now Syria, Lebanon, Palestine, Jordan, and Israel. Many of the products of that time reflected their cultures, so the goods that we sell will also reflect the influence of the ethnicity from that time. Vendors will wear the clothing, jewelry, and hairstyles of that day."

"We have a baker who will make traditional flat bread," Markos added, "and he will also sell the simple foods of that time - olives, goat cheese, fruits and vegetables. We will sell Mediterranean wraps, somewhat like a burrito. We will cheat a bit and have refrigeration hidden somewhere in the back of his shop. We *will* have tables and chairs, for Greece was the first culture to use dining tables. And, Michael, I regret to tell you this, but you will not be able to sit down to a spaghetti dinner in the village."

"Barbarians," Michael disgustedly said. "Any wonder a volcano covered them up? I'll show you - I will bring take-out from my favorite restaurant in Oia."

"Well, if you do, we will have the faux Akrotiri police arrest you and put you in our mock prison cell," Markos said. "And for eating Italian food, in a take-out container no less, we will force you to wear a chiton and sandals, so you can pose as an authentically dressed prisoner for the tourists to jeer at. We'll even provide rotten tomatoes for them to throw at you."

As if on cue, the server arrived and put a plate of spaghetti in front of Michael. He blushed at the random snickers around the table. Sophia gave him one of her many looks. "It's Bolognese," he said. "Hey, if we go Irish, I have corned beef…" Sophia began mouthing the words with him. "Mexican, I have enchiladas. If it's Italian –"

"Spaghetti," everyone said in unison.

"I admire a man who knows precisely what he wants, dear boy," Darius said.

The server arrived with their dinner and two more bottles of Merlot, and for White Buffalo, an Italian Smooch. Everyone dug in, agreeing that their misfortune at the hotel had turned into a much better experience in town.

"Now that we've settled this spaghetti issue," Sophia said, "perhaps we can allow Markos to finish his thought?"

"What thought?" Markos said, enjoying his lasagna. "I don't remember what I was saying."

"I'll help," Christofer said with a laugh. "We plan to have a weaver who will make rugs on a loom, and a potter will make some of the interestingly shaped pots and pitchers from the pottery styles of that era. And – Sophia, you'll love this - we even have a healer who will sell her herbal concoctions and essential oils in little glass bottles that look like something from thousands of years ago, similar to what you would have used - or should I say, Roxana."

"Oh, that is marvelous!" Sophia said. "I must meet her!"

"She is an enchanting young woman," Markos said.

"So, the village is still in the planning and development stage," Christofer said, "but our projected unveiling for next year is already creating quite a draw to Santorini. We have several wealthy patrons on the island who are promoting a spirit of community involvement. We are keeping the village at its pure state, as best as possible. We will not allow any souvenir shops with tourist paraphernalia, T-shirts, postcards, and the like. There are plenty of other places on Santorini where those can be sold."

"I can't wait to see it," Sophia said, "and I'm excited to add anything I can. Shoshana, what do you think of it?"

"It is quite ingenious," Shoshana said. "This will draw more people to Santorini. As a result, more tourists will come to see Akrotiri and learn how it would have looked back in the day. I am sure you all know that what we have revealed is all in dusty gray tones. The mock village will be in full color."

"Oh, I almost forgot," Christofer said. "There's one more thing, Sophia. We are re-creating the temple, with the vesica piscis pool, the stone dolphin, the standing torchiers, and crystal lights against the indigo ceiling."

"That is a stunning undertaking," Sophia said. "I think I can recall most of the details."

"That is where you will be of great help in the design," Christofer continued. "You remember the details of the building as no one else can. Of course, we will not build it high on top of a hill, as was the original temple, but off to the side of the village grid instead. I will paint frescos on the walls, but I need you to help me remember the illustrations. Very few of the houses will be of interest because most were rather ordinary, created specifically for function and not design. The temple, however, will be something for people to remember, because of the unique features."

"Michael can help with the temple design, since he, as Yiorgos, built a replica on Mt. Parnassus."

Michael nodded, his mouth a bit too full of spaghetti to speak.

"We'll take that as a 'yes'," Markos said. "It looks like we all have a lot to talk about before we return to Santorini."

Their server began clearing dishes as everyone sat back and savored the fine meal. No one went for dessert, but several ordered an after-dinner coffee.

"And how about you, White Buffalo?" Christofer asked. "What's new in your world?"

"Michael and I have a surprise for all of you. So, until then I will wait to share. For now, this old buck is ready to return to the hotel. Hopefully, they have not run out of water, so I can brush my teeth before bedtime."

"Well, if that is the case, you can just pray rain, and we'll put out a pan to collect it for you," Michael said.

"My friend, I know you are joking, but if I pray rain, the rain will come!"

"I have no doubt of that!" Michael smiled and nodded to White Buffalo as a gesture of affection for his elder. Everyone left the restaurant and began to load back on the van to return to the Lodge.

CHAPTER
Twenty-four

Michael put his arm around Sophia's shoulders just as she was about to step into the van. "How would you like to go for a walk through town? It is such a beautiful night. We can catch a cab back to the hotel before too long."

"That sounds nice. I could use a walk after that big dinner."

Around the corner from the restaurant was a small liquor store. Michael left Sophia on a park bench and went inside to buy a bottle of champagne.

"What 'cha got there?" she asked.

"Just wait. You will soon find out."

They walked hand-in-hand along a path that ran parallel to the river behind several buildings that flanked East Elkhorn Avenue. They talked about the last few days, and other than their snag at selecting the Lodge at Estes Park for their stay that night, everything else had gone well. They anticipated the same success during the remainder of the tour through Colorado. They had already walked a couple of blocks, and Michael was limping badly, clearly in pain. Sophia thought she would take the opportunity to talk with him about proceeding with hip replacement surgery - again.

"The entire time we have been together, since the

beginning of time number four, your hips have been getting worse," she said. "As a matter of fact, Michael, you are the only guy I know who limps on both legs because you are in such tremendous pain. Instead of walking in strides moving forward, you rock back and forth like a penguin."

"Sure is a beautiful night, isn't it?" Michael said.

"Selective hearing loss again? C'mon, Michael, you know you're going to have to do something about this sooner or later."

"I know, I know," Michael said. "The doctor said, when it gets bad enough-"

"That was over two years ago. How bad is bad enough? We are to the point where we are limited in what we can do together, and where we can travel. You are way too young to be so physically impaired. Tell me this, just where do you see yourself in five years?"

By that time, they came to a large footbridge across the Big Thompson River. The silvery full moon shined from the southwest onto the bridge where they stood. Michael did not say anything in response to her question. He merely pulled out of his pocket two champagne flutes and handed them to Sophia.

She smiled with a sigh. "So that's what you were up to; self medication. Good idea!"

He took the champagne from the paper bag and popped the cork. The champagne fizzed all over his hand. "Whoa!" he said as they both jumped back to avoid getting it all over them. He filled their flutes and placed the bottle on the bridge railing.

"To my love!" He raised his glass in a toast to Sophia, and her glass met his in return. After they took a sip, he placed his glass on the bridge railing next to the champagne. He struggled to get down on one knee, while he pulled out of his inside breast pocket a small, hinged box.

"Michael? What are you doing? You're gonna get all dirty."

As he opened the box to reveal an antique diamond engagement ring, he asked, "Sophia, to answer your question, I see myself married to you for the next five years, and for the rest of this life. My love, will you make me an even happier man than I am now by becoming my wife?"

That shut her up.

She simply stood with her jaw dropped in astonishment. She had long adjusted to the idea that they would never marry and just remain *registered domestic partners,* according to the State of Colorado.

She finally processed his question. "Oh, yes, Michael! Yes, yes, yes! Where did you get the - how did you know - I didn't think we would ever get married!"

"Can I get up now?"

She laughed and helped him rise to his feet, but not before they hit heads, knocking Sophia off *her* feet - but she didn't spill a drop of champagne. Giggling she quickly got up and wrapped her arms around Michael's shoulders, accidently spilling her champagne down his back.

"Oh, I'm so sorry!" She continued to giggle.

He took off his coat and tried to wipe the wet off with

the liquor store paper bag. "I guess being baptized in champagne is as good an answer as any. I hope this isn't a sign of what's to come in our marriage. We're getting off to a rocky start here, but hey, it can't be perfect all the time, now can it?"

"Oh, nothing could be *more* perfect – concussion and all!"

After putting his coat back on, he pulled her close and kissed her. She stood on her tiptoes, meeting his lips with hers. Moonlight reflected in her gleeful tears of joy. He handed her a handkerchief and filled their glasses with more champagne.

They both suddenly noticed they were not alone, the scent of cigarette smoke drifting by. About twenty feet away on the riverbank, two rather harsh-looking older women were seated in plastic lawn chairs, heavily puffing away and intently watching Sophia and Michael as if the bridge were a stage in the spotlight of the full moon. The romantic mood suddenly fizzled away.

"Maybe we should head back to the hotel," Michael softly said. "Those two look like they could beat me up."

Sophia giggled as he calmly slipped the bottle back into the bag and turned away from the onlookers. He gallantly put his arm out for Sophia to take, and they strolled away in the silver moonlight, now officially engaged to be married. They caught a cab to the hotel, where they made love. The Lodge at Estes Park would leave them with better memories after all.

A nocturnal soul, Sophia was not going to be able to sleep with wedding plans already filling her mind. "Where will we get married? At the cabin? When? Who shall we invite? I have so many ideas." Her mind raced and her words could not catch up.

"I already have a plan," Michael said, gently grabbing her hands as if he could stop her. "I would like to surprise you, if you will let me."

"Wait," she said. "If I let you, how will it be a surprise?"

Being the creative sort, she always had to plan every detail, but Michael wanted to ease her away from her constant busyness. "Well, the art of the surprise is in the timing. You know we're going to get married, but *when* it happens is the mystery."

"You aren't thinking about one of those ten- or fifteen-year engagement things, are you?"

"No," Michael said. "In fact, I want to marry you now – on this trip."

"Now?" Sophia said. "On this trip?"

"There's an echo in here."

"But a wedding requires planning, inviting, shopping, more shopping-"

"I'm just thinking a more unconventional – but timely - approach might be appealing. The people we want to attend are already here. You and I are here. What more do we need? Just leave everything to me. What do you say?"

"Hmmm," she paused, thinking about it for a moment. "That *would* make it nice and easy. Okay, but one thing – we are *not* leaving out the shopping. I want to dress the part."

"Of course, we need to be married in style. I have an idea. Early in the morning, let's go to town and find some wedding clothes while everyone else is eating breakfast. I know of a diner where we can catch a bite afterwards. The van can come to meet us, say - eleven."

"Perfect. And you actually spending money on nice clothes will convince me that you are truly committed to marriage."

Michael shrugged, and they kissed to seal the deal. Finally, he could get some sleep, and he hoped she would let her mind rest, free of the worry of wedding details. Secretly, he had already made extensive plans for an exceptional wedding, so it was a good thing she said yes. Sophia hoped she wouldn't have difficulty sleeping that night, but then again, she did have to find the perfect dress and shoes the next day. She spent the next couple of hours staring at the wall, while Michael snored like a freight train . . .

Marriage cast a completely new perspective on their relationship. All along, Sophia felt her total commitment to Michael, but to join with him in a ceremony of sacred union would create a deeper, more spiritual honoring to carry them forward with greater purpose. However, the circumstances in the hotel that night did not leave Sophia in a calm, contemplative atmosphere.

Their room was located on the third floor, and the old hotel had no air conditioning. The windows were wide open to cool the room down from the unseasonably warm, 84-degree day. One of the wedding receptions blared well beyond midnight, two floors below in the hotel courtyard. Green LED flash strobes burst across the courtyard, flashing green light into their room, making Sophia feel like she was in a scene from Hitchcock's *Vertigo*. The DJ cranked up the music base tones to the max, which reverberated through the thin walls and down Sophia's spine. The party lasted well into the early morning hours, but the many other hotel guests were not as enthusiastic.

She tried calling the desk to complain, but she got an answering machine.

Then, there was Michael's snoring. He had the uncanny ability to fall asleep anywhere, under most any circumstance. When Michael was especially tired, his snore could keep the surrounding wildlife away. One advantage was he scared the squirrels away from the attic at home. Michael could be a quiet, introspective man, but he made up the difference when he slept.

Throughout their relationship, he tried most everything to keep the volume down. Snore strips were true to their name, for instead of opening his nasal airways, they stripped the skin off the bridge of his nose. He tried a rubber mouthpiece that he saw advertised on TV, which was designed to shift his jaw while sleeping, but instead the piece loosened his lower teeth. The CPAP mask was the next attempt to help him sleep without snoring, but it made him sound like he was breathing in a deep cave. He didn't really snore *per se*, but she was tired of him kissing her goodnight and saying, "Sophia, if you only knew the powah of the dark side." Scratch another remedy off the list.

Sophia got very little sleep, and instead nudged Michael throughout the night, making him roll on his side so the roar would temporarily cease until he turned over again. She fantasized about plugging his nose with her fingers like she saw a woman do to her husband in a movie one time, but she decided that would not be the best way to begin their engagement.

Michael must have been especially tired, evidenced by the amped up reverberation of his retched uvula. Sophia sat upright and completely awake as the walls quaked and the window glass nearly shattered. For a moment, she considered going downstairs to find a comfy chair in the lobby, but then again, *that* was not an option because of the overflow of partying wedding guests. The only thing she could do was twist her earplugs tight before shoving them in her ears. She resigned herself to being stuck in the room with her big bear of a man.

Sophia shut out the green party glow in the room by putting her sleep mask on, and she buried her head between two extra pillows, which was one thing in abundance the hotel *did* provide. But then, there was no escaping her constant, steady heartbeat that reverberated within the layers of pillows.

One consolation was that Michael didn't need many hours of sleep and was an early riser, which afforded Sophia several hours of solace in the early morning hours. He woke Sophia up to the smell of coffee around eight. Out of a deep slumber she came, with both her arms holding her head wedged between the pillows.

"I don't know how in the world you can sleep all suffocated in those pillows like that," Michael said, putting her coffee on the nightstand.

Curled in the middle of the bed in a mess of rumpled sheets and covers, she pulled down her sleep mask and gave him a Vulcan death stare. Not quite sure where she was yet, she propped herself up with her back to the padded headboard and pulled off the mask. Her hair was twisted in a blonde bird's nest, her mouth parched and dry. She smacked her lips and squinted at the bright sunlight streaming into the room. Quite certain she was a remarkable sight, she said, "*Now* tell me you want to marry me."

He laughed. "Well, your appearance this morning is nothing compared to the way you woke me up."

"The way *I* woke *you* up - what are you talking about?"

"You were snoring so loud, you woke *me* up!"

"No!"

"Yes!"

"Nah, you're kidding me."

"I am not! I woke up to this strange muted muffled sound, wondering what it was. I had to turn on the light, only to find that the noise was coming from your face buried in the pillows, and you were snoring away. It was so funny, I took a video of you on my phone - sound and all."

"You *what?*"

"I left it there while I showered and then went for coffee. I now have evidence that you *do* snore. So beware, my bride to be - if you ever cross me, I will post the snoring queen on Facebook."

She jumped out of the covers, giggling, and crawled across the bed and tried to pry the phone out of his hands. He dropped the phone and grabbed her. They rolled back on the bed, and he tickled her as she squirmed and laughed until she cried.

"Okay, okay, I give, I give!" He let up and embraced her

with a kiss. "So that's how it's going to be?" she said. She was beginning to wish she *had* used the two-finger snore-stop method, but she would have to think of a better approach by which she could play in a game of strategy.

"I was just kidding about the video," he confessed.

"Too late, pal," she said. "All I can say is that I am gettin' *even*. You know what they say about paybacks." She rolled over to grab her coffee from the nightstand, showing off her long legs and slender body in her tank top and sleep shorts. With her coffee in hand, she walked around the edge of the bed and sat next to him. She took a sip before she attempted to smooth down her hair with her hands, as if it was at all possible to look decent.

Michael just smiled and shook his head.

CHAPTER
Twenty-five

The grand tour proceeded through Colorado's crown jewel, Rocky Mountain National Park, established in 1915. They drove the 48-mile Trail Ridge Road, the highest continuous paved highway in the United States and a destination spot all in its own. From Estes Park, they rose in elevation over 4,500 feet to its highest point on the road at 12,183 feet above sea level.

White Buffalo served as tour guide along that part of the ride. "Long before the white man came, the Arapaho people carved this route from the mountains to the hunting grounds in the east. They called it the Dog Trail. The highest ridge is named, 'Taienbaa,' which means 'Where the Children Walked' because the terrain is so steep that women could not carry their children, who had to climb by themselves. In honor of Gaston, I declare a new name, 'Where the Nose Bleeds.'"

"I am so deeply honored, my Indian friend," Gaston said, laughing with everyone.

On the mountaintop, the wind was brisk and the temperature 40 degrees colder than where they left town at noon. They only brought sweaters with them, and did not spend much time outside the van taking photos throughout Rocky Mountain National Park, which contained 95% wilderness area.

They stopped at several vista points along Trail Ridge Road to photograph the rugged eastern and western slopes of the Continental Divide, where rivers and streams flow to the Pacific Ocean on the west, and to the Atlantic Basin on the east. The snow-covered peaks soared high into Colorado's blue skies, above the deep and heavily forested evergreen valleys below, which was home to elk, mule deer, bighorn sheep, bobcat, moose, fox, otters, marmot, pika, and various bird species.

For eleven miles, they drove above timberline, where the multi-colored quilt of ground-hugging alpine tundra, similar to the tundra in Alaska and Canada, had a growing season of only forty days per year. Signs warned visitors to walk only on the designated trails, for any damage to the tundra growth took decades to repair. Depending on where they stopped at the turnouts along the road, they could see primarily the plains of the Front Range to the east, and Wyoming to the north. A month later, in mid October, the road would close down for the winter season, for well over twenty feet of snow would accumulate over the next several months.

On their way down to Grand Lake, they came across a herd of bighorn sheep. Sam stopped while the herd made its way across the road, giving everyone a close and personal look, nearly eye to eye, with a few adult males taking their time to catch a bite next to the van. Each one weighed about 300 pounds, standing four feet high with their big spiral horns.

"That is not something you'll see in Bali. Right, Lestari?" Michael said, noticing her wide eyes as she pointed her camera directly at a bighorn that stood outside her window.

"Yes, but we do have whales and sharks," she responded.

As they descended into lower elevations, they marveled at full mountainsides of brilliant gold aspen trees shimmering like golden coins backlit by the afternoon sun. The group wore Sam out, requesting he stop every quarter mile or so for another photo op.

By dinnertime, they arrived at Grand Lake, the largest and deepest natural lake in Colorado. There they settled for the night at Spirit Mountain Ranch, a popular bed and breakfast. At the Grand Lake Brewing Taphouse, they enjoyed dinner and many samplings of genuine Colorado brews. Sam decided to join them that evening for a burger and a handcrafted beer.

The waiter delivered beers to the group, and finished with White Buffalo. "Here you go, sir, a Virgin Bloody Mary."

"Thank you," White Buffalo said. "Occasionally, I have to be true to my Catholic upbringing from the Mission school - you know, the virgin-thing."

Markos raised his beer stein. "To the virgin thing."

Everyone laughed and raised their glasses. "The virgin thing!" they said.

White Buffalo quickly segued to pass the buck to Anja. "Dear, so it is now your turn. Tell us something about yourself that we don't know."

"Alright," Anja said. "I am not a virgin."

The group roared with laughter. "We have a winner!" Michael said.

"Oh, dear me," Anja said, wiping away a tear of laughter. "And I am only drinking water!"

"It's alright," White Buffalo said, "we teetotalers must keep these people on their toes. Please continue."

Well, to begin – I am from Senegal, a country in West Africa, which is predominantly Muslim. I am married to a man named Ibrahim, who also has another wife, named Bintou."

"Good gracious," Darius said. "I had a full-time job with just the one!"

"If you ask me," Anja said, "I believe women should have more than one husband – just to keep things balanced." All the women at the table agreed, while Anja showed her big grin. "Ibrahim and I work in art and trade. We live several places in the world - Senegal, New York City, London, and San Diego. Bintou lives in Senegal."

"Well, that is quite a convenient arrangement, now isn't it?" Shoshana said, giggling.

"Yes!" Anja said with a satisfied smile. "Ibrahim and I work art fairs, selling handmade African crafts in United States and London. During our travels, we also purchase clothing and art designs that our company can reproduce. We take them back to Senegal when we travel there at least twice each year. Bintou directs our sixty-person community that mass-produces these items for distribution around the world."

"How creative! Someday we must come and visit," Sophia said.

"I had not thought of it until now," Anja said, "but we could make beads for your jewelry - even silver and gold beads at a much cheaper cost to you. They are very fine craftspeople. We can plan your visit when Ibrahim and I will be there."

"Make sure Bintou is there so we can meet your other third," Michael said, smiling.

"Wouldn't that be fun?" Sophia said. "It will be quite an adventure! We *have* talked about taking a trip to Egypt. We could come to Senegal, and then go on to tour the Egyptian temples. Michael hasn't been there for many years, and I never have been there - at least not in this lifetime." Sophia gave them wry smile.

As the waiter brought coffee and dessert, Yesinia spoke. "I will go next. I am from Peru. My brother, Juan Carlos and I have a touring business in Lima. We offer tour packages throughout Peru, starting in Lima, where we fly to Arequipa. On the way, we take an aerial excursion over some of the Nazca Lines, which are best seen from a plane. From Arequipa, we then go onto Colca Canyon, an ancient canyon beautifully terraced for farming that was sculpted before the Incas. Oftentimes, we see the largest flying bird in the world, the Giant Andean Condor.

"Then we travel to Lake Titicaca on the edge of the Andes Mountains. It is the largest freshwater lake in South America, and the highest navigable lake in the world, where many Incan ruins are nearby. A few years ago, divers discovered a large temple, 50 meters by 200 meters, at the bottom of the lake, which is about 1,000 feet deep."

"I read about that," Shoshana said. "Isn't the temple something like 1,500 years old?"

"Yes," Yesinia said. "That would be before the Inca period. Archaeologists believe it may have been built by the Tiwanaku people."

"Michael," Shoshana said, "there is our next project."

"I'll bring my snorkel and fins," Michael said.

Yesinia continued, "From there, we go on to Cuzco to see Incan ruins and the Sacred Valley of the Incas, and then on to Machu Picchu. Along the way, we enjoy the wonderful hospitality in each city with its delicious Peruvian food, the incredibly warm and loving people who sell their crafts, and many sites at each stop. We offer cruises to the Galapagos, and tour packages that cross the Andes into the Amazon. There is never a day without adventure, and we meet hundreds of people from all over the world."

"I want to take one of your tours," Ananta said. "I am from India and would love to see South America."

"We will give you the special friend and family discount," Yesinia said. "We also offer trips to São Paulo and Rio de Janeiro, two of South America's must-see cities."

"I am very interested in Peru," Ananta said. "Tell us about one of your favorite ventures."

"Oh, let me think," Yesinia said, pausing for a few moments. "Okay, yes, you will like this story. One time, while we were leading a tour, we stopped for two days at Lake Titicaca, and I receive news of a friend who died unexpectedly. I needed some quiet time to get away from our group and grieve. It was a moonless night, and quite late. I stood at the shoreline, which was almost completely dark, and I look up at the stars. For many centuries at Lake Titicaca, there are folktales of sightings of peculiar objects in space that are not of this world. And I have to say, perhaps I am one who has seen such a thing."

"What was it?" Ananta asked.

"Well, I was so sad to lose my friend," Yesinia said, "and so I spoke out loud and asked her why she died. Then, I saw the most wondrous comet, or so it seemed. It flew from right to left, parallel to the surface of the lake, and very low in the sky. You know how big and bright Venus can get in winter? Well, this light was ten times that size, and much more brilliant - a fireball flying across the heavens. From where I stood, the fireball slowly faded out when it reached the north side of the lake. Then it came to me that it may have been my friend, because she was so fiery, with energy that never seemed to stop. At that point, I heard her voice. She said to me in Spanish, 'Yesinia, I am fine. Go on to live your life. Know that I am happy.' I was finally at peace, and whether or not that shooting star was her, I will never forget how its light healed me."

Everyone looked at each other with a sense that something otherworldly had passed between them.

"I believe Peru goes on all of our lists of places to see," Ananta said.

"Indeed," Gaston said. "Perhaps a wonderful prospect for the next gathering of Apeiros . . ."

Early the next morning, following breakfast, the tour headed southbound to I-70, which took them west, where they stayed at the Glenwood Hot Springs Lodge. They enjoyed the natural thermal hot springs in the cool afternoon autumn temperatures. Even though it was late afternoon with steam billowing everywhere, Darius, Gaston, and White Buffalo wore their sunglasses as they soaked in the healing waters and checked out the views at the pool. Darius and Gaston enjoyed a lovely Stranahan's single malt, while White Buffalo sipped on a Shirley Temple.

A stunning young woman walked by and smiled as she slowly sat at the edge of the pool and dipped her feet into the 90-degree water. The boys' heads turned together, White Buffalo peering over his sunglasses.

"Thank the Lord I shall never be too old to appreciate breathtaking scenery," Darius said.

"Please, God," Gaston said. "I shall be forever in your service if you choose not to strike me blind at this very moment."

White Buffalo just nodded, quite satisfied. "The Ute people, who ranged through these mountains, called these springs 'Yampah.' It means 'big medicine.' I don't know about you, but I feel pretty good right now."

Christofer and Markos also enjoyed the scenery, but they were even more intrigued by the 405-foot-long pool that came from natural underground springs. There were fifteen healing minerals in the 3.5 million gallons of hot water that flowed through the one million-gallon pool every day. The 122-degree mineral water, mixed with fresh water before it reached the pool, cooled to a luxurious temperature of 90 degrees.

"Our volcanic heated pools in Santorini are

wonderful," Markos said, "but this is so magnificent."

"Indeed," Gaston said, still hiding behind his sunglasses. "Magnificent."

"I'm talking about the pool," Markos said.

Christofer looked around and put his hands out, framing the pools. "I can envision something like this back home."

"As can I," Markos said. "Indeed . . ."

That night, they all enjoyed another wonderful Rocky Mountain dinner and discussed the next route they would take through the Colorado Mountains, while visiting many picturesque sites along the way. They would have to wait to visit some of Colorado's finer locations another time, like Telluride, the Great Sand Dunes, and the Colorado National Monument - a mini version of the Grand Canyon - for they only had a few days to take it all in.

"Another time we could all gather in New Mexico to visit Taos, Santa Fe, and Chaco Canyon," Michael said. "Or we could charter a longer bus tour and visit a number of sites like Monument Valley, Bryce Canyon and Zion National Park, and another wondrous site - Antelope Canyon. I know you have all seen the photos of the red Navajo sandstone sculpted by flash floods. From any of those sites we could go on to the Grand Canyon. From there we could head west to Lake Mead and Hoover Dam, and end up in Las Vegas, where we could fly back to our individual destinations."

"There are so many places to gather," Gaston said. "We have already thought of going to Peru. Another idea would be to cruise along the Black Sea, stopping in Constanta, Irina's territory. I suppose we will never be without places to visit."

Toward the end of dinner, Michael stood while their servers brought in champagne and some sparkling apple cider for White Buffalo and Anja.

"What is the occasion?" Darius asked.

"I have an announcement to make," Michael said. "After all these years, I am the happiest of men finally to announce that Sophia has agreed to marry me!"

Everyone cheered with hugs all around. Darius even dabbed a few tears of joy.

"A toast! To my lovely Sophia!" Michael said, raising his glass. They all lifted their glasses toward her and took a sip. "And furthermore, you, our dearest friends and family, will be our guests. We will marry during this time together, but the destination is a secret. Only White Buffalo and I know when and where the wedding will take place. For once, Sophia has no say in the matter, except, of course, to say I do."

"And I did!" Sophia said, nodding her head and grinning from ear to ear. "I knew you two were up to something. Well, I can't wait. Everywhere we go now, I will be wondering if that is THE place."

White Buffalo sat peacefully still, watching everyone at the table, especially taking in the joy between Sophia and Michael.

The next day, the van left at 10 a.m. and drove through Carbondale, Paonia, and on to Delta in the western region of the state. They stopped for a snack at a drive-through to eat on the van, and in the late afternoon, they arrived in Ouray, nestled among some of the most lofty, rugged peaks of the Rockies. The next morning, they departed early for scenic Silverton, named in the late 1800s for its rich silver mines. In Silverton, they caught the Durango and Silverton narrow gauge train in the morning, which arrived in Durango mid-afternoon. Sam drove the van to meet them there the following morning.

The train traveled along the Animas River, through wilderness areas not accessible by road. Along the way, they saw spectacular views of rich farmlands, old mining camps, and stagecoach roads of the Old West, all highlighted by aspen gold. Some of them spotted a black bear making its way down a hill, preparing for a long winter hibernation. The pinnacle of the train trip was the High Line, a shelf blasted from solid red granite to create the railway. At the time, in 1881, the construction along that section of the railroad was a prohibitive cost of $100,000 per mile. From that point on the roadbed, the Animas River dropped 400 feet down to Durango.

In Durango, that evening at dinner, the group began by reviewing the wondrous views they all witnessed that day. They then gave their attention to Ananta, who took a turn telling her story.

"I am from India," she said, "where I now live in Dharmshala, which means 'spiritual dwelling' or 'sanctuary.' His Holiness the Dalai Lama lives in Dharmshala, and I am one of his chefs."

"What? How long have you worked for the Dalai Lama?" White Buffalo asked.

"For nine months."

"Such a marvelous revelation. Why did you not tell us before?" Gaston asked.

"No one asked me," Ananta said, humbly.

"Tell us more," Irina said. "How did you come to work there?"

"Following culinary school in Chicago, I worked at an inn in Saugatuck, on the west coast of Lake Michigan. I was a sous-chef at the time, when His Holiness' assistant came to stay at the inn for a few days. The second day of his stay, the executive chef became ill and I served as the acting executive chef until he recovered. His illness is the best thing that ever happened to me." She covered her mouth and laughed with everyone.

"The meals I prepared evidently impressed him. On the last evening he spent with us, he asked to meet the chef, and when I came out of the kitchen, he applauded me. He gave me his card and asked for my phone number and email address. He seemed to be impressed that I was from India. A few weeks after this group met in Santorini, I received a call from his office, asking if I would fly to Dharmshala for a job interview to be a chef for the Dalai Lama. I could not pack fast enough. Obviously, I got the job.

"I was fortunate to have the opportunity to meet His Holiness about three months after I started working there. He asked me what else I do besides prepare meals for him and his guests. I told him about the Order of Apeiros. He was most impressed, and asked if I would be interested to meet with him again to tell him more about what we do. I already have an appointment scheduled for our chat when I return. So, I have something more to look forward to. I couldn't have a happier life."

"Well, we will want a full report from you after you meet with him," Darius said. "I think I can speak for everyone - we are quite impressed."

"Thank you, but I have done nothing. The Universe simply has smiled upon me, and I am quite a fortunate woman - greatly blessed. I cannot wait until I have the opportunity again to have an audience with His Holiness. I will certainly let you know what he has to say."

Darius had the fleeting thought that he later shared only with Sophia, for he did not want to impose on Ananta when she was still so new to her job. "I wonder if it would be possible for the Order of Apeiros to have an audience with His Holiness. There could be no better way we serve the world than to be in counsel by he who has taught the world about compassion and forgiveness." Sophia agreed to the possibility that Ananta would someday be able to make that happen.

Toward the end of the meal, Christofer walked around the table, re-filling wine glasses. "Michael, we have known you for some time, but I don't think we know many details about your past. Tell us more about your fine self."

"Well, I got my masters degree in archeology from the Australian National University. Later, I returned to earn my doctorate. While in Australia, I often went to the beach, and on one particular day, I went surfing with a couple of friends when a helicopter flew overhead. From their vantage point, they sighted an enormous great white shark not far from where we were in the water. They later reported it to be the about the size of the shark in the movie *Jaws*. They had never seen a shark that size before. Great white sharks get to about twenty feet in length, but they said this one was three or four feet longer. Don't ask me how they know that from so high above the ocean's surface.

"The Royal Australian Navy, Australia's version of the Coast Guard, soon came along announcing the shark sighting and ordered everyone to get out of the water. I've never paddled so fast. All I could hear was the infamous shark music running through my head." He got a few smiles when he mimicked the music. "Luckily for us, a good-sized wave came along and we rode it to shore.

"I guess what might interest you more is my work as an archeologist. My father worked in the same field. My mother and I traveled with him to live wherever a grant enabled him to work. I have seen every continent, with the exception of Antarctica, and many of the excavation sites that most people are familiar with, such as Giza, the Great Sphinx, and the city of Thebes in Egypt. I have studied many of the temples in Mexico, some in Asia, Turkey, and the Middle East. My parents either worked or vacationed all over North, Central, and South America. Throughout their prime, they saw far more historical sites and temples than I ever have."

"Then how did you come to meet Sophia in Colorado?" Darius asked.

"My dad taught at the University of Colorado during my high school days, where I met and nurtured a large crush on her for three years."

"Yeah, it was more like a large crush on my feet. He took me to prom and stepped on my toes for three hours," Sophia said.

"Ah, yes," Darius said. "I believe that was your romance number one?"

"It was," Michael said. "I did my undergraduate work at C.U., which began that long journey Sophia and I took in and out of each others' lives. As I became more mature, I developed a greater appreciation for the skills it took to create and build incredible ancient structures. One of my favorite places is Petra, in Jordan, once a primary trading center, with its ornate detail both carved and built out of sandstone. Only 15% of the city has been unearthed, with so much more history left for discovery.

"The ornate temples of Palenque, in Mexico, are an incredible sight, as they were not built with metal tools. The design precision is quite astounding. There, hundreds of temples remain in the jungle, not yet revealed. Yesinia - you know this one well - to me, one of the most interesting sites is in the Sacred Valley of the Incas, near Cuzco, Peru. The stones of many walls meet perfectly together with no use of mortar. The builders rounded off each stone surface, leaving no sharp edges.

"Like you, Yesinia, in many of these ancient places, I too have seen light-beings and felt a presence that is not of this world. It is as if the Ancients carved their mystical world into the rock. Now, it seems, some people are able to tap into the mystery they left behind.

"I was once alone in Teotihuacan, late at night, long after it closed. I had a sense to remain there for some reason beyond what my logic told me, and what I experienced I will never forget. I felt compelled to climb to the top of the Pyramid of the Moon and soon felt an energy envelope me that took me into an entirely different level of awareness -

and no, I was not doing mushrooms or any form of hallucinatory drug. If anything, I was dehydrated," he said, laughing at himself.

"But, instead of telling you about it, I would rather have you experience it yourselves. White Buffalo and I have a surprise for all of you. When we get there, I hope to create an experience similar to the one I had when I was in Mexico. Are you game?"

They all agreed, always ready to try something new.

"One thing you all may not know about Michael," Sophia said, proudly, "he has written twenty-seven books, all on his vast knowledge of archaeology."

"Really! Why did you not tell us this?" Darius asked.

"No one asked," Michael said, smiling at Ananta.

"He never toots his own horn," Sophia said. "He lectures all over the world. You probably are not aware that he is also an architect. So, his knowledge of how the ancient temples were constructed helps him to better teach about the Ancients' mindset when they built their temples and villages."

"The Ancients *are* quite intriguing," Michael said. "None of the buildings constructed today would last hundreds of years - or thousands, for that matter. Did you know that in the United States today, the construction of many public buildings is intended to only last for fifteen years? With the western need for immediate gratification, we always seek something new. Contractors build semi-permanent structures out of cheap materials, sometimes out of coated Styrofoam, for easy destruction when the style of the architecture phases out and its popularity wanes. New buildings in contemporary designs then rise with the same premise in mind. It is such a waste of talent and money, but that is the way of our society today. Okay, I will now get down off my soap box."

"You know, if you went ahead with your hip replacement surgery, it might be a whole lot easier for you to get down," Sophia said, smiling at him with a reprimanding look.

"Ah," Gaston said. "I *have* noticed a slight hitch on your get-along."

Michael sighed. "Too many years climbing ruins and digging on my knees. That, and pick-up games of basketball wherever I could find one."

"You should treat your body as your temple," Ananta said. "It might be time to see a doctor?"

"Thank you," Michael said. "My bride-to-be reminds me every day."

"He's a big baby," Sophia said. "Whenever we talk about him getting surgery, he changes the subject."

"So, what's the plan for tomorrow?" Michael said.

They discussed the agenda for the next couple of days and concluded their meal with homemade ice cream served on warm brownies, accompanied by a good, hot cup of coffee.

CHAPTER
Twenty-six

The next morning, Sam drove the group to Mesa Verde National Park, a designated World Heritage Site and the largest archeological preserve of ancient Native American cliff dwellings in the United States. White Buffalo knew one of the park rangers, who agreed to take them on a private guided tour of a few of the better-known dwellings. White Buffalo also had a secret ulterior motive, for he had long harbored a strong intuitive hit that his friend might be a perfect match for Irina.

Sam checked everyone into the Far View Lodge, so their bags would be in their rooms when they returned that evening before dinner. In order to maintain the tranquil atmosphere of the sacred park, the group requested that none of the rooms had TVs or phones. Every room had a balcony with grand vistas of Colorado, New Mexico, or Arizona. They all looked forward to stargazing with no city lights to impede the view.

After the group ate a quick lunch, they met at the Chapin Mesa Archeological Museum, where they looked over the exhibits and watched an informative video of an overview of the park. Afterwards, they bought tickets to tour Cliff Palace and Balcony House, lead by White Buffalo's park ranger friend. Outside the museum, White Buffalo made the introductions.

"This is my good friend, Chayton Blackwood, who will be our tour guide for the next couple of days. He is a fellow Lakota, who I met many years ago at a speaking engagement and found common ground through our Native American blood. We have remained in contact ever since."

"Blackwood," Darius said. "If I am not mistaken, that is Scottish?"

"It is," Chayton said. He stood six feet tall, with striking dark Lakota features and long thick straight black hair braided down his back. If Irina wasn't interested, White Buffalo would have no trouble recruiting any of the other six women in the group. "My mother is full-blooded Lakota, and my father's grandmother was Oglala, but my grandfather was a true Scotsman from Edinburgh."

"Chayton, we have two archeologists in our group," White Buffalo said. "Shoshana is the lead archeologist at the reveal of Akrotiri, in Santorini, Greece, and Michael is both an archeologist and an architect."

"Ah, Shoshana, I have heard of the work you are doing in Akrotiri. It is on my bucket list to visit."

"You must let me know when you are coming, and I will personally tour you through parts of Akrotiri, not open to the public," Shoshana said. "Christofer, Markos, and I all live on the island, and we would be happy to have you as our guest."

"Indeed," Markos said. "You are welcome to stay with me. I am sure you know that the cave homes go back to the days of what we know as Akrotiri. The cave home I live in is around 1,000 years old."

"Is that right?" Chayton said. "I have read much about the Santorini caves."

"Christofer owns a boutique hotel with 25 refurbished historic cave homes in northern Santorini," Markos said. "You must promise to come and visit. You, more than most, will have a great appreciation for the island and its history."

Michael curiously looked at Sophia, who stared dreamily at Chayton. "Honey? You look like you're drifting off in one of those flashbacks. You ok?"

She sighed at Chayton. "Oh, I'm having a dream alright..."

Chayton turned to Michael. "Michael O'Hara, I recognize you. I have attended many of your lectures. I hope we can talk in greater detail when the tour is finished."

"Absolutely," Michael said. "You've met Sophia MacPhaidin Delacroix Delaney Gallagher?"

"Hello, Sophia. That's quite a mouthful. You must have quite the challenge signing checks," Chayton said.

Sophia knew she said something, but it was unintelligible. Then, she just giggled.

White Buffalo had one more introduction to make. "I would especially like you to meet Irina, from Constanta, Romania. Chayton is fluent in every Romance language, including Romanian. Something tells me you two should get to know each other."

White Buffalo walked over to Irina and winked. He took her by the shoulder and guided her to stand directly in front of Chayton. He could not have been more obvious as a matchmaker, getting a few grins from others in the group.

Chayton spoke to Irina in Romanian. "Constanta - I have been there - a lovely city. It is a pleasure to meet you, Irina. When we are finished here, I would like to hear more about your country."

"I would be happy to tell you." Irina blushed and found herself immediately enraptured by his charm. She quickly made a personal assessment of herself. Rarely did she show emotion when meeting someone new. Every year she met hundreds of people in her job, but there was something unique about this man, and she was intrigued.

Chayton slightly smiled and then turned his attention back to White Buffalo. "Since I am your guide here, I guess I should start guiding."

"Lead on, bwana," White Buffalo said. As they began to walk, he gave Irina a gentle shove toward Chayton. Embarrassed, she slapped his hand away.

"Very subtle," Michael whispered.

"To begin," Chayton said, "I have worked here for eighteen years, and while park rangers do not make much money, I love it here and have a very satisfying life. I think of myself as one of the keepers of this historic site. I help to educate visitors, hopefully to leave them with a lasting impression and appreciation of the history of Mesa Verde and its people."

"I am curious," Gaston said. "If you do not mind my asking, what education is required to be a park ranger?"

"Dear brother," Darius said, "are you thinking of a new

career when you sell your antique store and retire?"

"No, I was thinking of you. I thought you might fit in here since you are old enough to be a part of Mesa Verde's ancient history."

Chayton laughed. "Well, I-" He stopped short when White Buffalo 'accidentally' bumped Irina into him. "Oh, excuse me."

"My bad," White Buffalo said. He winked at Irina and tossed his head toward Chayton several times. Irina's face turned multiple shades of red, as she gave White Buffalo a stare and clumsily retreated to the back of the group.

Gaston continued, "As I was asking - before I was so rudely interrupted - I am always impressed that park rangers are so well-spoken and well-educated."

"Well, what did you expect," Darius said, "Yogi Bear?"

"Of course not. It is just that Chayton said rangers don't earn a high wage, which to me is an anomaly considering the level of education they must achieve to speak with such authority about a marvelous historical site like this."

"Your question, Gaston, is actually a common curiosity of tourists," Chayton said. "It seems to some that this is an easy job, but there is more to what we do that people do not realize. A general park ranger must have at least a bachelor's degree in one of a variety of areas relative to the numerous jobs in the park service. Some people have a degree in forestry, horticulture, archeology, anthropology, sociology, or many other related areas."

"That is impressive," White Buffalo said. "Isn't that impressive, Irina? Irina? Where did she go?"

"She's hiding behind me," Sophia said, rolling her eyes at White Buffalo.

Michael joined in. "Where did you study, Chayton?"

"Well, additional training is required for the jobs in National Park Service. I majored in history and secondary school education as an undergrad at North Dakota University. I taught history at a high school on the Rosebud reservation for a few years, and then I earned my M.S. in American Indian Studies with an emphasis on Tribal Leadership and Governance at Arizona State. A good majority of us who work here have at least a master's degree."

"Splendid," Darius said. "And what a marvelous classroom this is."

"It takes a certain type of person to commit to this kind of work," Chayton said. "It is not just a summer job for a college student looking to make a few dollars working outdoors. Our student interns take their work very seriously. Park rangers are committed to the numerous levels of service we provide. It is satisfying to educate people from around the world about Mesa Verde, where the indigenous people who lived here were creative innovators from the time they were hunter/gatherers, to later as they evolved into successful farmers."

"Who were the people that lived here?" Anja asked.

"That will be a lesson for tomorrow during the grand tour," Chayton said with a laugh. "We don't have enough time this afternoon to cover the many civilizations that dwelled here, but I will tell you a bit about Spruce Tree House, which we can see from here. It is the third largest cliff dwelling on the site, with 130 rooms and 8 kivas."

"What is a kiva?" Ananta asked.

"Kivas are round subterranean ceremonial rooms, built three to four feet into the ground with brick and mortar walls slightly extended above ground level. The ceilings were finished off with horizontal logs and small timber placed on top of the walls to cover the round room below. The builders mudded the log surface with adobe to seal it off. An open door at the top allowed ventilation for when a fire was set inside. The door also provided access to and from the subterranean room with the use of a ladder. The year-round temperature in the kiva is 50 degrees Fahrenheit, leaving the atmosphere cool during the summer months. In winter, it took only a small fire to heat the space. We think 30 to 80 people lived in here. Unfortunately, we are currently unable to go through Spruce Tree House, due to rockslides, but you will discover as we tour through the park, it is one of the better preserved cliff dwellings in the entire area."

"Now that it is after 3:00, it is too late to tour the cliff dwellings," White Buffalo, said. "We will meet back here again at 9:00 in the morning, and Chayton will guide us through the major sites of the park. And Chayton - I promise not to be on Indian time." Chayton smiled at White Buffalo with a knowing glance.

"Indian time?" Irina said.

"Late," Michael said, draping his arm around White Buffalo. "It is also known in my culture as 'Sophia Time.'"

White Buffalo chuckled with a shrug. He then turned his attention back to the group. "Sam already checked you into your rooms, so you can return to the hotel, or if you would prefer, you can take the walking trails to see many of the archeological sites in the park that do not require a guide. We will join for dinner at the hotel at 7:00, white man time." Everyone laughed. "Irina, I think it is your turn tonight to tell us your story."

"Yes," she said, glancing at Chayton, who smiled back.

"Chayton," White Buffalo said, "will you join us for dinner?"

"Oh, well yes, thank you."

White Buffalo turned to join the group as they walked toward the van. He nudged Chayton in the ribs and chuckled . . .

That evening, everyone gathered at the Metate Room Restaurant. They sat at a long table along a curved window that overlooked the peaceful sprawling plains in sunset colors of gold, persimmon, shadowy heather, and smoky mauve. Sophia looked out, envisioning the ancient Anasazi people who once roamed this land by the thousands. She took in the vision, ever grateful and amazed that she could witness both the future and the past.

They passed menus around just as Chayton joined them. He took the last seat available, smiling at Irina sitting across from him. "I apologize for being late. I guess I am the one on Indian time."

"Not at all," Markos said. "Did we mention we have a custom of passing the check to the last one to arrive?"

"Did I mention that park rangers are not paid well?"

Chayton said. Markos laughed and playfully pointed at him. Chayton had shed the ranger's uniform and instead he wore a sports jacket, woolen slacks, white shirt and bolo tie with a large turquoise slide.

Sophia noticed his boots. "Chayton, your boots are exquisite. Where did you get them?"

"Oh, thank you. These are custom made by an old Navajo man in Mancos, not far from here." He looked at Irina and caught her admiring more than just his boots.

She pointed at his tie. "I love that stone."

"Oh, this – it is turquoise – a Navajo thing, too. You cannot live around here if you do not own any turquoise." The waiter arrived to pour wine and take their orders.

White Buffalo then lifted his Paloma Fizz and proposed a toast. "We welcome our guest, my good friend – my brother - Chayton Blackwood, we are all in the circle of life together, Aho, Mitakuye Oyasin."

Everyone toasted by touching glasses and speaking the sacred Lakota words, "Aho, Mitakuye Oyasin," meaning *All my relations.*

"Aho, thank you," Chayton said.

White Buffalo turned to Irina. "Irina, while we wait for our food, how about you tell us an unusual tale about yourself."

"Oh, I have been trying to think of what to say," she said. "I cannot top what Ananta told us last night, but thirty years ago my brother, Gabriel, and I represented Romania in the 1984 Summer Olympics."

Everyone at the table looked at each other, obviously

impressed. "Oh, okay," Michael said, "I'm glad you could at least come up with *something*."

"Irina!" Ananta said. "How extraordinary!"

"My dear girl," Darius said, "what were your events?"

"Gabriel was a weightlifter, and I was on the swimming team. At the time, he was twenty-one and I was seventeen. Ever since we were children, we trained most every day, and over the years, we both won many awards, but neither of us was fortunate enough to win an Olympic medal. We were expected to return four years later, but Gabriel had different plans."

"You did not compete in the next Olympics?" Chayton asked.

"No, we – shall I say – took a different path. We lived in Constanta, which is the largest port on the Black Sea. Romania was under a communist dictatorship back then, and Gabriel always told my mother and me that there would come a day when he would be gone. He would just disappear. We would not know when or how, so that the authorities would not hold us responsible.

"On one freezing cold winter night, I sensed I must go to Gabriel's apartment. He had been acting strangely, and I knew something was not quite right. Just as I was walking up the stairs, he came out of his apartment in a hurry, carrying a large duffle bag. He was dressed in black, and he never dressed like that. I begged him to tell me where he was going, and I refused to allow him to leave until he did. He confessed that he was defecting – with the help of a friend, he was going to stow away on a freighter bound for Greece."

"My word," Gaston said. "What did you do?"

Irina shrugged. "I don't know what came over me, but I said I wanted to go with him. I had never seriously considered defection, but Gabriel was obsessed with the idea since spending those three weeks in Los Angeles at the Olympics. I briefly hesitated in going, because our poor mother would feel abandoned and left to question what happened to both of her children, but she once told us, if we ever had the opportunity to flee, we should take it.

"He didn't hesitate to take me with him, but he warned that it would be very dangerous – and terribly cold. I was dressed warmly, and he told me we would escape with just the clothes on our backs and what little supplies he had in his bag. We lived very close to the port, so we tiptoed along the sides of buildings to the edge of the pier where the freighter was docked. I remember it was snowing very hard, but that was to our advantage, for it was more difficult to see or hear us in the darkness. In the shadows of the ship, he told me to take off all my clothes - to strip naked-"

"Oh, my God," Sophia said, "whatever for?"

"We were going in the water," Irina said. "It was the only way we could board the ship undetected. He had a large can of heavy black grease in his duffel bag."

"Ah, yes," White Buffalo said. "You greased your bodies to protect you from the freezing water."

"Yes. So, we wrapped our clothing in plastic and packed it in the duffel bag. Then we greased our bodies, which also helped to camouflage ourselves in the black water. He handed me his black swim cap to put over my hair."

"Ah, a gallant man," Anja said, laughing.

Irina laughed. "Well, his head was shaved, so he could grease it for protection. So, then we did it – we jumped into the water."

"It must have still been quite a shock when you hit that water," Michael said.

"Oh, yes! It was so cold, but the grease did help create a barrier so our bodies would better retain heat. It was a good thing that I sometimes trained in the icy waters, or I do not think I could have done it. By then, our hearts were racing and we were so afraid – I think that made me forget about how cold I was."

"How did you get aboard?" Chayton asked.

"Gabriel, who is a big, very strong man, hauled the wet duffle bag on his back, and we swam to a point near the back of the ship, where a sailor friend of Gabriel's was waiting. He threw a rope ladder over the side, and we climbed up – just like that."

Markos laughed and snapped his fingers. "Just like that! In a blinding snowstorm, in frigid, icy water, buck naked and covered in Crisco, you hopped a freighter bound for Greece!"

"That is most remarkable," Darius said.

"By the time we climbed onto the deck, it was about 2:00 a.m., and everyone on board was asleep, except for the night watch – Gabriel's friend. He led us down to the ship's hold, which was stacked high with thousands of big bags of cement mixture on wooden pallets. We dried off, cleaning off as much grease as possible, and then we put on our dry clothes, coats, hats, shoes and gloves. We tied bandanas over our nose and mouth to protect us from breathing in the cement dust.

"We waited until the ship left port before we climbed over the bags of cement to the back of the hold, away from both the hatch and the doorway. Gabriel lifted those hundred-pound cement bags as if they were filled with feathers, building a little fortress just wide enough for us to hide inside. We sat on the cement bags instead of sitting on the cold metal floor."

"Hardly five-star accommodations," Gaston said. "And we thought the Lodge at Estes Park was inadequate. I don't suppose you had room service either?"

"Gabriel brought a flashlight and extra batteries, some bologna sandwiches, a thermos of hot coffee, a liter of water, and homemade cookies!"

Everyone laughed. "My gosh," Sophia said, "he thought of everything!"

"Oatmeal," Irina said, "which happened to be my favorite. Of course, he only packed food for himself, but my big brother generously shared. I remember one time, we heard someone moving about. Gabriel shut off the flashlight when he heard the metal door swing open. We were silent - barely breathing. After some time, Gabriel climbed out of our cement fort and crawled over the stacks of cement to the same doorway. To our relief, the visitor was Gabriel's friend, who left two wool blankets and a paper bag with four apples and some cheese. It seemed as if we were in that dark cold cargo hold forever, waiting for the ship to arrive in Athens."

"How long did it take?" Ananta asked.

"I'm not really sure. It must have been around 24 hours, for the ship docked at night, and we were not aware of the time until we came up on the deck after being in port for at least an hour. We were able to disembark without anyone seeing us. When we walked away from the dock to where more people were moving about, we quickly noticed how they stared at us as if they had seen a ghost. We looked at each other and could only laugh, because we were completely light gray, covered in cement dust. We truly did look quite ghostly. It was such a relief to finally arrive in Greece, where we were free for the first time in our lives. Feeling such relief, all we could do was laugh and cry!"

"Such a remarkable story," Shoshana said. "Here we all have spent many hours together in our past gatherings without really knowing who we are."

"So curious," White Buffalo said. "You defected, but you now live back in Romania?"

"Yes, I suppose it is the full circle of life," Irina said. "We defected in 1986. We sought asylum at the U.S. consulate in Athens, and they helped us immigrate to America. From Athens, we flew to Florida and then later to New York. We were able to connect with others from our country who had established themselves in Manhattan. Gabriel became a U.S. citizen and is now married, a father of three, and a successful owner of a gym, where he trains athletes. He never returned to Romania, but after the revolution of 1989, I did go back, for our mother was quite elderly. I took care of her until she passed on. While I love America and am grateful for the freedom it offered, Romania is my home, and I wanted to stay after we became free."

"What do you do there now?" Shoshana asked.

"I'm the Head Concierge at the Hotel International in Constanta. I am a member of Les Clefs d'Or, a worldwide organization for professional concierges. I have worked at the hotel for many years and have met some very interesting people. Through Les Clefs d'Or, I have been able to travel throughout the world."

"Who was your most interesting guest?" Lestari said.

"Oh, there are so many. One time, I took care of two children of a very wealthy man from Saudi Arabia. The father was in Constanta on business, and I took care of two of his children for the day, or I should say, I came along for the ride. We had a limousine for the day, and along with the driver, we had two bodyguards, each one bigger than a house. One of them was from Saudi Arabia, and the other was originally a member of the IRA in Northern Ireland. I could not get a smile out of either of them. I must say they were two frightening personalities!"

"I have had middle eastern royalty stay at my hotel in Oia," Christofer said. "Our little island turns into a fortress – some say a prison – whenever they visit."

"Oh, yes," Irina said. "We had a lead car ahead of us with two men from the Romanian Intelligence Service. They communicated with us by car phone - there were no cell phones in those days. Both bodyguards and the two men in the car ahead of us carried guns, of course. Before we left the hotel, I was required to sign a release, saying that if the limousine was attacked, the children would be taken away in the lead car, and I would be left behind. If I happened to be killed, my family could not sue the Saudi government. Of course, without much choice, I signed.

"The boys were ages ten and seven. The older one spent much time in the limo, sitting next to the male nanny, whose name was Rashid. He read the newspaper aloud to keep the boy abreast of world events, I suppose because the older boy was destined to someday be his father's successor. He could not have been more disinterested in our tour that day if he had tried. The younger boy, however, was sweet and kind.

"Rashid gave each boy the Romanian equivalent of about 500 American dollars to spend that day. The older boy spent it all on himself, but the younger one bought his mother a blue topaz ring set in gold, after which he had very little money left to spend on himself. But he was as happy as he could be. Rashid was their caretaker, nanny, their teacher, and disciplinarian - and he flirted with me the entire day." Irina giggled, a bit embarrassed.

"One could see why," White Buffalo said. He turned to Chayton. "Could you not see why, Chayton?" He looked then at Sophia's scolding eyes. "What?"

"He invited me to stay with him at the family's mansion in Switzerland," Irina said. "I finally told him I was married, but he said he had several wives and it did not matter to him."

"I have empathy for you," Anja said.

"Yes you would, wouldn't you," Irina said. "I said to him, 'So, your wives will welcome me if I come to visit you? How do you think that will that work?' – and he just laughed, but I do not think he thought I was very funny. I told him that my husband *did* matter to me, and then he complimented me and said he hoped that my husband realized what a fortunate man he was.

"The itinerary I planned had to be approved by the boys' father before we could leave. To begin with, I did not know the ages of the boys when I planned the itinerary, and most of the arrangements I made did not suit them. They traveled so much with their father, and they were soon bored by my choices, because they saw so many of the same type places wherever they traveled. So, I changed the plans the morning of our excursion while we were in the limo. Calls in Arabic went back and forth from Rashid to their father, to the lead car, and back again, before we could continue our tour. We first went to the Dolfinarium."

"The who?" Gaston said.

"It's an aquatic park," Michael said. "You know, dolphins."

"We also went to the Planetarium, the Aquarium, and the Micro Delta. At the end of the day, we went to the beach, where the boys ran around and played in the water - and *I* ran around, trying to avoid Rashid. We were busy the entire day, but I was more tired than the boys were, from fending off the nanny.

"The next morning, the assistant to their father came up to my desk in the hotel lobby and said, 'The Prince would like to know why you changed the itinerary yesterday.' I thought, *The Prince?* I hoped I had not overstepped diplomatic protocols. Until that moment, I was not aware that I toured two of the royal children of the heir to the Saudi throne. Evidently, the changes did not go over well with the boys' father. I explained that the boys were disinterested, and I wanted to be certain that they had a good time, which they did. He apparently was satisfied, because he gave me a gift of a narrow green leather box.

Inside was a 24-karat gold watch made by Queen Elizabeth's London jeweler, with the Saudi Arabian national symbol of the palm tree and two crossed swords on the watch face. I still wear it." She held up her arm to show off the impressive piece.

"As they were about to leave later that morning, the younger boy came up to me and smiled, while the older one ignored me, which was no surprise. Then, Rashid took my hand in his and kissed it, which was certainly not a common gesture in his country. Today, it is an act considered controversial. In the practice of Sufism, kissing the hand shows devotion to the inner mystical dimension of Islam. I have to say, I was flattered by his gesture. He was a very handsome man and quite charming, even though he was a wolf."

"Tell us about your husband," Lestari said.

"Oh, that! I was not married. I just needed a graceful way to avoid Rashid's advances. I have never married, but I do enjoy meeting many interesting men throughout my travels." She smiled and gazed downward to avoid looking across the table at Chayton.

White Buffalo shook his head and looked at Chayton. "Hmmm. Never married. You are a bachelor yourself, are you not?"

"Yes, my friend," Chayton said. "Something you have known for – how long have we been friends?"

Irina blushed and shook her head at White Buffalo.

"What?" he said.

"I had no idea we were all such interesting people!" Gaston said. "I know *I* certainly am. Of course, nobody has asked about *me* yet."

"With good reason, dear brother," Darius said.

"I am tired of talking," Irina said with a laugh. "I would like to hear from Lestari."

"Hear! Hear!" Christofer said.

"Alright, I will be next," Lestari said. "As you know, I am from Bali, a tiny island in Indonesia. You may not know this, but when people are born in Bali, they are given only one of four names at birth whether they are a boy or girl. The name of the first-born is Wayan. The second child's name is Made. The third is Nyoman, while the fourth child's name is Ketut. For those born in the higher caste, Putu or Gede is the name of the first-born. Kadek is the name of the second-born. Komang, for the third, and Ketut is the name for the fourth-born child, no matter which caste they come from.

"If there are more than four children, we start over and sometimes add Balik to their name, such as Ketut Balik, meaning 'another Ketut', and in that case the child would be the eighth in the family." They all laughed, enjoying her explanation. "Most of us have second and third Hindu names. My first name is Kadek, and my second name is Lestari, which means everlasting or eternal. Now that I am married, some may call me Ni Kadek, which means Mrs. Kadek. Likewise, men go by I Wayan, meaning Mr. Wayan.

"I am married to Putu Balik Darma. I call him PBD. We have two children in college, of course named Gede - a boy, and Kadek - a girl. My husband and I work for the World Wide Fund for Nature, the world's largest conservation organization. Its mission is, 'To stop the degradation of the planet's natural environment, and to build a future in which humans live in harmony with nature.' We work with the six different countries that endeavor to preserve the Coral Triangle, one of the earth's most biologically diverse and ecologically rich regions affecting millions of people's livelihood."

"Where is that?" Sophia asked.

"It covers Malaysia, Indonesia, and the Philippines, and as far east as Timor-Leste, Papua New Guinea, and the Solomon Islands. There are species of coral and marine life within the Coral Triangle that live nowhere else on the planet. The importance of my job coincides well with what we do here in Apeiros."

Just as she finished telling about herself, the food arrived and everyone dug in. The evening concluded with most everyone strolling back to their rooms.

Chayton caught up with Irina and asked if she would like to join him for a nightcap. Of course, she agreed.

In the lounge, she ordered a Prickly Pear Margarita, and he had an Avalanche Ale from the Breckenridge Brewery. They strolled out onto the deck to look at the stars. In the night air, being quite chilly, Chayton removed his jacket and placed it around Irina's shoulders.

"Thank you. We will not stay out here for long, or you will catch a chill," Irina said.

"I am quite warm. I rarely wear a jacket." They stood, looking at the stars for an uncomfortable moment. Finally, Chayton took the plunge. "White Buffalo has a big mouth, does he not?"

Irina burst into laughter. "I love him dearly, but he

embarrassed me so!"

"Do not get me wrong, I love him too, but he has all the subtlety of a charging bison."

"Bison?"

"You know-" He pointed his fingers from his head as if they were horns, "-some call them buffalo."

"Ah!" Irina said. "Buffalo - Dances with Wolves!"

"Yes!" Chayton said with a laugh. "They are actually called bison – but, I'm boring you."

"What? No!" Irina said.

"Look, White Buffalo was pushy because he treats me like a son – he always wants the best for me, and he always bothers me about the fact that I am single. I do not want you to feel like you are being pushed into getting to know me, or-"

"What is Indian time?" Irina asked.

"What?"

"Indian time. You and White Buffalo talked about it."

"Oh, that is something very few people outside of my culture understand. Native Americans did not have timepieces, nor did they comprehend the concept of time until the end of the 19th century, when they began to assimilate into the white man's world.

"Our people lived by the passing sun and moon, the changing seasons, animal migration patterns, and the shifting weather. We all retain in our cellular memory the history of our ancestors. Indian time is not a detachment from time, but rather a joining with it in the purest sense. In other words, we 'go with the flow,' which is a different way of being. What I find interesting about living without time is I tend to live more from my intuitive guidance. I do not get caught up in the effects of the world around me as much. People on Indian time do not live by expectations based on schedules."

"Oh, that is so different from the Europeans, whose lives are so attached to schedules and timetables."

Chayton agreed. "Americans, even more so. While it is in my DNA to measure time by the rising or setting sun, or the phases of the moon, I have a responsibility to my job. I give tours, lectures, attend seminars – I prefer to watch the moon, but I have to I admit that I wear a watch!"

"I come from a very strict, rigorous, scheduled background," Irina said. "You heard my story at the dinner table tonight. I cannot think of any activity I participate in where time is not important. In all my activities as a young girl, I lived by a schedule - school, studies, training and competitions. I went to sleep by the clock."

"Yes," Chayton said, "and you were a competitive swimmer, which was all about keeping time."

Irina smiled. "My job as a hotel concierge also concerns the time and schedules of hotel guests. Your concept of Indian time has me intrigued. I am not sure I would be able to live free of the clock."

"It is a different mindset. Everything I do in my work here in MesaVerde has to do with time. We begin and end our tours with very little leeway of the schedule. I have to say, the only activities where I slip back into Indian time is when I participate in Native ceremonies, where time does not exist. Perhaps, if you have an opportunity, you would like to join me during one of our ceremonies. Then you will understand."

"I am intrigued. Let me know so I will be able to find time for it," Irina said, laughing.

"Very good," Chayton said. He inched a bit closer, presumably to keep Irina warm from the chilly breeze, but they both seemed to know better.

"So, Chayton Blackwood, tell me more about yourself. Do you come here often? What is your sign? What is your favorite color? Are you married? Do you have any children?" Chayton began to laugh. "What kind of car do you drive? Do you have a felony on your record? Do you have your own teeth?"

"You *are* funny!" Chayton said. He enjoyed a challenge. He had to think fast around her, for Irina would keep him on his toes.

"I am sure White Buffalo is going to be certain I – how do they say it? – cross-examined you."

"Well, to answer your barrage of questions, in order - no, Aries, green, no, no, Jeep Cherokee, no, and yes."

She had to remember the order of her queries, and she began to laugh. "Very good! You may not know what time it is, but you do have an excellent memory. Isn't it awkward to find out some of the important details when we first meet new people? I don't have a felony either, by the way."

"That is good to know, but what about children, and are those *your* teeth?"

"No and yes, but I do have veneers, so that answer should be no *and* yes."

"Smile for me." Chayton looked into her lovely eyes. "Ahhh yes, you have beautifully perfect white teeth."

"You are not looking at my teeth."

"I do not have to, they are glaring in my eyes. So, I already know you do not come here often, but to stay on an even playing field, what about your favorite color and sign?"

"Red and Cancer."

"Good, now that we have the preliminaries out of the way, what do we do from here? I would like to get to know you better. How much longer will you be here in Colorado?"

"I thought time did not matter to you."

"Indians are flexible."

"I have four more days with the group, and I have a week after that before I must return to Romania. I planned to rent a car and drive to Taos and Santa Fe, where I will fly home from there."

"Where were you planning to get a rental car?"

"Michael is going to drive me to Boulder."

"What would you say if I drive you to Taos?" Chayton said. "I have two weeks of vacation time coming, and this is the start of our slow season. I know I can get away. Do you think Michael would be too disappointed?"

Irina giggled. "I believe he would forgive me."

"I know White Buffalo will approve."

"Oh, yes!" Irina said. "He probably will want to go with us. Well, this sounds wonderful, but it is so sudden."

Chayton looked at his watch. "Do you need time to think it over?"

"Yes," she said. "Alright, I thought about it. I accept your offer. I could use a good tour guide in Taos."

"One more thing - I don't know if you noticed, but I am quite attracted to you."

"Yes, the feeling is mutual, Chayton."

"So, Irina, may I kiss you?"

"I thought you would never ask."

He drew the tall brunette into his arms and kissed her. If the energy was visible, sparks would have lit their hair on fire.

It took a moment before it ended. "Well, then," Chayton said. "That is a good start."

"Yes, I quite agree."

They went inside and ordered two Irish coffees to warm up, and they sat talking for a couple more hours in front of the burning fireplace, getting to know one another better. Before long, they went to her room to enjoy the intimacy of each other's company. They fell asleep about 3:00 a.m. with thoughts of each other on their minds.

Chapter
Twenty-seven

The next morning's itinerary began far too early for both Chayton and Irina, who had so wished to spend more Indian time together. After getting less than three hours sleep, Chayton left her room at the lodge before dawn to shower and shave before going to work. Irina, bleary-eyed and emotionally drained, showered, dressed, and put on her face quite slowly, bolstered by a pot of rich, dark coffee delivered by room service.

When the group met for the tour, White Buffalo noticed how their eyes briefly met with a gleam that was not there the day before. His plan had evidently worked. *Great Spirit, I am good!*

"Aho, everyone," Chayton said, looking worn out but happy. "I trust you all had a good night's rest."

"I would say, most of us slept well," Lestari said under her breath, just loud enough for Irina to hear. Irina rolled her eyes in Lestari's direction.

Chayton quickly interjected, "To pick up where we left off yesterday, I will give you a short synopsis of the history here. Since around 9500 B.C.E., various indigenous people emerged here from nomadic Paleo-Indians to the Basketmaker culture, and eventually to the Ancestral Puebloans we call the Anasazi. They lived here around 750

C.E., distinguished by their inner-connected year-round dwellings, called pueblos. They were both hunter-gatherers and farmers who grew many sustainable crops of corn, beans, and squash. The population of the area, at that time, was from 1,000 to 1,500 people. Now, that sounds quite crowded, does it not?

"By 860 C.E., the population grew to approximately 8,000. They built the first rock shelters in and around the mesa and created large pit structures for central gathering places, which were the precursor to the buildings later constructed not far from here in Chaco Canyon, New Mexico. By 880, the population began to substantially decline as they immigrated south to Chaco Canyon. Over the next 400 years, people moved back and forth between Chaco Canyon and Mesa Verde, dependent upon the rainfall patterns. If the people lived in drought years, the population declined. In those of abundant rainfall, the population increased.

"Four hundred years later, they began to build substantial cliff dwellings, some of which you will see today, made of rocks about the size of a loaf of bread and held together with mortar. The park includes over 4,000 known archaeological sites, with 600 cliff dwellings. At the start of the 13th century, the population was about 22,000 people – very crowded conditions."

"Chayton," Markos said, "you mention droughts. Was that a common occurrence?"

"During the 13th century, the region experienced 69 years of below average rainfall, followed by severe cold temperatures in 1270. Tens of thousands either emigrated to what is now New Mexico and Arizona, or they died of starvation. The last inhabitants left around 1285, after 700 years of continuous human occupation in Mesa Verde."

He led them through the Cliff Palace, with 23 kivas and 121 rooms, originally with brightly painted interiors. "This is the largest of the cliff dwellings here and in North America as well. As you can see, the structure is made of sandstone, wooden beams, and mortar. They used fibrous plants to mix with the mortar, making what we now know as adobe, which is much stronger than using only dirt and water."

They walked along the trail to the nearby Sun Temple. "This was to be a ceremonial structure. It was never finished and abandoned around the late 1200s when the Anasazi left Mesa Verde. There were no timbers found here. A ceiling would have indicated a finished structure.

"I would like you to come around here to the outside of the wall. Take notice of this area that looks like a shrine with short parallel walls on the ground. In between the walls is weathered sandstone on the ground, naturally carved by the elements. It appears like a sunburst, which led to the name of the building, Sun Temple. Some archeologists believe this sandstone sunburst was a sundial."

Chayton pointed out toward the House of Many Windows. "They are actually doors instead of windows that originally would have been covered with animal skins or a stone slab. There are eleven rooms and a kiva built on a ten-foot-wide ledge. Above to the right you will see another two rooms. They used toeholds in the stone along the mesa's edge to access these rooms from the top of the above mesa.

He took them through Long House, the second largest cliff dwelling, and to the Square Tower House, the tallest structure in Mesa Verde. "We are unable to tour through this cliff dwelling, because some of the walls are quite fragile."

Lastly, they visited the Far View Sites Complex, away from the cliff dwellings. "These structures were built like those in Chaco Canyon, much like today's pueblos in Taos. This was one of the most densely populated areas, with fifty villages in a one-half square mile area. Hundreds of people lived here, two hundred years before the cliff dwellings were constructed, and many remained living on top of the mesas long afterward. The Anasazi were a developed civilization, with engineered water reservoirs and sophisticated irrigation systems for organized farming of corn, beans, and squash. They supplemented their diet with wild plants and hunted wild game."

"This area was evidently a vast trading network. Here we found Chaco-style pottery, along with macaw-feather sashes, and copper bells, none of which came from local materials. Jewelry made of shells came from the Gulf of California, along with pieces with red coral, shell, and turquoise. One unearthed black and white painted mug is the same rounded shape as the mugs we use today, with a large handle on the side of the cup.

"There are many areas we did not see, but if anyone is interested in taking any of the backcountry hikes, to get to Balcony House, you will have to walk a 100-foot stairway just to get to the start. Then you will climb a 32-foot ladder up to where you must crawl through a twelve-foot, 18-inch-wide opening to reach the cliff dwellings. There are footholds in the rocks and narrow 'hallways' to traverse. It is quite spectacular, and the altitude is at 7,000 feet. If you are interested, it is well worth the effort."

"I do believe I will pass that up," Darius said. "But, Gaston, that sounds like your cup of tea, does it not?"

"I agree," Gaston said, "it does not."

"Shhh!" Sophia scolded.

"Over there is Mug House," Chayton said, "so named because inside one of the rooms were four mugs tied together with yucca rope. It is one of the largest of the cliff dwellings, built on two ledges, with 94 rooms, a large kiva, and a nearby reservoir. You may see Mug House and Fire Temple only through a guided tour. In addition, there is Oak Tree House, Spring House, and Adobe Cave, among many other sites to see if you want to hike."

Chayton concluded the tour and opened the floor to discussion. He took the time to answer many questions, especially those from Shoshana and Michael, who never tired of visiting archeological sites. In fact, everyone asked many questions.

When their conversation was over, Michael said, "Tonight, we have a special surprise for you. Chayton is going to bring us back here after dinner when the park is closed. That is all I am going to tell you for the moment. When we come back, be sure to wear comfortable clothes and bundle up. At night, the temperature gets close to freezing this time of year . . . "

At sundown, Chayton and Sam joined the group for dinner at the Far View Lodge, where they enjoyed the flavors of fine southwestern cuisine. Throughout the meal, their conversations were rich, covering the many interesting points they learned during their tour of Mesa Verde. Chayton filled in many details he had not shared earlier that day. Shoshana and Michael made comparisons of Mesa Verde to many of the archeological sites they had worked in. She was also interested in the artifacts that were left behind in the cliff dwellings.

Michael then turned to Sophia. "Okay, Soph, it's your turn to share something we might not know about you."

She paused, looking at Michael with wide eyes. "Oh, well put me on the spot, will ya. Okay, this you might find interesting. I once went skydiving!"

"I didn't know that!" Michael said.

"Hence, your instruction to tell something you didn't know about me."

White Buffalo rubbed his chin and sipped his Roy Rogers. "That is as good as Irina stowing away on a freighter naked with grease all over her."

"That is *my* favorite," Chayton said.

"Oh, dear granddaughter," Darius said, "always full of surprises. Please, do tell."

"I always had a desire to learn how to skydive," Sophia said. "In Colorado, if you are not a certified diver, you must dive in tandem with a certified instructor. At least that was the law when I went skydiving years ago. Some of my friends, at the time, thought I *was* certifiable when I told them I was going skydiving, but I digress.

"To get certified, it costs about $1,500 for eight hours of

classroom time plus equipment. Then to complete the certification process, you must do 25 jumps. After certification, for about $25.00 each, you can skydive anywhere in the world. I first wanted to try it out before I committed my time and money.

"So, I went with a friend to a small airport on the west side of Pikes Peak in Colorado Springs. The tiny plane, completely stripped out, with the exception of the pilot's seat, had a capacity for six people. The pilot circled the plane up to 14,000 feet while we all sat on the floor. I was sitting inside the legs of my tandem instructor while being hooked together at our sides, just waiting for our turn to jump. For me, it was not about the adrenaline thrill, but more so about complete surrender. I had to let go and trust that all was well."

"Were you frightened?" Anja asked. "I would be!"

"I truly was not nervous until I saw my friend, who *was* a certified diver, jump out of the plane by himself. He just kept getting smaller and smaller as he did his freefall. Then my adrenaline kicked in. Not allowing me to panic for long, my tandem scooted us up to the open door of the plane, as I sat there with my legs dangling out the open door looking 14,000 feet below me. Yikes!

"My tandem kept talking in my left ear, instructing me about what to expect. Mostly, he told me to cross my arms and not grab the doorway on the way out of the plane; otherwise, we would tumble through the air. He was a huge man, about 6'4" tall - big like a bear. I felt very safe strapped to his body. I listened carefully to his instructions, then we jumped.

"We were almost at the same altitude as the top of Pikes

Peak. I watched the mountain rise above us as we quickly fell through the air at 120 mph – what is called 'terminal velocity.'"

"That term alone is reason for me to never try it," Christofer said.

"My tandem yelled at me to arch my back so we would more easily fall parallel to the ground, and I did. It seemed as if I could not breathe, flying at that speed. Before he pulled the ripcord, he tapped a warning on my shoulder, and then the chute came out of his pack, jolting us to 35 mph. Later, I noticed the front of my shoulders and chest had bruises from where the harness wrenched my body.

"Until we got down to a lower altitude, where we were at the same level of buildings and trees, it didn't seem like we were going very fast, but the ground was not far away. He yelled at me to land on my feet running, and so I did. Otherwise, I might have landed on my face, as did one of the other people of our group. From 14,000 feet, it took less than three minutes to reach the ground, but what an astounding few minutes it was. It was one of those experiences where time does not exist, because I was aware of every second - completely in the here and now. It is truly my favorite way of being!"

"My dear girl," Darius said, "did Patrick know you did that?"

"Oh, he knew about it," Sophia said. "That's the punch line to this. Remember I said I went with a friend? That was Daddy. He jumped out of the plane before I did!"

Darius and Gaston laughed out loud. "That *is* my Uncle Patrick!" Gaston said.

"Oh, I want to do that!" Irina said. She looked at Chayton. "Have you ever?"

Chayton laughed. "I am happy on the ground, thank you."

"It was perfect - and I have to say," Sophia said, "the thrill of it was better than an orgasm! Sorry, honey!" Sophia looked at Michael and gave him a cheesy Cheshire grin. All of them burst out laughing, catching the attention of people seated at the tables nearby.

"Well, on that note – celebrating the insanity of the white man - we should conclude dinner," White Buffalo said. "It is time to go back to the park. Let us all get our coats and hats, and meet in the lobby in fifteen minutes. Be sure to wear your aquamarine rings."

Before they left the hotel, Michael asked everyone, including Sam and Chayton, to join him and White Buffalo on the balcony, which faced south. Lit with candlelight, on one table sat a large basin filled with warm water. Michael stood on the left side of the basin, and White Buffalo stood to the right. Michael asked each person to come up and place his or her hands over the basin. To each one he said, "With this sacred element of water - the life force of the earth - you are now purified." He took a ladle made from a gourd, dipped it into the water, and poured the water over their cupped hands.

White Buffalo took their wet hands in his and dried them with a white terry cloth towel. When they finished, Michael and White Buffalo performed the same cleansing ritual for the other.

Chayton arranged to have the gate unlocked so Sam

could drive the bus to the parking area inside the park. With flashlights in hand, they walked the trail to the Cliff Palace, where they gathered around one of the kivas, facing each other.

"Please shut off your flashlights and remain still," Michael said.

The night held no moon, leaving the heavens to reach down, gently bathing them in crystalline starlight. The silence, engulfed in darkness, was pregnant with anticipated promise.

White Buffalo began to sing in Lakota, and soon, Chayton joined him. The deep resonance of their voices echoed off the rock overhang, emphasizing their prayer to Wakan Tanka - Great Spirit. Grandmother Earth held each one securely in her compassionate embrace. The Grandfathers were present and listening, while the ancestors of all time joined them in celebration. Each person communed from the heart with their own god, for never before had they felt Spirit's presence more than they did that night, which was truly Apeiros - the cause of all unity and the measure of all things. The spirit and soul of each joined in union, in the atmosphere of eternality, as the Ancients welcomed them home once again.

Michael looked up and opened his hands to the sky in a gesture of receptivity. He felt the electric energy fill his hands. The energetic power grew, surrounding him in its stimulating pulse of the earth's life force within the essence of the entire universe. He looked around the circle, barely making out each person's face in the dark, feeling great love and respect for each one of them. From deep within, Michael enveloped them within his life force energy as he felt a shift occur. All were ready, whether they were consciously aware of it or not, including Chayton and Sam.

"Everyone, place your ringed hand toward the center of the circle," Michael said. They all faced to the left with their right hands extended. "Chayton and Sam, if you choose, you may join in. Concentrate on the love you have for the world and for Grandmother Earth. Join your thoughts, feelings, and emotions, and energize that love with the Universal Intelligence to its full force. Feel that force clear down into your cellular level. See it in your mind's eye working for the good of all. Clearly know, without a doubt, that your calling of love is now a manifest reality in the lives of those you serve. Now join your energies at the center where your hands meet." He waited until he felt their energies merge as one. "Beginning with Darius, to my right, name your previous calling and feel its power within your heart as it is enjoined with Love throughout this ceremony."

Around the circle, each spoke out in turn, "Balance," "Truth," "Health," "Harmony," "Order," "Abundance," "Peace," "Oneness," "Grace," "Joy," "Beauty," "Compassion," and "Love and Absolute Awareness."

"Now, extend this love for every person standing in this circle, here within this ancient holy land," Michael said, exuding great passion. "Continue to expand that energy out to the surrounding counties throughout the Four Corners, where the four states of Colorado, New Mexico, Arizona, and Utah meet. Now include the Americas. Extend your energies to surround the Western Hemisphere. See your energy flowing through every continent on earth and every land mass, including the polar regions surrounded by the seas. You now hold your consciousness for every being that lives upon Grandmother Earth in her entirety - for every human, every four-legged being, each winged one, finned one, the creepy crawlies, all trees, plants, and every rock, sandy shore, hill, and mountain.

"You hold the universal energy for the land, sea, fire, air, and ether as you extend it out to the edge of the earth's atmosphere. Going further, include our moon and beyond to all the planets and stars in our galaxy, and as you witness the heavens above, send your energies to every star, planet, nebulae, and all the cosmos. Hold your energy there - hold the entire universe in your hearts. From this place, beginning in this moment, this is how we are to go about doing our work from the Mind of Love."

In that moment, the familiar radiance returned, beginning as a wisp of light, incrementally gaining. The illumination grew in intensity, so bright that it bathed the Cliff Palace as if the sun was shining at midday.

"Keep your eyes on the light," White Buffalo instructed. "It will not harm you, and hold your intention to keep the universe in your embrace."

With their individual concentrated energies, the light extended from their hands, meeting at the center of the circle and forming a single vertical column of light, with its central core seven feet wide in diameter.

"Remain standing with your hands toward the center," Michael said as he watched the intensity on the face of each person. "Feel the increasing life force as it flows into your crown chakra from directly above you. Grandmother Earth, whose back upon which you stand, fills you with her heartbeat. Feel that pulse continue up your legs and through your body as the two energies meet at your heart. Remember, it is the same divine energy coursing through your bodies, coming from two different sources. One is of the ethers, and the other of the earth. The life force energy pulsates from your hands, where it meets at the center of the circle, which now rises into the heavens. Keep your stance strong. Now, look up."

The light extended down through the kiva floor. All at once, the radiant shaft of light, filled with the attributes of the Divine, shot into the heavens as their own signal of starlight beamed throughout the universe from Grandmother Earth herself. Chayton smiled, witnessing the sight, while Sam caught his breath, eyes wide in total astonishment. The radiance lit up each person in the circle - body, mind, and soul.

Then they witnessed an even more astounding sight, as the heavens grew vibrantly alive. Starlight flashed throughout the skies in response. A brilliant meteor came down from the heavens, appearing as if it would strike where they stood.

"Do not move!" Michael said, with a voice of authority. "We are safe, for all is well. Stand still, anchored to the earth, right where you are."

The fiery ball of radiant light soared through the sky until it came into their vicinity. Then it stopped. Overhead, the ball of light hovered with a force of energy so bright, they could see details of the distant mesas in light and shadow. The column of light at the center of their circle then joined with the light above as it burst into a massive array in rockets of light arching down to the earth's surface.

It appeared as if the grand finale of a New Year's fireworks display combined into one single massive crystal chandelier pattern.

Everyone cheered. They all looked into the starry skies, witnessing the union of the Universe in its entirety. The memory of this night would propel each person forward, even when in their darkest of days ahead, as they knew deep into their cells that they were never alone.

As the starlight returned to its natural glow, Michael said, "We thank the heavens, all planets, and celestial bodies. We are grateful to all the Ancients, the Grandfathers, the Ancestors, and we thank God, in all the names we give It. Tonight, we welcome all souls yet to come and send them blessings, for they are already an idea in the Mind of God - that of Apeiros.

"Now, each of you send one last silent message into the heavens." A few seconds passed as the light glowed in its golden-white radiance. "Now, gently pull your hands away from the center." The light force at the center of their outstretched hands diminished to a soft glow until it left them with a feeling of love beyond comprehension.

Their evening concluded as everyone silently walked back to their rooms to sleep in the wonder of what they just witnessed, for it was an experience where heaven and Earth bathed in Love's oneness, and whether or not they were aware of it, all beings everywhere felt a vitalizing shift in the universal presence.

CHAPTER
Twenty-eight

The next morning, they overheard their breakfast servers talk about the column of light that shot into the sky the night before. Some believed it was a meteor. Others exclaimed that they saw the largest fireworks display they had ever witnessed. Evidently, the event was all over the news that most of North America could see the light beaming far into the heavens, because the northern part of the western hemisphere experienced a cloudless anomaly from 9 p.m. to midnight. Of course, none of the group had a television in their room to see the reports. Besides, after they concluded their evening, they were physically and emotionally exhausted and immediately went to sleep.

At the breakfast table, White Buffalo asked, "If you all will indulge me a minute? I spoke to Chayton this morning, and he told me he is taking some vacation time, beginning today." He winked at Irina. "Since he suddenly has free time on his hands, I wonder if it would it be alright with everyone if I invited him to join us for the remainder of our Colorado tour?"

Everyone agreed enthusiastically.

"Irina, would you like to call him?"

Irina smiled and threw her arms around White Buffalo and kissed him on the cheek.

"I can call him if you want," White Buffalo said . . .

Chayton met them an hour later, ready to go as if he had already packed the night before. He was definitely not on Indian time that morning.

Irina hopped into his Jeep Cherokee and rode with Chayton as they followed the van toward its next destination. They caravanned back through Durango, and on through Pagosa Springs, northeast to South Fork, then eastbound to Highway 285. Northbound through the Upper Arkansas River Valley, they followed the eastern valley of the gorgeous Sawatch Range, which included the Collegiate Peaks, one of the highest mountain ranges in Colorado. From Nathrop, they drove along Chalk Creek Drive, into the hills until they reached St. Elmo, a ghost town that sat at nearly 10,000 feet in elevation.

Michael wanted everyone to see another part of Colorado history in this authentic old west gold mining town. Sophia secretly hoped this was not the location of her surprise wedding, albeit charming in its own dusty sort of way. She had to admit, the surrounding mountains were beautiful, especially that time of year with the aspen gold at its peak. A week later, leaves would fall, and the gray pallor of winter would settle in until the end of April, five months away.

At the end of the 19th century, St. Elmo was once a booming gold mining town with a population of 2,000. Out of 150 patented mine claims, four principle mines operated in that area, one of which was the Mary Murphy Mine. It produced 50 - 75 tons of ore daily. Until 1922, when the mine closed, it produced $60 million in gold, nearly $1.5

billion in current value. The buildings that remained standing in St. Elmo were a schoolhouse, telegraph and post office, hotel, several cabins, and the general store, complete with a boardwalk running along Main Street, which remained a dirt road. Sophia could faintly see horses lined all along the road, tied up to where railings once lined the boardwalk.

The group enjoyed taking pictures as a digital framework of a town where old west history was rich. They could only imagine life back in the day, when several men on horseback rode into town after a long day's work in the mine. At that time, there were fewer restaurants than there were saloons, dance halls, and brothels, which were brimming with the West's soiled doves for the miners' temporary pleasures. These women were some of the first to occupy the town to set up a booming business where lonely men and plenty of gold flowed abundantly through the doors of their establishments. They were the ones who prospered when the men lost their shirts to gambling and their pants to temptation.

On Main Street, they toured through the historic three-story hotel, *The Ghost Town Guest House*, which operated as a bed and breakfast, offering both breakfast and supper. The homey interiors were furnished with antiques, making one feel as if they had stepped back into the late 1800s. Most of the tourists draw to the town, other than visiting an honest-to-goodness ghost town complete with its own ghost stories, was for the adventures in four-wheeling along the old mining roads above town.

One area Sophia found of specific interest was a pile of timber, where a building once stood next to *The Ghost Town*

Guest House. The layers of rubble became a chipmunk and ground squirrel hotel, with dozens of the little critters scampering about the layers of wreckage as if they were the striped, furry four-legged cast of a Disney movie. Several red hummingbird feeders hung along the front of the General Store, drawing swarms of hummingbirds in various colors. Sophia was in her element, watching the tiny wildlife.

The General Store was open for business, which sold grocery items, antiques, cabin rentals, and ATVs. While she and Michael sat on the edge of the boardwalk eating ice cream sandwiches, a hummingbird chase sent one of them right past Sophia's ear, causing her hair to fly in its wake. Another hummingbird on the chase dive-bombed and nearly flew into Michael's face. They both burst out laughing, and Sophia dropped her ice cream onto the dirt road. It did not remain there long before a couple of ground squirrels, similar to a mini clean-up crew, came to the rescue, scampering over Sophia's feet to carry away the remains.

The daylight soon dimmed, and they left St. Elmo in their rear-view mirror and headed to Buena Vista at the foot of majestic Mt. Princeton, where they spent the night at the *Two Sisters and their Husbands B, B&B*, a large Victorian house with many rooms to accommodate the group.

A month before, Michael could not resist calling the establishment with the creative moniker to see if it would be a good place for them to stay.

"Two Sisters, and their Husbands, how may I help you?"

"Is this one of the sisters speaking?" Michael asked.

"No," the woman on the line said, "you sound like a man."

Michael laughed. This will be fun, he thought. "Then are you one of the sisters?"

"Yes, I am," she answered.

"To which sister am I speaking?"

"To the one you are speaking with."

Not getting anywhere, he asked, "May I ask your name?"

"Yes, you may."

"Well, how about it?"

"How about what?"

Just for the heck of it, he said, "Who's on first?"

"Yes."

"I mean the fellow's name."

"Who."

"Ahhh, you know the routine."

"I am happy to go through the rest of it if you want, but I imagine you're calling to make a reservation."

"No, you're not imagining it, I really *am* calling to make a reservation."

"Well, now I have reservations about *you*."

He was impressed. After trading a few more one-liners, Michael made reservations for the group for a two nights stay, hoping he would get to meet the proprietors, or at least the one sister who bested him.

By the time they reached *Two Sisters and their Husbands B, B&B*, it was nearing sundown. They checked into their rooms, appointed with handmade wooden furnishings and artfully hand-painted tables and chairs. The small end tables, some with mosaic tabletops, held artistic lamps that befit the surroundings. Throughout the room were special touches, like handmade quilts and original paintings on the walls. Each room had a small gas fireplace in the corner. The entire place was an artisan's dream - perfect for Sophia's creative mind.

The group soon gathered on the riverside deck outside, which faced the Collegiate Peaks. They were happy to discover that the B, B&B also served dinner - *the best New Mexican food on this, or any other planet,* a sign in the window said. The weather still held out for this time in the fall, warm enough for them to eat outside while enjoying the sunset, augmented by tall propane patio heaters. The two sisters, who would serve and cook that evening, must have been twins, greatly resembling each other both in appearance and humor.

As one of the sisters took cocktail orders, Michael said, "Who's on first?"

"Yes."

"I mean, the fellow's name."

"Who."

"It is nice to finally meet you."

"Well to do that, we have to first exchange names."

"Alright. I'll call you Michael and you are…?"

"Smartass."

The group watched the two volley back and forth as if they were fans at a tennis match.

"Okay then, may I introduce myself – I'm Michael O'Hara."

"Michael is a good name. It's Hebrew, meaning 'who is like God.' Tell me, is it true?"

"Is what true?"

"Are you like God?"

"You will have to ask Sophia, who is soon to be my wife."

"Ohhhh, yeeees, it is quite true," Sophia said with an obvious face-contorting wink.

"Well then, Michael, who is like God, my name is Lou Ella Costello - kinda rhymes, doesn't it?"

"Lou Ella Costello," Michael said, flatly.

"Yes."

"Okay, I'll bite. And your husband's name?"

"Abbott."

"Of course. Why did I ask?"

"His parents had quite the sense of humor."

"They're not the only ones," Michael said. "So, tell me, Lou Ella, Abbott must have sought you out for many years."

"One would think so."

Darius joined in, "My dear-"

"Darius," Michael interrupted, "I got this. Now, we have to stop for a minute here. Is your name really Lou Ella Costello?"

"No, not 'Really Lou Ella Costello,' just Lou Ella Costello."

"And your husband's name is Abbott Costello?"

"I told ya, his parents were a couple of pills."

"How did you meet?"

"He put an ad in the personals." She moved her hand, spanning her palm outward as if she were reading the words on a majestic theatre marquis. "'Abbott looking for his Lou,' the ad read."

"Oh, come on!"

"You asked. Seriously now, if you were me, wouldn't you answer such an ad? We've been married forty-eight years next March, four children, sixteen grandchildren, five great-grandchildren."

"And a partridge in a pear tree," White Buffalo sang.

Lou Ella glared at him. "Hey, I work alone here."

"I'm afraid to ask your sister's name," Michael said.

"Don't be afraid, but you'll have to ask her."

"Don't," White Buffalo said, "we'll be here all night."

She turned to White Buffalo. "OK, it's your turn. What can I get ya?"

"I feel like a Virgin Mojito."

"What the hell?"

Everyone laughed, and White Buffalo tried his luck. "Virgin Mojito. If you do not know how to make it, I would settle for an Arnold Palmer."

"No, no, I can make your Mojito a virgin. Not a big

drinker, huh?"

White Buffalo shrugged. "Just the opposite. You know, one is too many, two are not enough."

"Okay, I get ya. Virgin Mojito comin' up."

During their meal, Shoshana said, "Alright, now that the floorshow is over, we have not yet heard stories from Darius, Gaston, or White Buffalo. Who's on first?"

That brought laughter *and* applause.

Chayton leaned over and whispered in Irina's ear, "This sure is a kooky bunch of people you hang out with."

Darius leaned forward, placed his elbows on the table, and casually folded his hands together. "I shall take the floor, with your kind permission."

"Kindly granted," Shoshana said.

"It sounds as if many of us are in the reconstruction business. Gaston and I have a new building project of our own. You all are aware of my ancestral grandparents' hotel, The Hibernia, yes? The abandoned building has sat for many years with the area surrounding it in ruin by the floodwaters of Hurricane Katrina. New Orleans is still in reconstruction after 80% of the city was under water, with 90,000 square miles of damage, 2,000 lives lost, and almost total devastation to the area.

"Fortunately, the Hibernia sustained relatively minor damage, and now much of the surrounding area is under new construction. Gaston and I decided to renovate the building and create a boutique hotel close to its original fashion. Of course, it will join the Delaney Hotel chain, but it will be set aside from our typical type of hospitality."

"How wonderful!" Sophia said. "Hey, you'll need a lot of artwork, won't ya? Huh?" She winked – about ten times.

"Of course," Gaston said, "and I'm sure you have some ideas where we can find it."

"The five-story hotel originally had sixty-eight rooms," Darius said, "and we are enlarging some to make suites, leaving us eleven rooms on each floor, now forty-four in all. The hotel is somewhat like a large bed and breakfast."

"And from what I have seen tonight," Gaston said, "we would be remiss if we did not offer Michael and Lou Ella Costello a job entertaining in the lounge."

"Indeed," Darius said, laughing with everyone. "Other than the brick exterior, every bit of the hotel is brand new, but styled as if it were from the early 1800s. We *do* have modern plumbing and bathrooms, so our patrons will not have to use the his-and-hers, two-hole outhouse behind the building."

"That's good thinking," White Buffalo said.

"And, of course, we have electricity, but the lighting throughout the building will have decorative vintage gaslights. We plan to appoint the hotel with every modern convenience, such as elevators, air conditioning, telephones, Wi-Fi, and a television hidden inside an armoire. It is a most charming hotel, one of which I believe my ancestors would truly be proud."

"It sounds so wonderful," Irina said. "Perhaps I should reconsider and come work for you!"

"If you ever need a job in America, we would be delighted," Darius said.

"What about furnishings?" Christofer asked.

"I am providing most of the furnishings from my shop," Gaston said, "complete with crystal chandeliers, and porcelain and crystal stemware for the dining room that are replicas of the antebellum period. The restaurant and room service will serve good old southern cooked meals, similar to the diet at that time - actually, meals not too different from our traditional New Orleans fare."

"We are working with an interior designer that specializes in historic renovations," Darius said. "He found beautiful fabrics for curtains, bed linens, and rugs appropriate to the Regency style of the day. It is quite posh. We will cater to a high-end clientele with the elegant personal touches of the Old South."

"As a matter of fact," Gaston added, "the meals will be served on a variety of tableware, with unusual china, cloth napkins, tablecloths, and such. We want this to be an experience that our customers will want to repeat and share with their friends. The best business is through word of mouth."

"We are also adding a building off the main level, which will face the street to welcome the community," Darius said. "It will be an elegant contemporary day spa, with an indoor swimming pool, where we will offer poolside yoga, tai chi, and qi gong. There will be a steam room, sauna, and Jacuzzi, and for extra pampering, one can enjoy a facial or body wrap, topped off with salon services, complete with beauticians and cosmologists. We shall have candlelit massage therapy, including hot stone massage, and acupuncture for those wanting to deeply relax and relieve tension."

"Can we go there right now?" Christofer said.

"Soon," Gaston said, "very soon."

"We want no one to leave the hotel without feeling they have been well pampered," Darius said. "The theme is Southern hospitality, welcoming guests to visit New Orleans anytime of the year, and not just for Mardi Gras."

"I think we know where one of our gatherings for Apeiros will take place before too long," Shoshana said. "I love the idea of being well pampered."

"Indeed," Gaston said. "And with that, I believe our fine Lakota friend should share."

"Yes, White Buffalo, what about you?" Anja asked.

"Yes, I'm all for a massage and hot rocks."

"No," Anja giggled. "What I meant was, do you want to tell us your latest news?"

"Not tonight. Tomorrow I will share with you. It is time for me to go to bed. Good night all. Michael, would you carry my bag up the stairs, please?"

"Of course. You go on and I will be up in a few minutes."

Dinner was over, and the other sister came into the dining room, offering coffee and a plate of homemade cookies.

Michael could not resist, and everyone sat back for the show, waiting to see if her sister had as good a wit as Lou Ella.

"So, your sister would not tell me your name," Michael said.

"Yeah? What else did she have to say?"

"She told me I would have to find out from you. What is the big secret?"

"There's no secret, I've known my name all my life."

"Oh, jeez, here we go. So, what about it?"

"So, what about what?"

"What is your name?"

"Mary. See? That wasn't so hard."

"Why wouldn't Lou Ella tell me your name is Mary?"

"The whole name thing is not about me, but who I am married to."

"Okay, I'm the straight man. What's your husband's name?"

"Joseph."

"Mary and Joseph. Drum roll, please. Don't tell me you have a son named Jesus."

"Okay I won't tell you that, but..."

"But what?"

"We have a son named Joshua, which it is believed that the name Jesus was derived from."

"I'm afraid to ask what your last name is."

"Go on. Ask."

"Okay, what-"

"Christello."

Michael deadpanned. "Mary and Joseph, and your son's name is Joshua Christello? Well, Ollie, I can see why you didn't name him Jesus."

"Yeah, we aren't as funny as Abbott's parents."

"And your sister's last name is Costello."

"Nothing gets past you, does it?"

"So the Christellos and the Costellos own a B&B and-"

"In town they call us the Ello sisters. And it's B, B&B."

"Yeah, that's right. What is the extra 'B'?"

"Bakery."

"Oh, now we're getting somewhere!" Markos said. "You have a bakery?"

"Yes, I know."

"I am staying out of this," Markos said.

"There you will find our bakery case full of Ellos."

"I'm all-in," Michael said. "What are Ellos?"

"The greatest pastries on this, or any other planet. There you will find Danny A-ellos, B-ellos Lugosi, Ladies and F-ellos, H-ellos, J-ellos, M-ellos - our gluten free carob bars, O'th-ellos, P-ellos, Tom S-ellos - which are sale-of-the-day items, W-ellos, Y-ellos - our yummy lemon bars, and Z-ellos, which are the most colorful of all - our cupcakes."

"Or – cup-kellos," Michael said.

"Don't help. Here on the tray in front of you are our H-ellos, our cookie du jour, one of our bestselling items. People come weekly to purchase the next new cookie, even if they don't have the good sense to rent a room."

"Okay then, I guess I can say that you had me at-"

"H-ello? As if I haven't heard that one before. You have to be quicker than that," Mary said.

"Oh, you're good!" Michael said.

"How about I pour you some coffee?"

"Yes, thank you."

"It is my pleasure!" Mary laughed as she walked around the table, offering coffee to the rest of the group, who thoroughly enjoyed the tête-a-tête between the two.

Michael finished his H-ello and coffee, and he wrapped one in a napkin to take up to White Buffalo. When he arrived at his door with his suitcase, it took a minute before White Buffalo answered, slightly bent as if something ached.

"Hey, are you all right?" Michael asked.

"This getting old is not for sissies," White Buffalo said, wincing in pain while holding his belly.

"Eat too much? Can I get you anything?"

"No, but I am about to take up drinking," White Buffalo said with a laugh.

"That bad, huh? What's the trouble?"

"Nothing, I'm alright. Put the bag over there, will you, please?"

Michael walked in and put his suitcase on the stand. White Buffalo winced again. "That sure doesn't sound like nothing."

White Buffalo gingerly sat on the bed and rubbed his abdomen. "It comes and goes. Thank you, bellhop, I will get your tip later."

Michael sat down next to him in silence. He looked at him for a moment, and then quietly said, "Are you sick?"

White Buffalo drew a long sigh and finally nodded. "Let's just say that it will not be long before I am one of the ancestors." He looked directly at Michael, who grew suddenly pale. The old Lakota elder put his hand on the back of Michael's head and gently rubbed.

"Cancer?" Michael barely whispered.

"Please, my son, do not to say anything to anyone."

"Doctors? Have you-"

"There is nothing to be done. Stage four – it is in my pancreas."

Michael dropped his head and covered his mouth, tears pushing through his closed eyes.

White Buffalo drew him near. "I am going to live out my days enjoying every one of them. You and Sophia will make those days be like sunshine."

"Are you beyond treatment?"

"I will not have chemotherapy or radiation. I came into the world with this body, and I will leave with it as it is. Besides, the ancestors would laugh at me if I came to the Spirit World without my hair."

Michael composed himself and took his hand. "What can we do for you?"

"Be who you are. Great Spirit has given me life's greatest blessing in you and our darling Sophia. Just help me live out my days well. Can you do that, my friend?"

"Of course. Anything - anything at all."

White Buffalo embraced Michael. "Thank you, my son. I will wait until the end of the trip before I tell the group about this in my own way. Until then - promise me that you will not blubber like the bighearted Irishman you are?"

Michael sucked the tears back and dried his eyes. "I promise."

"This is Sophia's time to rejoice in our hearts. You entered her life to set her free, Michael, and she entered yours as salvation."

Michael could only nod in reverence of the man he regarded as a second father. Only a few short years before, he was with both of his elderly parents when they laid down their bodies. "I love you, Chief," he said.

White Buffalo interrupted Michael's contemplation. "I love you, too. Now, let us talk about our plans for tomorrow. It will be a good day to remember . . ."

Michael took a walk under the stars, and he joined Sophia an hour later in their room. She was already asleep. Michael noticed that she had been quieter the last few days since he proposed. He hoped she was not having second thoughts about getting married. He knew that she would tell him if something was wrong. *Perhaps she's just getting tired,* he kept telling himself, so much had been going in the last few weeks. *Perhaps I'm just feeling the shock of the news White Buffalo just gave me. Or, perhaps I should just relax and know that everything will turn out just the way we planned.*When he got into bed, she stirred enough to wake up.

"Hi, sweetie," Michael whispered, rubbing her back.

"Hi."

"Is everything alright, Soph? You've been rather quiet,

especially since we did the ritual in Mesa Verde."

"I'm fine, really." She stirred and turned toward him. "I've just been thinking about my parents. I can't help but think about my mother, now that I know more about her death, and the man that loved her - Tommy. I just wish Daddy and I could have talked about it."

"You can, you know?" he said with a smile.

Sophia nodded. "Oh, yeah - I guess everything is still so new that I forget sometimes. When we settle down again - when we are not so busy - I would like to call in their spirits so we can all communicate." She sat up in bed. "And you know who I would like to have with us?"

"White Buffalo," Michael said, fighting a lump rising in his throat.

"Well, yes, naturally, but I was going to say Gaston and Darius. Michael, I want to tell you something about a dream that keeps coming to me."

"Uh-oh, this doesn't have anything to do with Chayton, does it?"

"No, no, you're safe there - Irina already claimed him," she said, slapping him on the arm. "You know that teacup and saucer we found in Gaston's shop?"

"The one from the *Titanic*? Yeah, I'd say I remember it. We could make a fortune selling it, if you didn't threaten my life every time I suggest it."

"I was on the ship."

Michael's eyes darted back and forth. "You're kidding."

"At least, I've been on it in my dreams the last few weeks. I see it all from the eyes of a beautiful woman named Jocelyn Brewster Davis, and there on the ship she met and fell in love with a Frenchman named François Delacroix."

"Delacroix? Have you told Gaston about this?"

"Not yet, but remember when Gaston gave us the teacup? He said something about its story would someday reveal itself."

"Then this Delacroix in your dream could be – his grandfather?"

"That's what I'm thinking, because François' middle name was Gaston."

"I guess it doesn't take Albert Einstein to do that math, huh?"

"I believe Gaston knows the teacup belonged to his grandparents, but he may not know the intimate details of their lives. In my dream - I don't know if I was Jocelyn, or if I'm just reliving the life of Gaston's ancestors – who would also be *my* ancestors. It's confusing, but also quite exciting."

"Why don't you ask Gaston?"

"Because I want to see how it turns out first."

Michael laughed. "Honey, you *know* how it turned out! It wasn't pretty."

"But we have the teacup, and I know that Jocelyn took it with her the night of the sinking. And, get this, when François asked her why she put the teacup in her bag when they were obviously scrambling to save themselves, Jocelyn told him it was something they will someday show their grandchildren when they would tell them about that terrible night."

"But you said her name was Davis."

"She was pregnant by François."

"Oh, then clearly they both survived and had a family."

"No, she got pregnant that night on the ship."

"Boy, François moved fast. You know the French," Michael said. "Wait, how did she know she was pregnant if it happened that night?"

"Because women just know, Michael."

"O— —kay." Michael decided to let that one go.

"There still are missing pieces to their story," Sophia said. "The ship struck the iceberg, and it was sinking fast. Jocelyn got in a lifeboat, but she had to leave François behind."

"Very few men survived," Michael said. "If François didn't get to a lifeboat himself, then he didn't make it. Do you know if he did?"

"Not yet. It was so horrifying," Sophia said. "I just hope I can learn his fate, so I can tell Gaston the whole story. François was an incredibly gallant man. Did you know that some men were allowed to board the lifeboats? But he refused. He wouldn't go ahead of any woman or child."

"And could you imagine Gaston acting differently?"

"No," Sophia said, her voice quivering. "Jocelyn was a medium. In fact, François also was highly intuitive. They both sensed something terrible was going to happen that night, but they couldn't identify what it was. Can you imagine?"

"Well, Gaston's real name is Delacroix. That could be a good sign that François survived."

"Or, he didn't, and Jocelyn gave her child his name to honor him. But what confuses me is - Jocelyn was Gaston's grandmother. If I'm not just dreaming about her life, but rather, I actually *was* her, that would mean I was Gaston's grandmother in another life. I would be my own great-grandmother."

Michael stared and blinked five times. Sophia knew him well enough simply to keep on talking, because his mind would remain on 'hold' until he could process what she was saying. He would eventually catch up.

Sophia slumped back down in the bed. "This is just too weird to give it any more thought tonight. I just hope my dream completes, so someday we can sit down and discuss this with both Gaston and Darius."

And White Buffalo, Michael thought. "Let's get some sleep. We have a big day tomorrow."

"What are we doing tomor—" Her voice trailed away, for she had already fallen asleep.

CHAPTER
Twenty-nine

There was a knock at the door at 8:00 a.m. Sophia stirred under the covers, wondering who it could be, but Michael, as usual, was already up and ready for action. The group was not to meet for breakfast until 9:30, so Sophia submerged back into her cocoon. Michael opened the door, and Lou Ella Costello rolled in a service cart with a beautiful breakfast for two.

"Rise and shine, the day's half gone," she said.

Michael smiled. "Lou Ella, you are radiant this morning."

"You're looking snappy there yourself, sport," Lou Ella said. "You clean up good."

"Look, Soph, breakfast." Sophia peered out from under the covers.

"On the house this morning," Lou Ella said. "A little gift from the two sisters and the husbands, yada yada."

"How sweet," Sophia mumbled.

"We wish you two all the very, very best," Lou Ella said with absolute sincerity.

"What's the occasion?" Sophia asked.

Lou Ella looked at Michael, who gave her a stupid smile. "Oh, occasion? I get it. Who needs an occasion?" She poured the coffee, and before leaving the room, she removed the cloche, in style - the silver dome that kept their food warm. Michael gave her a tip before he closed the door behind her.

"I'll ask again - what is the occasion?" Sophia said, sitting up in bed and running her fingers through her nest of blonde hair.

"My love, today is our wedding day," Michael said.

"Really! Today?"

"Fasten your seatbelt, baby, this is it!"

"Oh, I can't wait to marry you!" Sophia said. "Where are we getting married? Is everybody coming? God, my hair's a mess! What time is it?"

"Hold on! Take a breath. After breakfast, we're all going up to the Mount Princeton Hot Springs Resort. We have day passes for a soak in the hot springs, and then off to their spa. I have a full body massage, hand and foot massage, and other treatments lined up for you. We just have to be back here by two, when we get all gussied up for the wedding. The rest is a surprise."

"Has everyone known about your plan all along?"

"They all knew we would get married in Buena Vista."

"They're pretty good at keeping a secret."

"So, you are happy?"

"Yes, of course. Were you concerned?"

"Well actually, I am relieved. You've been so quiet lately - so introspective. I was wondering if you were having second thoughts."

"Oh Michael, it's not that at all. My mom and dad have been on my mind. The whole revelation about how they died has turned me around. You know, it's the same as when I tap into a past life. I gain a new perspective that fills in the gaps in my life, and I need to rearrange my thinking, because the new revelation alters my current outlook. My mother died because she was trying to protect me, and my father died seeking vengeance for her death."

"Yes, that's one way to look at it. It sounds perhaps like guilt has overtaken you. Would you not fight to protect one you love so dearly? And can you blame your dad for what he did?"

"No, of course not. My first thoughts would be to do the same as they did."

"I don't want to sound smug, but Elizabeth was one of many in Algernon's path of destruction. He is the type who sucks the life force right out of another. The only thing that she did wrong was not listen to what may have been strong intuitive nudges to stay away from him in the first place. Predators like Algernon seek out sensitive people. Your mother, I am sure, had no idea what was coming. Once she was involved with him, no matter what she did, her involvement would have been detrimental, because he was so insidious. And your dad was the collateral damage that resulted from her murder.

"That's why we must pay attention to the wisdom of intuitive guidance. If anything, it's a lesson we all learn from the death of your parents. It's not what happened that matters, but how we handle our response to what we learn."

"You are right, my wise sage," Sophia said, gently

placing her hand on his face. "It's all about how I live my life in a better way, knowing what I now know."

"We can talk more about this later. Are you alright for now - for today?"

"Yes, thanks. I feel better. I didn't mean to cause you any concern."

"We're a team, you and me. When you are uneasy, I am here for you in the same way you are for me," Michael said, reaching out for her to come to him.

He wrapped her in his big arms and rested his chin on top of her head, which always made her laugh.

"I love you so deeply, my sweet Sophia."

"And I love you!"

After a day of pampering at the spa, everyone dressed their best for the wedding and then boarded the van, with the exception of Sophia and Darius. Sam drove the rest of the group up to Cottonwood Lake at the east dock, which was just big enough for their small wedding party. Chayton followed in his Jeep, driving Sophia and her beloved grandfather.

As Darius offered his hand to help her out of the Jeep, Chayton waited with a beautiful arm bouquet of fall flowers in shades of red and burgundy roses, gold alstromeria, rust lilies, persimmon tones, and purples with trailing ivy and springeri.

"Michael had this bouquet made for you."

"Oh, they're beautiful. Thank you, Chayton." Sophia smiled, ever amazed at Michael's thoughtfulness.

They walked to the dock, her hand resting in Darius' arm, where Michael waited for her with their friends. They all stood in a circle. White Buffalo stood facing them as the officiate, with his back to the lake.

There could not be a more beautiful setting for our wedding, Sophia thought, as she looked out over the gleaming late afternoon waters with reflections of the aspen gold that surrounded the lake.

When Sophia saw Michael standing to the right of White Buffalo, dressed in such elegant fashion, she paused for a brief moment just to take in the sight of him. He was so handsome and gallant. She half-expected him to be dressed in his blue jeans, white shirt, and leather belt, with newly polished cowboy boots, which would have been fine by her. Instead, he wore a dark gray suit with a dark gray brocade double-breasted vest, and an ivory shirt and gray silk tie. He looked like a version of Cary Grant from a 1930s film, and since Cary was one of Sophia's favorite actors from that era, Michael was more than satisfied to be dressed in all his regalia.

Michael held out his hand to take her from Darius' arm, looking at her as if he was seeing her beauty for the first time. She was dressed in a long antique ivory velvet gown, with a slight train trailing behind her. On her feet were delicately beaded gold slippers. She wore her blonde hair tied at the base of her neck in loose chignon, anchored with her grandmother's pearl comb, and dangle earrings of her own making in pearls and gold. Around her neck was the pearl necklace her father gave her mother on the day Sophia was born. Michael slipped several of her favorite pieces into his bag before they left the cabin, knowing she would like to make her own choice of which ones to wear.

Sophia was all smiles. A few people who were fishing on the east end of the lake took notice of the gathering. Some put their fishing poles down and sat back to observe.

Sophia looked around their circle of friends. Then, spirits of those who had passed on appeared in her awareness. Standing behind Markos was her father, Patrick, and next to him was her mother and birth father, Elizabeth and Tommy Gallagher. They were all vibrant and young as she imagined them at an age when she was quite small. Sophia beamed at their presence. Michael's parents were there, so happy for their son. Others came as well. She saw the spirits of Jocelyn and François, Rachel and Yeshua, Hypatia, Luciana and Michele du Nostredame, Roxana and Yiorgos. For a split second she thought, as she laughed to herself - *Yeshua and Nostradamus came to our wedding. I would like to see someone top that one!*

The faint outline of colors and shapes of countless souls she recalled from somewhere deep in her memory surrounded them. Her animal spirits were sitting inside their circle of friends, every one of which she had been blessed to be their human, and she smiled a loving smile in their direction, realizing that they ever surrounded her in a ring of loving protection.

By that time, in their shared history together, the other twelve understood that Sophia could see beyond the physical world. In this case, they knew she was aware of beings they could not see, and yet they sensed the high vibration of their loving presence.

White Buffalo was dressed in traditional Indian garb, in dark pants, with a vest and shirt in many bright colors of the earth and sky. He wore beautifully handmade deerskin moccasins, beaded in colorful seed bead designs. Sophia was so pleased that he was the one Michael chose to perform the ceremony.

White Buffalo closed his eyes as he opened up the ceremony with a prayer spoken in Lakota. Sophia thought nothing else could be more perfect. Even though no one, with the exception of Chayton, understood what he said, the resonance of White Buffalo's words filled the hearts of all.

Then, White Buffalo spoke in English, so everyone could understand, "Wakan Tanka, it is I, your grandson, Tatanka Ska, White Buffalo. Thank you for this day and for all creation. We have all come here today to celebrate, and I ask that you hear our prayer.

"To the West, the element of water, and the color black, be with us. We ask for healing for the people, for all beings, for Grandmother Earth, and for ourselves. May we live in balance within the physical, emotional, mental, and spiritual planes, so we are able to know our place on this earth - in life and in death. We ask for healing of the body, and for the mind, to bring light, joy, and awareness to our spirits. To the West, we ask for its inner seeing, emotional understanding, deep introspection, and reflection to come to this marriage.

"To the North, the element of wind and air, and the color red, be with us today. As each day passes, help us surrender, so that the things that hold us back will be cleansed and released with grace and ease. May we be given patience and endurance. Help us to listen to the quiet with both ears, and find serenity and comfort in the silence as it extends into the stillness. Give us all wisdom so we will be able to make wise choices in all things that are placed at our feet in front of us, so that we may walk the red road - the sacred way.

"To the East, which is fire, and the color yellow, be with us today. East is far seeing or seeing into the future, which focuses the connection to the physical. We ask that the Spirit of the Eagle to be with us as it flies high while carrying our prayers to the Creator. May we see with our two eyes the clarity of vision - to have eyes as sharp as the Eagle - so we are able to see truth for the path we have chosen. Guide our steps and give us courage to walk the circle of life with honesty and dignity.

"To the South, the element of earth and the color white, be with us today. Help us to remember compassion for ourselves and for all beings, as we remember the truth of innocence. May we all walk with love and joy for the two-legged, the four-legged, the winged ones, the finned ones, the creepy crawlies, the plants, and all creation upon Grandmother Earth. Help us to grow and nurture our hearts and our self-worth in integrity, honesty, and in truth.

"Grandmother Earth, we thank you for your abundance and beauty of all the green that surrounds us. We thank you for holding all the bodies of water, the life force by which we thrive. We thank you for all you have given us. Remind us never to take from you more then we need, and remind us in all ways to return to the Earth more than we receive.

"To Creator, Wakan Tanka, we look into the blue skies above for inspiration. We ask that Sophia and Michael will walk on Grandmother Earth in a good way. When all these directions and elements come together in the life of the individual, then perfection of humanity is realized within the eternal realm of Great Spirit, which has ever been, and will never cease. This is one of the gifts of marriage, when the love for each other merges the journey of their souls, and through their love, together they will walk as one."

White Buffalo turned to Sophia and Michael. "Your mothers and fathers, along with your grandmothers and grandfathers are here. Sophia, Grandpa Napayshni wants you to know he is here. He is very pleased in the choices you have made, especially in choosing Michael to be your great love. All the ancestors and relations are smiling. They have gathered in this sacred and holy place by the water's edge on the back of Grandmother Earth, for this is a good day.

"We, as your community, have gathered here today, to celebrate the union of your souls. Each of us now has a deeper calling - we will continue to honor you and to support you in your marriage. We are here to *remind* you of your commitment to each other and to Great Spirit. We honor fire, which is energy, power, passion, and creativity - ever lighting the way to new journeys. We honor the wind and the air, which is change - bringing in the new and sweeping out the old. We honor sacred water, as reflection, clarity, intuition, and life itself. Water is a symbol of transition as it moves from liquid, to ice, and to the mists. We honor Grandmother Earth, for she holds us, and allows us to walk upon her back, while providing us with food to nourish our body, mind, and heart.

"True marriage is the holiest of unions, for love has no limits, as the stars never cease to shine. Love is like a river that will cut a new path, for water always finds its way to the ocean. The flame of love burns through all things that are unlike it, leaving to remain only the undying embers of love's glow. Love is one song, which sings with clear resonance far into the heavens, and deep into the core of Grandmother Earth. Marriage is a union of souls. There is nothing greater for two people than to join in the highest order of love.

"To quote Voltaire, 'God is a circle whose center is everywhere and circumference nowhere.'" In his cupped hands, White Buffalo held their two rings. "These rings that I hold represent the eternal circle of the wholeness of life, which is holy, that of Wakan Tanka - Great Spirit - that which is love. The circle is who you are. You are everywhere and endless. You are one with Great Spirit, as a living, breathing, earthly example of Apeiros - the cause of all unity and measure of all things.

"When you join in marriage, you bring together your two circles. That place where the two circles meet is the vesica piscis - the union of souls - the place of creation where both of your hearts and minds join in oneness. That place at the center is also a place of neutrality, where all things are healed, whole, and holy. This union is the place where your relationship thrives and flourishes within the heart of Great Spirit - the Divine - the Infinite Intelligence. It is where you come together in joy, peace, and harmony - and in all the aspects of Wakan Tanka here in the earth realm, in what we know as Love.

"The Grandfathers advise you to keep Great Spirit at the center of your union. Always ask the Grandfathers and the angels for guidance, and trust that it is given. In trust and wisdom, you will step between the veils to witness what seems like miracles, when in truth you are living in the cosmic consciousness that is ever available to us in every moment of each day.

"Marriage is a sacred pact, with Love being the remembrance of your blessed uniqueness, both as individuals and in your union. When you agree to first honor each other, marriage can be easy. In this, you choose right decisions, which benefit you both. By honoring the other, you avoid harsh words. Instead, you choose loving and supportive thoughts, which then translate into actions that create a long and lasting relationship of kindness and compassion. In making choices to honor the relationship, one bypasses thoughts and words generated from the voice of the ego. Loving and life-giving thoughts transform into actions toward each other that expand into grace and compassionate elegance, which extend outwardly to family, friends, and into the communities of the world.

"Where you are in need, Sophia, Michael will fill that yearning with his wise heart, strength of character, and his humor. Michael, when you desire tenderness, care, compassion, and the zest for life, Sophia will lovingly give it. We only have two choices, either love or fear. In choosing love, fear cannot thrive, and therefore it can never turn you against your lighthearted, joy-filled, and tender ways.

"We become what we do not forgive, so it is wise to let the small things go so they do not grow and become something they are not. Be straightforward and honest. Talk about your concerns with kindness. Settle your differences, so you can love and respect each other, for the effect you have on each other is the most precious exchange there is. Live in the now, the timeless dimension of the presence, and always be grateful. As you express your gratitude, more will arise for you to appreciate. In marriage and union, love and be loved, give and receive, allow and support the other, always within the sacred circle of the spirit, heart, mind and body. Live within the Knowledge, which is the essence of your soul, that when you breathe in that Love, you are ever safe, ever sourced, and supplied with all you need. Trust Love, for Love will in all things lead the way."

Sophia handed her flowers to Ananta and Markos handed the rings to White Buffalo. Then Sophia and Michael joined hands.

"Do you Michael O'Hara, promise to love and respectfully support Sophia - to hold her with a generous and compassionate heart? Will you sustain your good mind with wisdom, tempered by humility, and prayer - living in gratitude and forgiveness? Do you agree to keep your body temple as sacred, never forsaking her - keeping yourself honest and true to your word, first to Great Spirit, and therefore to Sophia?"

"Yes, I do."

"Michael, as you place this ring on her finger, you may speak of your love to Sophia."

"I have loved you for many lifetimes, Sophia, and I will for many more to come. It seems that you just can't get rid of me." He laughed, as Sophia smiled, listening intently to his every word. "You are a remarkable woman who never ceases to amaze and astound me. You are compassionate and kind, I love your bohemian gypsy ways, as you truly are the Oracle. You not only see into the future and the past in ways I cannot understand, but you see the good in all situations, and all people. You are the alchemist, as you transmute everything in your awareness to the splendor of golden truth. The miracle of you is the healer within.

"Life with you is never without excitement and discovery. I promise you, my love, to be your rock to stand on; to be your protector; your listening ear, supporting you and standing by your side in all you do. I will never disappoint you, keeping true to you in every sense of the word. From this day forward, I will continue to love you more each day, to adore you, further cherishing you as the years pass, and I will hold you both in sorrow and in triumph until we leave this world - and I am most certain we will find each other again - each time living life at its best. I am so greatly honored that you agreed to marry me. Sophia, you I adore, for you are my love and my beloved." He placed the ring on her finger.

White Buffalo continued, "Do you Sophia Delaney, promise to love and respectfully support Michael - to hold him with a generous and compassionate heart? Will you sustain your good mind with wisdom, tempered by humility and prayer - living in gratitude and forgiveness? Do you agree to keep your body temple as sacred, never forsaking him - keeping yourself honest and true to your word, first to Great Spirit, and therefore to Michael?"

"Yes, I do."

"Sophia, as you place this ring on his finger, you may speak of your love to Michael."

Sophia had very little time to prepare, and so she simply said what was in her heart. She was radiant as she looked into Michael's green eyes. "Michael, my love, I stand with you today with our friends and family to celebrate this sacred love that we share. We stand here in God's creation of grand beauty surrounding us, at the edge of this pristine mountain lake, with golden aspen amidst the pine and spruce, all held in this valley of mountain splendor. The Colorado blue skies soar overhead as the sun sets to the west, with its golden orb bathing all in its brilliance. This place is a representation of the splendor of our love, and I will ever remember every cherished moment.

"Do you know what is most wonderful of all, Michael? I actually *like* you!" She smiled, while the others laughed. "How many married people can honestly say that? I am a blessed woman to marry my best friend, and my beloved. And in that, I promise to continue to hold your heart in my hands - these sacred hands - with which I will tenderly love, cherish, and care for you. I will support and guide you in truth, as you have done for me. I will continue to be your lover, your best friend, your listening ear, and your lifetime companion. Our souls have come together again, as we fuse our spirits, hearts, minds, and bodies - and I promise to love you more each day until time no longer exists."

She placed the ring on Michael's finger.

For a moment, she looked at Michael and saw Yiorgos. Markos was Theo, and White Buffalo was Makarios - the high priest who married them on Mt. Parnassus. She smiled at her mother and father and Patrick, to her animal family, so grateful that they came to her so she could be their human. She silently thanked all the souls who showed their presence to her. Sophia's heart was full.

White Buffalo then said, "And so, it is my honor to present to the world Michael O'Hara and Sophia MacPhaidin Delacroix Delaney Gallagher O'Hara," he paused, "did I leave anyone out?"

"No, that's it!" Sophia laughed with everyone.

White Buffalo resumed, "husband and wife! You may now kiss the bride."

Michael embraced her in a fashion true to his word as her protector. They lovingly kissed, as everyone, including those in nearby fishing boats, clapped and cheered. Chayton then took Irina's hand in his.

Sam took several photos of the group gathered together on the dock with the western sun setting in the background of aspen golden splendor. Then Chayton took over the camera duty so Sam could join the group.

Twilight was soon upon them. They returned to the inn, where a candlelight feast awaited, starting with chocolate dipped strawberries with a variety of cheeses, smoked salmon, homemade dark rye, and whole wheat bread with Irish butter.

The two wisecracking sisters continued to delight everyone with their silly humor and their heartfelt congratulations.

Michael earlier prepared a track of three hours of music for the evening, starting with the late 40s era of Sinatra, then onto Tony Bennett, and Dean Martin, to James Taylor, Bonnie Raitt, Sarah McLachlan, to name a few. They danced, which was not Michael's forte, but just this once, he told her. The rest of them joined in for dancing, great food, and a champagne toast, before the cutting of the cake, which was a small three-layer chocolate cake with chocolate frosting and chocolate curls on the top. Michael had to have something about the wedding that was mostly just for him.

After the fabulous meal, the sisters presented a table of many of Sophia's family favorites - recipes Sophia grew up baking for her father, strewn with flowers and candlelight. Both Darius and Gaston enjoyed goodies they had not eaten for some time, such as penuche cookies, and an old family recipe called Swanky Sweets - the best buttery, cinnamon rolls laden with gooey pecans. Dessert would not have been complete without a chocolate chip bourbon pecan pie, and Y-ellos, the sisters' lemon bars lightly dusted with powdered sugar.

Sophia felt Patrick tap on her shoulder several times throughout the day and into the evening. As she danced with Michael, she smelled the scent of her mother's perfume wafting through the air. Sophia suddenly recalled the small cobalt blue bottle that sat on her mother's dressing table.

When the party ended, Sophia and Michael returned to their room where they made intense passionate love, unlike they had ever experienced together. When they both climaxed, Sophia burst into tears. Michael understood. He gently wrapped her in his arms as she silently sobbed tears of joy and released emotions she had held onto for weeks.

That night, Sophia dreamt of her mother and father, seeing them happily together, viewing them as if she were a mere thought in the distant wind. At one point, Michael got out of bed to get a glass of water and noticed how sweetly Sophia slept. He found her curled up in the covers, and on her face was a gentle smile.

Their honeymoon in Ireland would have to be delayed for another month, because Sophia had unfinished business to settle in Louisiana before they trekked away. To finalize the closure of her parents' deaths, Sophia made the difficult decision to go to Angola State Penitentiary and confront Algernon Gillette.

On the final night at the cabin, all thirteen celebrated the coming year and their work as individuals and as a community. Their combined energies were more powerful than ever, raising the calibration of the planet to levels of healing beyond that of ancient pain. Chayton also committed to doing similar work of his own for the upcoming year, with plans to lead thousands of people through Mesa Verde, holding for each one a blessed life in their future.

Their vision of peace brought into play Love's gentle pulse and continuous rhythm of infinite knowing, spiraling into greater expansion beyond the thinking mind. They celebrated gratitude and appreciation in their last moments together, knowing the next time they gathered wondrous happenings would have occurred.

Before they concluded, White Buffalo asked for a few moments of their time.

"I want all of you to know how much I love you, for you all live in a good way. Each one of you brings to me the heart of Great Spirit." White Buffalo looked into the eyes of each one in the group. "I must tell you all something, however, it is something that I ask you to accept with courage in your heart. I will not be with you much longer. The Grandfathers are calling me home. Soon I will join with Grandmother Earth, and you will remember me in your continued journeys."

The room fell in stunned silence, except for the soft weeping of Michael, who simply could not hold back any longer.

"White Buffalo," Sophia said. "This can't be true."

"It is so, my love," White Buffalo said. "I am ill, and I have no choice but to leave sometime soon."

"Dear God," Darius said, embracing Sophia.

Some in the group broke down in tears, while others simply sat, stunned at the news.

With tears welled up in her eyes, Sophia walked up to White Buffalo and embraced him. "We will take care of you," she said. "You will remain with us until it is time for you to go. Michael, we will move White Buffalo's things here. He will live with us."

"Those are my thoughts exactly, Sophia," Michael said.

Each one in the group embraced White Buffalo and shared with him their sorrow and deep feelings for him. Because of this news, the conversation led to the necessity to meet again in six months to support White Buffalo. The increased intensity of the world's fast-changing times and the Earth's shifting energies also called for them to gather more often. The key to their order was, wherever they were throughout the globe, they held the collective power of Love for the world. In that, they would embrace White Buffalo from around the earth, holding him in their healing energy. Their love for him was the essence of Apeiros - the cause of all unity and the measure of all things.

CHAPTER
Thirty

The next day, Irina left with Chayton to tour Taos, Santa Fe, and Chaco Canyon. Michael and Sophia dropped Darius, Gaston, and White Buffalo at his apartment in Golden to gather his things, while they then took the rest of the group to the airport.

White Buffalo lived in a simple way, never accumulating much more than a few sacred mementos for sacred ceremonies. He lived in a furnished apartment, so it took very little time to pack his belongings. After Michael and Sophia returned to Golden, they loaded up his things and drove back up to the cabin, where they gave him his favorite corner bedroom to call his own. That room overlooked both the mountains to the west and the river below. He often said this room was the most beautiful of all he had ever stayed in. He would go to sleep each night as he listened to the river's never-ending flow, with all his memorabilia surrounding him - most importantly his sacred pipe.

Since most everyone had left, and they were not leaving for New Orleans until two days later, Sophia was able to go to bed early. She thought she would get a good night's rest, but while they toured through Colorado, she had not dreamt of Jocelyn. Sophia's dreams that night picked up right where she had left off, in the crisis of *Titanic*, leaving

Sophia with a restless night's sleep.

Jocelyn's lifeboat, nearly filled to capacity, made it easier for most of the passengers to maintain their warmth in the humid, frigid temperatures. Jocelyn sat in one of the outside seats, as she was one of the last people to board. Before they lowered the boat down to the sea, she wrapped herself in the eiderdown quilt to shield herself from the cold.

About 1:20 a.m., the final distress rockets were set ablaze into the black starlit skies. Most of the Third Class men, women, and children stayed below in Steerage, not wanting to leave behind what little they brought with them, for it was all they owned. Some simply refused to risk their lives on the lifeboats and chose to wait for a rescue ship that they prayed would soon come.

The majority of men in Second Class stayed behind as well, remaining inside the ship along with most of the crewmembers. All 25 engineering officers remained below deck and labored in the icy, flooding waters to keep the lights on and the ship afloat for as long as possible.

Of the 20 lifeboats, 18 launched successfully. Both Collapsible A and B floated away without any passengers aboard. It was not until all the boats were set afloat that the hoards of people from the lower decks rushed onto the Boat Deck in wild panic, finally realizing the ship was sinking. There was no way off the ship, other than jumping into near instant death of the freezing ocean waters. Some passengers and crew who were aware of the circumstances for the past two hours seemed resigned to their fate. Others panicked and jumped into the icy waters with the hope of swimming to a lifeboat.

In a brief moment, while leaning over the edge of the Boat Deck and looking for Jocelyn's lifeboat, François saw Frederick Hoyt jump from a lower deck into the sea. He swam to Collapsible D, where his wife was aboard. They pulled him out of the frigid waters into the boat. Hoyt was only one of nine people pulled from the water that night, of whom three later died.

With *Titanic* tipped at such a precarious angle, François frantically held onto the railing to keep from falling. He witnessed the terrible, inevitable power of gravity pull many down the deck like ragdolls sledding down an icy slope and plunging into the icy water below. *Titanic* continued to sink into the sea, 38,000 tons of water now filling her bow.

Reality slowly dissolved François' one last thread of hope, as a thought entered his mind as an advance epitaph to all who remained on board, soon to be no more:

Until now, the ten decks of Titanic separated three classes of people amongst those of European and American societies. There are hundreds of people from various countries and faiths, both men and women, who, like me, wonder what heaven is like, for our time here on Earth is done. Parents who brought entire families to begin again in the New World remain with no options left for their families' survival. Several couples are newlywed, and some are expectant parents. We are millionaires, impoverished, crewmembers, stowaways - all classes of people. Now we stand here clustered together, taking one last collective breath. There is now no division between us as people, nor is there a separation from our God. For soon, we will rest next to each other in aeternalis, thousands of feet below at the bottom of the Atlantic Ocean.

François looked up and said, in a deep resounding voice, "Dieu, pour vous je me rends - God, to you I surrender!"

His life flashed before him. His deceased wife, Madelyn - would she and their baby be waiting to welcome him? He immediately pushed away the thoughts of her, replacing them with the picture in his mind's eye of Jocelyn and their vision of a life together in New York. He thought of the new job awaiting him. A slight smile formed on his face as he thought of the dreams he had for his new life in America, briefly transporting him from his circumstances . . .

Jocelyn could not distinguish François from the other men on the ship. She checked her watch that was pinned to her jacket lapel. The ship's lights shined just far enough to reach her so she could see that it was 2:05 a.m. By that time, all the lifeboats had been deployed, and the last collapsible floated onto the water's surface as the bow of the ship sank deeper into the ocean.

Hundreds of people jumped into the icy water, where the temperature was colder than the air at thirty-one degrees. Jocelyn closed her eyes, attempting to block out the sight of drowning and dead people who jumped or fell from the ship, too far from a lifeboat for rescue.

The healthiest of humans could survive no longer than 15 minutes in water at that temperature, with most losing consciousness after five minutes. Upon entering the frigid sea, they felt the sensation of a thousand knives cutting through them. Hypothermia immediately set in, their teeth beginning to chatter, and their helpless bodies shaking uncontrollably. Those without lifebelts quickly and mercifully drowned, while those with lifebelts endured several agonizing moments while freezing to death. Thrashing about in the water only increased heat loss, as the feeling in their fingers and toes almost immediately subsided. Their legs and arms then went numb and lifeless, leaving them unable to swim and stay afloat. Finally, short, painful gasps for air subsided as consciousness at last flickered out.

Amidst the terror of what Jocelyn witnessed, she heard the orchestra play its last tune from the Boat Deck.

Titanic dramatically listed to portside from the flooding of Scotland Road, the long internal hallway located seven levels down on E Deck. The stern by that time rose rapidly above the water at a 15-degree angle. François tightly held onto the railing and placed his feet at the base of the railing's post to better stand upright as the ship tipped at a steeper angle into the water's edge. He wondered what more he could do. It was 2:13 a.m., and *Titanic* was sinking at rapid speed, the bow completely submerged below the waterline.

All was lost now, and Captain Smith shouted orders through a megaphone from the bridge, releasing the remaining crewmen from duty. "Do your best for the women and children, but now it's every man for himself!"

On the starboard side, Second Officer Lightoller saw a wave rising to wash him overboard, so he dove into the sea.

He first attempted to swim to the crow's nest that was still above water, but he then changed his mind. Water pressure pulled him under and held him to one of the ship's forward gratings as the sea rushed into the opening behind him. A sudden blast of warm air came from inside the ship and blew him to the surface. He gasped a breath of cold air and was immediately pulled under water once more, held again against another grating. Not knowing how he was able to resurface, he noticed Collapsible B floating upside down. He swam to it and grabbed the rope at the front.

As *Titanic*'s bow sank deeper beneath the sea's surface, the first funnel broke away from the ship and fell to the port side. Those who were frantically swimming in its shadow never saw it coming, and their fight for survival instantly ceased. Those in the lifeboats on the port side screamed at the sight, feeling even more helpless and paralyzed by utter shock. The dark ocean shoved the collapsible further away from the ship, pulling Lightoller along with it.

Lightoller struggled with every ounce of his being to climb on top of the collapsible, followed eventually by thirty other men. He calmed and organized them, directing them to shift their weight on the upside-down craft to avoid being capsized.

From a safe distance, all Jocelyn could do was silently pray as she watched *Titanic* tilt into the ocean at a twenty-degree angle. The front of the ship's superstructure slid under, lifting the stern higher above the sea, and the second funnel broke off and fell to the starboard side with a horrendous roar. Those close by in the lifeboats could not help but hear the deafening rumble of imploding interiors, but more so, felt the impact down to their bones.

The lights flickered as the ship's electrical system failed, and all the lights went out, dropping *Titanic* and her desperate human cargo into a black, icy void. François suddenly felt a deep rumbling beneath him. The hull began to break at mid ship, directly under the third funnel. Gravity took the enormous weight of the water-filled center of the ship and pulled it downward. Beneath the sea's surface, *Titanic* buckled inward as if it folded in half. Metal twisted with a sickening moan. The screeching bend of steel sounded like fingernails on a chalkboard amplified to unnerving levels for an ungodly fraction of time that seemed without end. Then the bow broke away into the sea, pulling the stern with the ship's hull still attached at the bottom. The stern rose high above the water at a precarious angle, lifting the three gargantuan 50-ton propellers entirely out of the ocean.

The bow then completely filled with water and tore away from the ship. As the bow separated and ripped away from the hull, the stern slipped back onto the ocean, briefly righting what remained of *Titanic*. All Jocelyn could do was sit in shock and stare as she observed the black mass of the remaining stern twist to the port side. The ocean then pulled the remainder of *Titanic's* disemboweled belly, and the stern rose once again to the sky, this time to an eighty-degree angle. Jocelyn could barely see the tan bands of the two remaining funnels as they broke away from the ship, crashing into the sea below. The remainder of the mighty ship loomed nearly perpendicular to the sea, blocking out the starlight as *Titanic's* stern stayed aloft for a brief moment, bobbing like a cork. The stern seemed to float peacefully for a short time, and in that moment, absolute silence held the last vestige of hope. Then the ship's interiors imploded under extreme water pressure, belching like artillery explosions.

With hundreds still clinging to the stern, the *RMS Titanic* rapidly dropped, sounding like a rolling thunder of muffled explosions as she sank into the freezing waters below. Those close by in the lifeboats, as well as those left on the ship, felt the pressure of the blasts concuss against their bodies.

Watching *Titanic*'s horrible demise, Jocelyn felt a palpable jolt of pain in her chest, a brutal yank of her own life force as it left her body. When the tip of the stern disappeared, in contrast to the thunderous roar just moments before, the last of *Titanic* went under in peaceful silence.

What took 3,000 men three years to build was swallowed by the sea in two hours and forty minutes.

Look for
SÍORAÍ
Continuum Book Three

available in paperback and e-book at
Amazon.com, BarnesAndNoble.com,
and other online stores

Visit ardyce.org for updated information on the
Continuum Series.

Acknowledgements

Writing *Aeternalis - Continuum Book Two*, during the entirety of 2016, has been a work of love and creativity that would not have occurred without the tremendous support of so many people to whom I refer as "family of the heart." Some of them walk the earth with me, and others have moved on to greater dimensions.

The publication of my written works and art expression would not be possible if not for the tremendous love and support of my husband, Kevin. I would not have the well-finished works, expressed from the heart, without his expertise and persistence, as well as his sense of humor, as my editor and publisher. Kevin's wisdom and guidance throughout the year has assisted me in the enrichment of the book's characters and in the many levels of the story of *Aeternalis - Continuum Book Two*. This book is a collaboration of our many hours of conversation, months of research in crafting the story, and numerous weeks of editing. In that, I feel that *Aeternalis* is his book as well.

Weekly conference calls with my Mastermind group have given me the support of three dear friends from across the United States. Rob Ciminelli, of Buffalo, New York; Susan Jewett Reid Walsh, of Chapel Hill, North Carolina; and Judy Matejczyk, of Leander, Texas have spurred me on, week after week, to stay in the creative mindset, allowing the writing of *Aeternalis* to come through me in grace, ease, and joy. When I think I cannot write another word, I remember there are others who believe in me. Their love and support remain with me, and so, I continue to write.

Aeternalis and the entire *Continuum* series would not be possible without the five years of support of my previous Mastermind group. I am so grateful for the support of Simon Shadowlight, and Robert Brzezinski, of Denver, Colorado. Jay Lang, of Napa Valley, California continues to be of support today as my prayer partner of eleven years. When the four of us originally met at the beginning of our five years together, none of us had yet achieved the vision we saw for our lives. Now, each of us has done so, as we held each other's highest vision through the love of God.

My dear and "oldest" friend, Jeanie McSwain Hardey, has been a continual promoter of my art for many years, and now she supports me in my writing. There is something to be said about friends who go through the thick and thin of life throughout the years, always standing tall to hold the light for the other in the dark times, while celebrating the many triumphs as well.

Chuck Barr has been of foundational support, this year in particular. He has held me in the constant pursuit of my destiny to write, teach, and speak through Love, which I believe is my deeper spiritual calling. In that, I write the essence of the *Continuum* series, for I believe that is the only reason we are here - to be and express Love.

Mile Hi Church, its ministers and philosophy, continue to teach me, as I am privileged to be in service to this community of heart that greatly enriches my life. Without it, I would not have the philosophical basis upon which I write the *Continuum* series.

I am also grateful for the foundational teachings that I grew up in until my adulthood, in the Community of Christ Church, in which generations of my family history is steeped. From there, I developed deep and lasting friendships that I hold dearly.

Thank you all for your love and for holding the high watch for me.

Both of my parents, Elaine and Robert West, encouraged my creativity from a very young age. Much of that time was spent at our family cabin, where I glean some of the storyline in *Aeternalis*. In honor of my parents' memory, I am so fortunate to continue the pursuit of my calling, doing what I love in my writing and art, while loving what I do.

In my ancestral heritage, I am blessed, for I stand on the shoulders of giants. Some were well-known poets and writers, artists, politicians, leaders, spiritual teachers, and business magnates. And some were parents raising children to the best of their ability, encouraging them to make wise choices for the betterment of their lives and for the greater good. May I also be one who leaves a legacy for generations to come.

Lastly, and most important of all, is the gratitude I feel for my readers who support me by patiently waiting, letting me know they, "can't wait to read the next book."

I would be remiss if I did not acknowledge the tremendous beauty of the great State of Colorado, where I live. The cover art for *Aeternalis* is a photo of a summer thunderstorm, taken from my library window, with a gilded cloud highlighted at the center. It is a metaphor for life, for there is always a golden light shining in the darkness leading us onward.

Author's Note

The question most asked of me by my readers is, what inspired me to write the Continuum Series? The reasons are multifaceted.

Many years ago, within a few months of each other, I took a couple of unexpected journeys through two different near-death-experiences, one of which was during a surgical procedure, and the other, from a car accident. While in the next dimension, after witnessing an abundantly beautiful, joyful, and peace-filled existence beyond human description, where it was made known to me that I knew everything there was to know, I then heard what sounded like my intuitive voice clearly ask, "Do you want to stay or go back?" My soul self immediately responded, "Oh no, I must go back. I have too much to do."

It was only upon my return to my earthly existence did I realize there was absolutely nothing of any negativity in the realm from which I just returned. Only Love and all its qualities were everywhere present, as I was left with a portal into the expanded awareness of the eternality of the cosmic universe. After years of pondering my soul's reason for my return - while in the question of *Just what was it that I returned to do?* - I began to put pen to paper.

I now write the best way I am able to convey, from my human perspective, what I witnessed while in the timeless realm of the Divine without the veils of my earthly existence. Everything I experienced "there" is here. The eternal *is* here, around us, within us, always and in all ways. It is in every moment - in each timeless moment of now. We experience it in the smallest moments - a tender gaze into the eyes of another as a gentle exchange of the heart, in the laughter of children, and when we take notice of nature's beauty. Each heart-filled experience adds on to the next, creating the sacred way of Love's eternal exchange, which beckons us on to the next moment of grace. We have access to the entire universe, which exists within each of us, and it is up to us to say yes to this magnificence within our own potential. From that place of knowing, we then take positive steps, which lead to giant leaps within the celestial enfoldment - the eternality of our lives.

Each of us is of importance, as in the metaphor of the big cosmic jigsaw puzzle. Each elemental being is an individual piece of the puzzle, shaped differently, in varied colors and textures - all fitting together perfectly to make the grand picture we know as our greater selves - as One. No piece is more important than another, and yet each is crucial in the importance of their individuality and to the whole.

The characters in the Continuum Series are everyday heroes, who face real life challenges while living in their individual part of the world, raising the vibratory frequency, both as individuals, and as a collective body of thirteen. They are wisdom keepers, oracles, light workers, sages, and shamans, some who have joined yet again in this lifetime as they all hold the high watch for the world - and for the universe as a whole. As we journey through each character's life story and witness his or her human challenges, it is my intention to illustrate that no one is without significance or value.

As a lover of history, I wanted to find a way to research and write about historic events and people of interest who have made a profound impact in the metaphysical (beyond the physical) nature of the world. Although I personally believe in past lives, it is not my intention for my readers to do so. I chose to tell the story of Sophia, the main character throughout the series, through her past lives so I could incorporate endless historic accounts for this ongoing tale, while weaving the sacred way of Love's qualities throughout the series. Those same attributes are the basis for the Order of Apeiros, enabling the thirteen to remember their individual soul's journey as they hold fast the highest consciousness for the world.

I have experienced many rich and diverse lifetimes in this singular life, at times through the dark night of the soul. I am so very grateful, for my life has rarely been boring. I live a life of great fortune, for I do what I love, and love what I do, through my writing, my art, and as a spiritual practitioner, life coach, and speaker. Each day I am ever more aware of how blessed I am to have people of tremendous value surrounding me. Everyone I meet is a sacred soul upon this precious planet. This is why I returned - to help people remember who they came here to be, so they can embrace and express their utmost potential, using their individual gifts and talents, which already exist within them.

With my highest intentions, I reach out through the written word, through my illustrations, and my photography, to create stories that bring to the reader joy, peace, hope, harmony, grace, compassion - all wrapped in love... sometimes with a bit of added intrigue and mystery as well.

Knowing for you that love lights your way,

~Ardyce West

About the Author

Ardyce West is an optimum blend of spirituality and transformation. She is a Licensed Practitioner for United Centers for Spiritual Living in Colorado, as well as a certified Life Mastery Consultant and DreamBuilder Coach. Ardyce has expertly chaired large retreats and facilitated transformative healing workshops, assisting others in living a full spectrum wholehearted life through the brilliant guidance and intuition she provides for individuals and groups. Also an extremely accomplished artist, Ardyce has conducted many art and jewelry workshops.

She is the author of the captivating metaphysical historical fiction series, including *Apeiros - Continuum Book One*, *Aeternalis - Continuum Book Two*, *Síorai - Continuum Book Three*, and *Ouroboros - Continuum Book Four*, as well as the beautifully written poignant non-fiction book: *I Never Heard You Cry - A Compassionate Journey Through Abortion*, which was written to give a voice to the many who are affected by abortion, either through personal experience or through that of a loved one. Ardyce has also written and illustrated a children's book, *There Once Was a Kitty Named Digit*, the first in her *Travels With Digit* children's series.

Visit ardyce.org for updated information

Praise for

I Never Heard You Cry -
A Compassionate Journey Through Abortion

"*I Never Heard You Cry* . . . never approaches political edict or social commentary regarding abortion. Ardyce West focuses rather on the substantial number of people who do struggle with complex and deeply emotional post-abortion issues." - *Publisher*

"For me, a great book is one that leaves me moved and tingling when I complete its final passages. Ardyce West's book, '*I Never Heard You Cry*', did precisely that for me. Not only will you be supported and inspired, you will find numerous springs of healing in this book. It is poignant as well as practical, offering compassion and insight in a controversial and troubled arena. Read this book and let your heart be touched." - *Dr. Roger W. Teel, Senior Minister and Spiritual Director, Mile Hi Church, Lakewood, Colorado*

"Ardyce West courageously shares her vulnerability in exposing her soul's journey of healing after her experience of abortion. Her insights give us all strength in moving forward after irreplaceable loss into greater awareness. '*I Never Heard You Cry*' is a significant and much needed work that will heal lives." - *Rev. Christian Sorensen, D.D., Seaside Center for Spiritual Living, Encinitas, CA*

"This is a book that will support healing and transform the way people look at abortion if they are willing to suspend fearful concepts. I highly encourage you to read this book and share it with your family, friends and even counseling clients. It will make a difference in how they view the experience of abortion and hopefully encourage them to open their hearts." - *Cynthia James, Author, What Will Set You Free, Revealing Your Extraordinary Essence*

"This extraordinary book isn't about pro-life, pro-choice, politics or religion. It's about people - the vast majority of us who understand that abortion is not a black-and-white issue that can only be addressed in absolutes. While it is an essential book for those who are struggling with unexpected and unattended post-abortion grief, it's also an excellent book for parents to share with their kids to help them learn about consequences and accountability." - *Kevin Cahill, Author, Sand Creek, Letters to a Rose, The Last Cafe, Knights of Harvest*

What reviewers are saying on Amazon.com:

"Few know how to heal the emotional wounds that accompany abortion. We don't talk about it much. This book is a good place to begin. It speaks with compassion, and offers signposts to acceptance, forgiveness, and healing." - *T. Nash*

"This book attempts to sort it out without all the screaming, finger-pointing and useless drama. I applaud this author for bringing some peace to all the pain on both sides of this serious and divisive issue." - *Jane*

"It has been written with such care and compassion while elevating us beyond the false oversimplification of this being a matter merely of either pro-life or pro-choice." - *Bruce*

"It was like finding Spring water in the desert of judgment that surrounds abortion and other such life decisions that many face in this complicated world." - *Suzanne*

"This book should be given to anyone considering or has been through an abortion." - *Susan*

"The book is about so much more than the journey through abortion, it speaks to me on many different levels about my own experiences in life." - *Frannie*

"I would highly recommend *"I Never Heard You Cry"* for anyone facing a healing process or anyone who works in an area of healing or spiritual counseling." - *Carol*

I Never Heard You Cry -
a Compassionate Journey Through Abortion
by Ardyce West

Available at
Amazon.com, BarnesAndNoble.com,
and other online stores.

E-book also available on Kindle, Nook, and other devices.